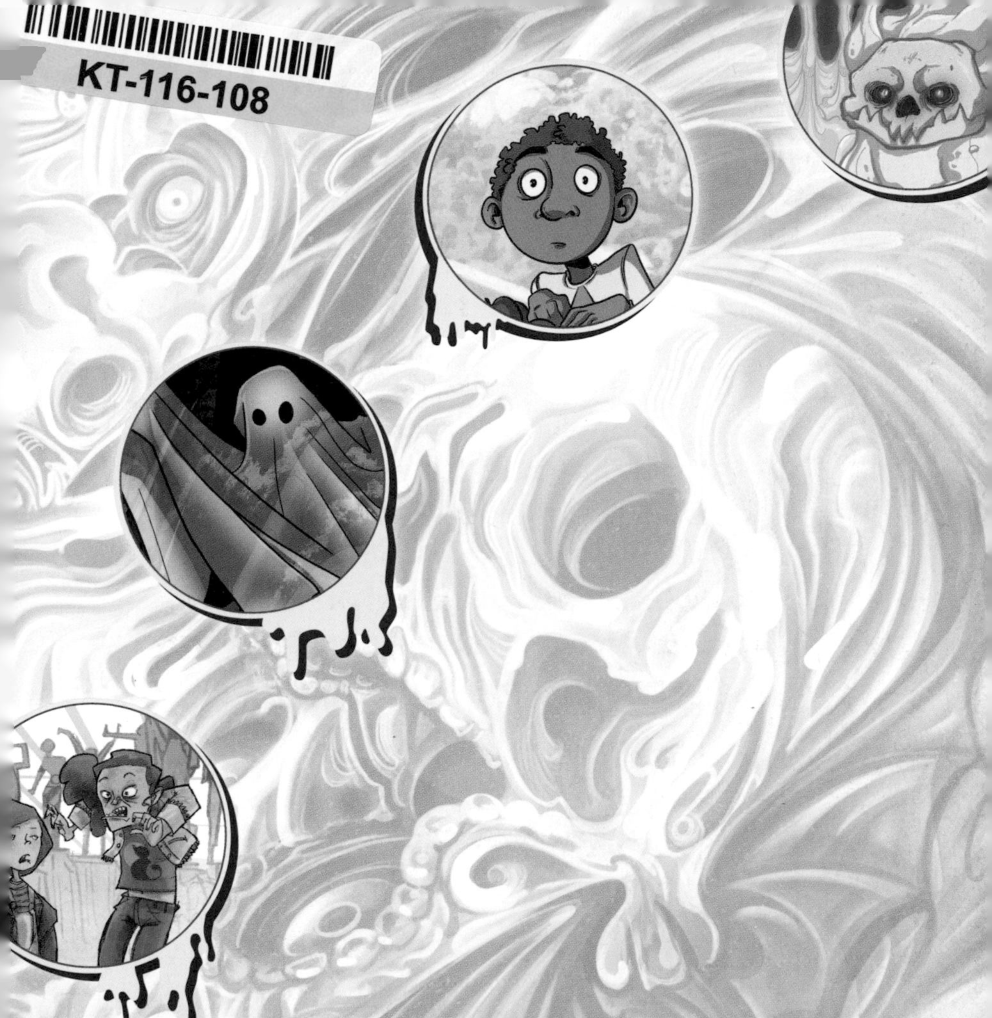

DEADMAN tells the SPOOKY tales

COURTNEY JORDAN Editor
STEVE COOK Design Director - Books
AMIE BROCKWAY-METCALF Publication Design
DANIELLE RAMONDELLI Publication Production

MARIE JAVINS Editor-in-Chief, DC Comics

ANNE DePIES Senior VP - General Manager
JIM LEE Publisher & Chief Creative Officer
DON FALLETTI VP - Manufacturing Operations & Workflow Management
LAWRENCE GANEM VP - Talent Services
ALISON GILL Senior VP - Manufacturing & Operations
JEFFREY KAUFMAN VP - Editorial Strategy & Programming
NICK J. NAPOLITANO VP - Manufacturing Administration & Design
NANCY SPEARS VP - Revenue

Deadman Tells
the Spooky Tales

Published by DC Comics. Copyright © 2022 DC Comics. All Rights Reserved. All characters, their distinctive likenesses, and related elements featured in this publication are trademarks of DC Comics. The stories, characters, and incidents featured in this publication are entirely fictional. DC Comics does not read or accept unsolicited submissions of ideas, stories, or artwork.

DC Comics, 100 S. California Street,
Burbank, CA 91505
Printed by Worzalla, Stevens Point, WI, USA. 8/19/22.
First Printing.
ISBN: 978-1-77950-384-8

Library of Congress Cataloging-in-Publication Data

Names: Aureliani, Franco, writer. | Richard, Sara, illustrator. | Price, Andy, illustrator. | Charm, Derek, illustrator. | Abbott, Wes, letterer.

Title: Deadman tells the spooky tales / written by Franco ; illustrated by Sara Richard, Andy Price, Derek Charm [and others] ; lettered by Wes Abbott.

Description: Burbank, CA : DC Comics, [2022] | Audience: Ages 8-12 | Audience: Grades 4-6 | Summary: Ghost host Deadman navigates the spooky, strange, and unexplained in this eerie 13-tale anthology.

Identifiers: LCCN 2022021820 | ISBN 9781779503848 (trade paperback)

Subjects: CYAC: Graphic novels. | Horror stories. | Supernatural—Fiction. | Humorous stories. | LCGFT: Horror comics. | Paranormal comics. | Humorous comics. | Graphic novels.

Classification: LCC PZ7.7.A8986 De 2022 | DDC 741.5/973—dc23/eng/20220505

LC record available at https://lccn.loc.gov/2022021820

Over the years, many writers and artists have lent their talents to Deadman.

But way back in 1967, a young artist brought the adventures of this strange character to life on the page for DC Comics, redefining what comics could do using his amazing layouts and the dynamic motion he brought to his figures.

On behalf of myself, all of the artists in this book, and all of the past and future artists who will bring the adventures of Deadman to life again, this book is dedicated to the memory of the legendary **Neal Adams**.

—Franco

CONTENTS

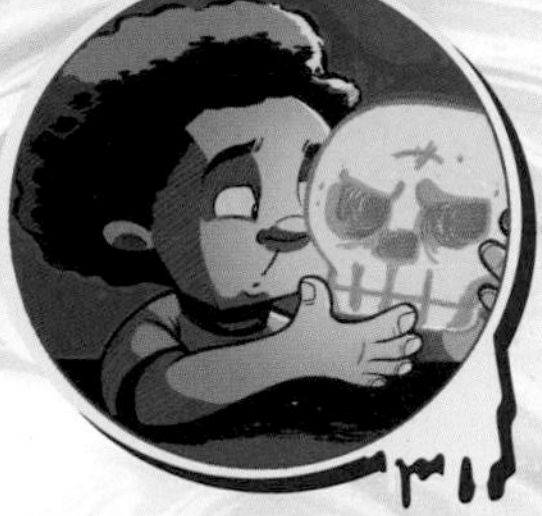

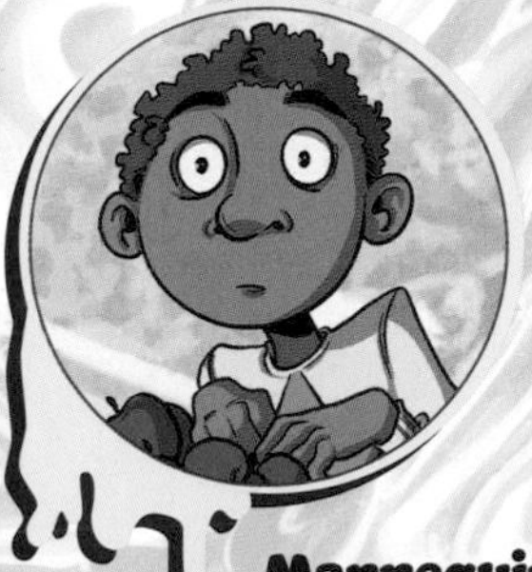

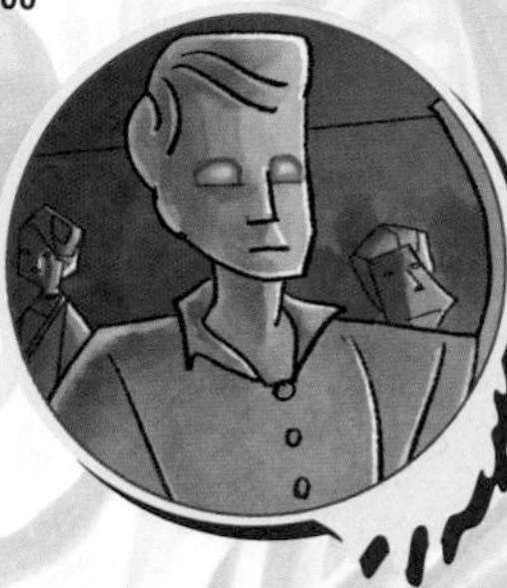

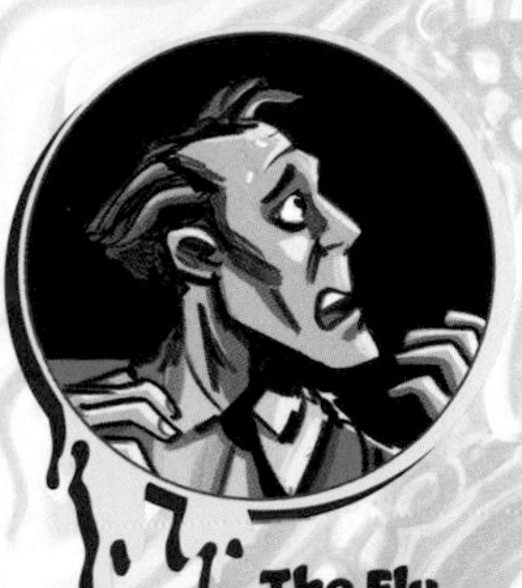

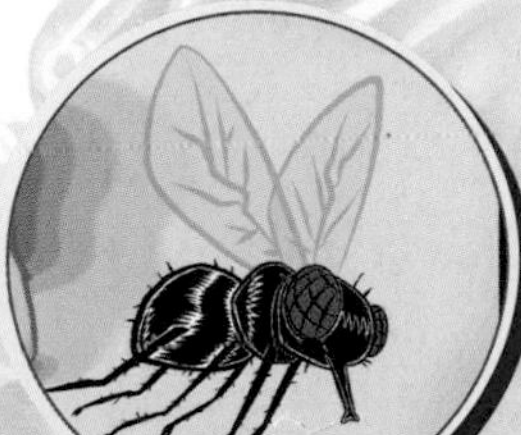

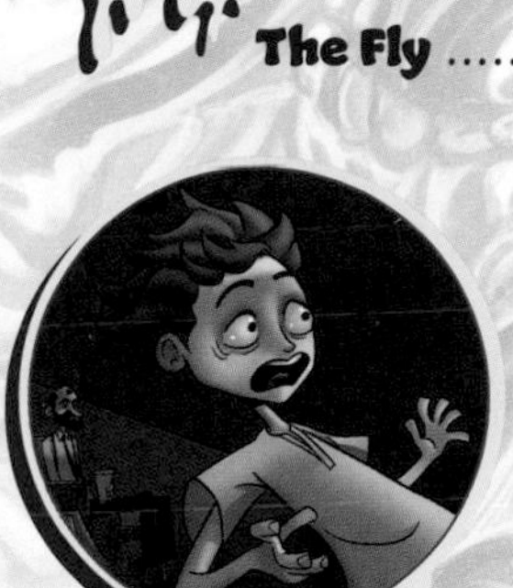

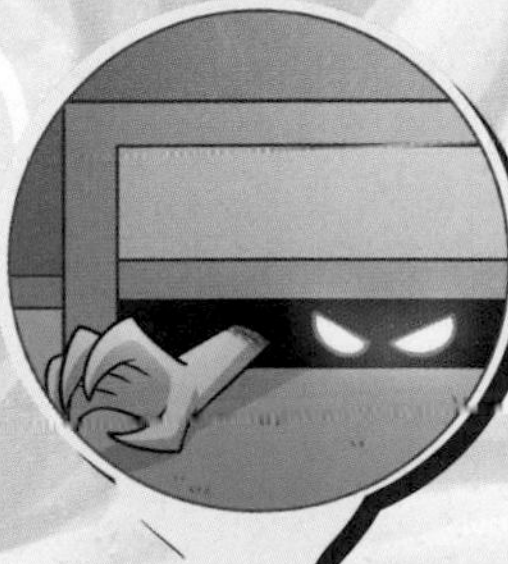

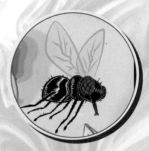

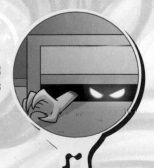

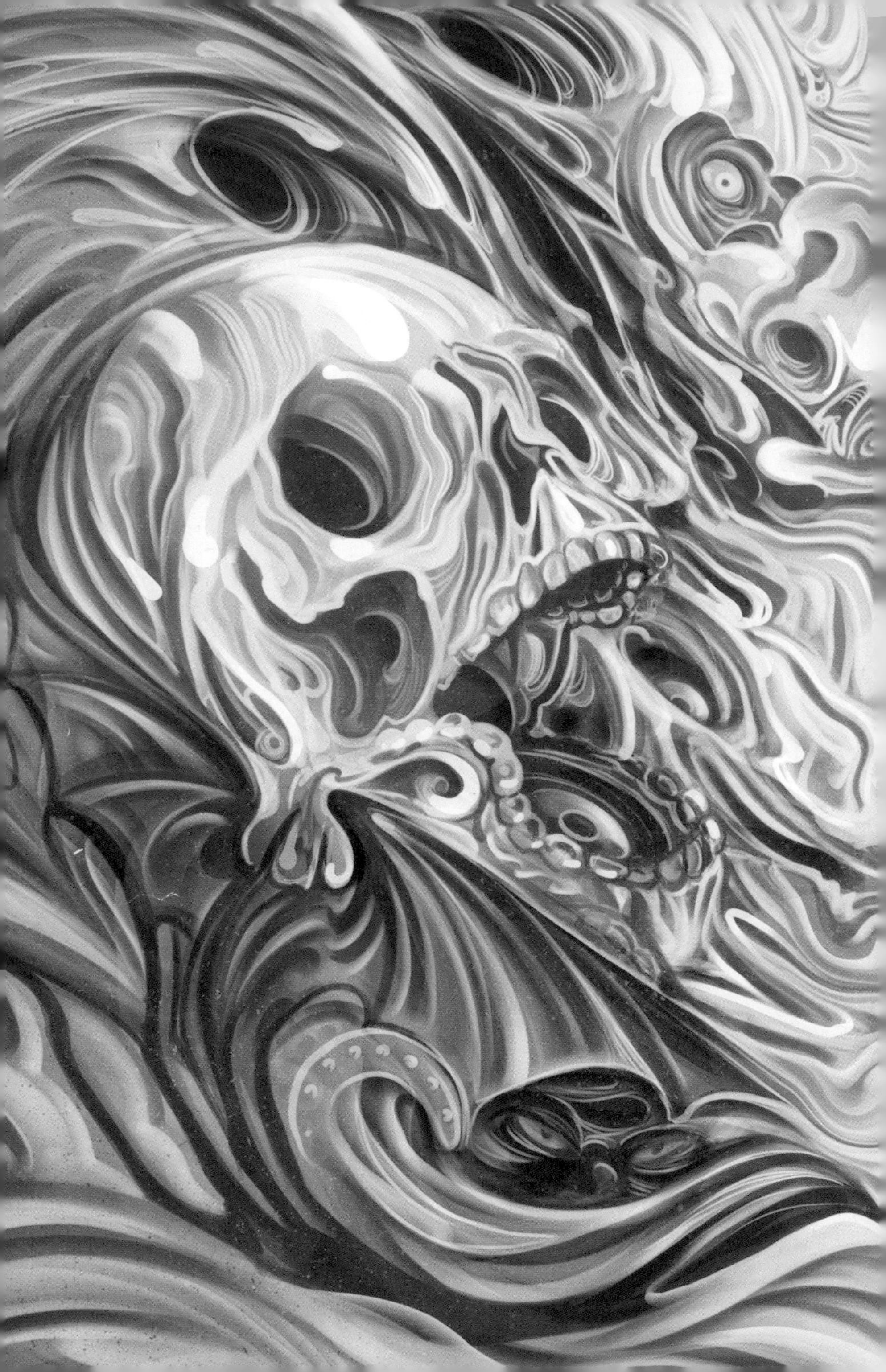

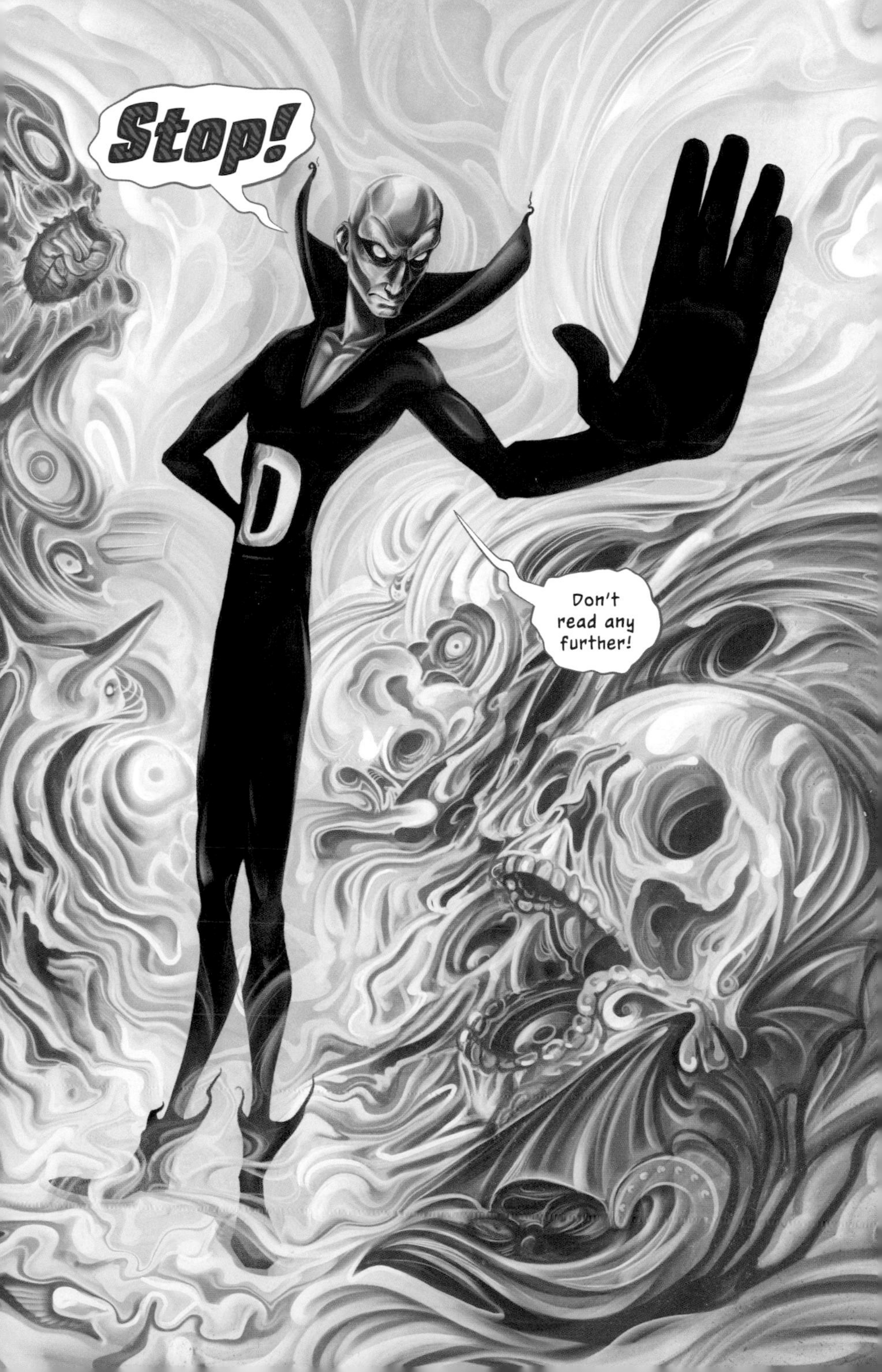
Stop!
Don't read any further!

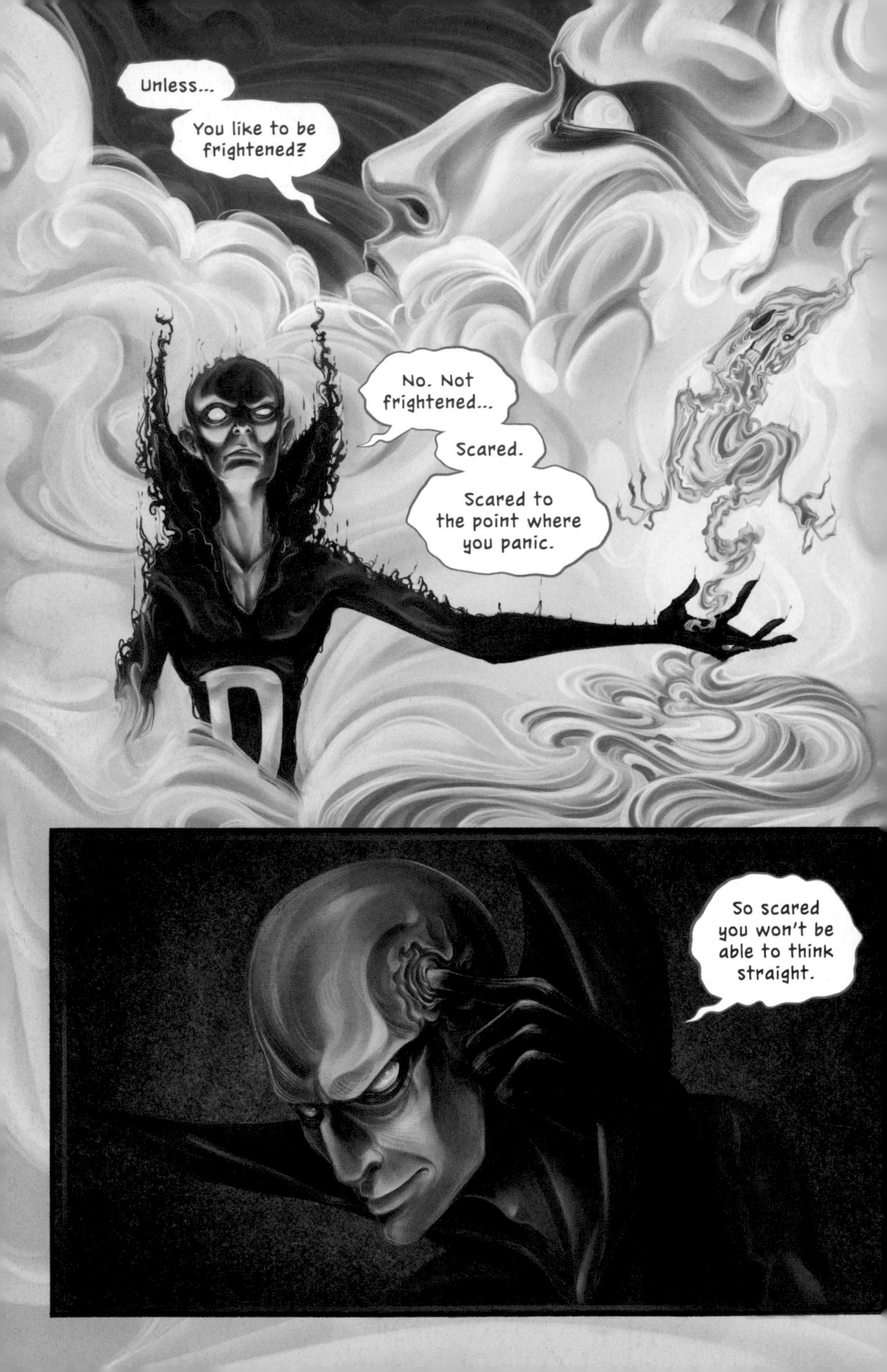
Unless...
You like to be frightened?
No. Not frightened...
Scared.
Scared to the point where you panic.
So scared you won't be able to think straight.

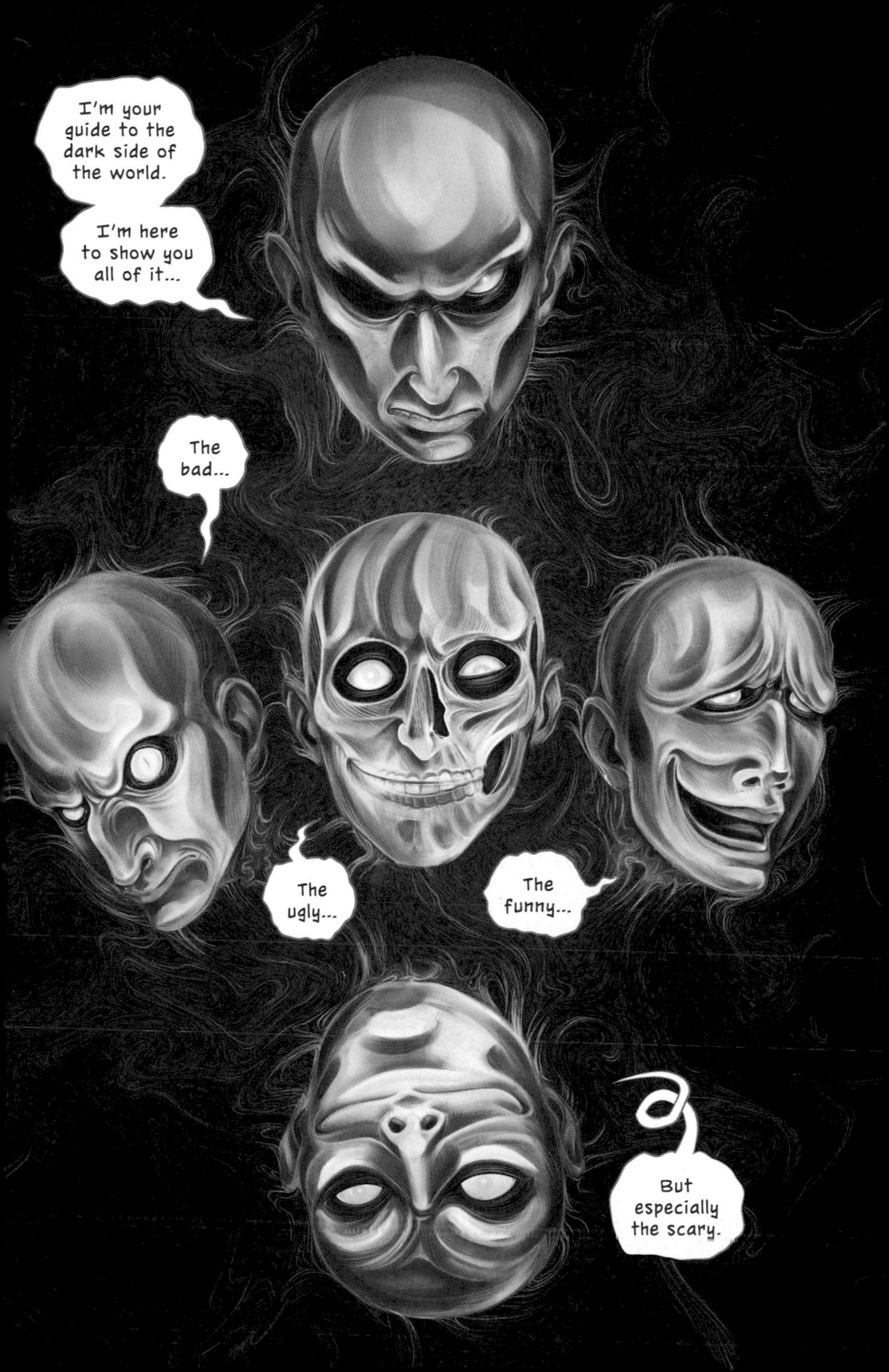
I'm your guide to the dark side of the world.
I'm here to show you all of it...
The bad...
The ugly...
The funny...
But especially the scary.

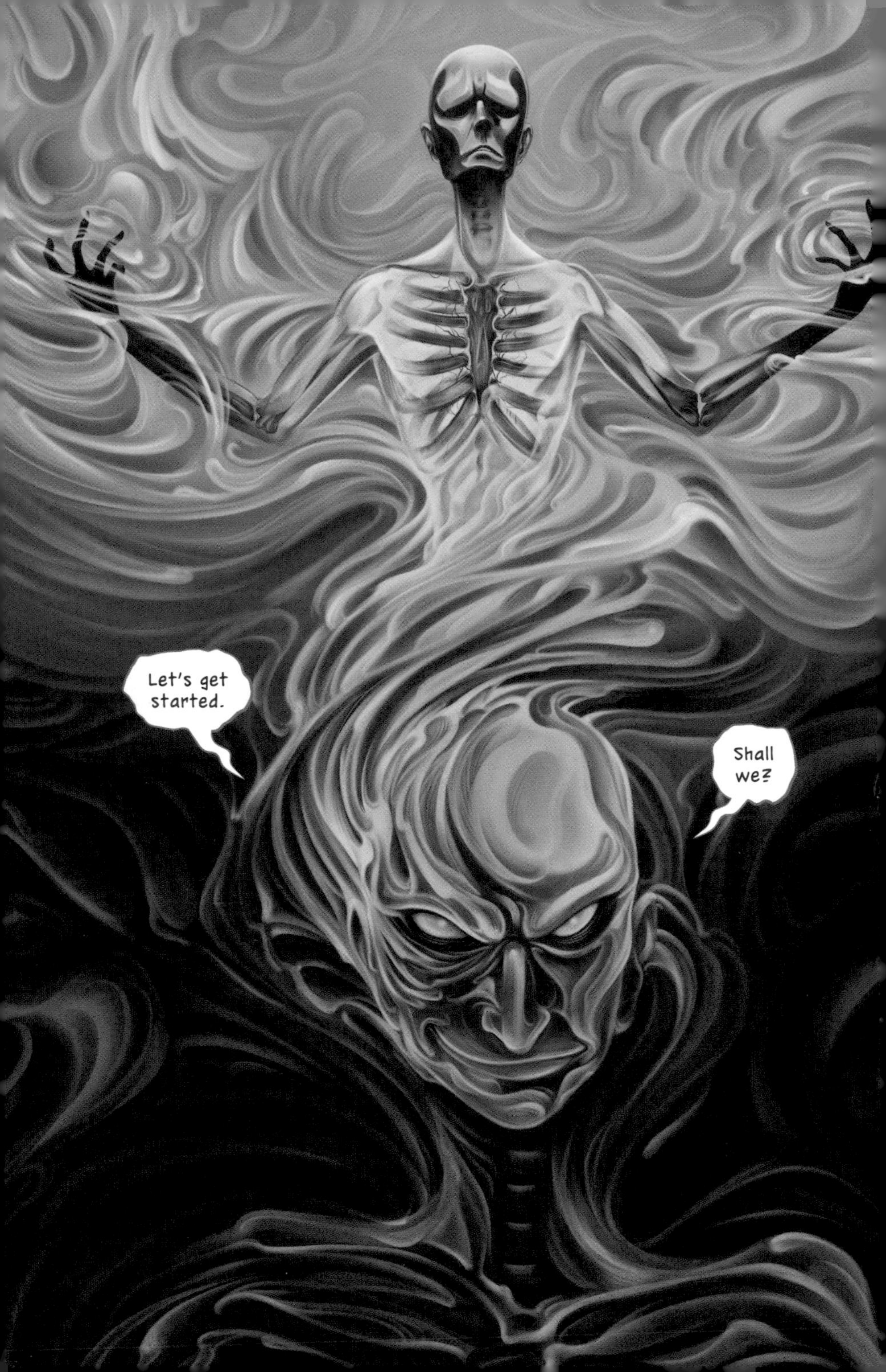
Let's get started.
Shall we?

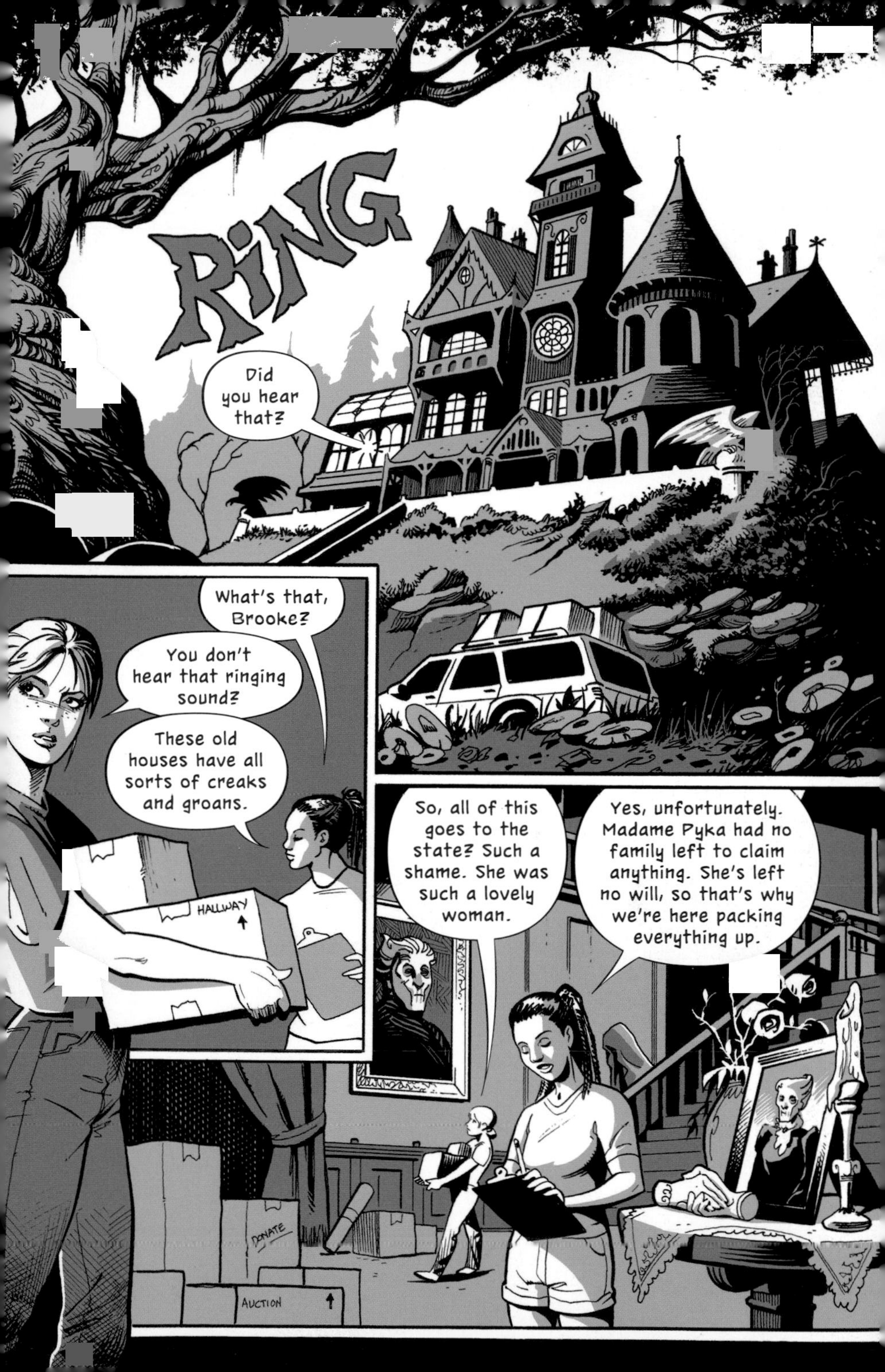
RING
Did you hear that?
What's that, Brooke?
You don't hear that ringing sound?
These old houses have all sorts of creaks and groans.
HALLWAY
So, all of this goes to the state? Such a shame. She was such a lovely woman.
Yes, unfortunately. Madame Pyka had no family left to claim anything. She's left no will, so that's why we're here packing everything up.
DONATE
AUCTION

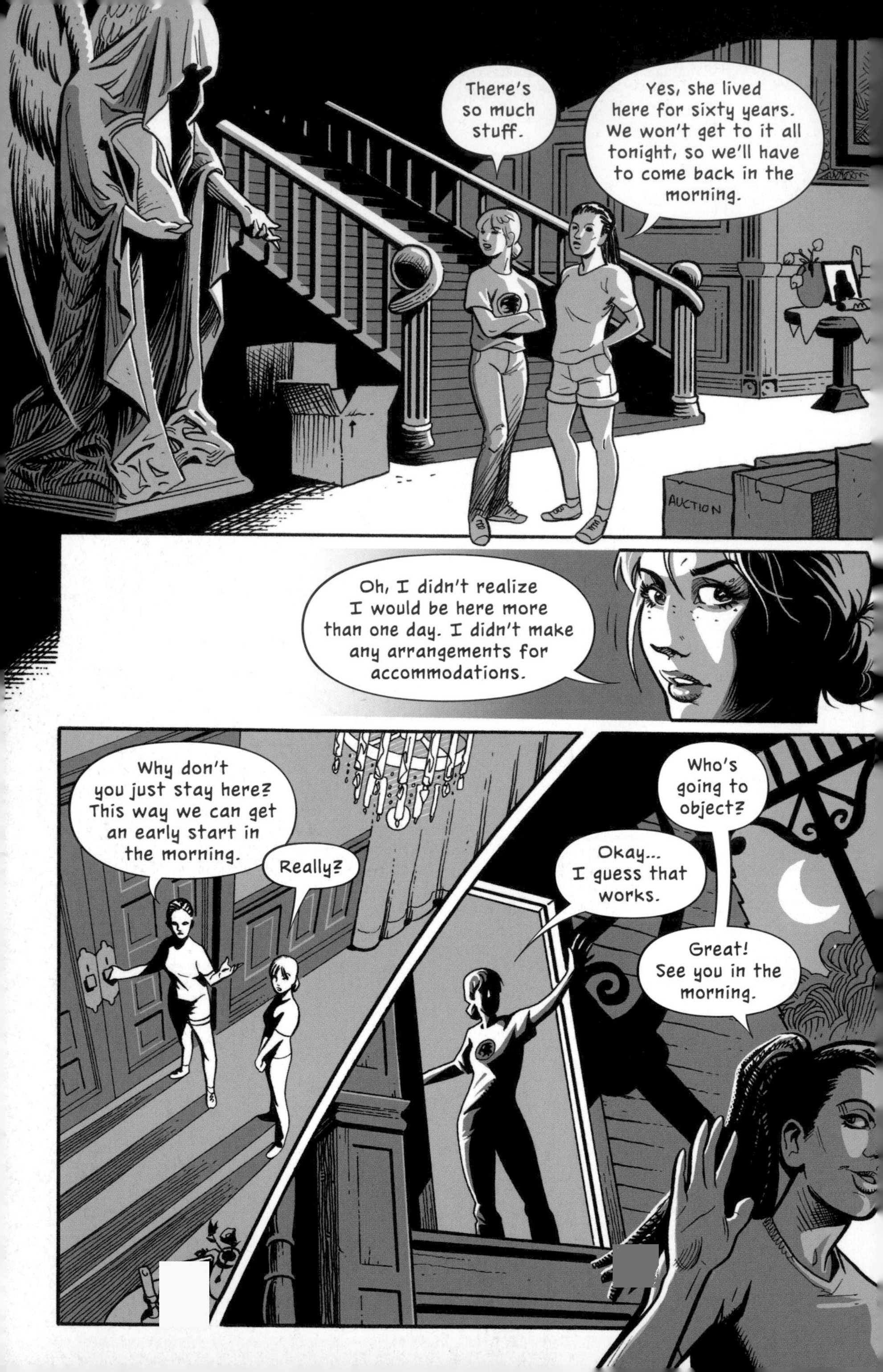
There's so much stuff.
Yes, she lived here for sixty years. We won't get to it all tonight, so we'll have to come back in the morning.
AUCTION
Oh, I didn't realize I would be here more than one day. I didn't make any arrangements for accommodations.
Why don't you just stay here? This way we can get an early start in the morning.
Really?
Who's going to object?
Okay... I guess that works.
Great! See you in the morning.

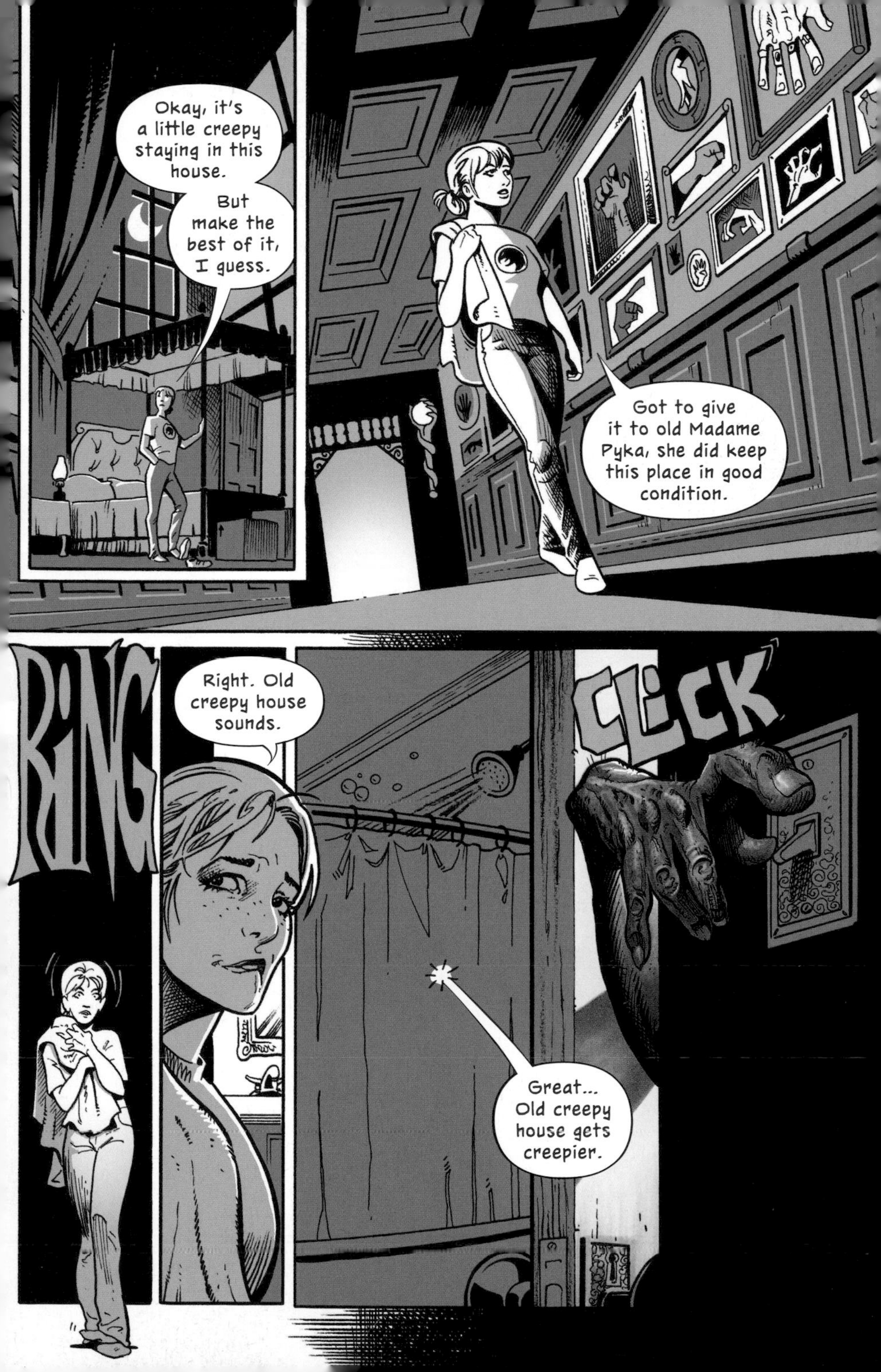
Okay, it's a little creepy staying in this house.
But make the best of it, I guess.
Got to give it to old Madame Pyka, she did keep this place in good condition.
RING
Right. Old creepy house sounds.
CLICK
Great... Old creepy house gets creepier.

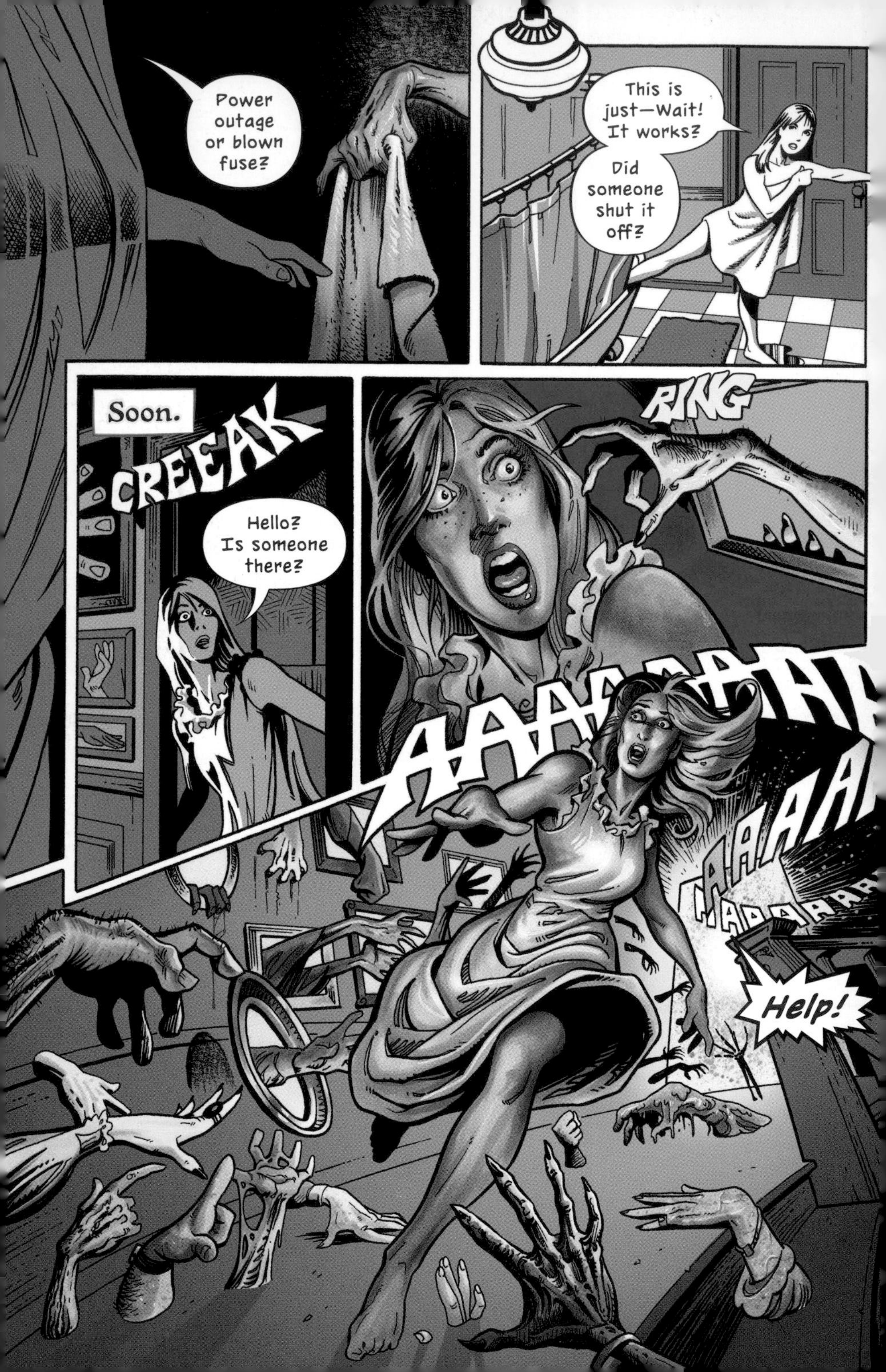

Power outage or blown fuse?
This is just—Wait! It works?
Did someone shut it off?
Soon.
CREEAK
Hello? Is someone there?
RING
AAAAAAAAAH
Help!

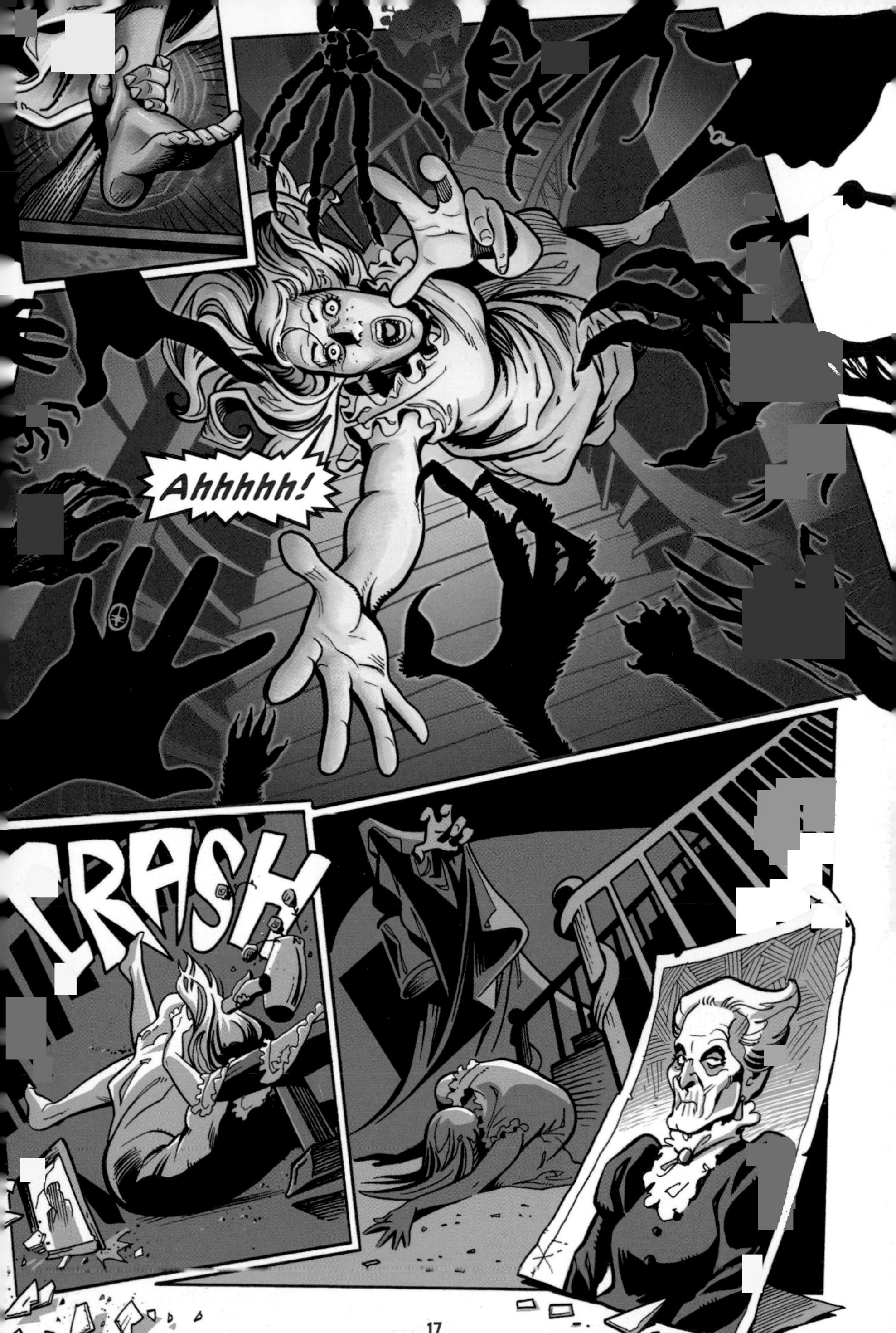
Ahhhhh!
CRASH

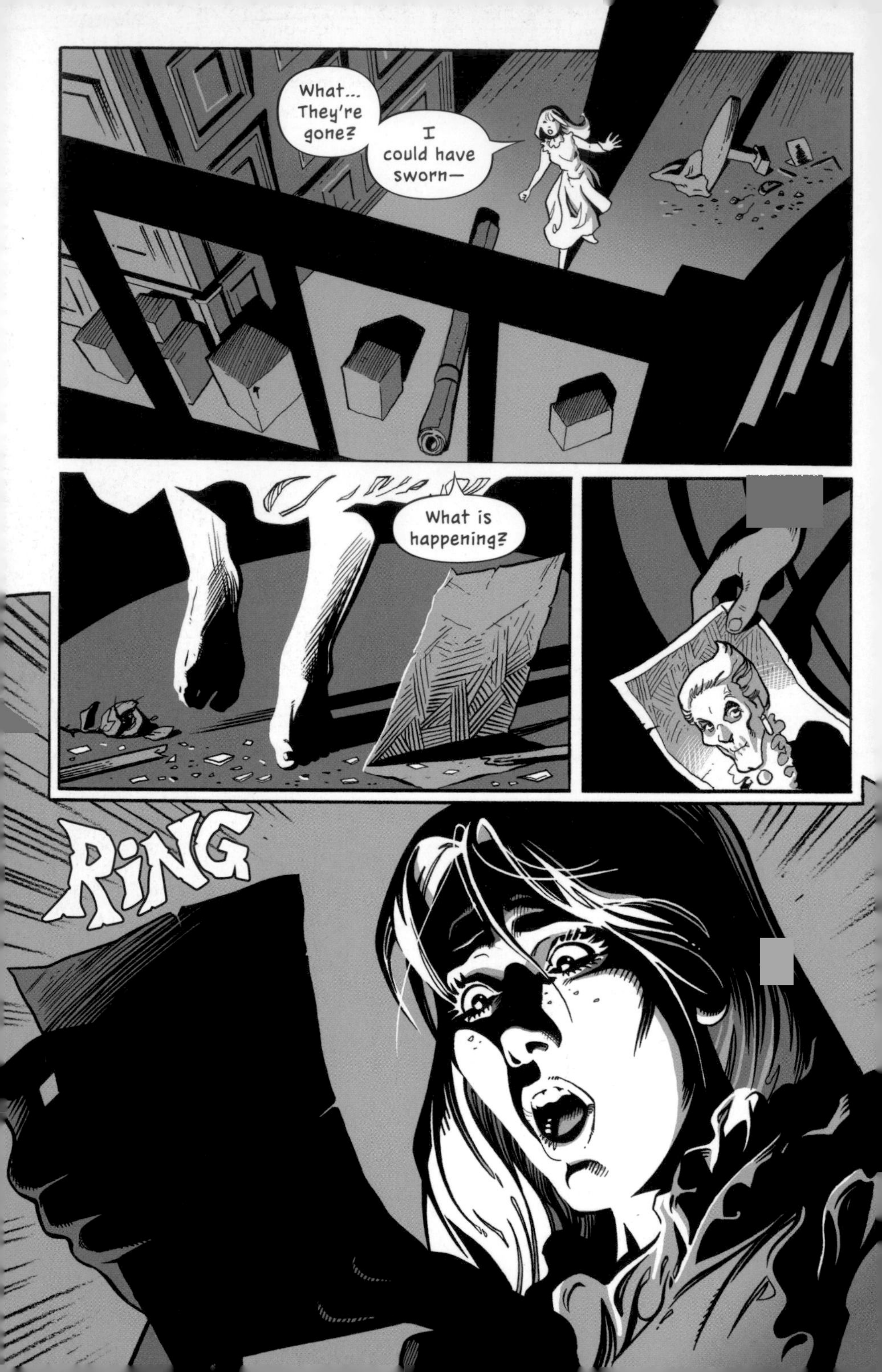
What... They're gone?
I could have sworn—
What is happening?
RING

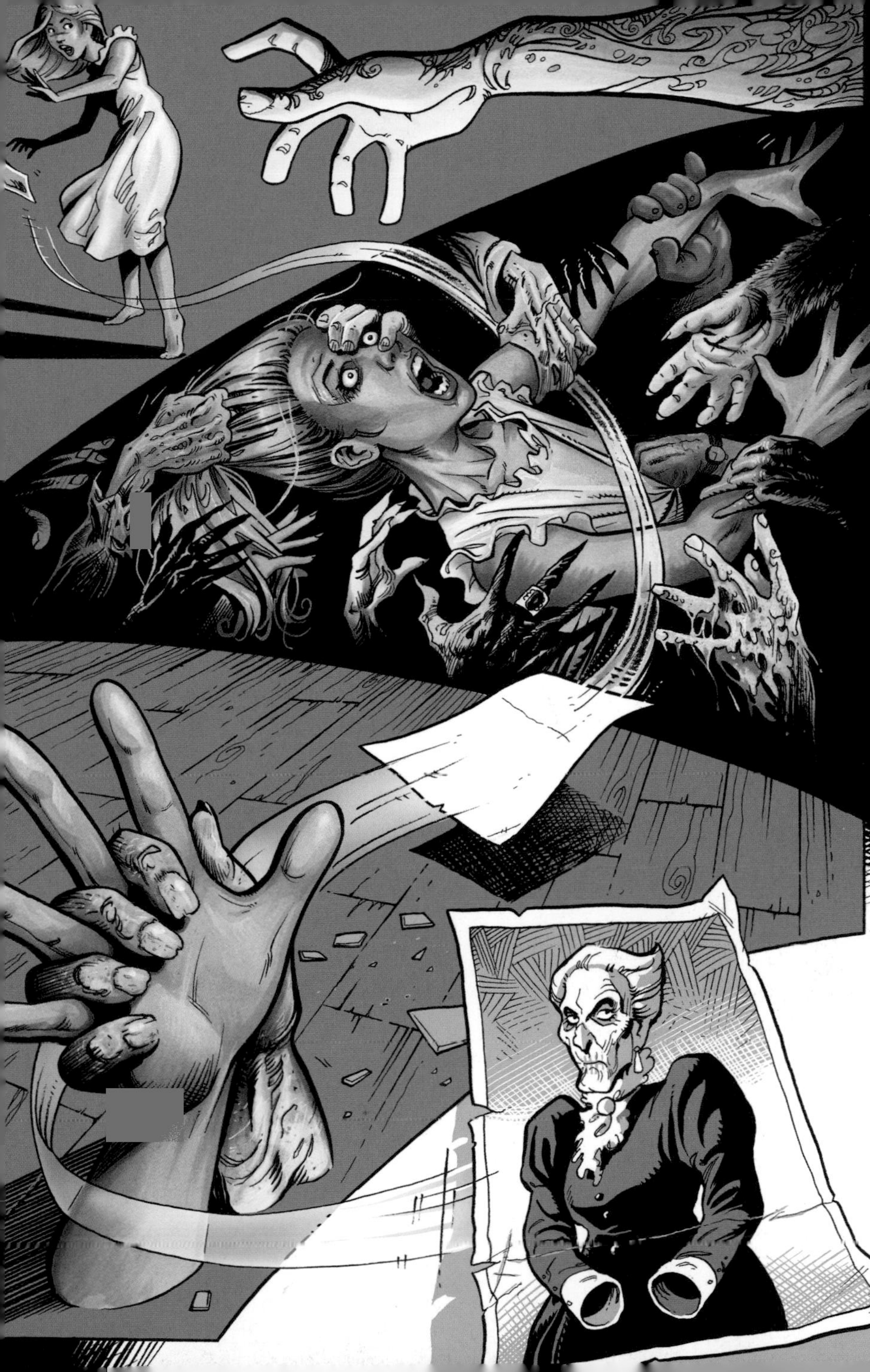

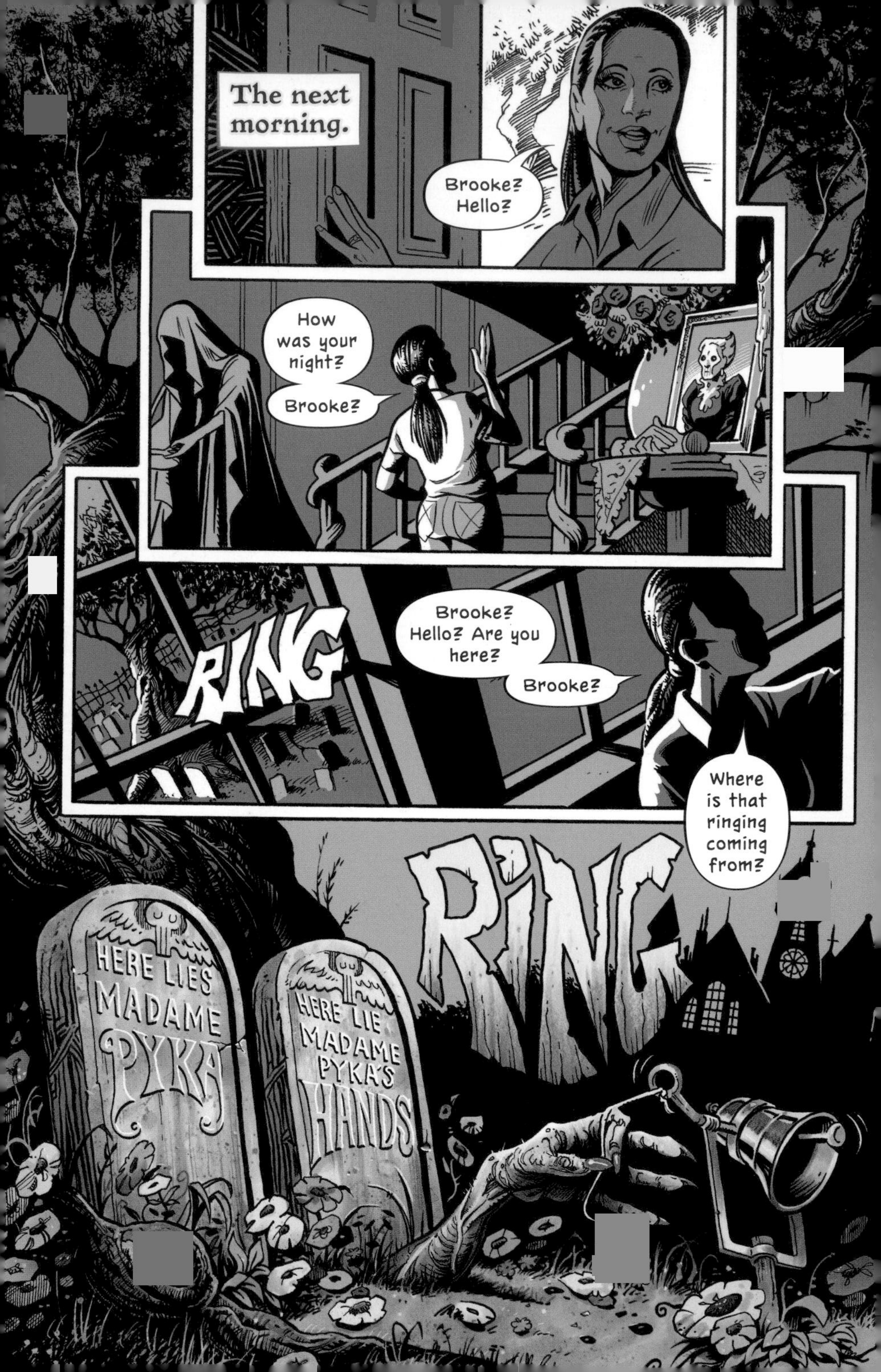

The next morning.
Brooke? Hello?
How was your night?
Brooke?
RING
Brooke? Hello? Are you here?
Brooke?
Where is that ringing coming from?
RING
HERE LIES MADAME PYKA
HERE LIE MADAME PYKA'S HANDS

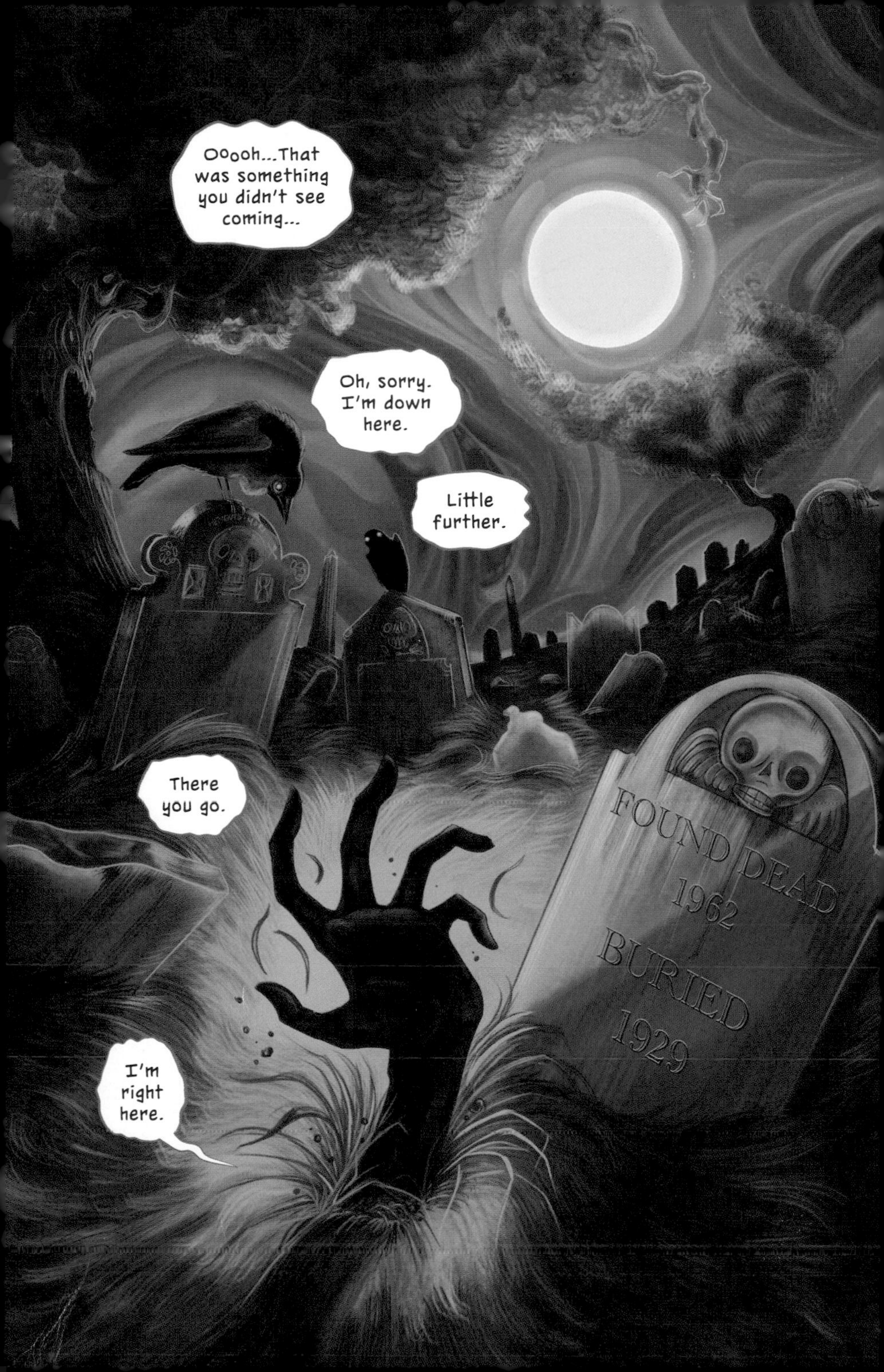
Ooooh...That was something you didn't see coming...
Oh, sorry. I'm down here.
Little further.
There you go.
I'm right here.
FOUND DEAD
1962
BURIED
1929

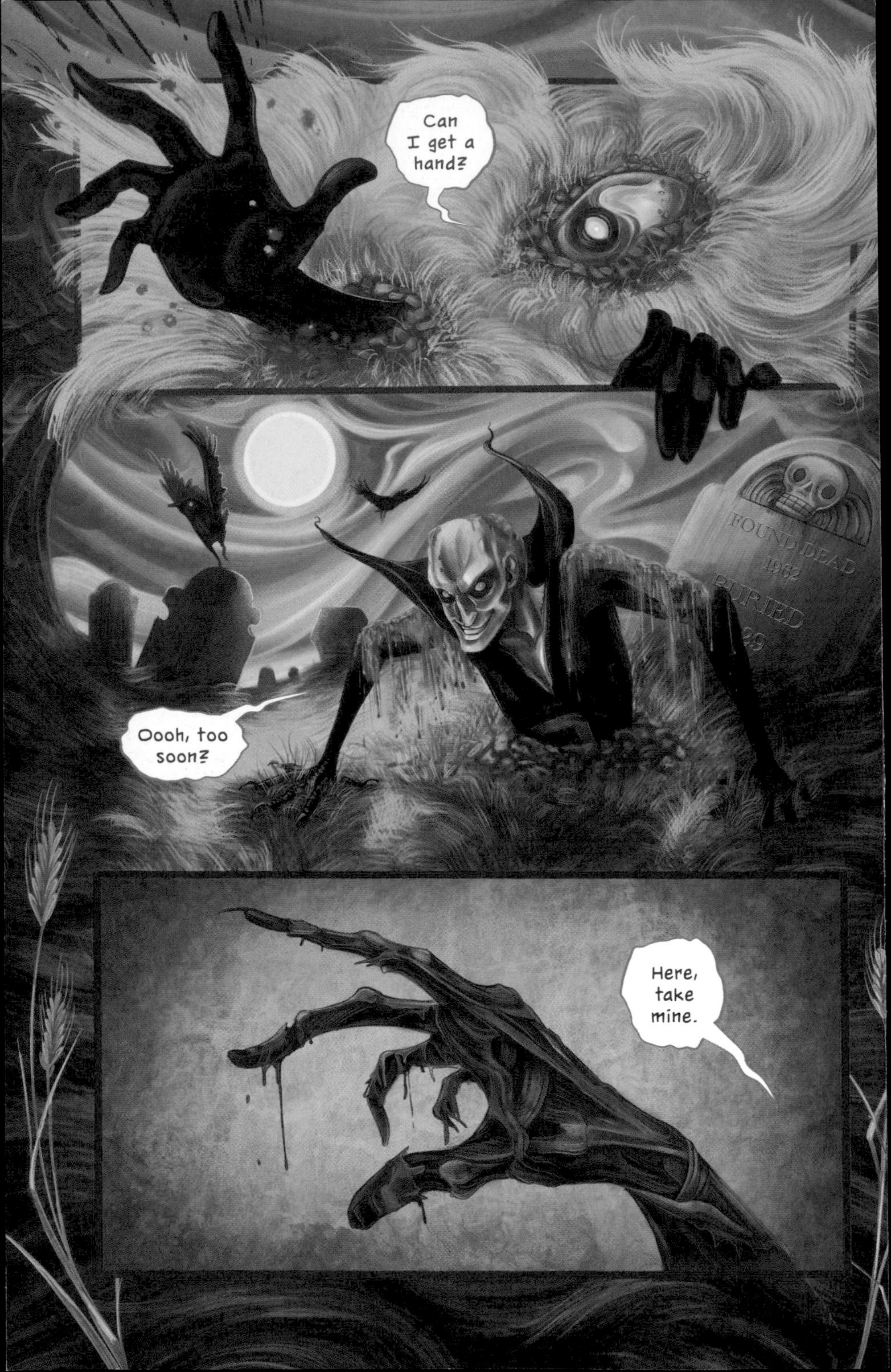
Can I get a hand?
FOUND DEAD
1962
BURIED
Oooh, too soon?
Here, take mine.

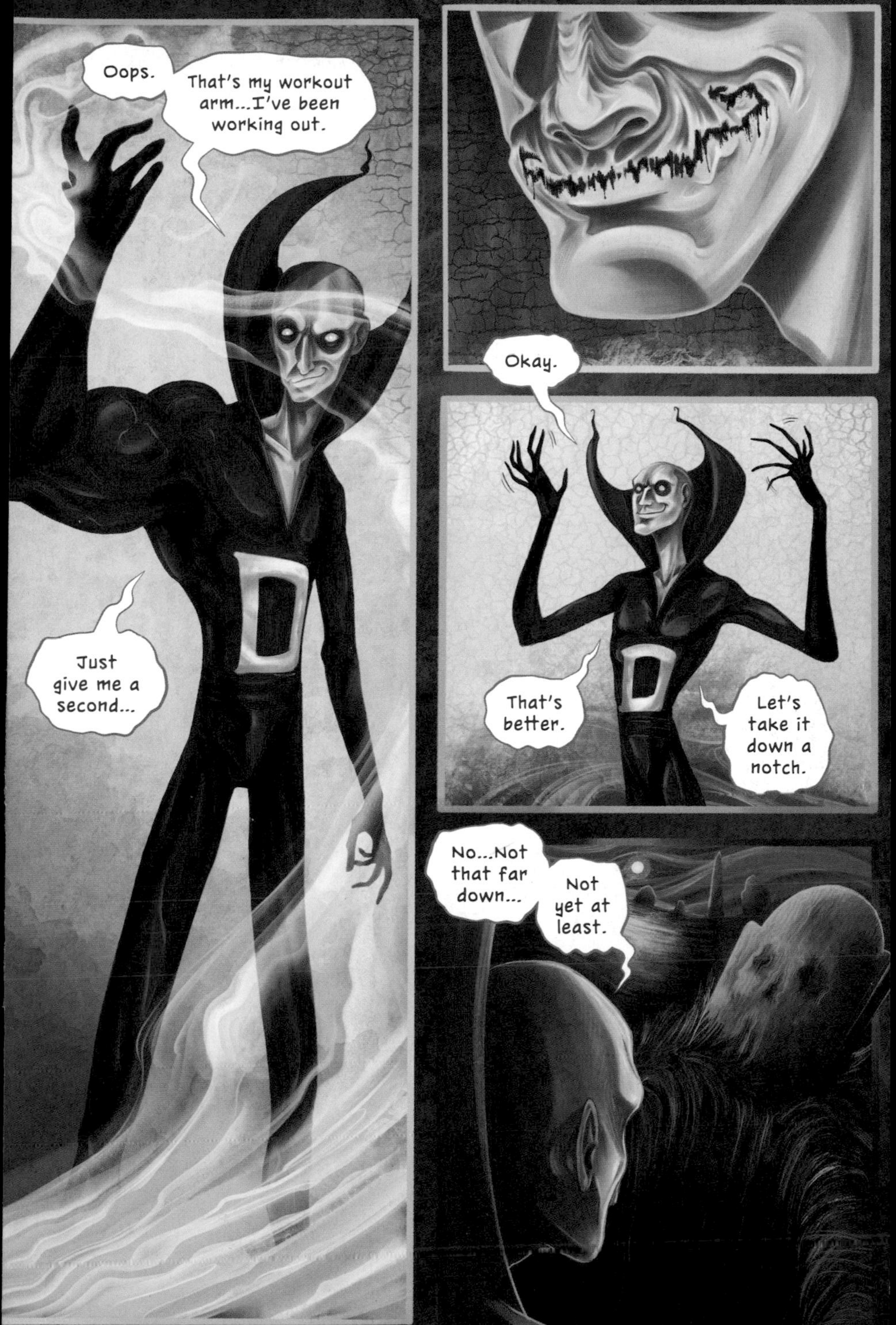
Oops.
That's my workout arm...I've been working out.
Just give me a second...
Okay.
That's better.
Let's take it down a notch.
No...Not that far down...
Not yet at least.

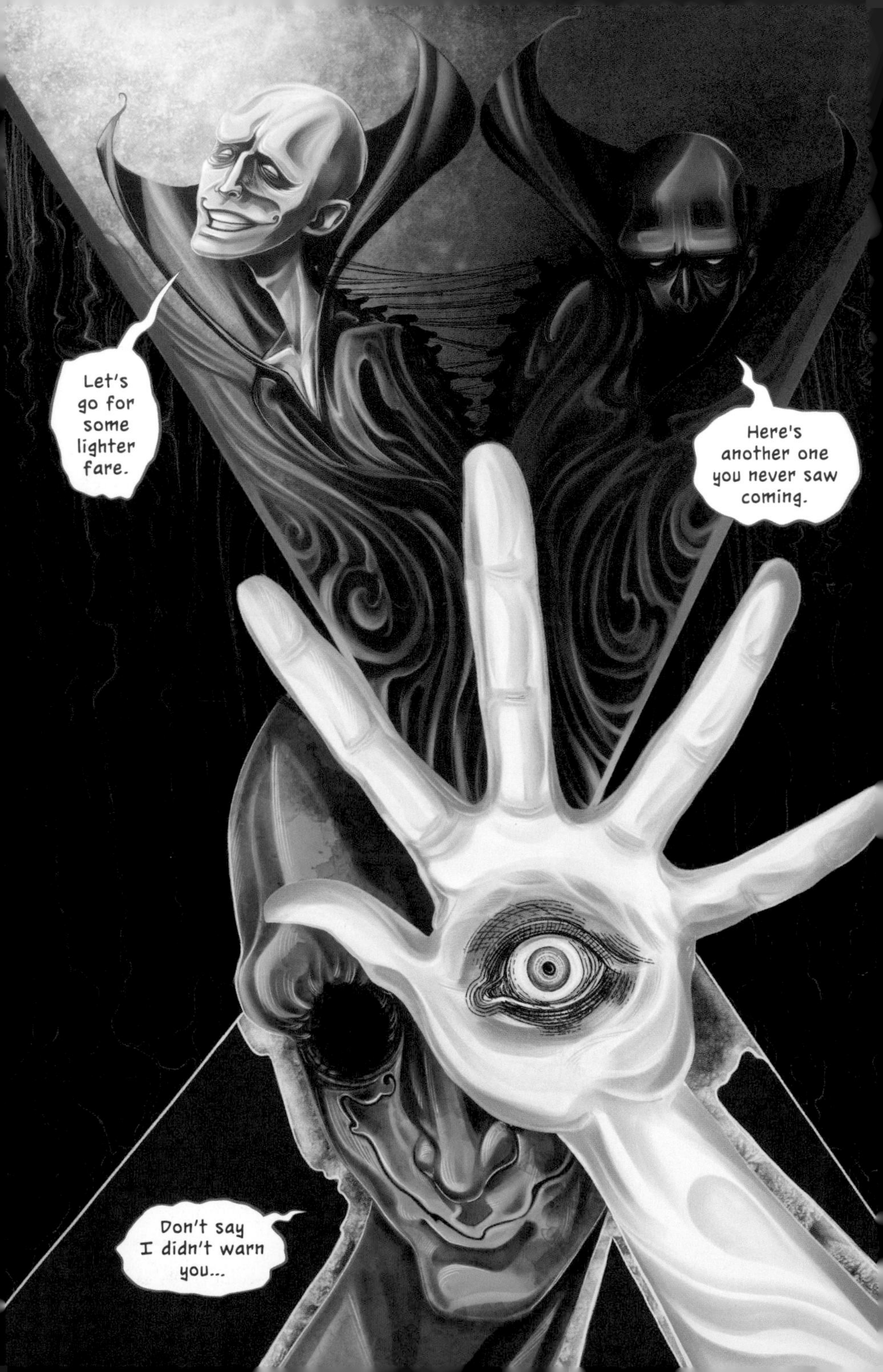
Let's go for some lighter fare.
Here's another one you never saw coming.
Don't say I didn't warn you...

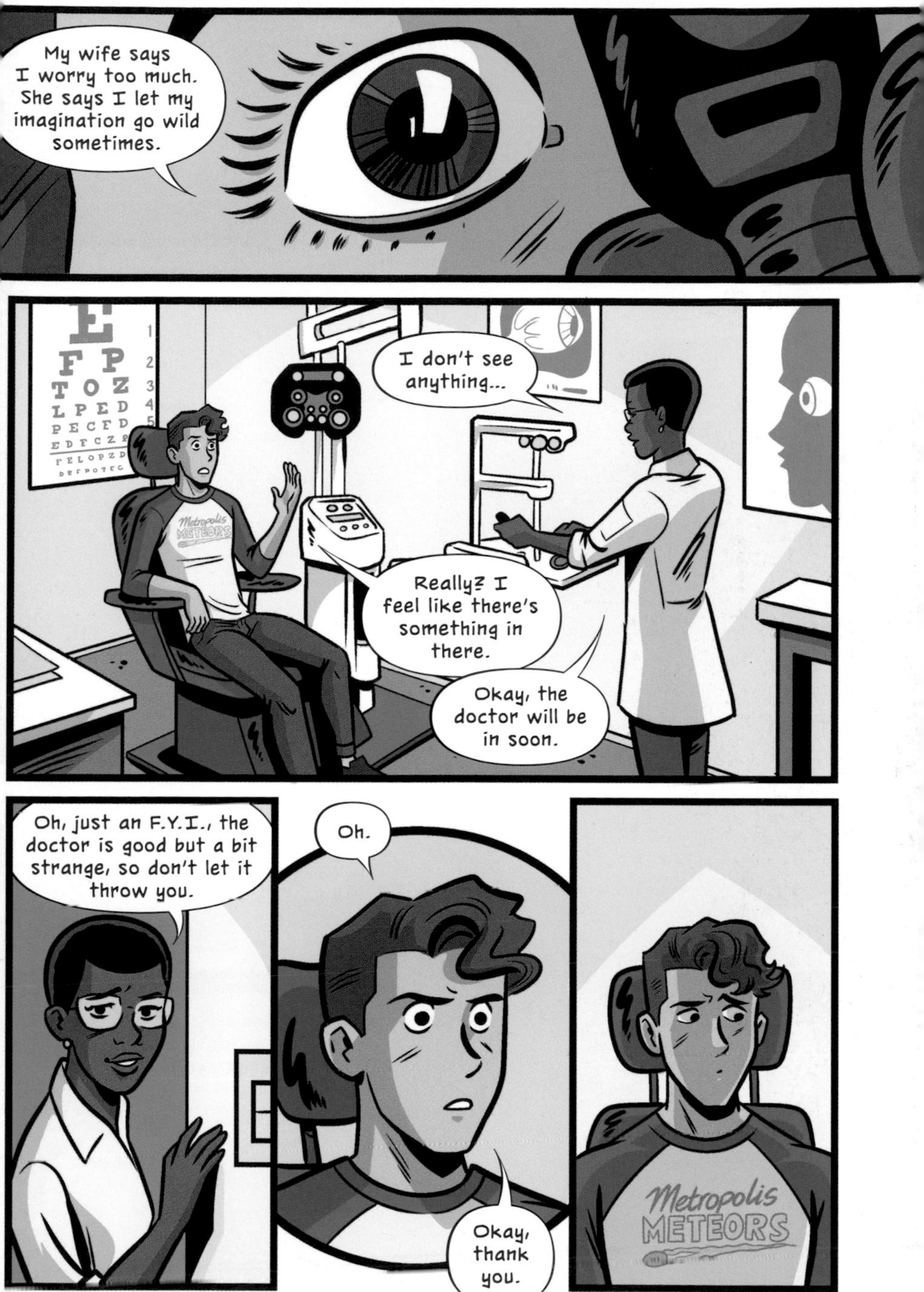
My wife says I worry too much. She says I let my imagination go wild sometimes.
I don't see anything...
Really? I feel like there's something in there.
Okay, the doctor will be in soon.
Oh, just an F.Y.I., the doctor is good but a bit strange, so don't let it throw you.
Oh.
Okay, thank you.

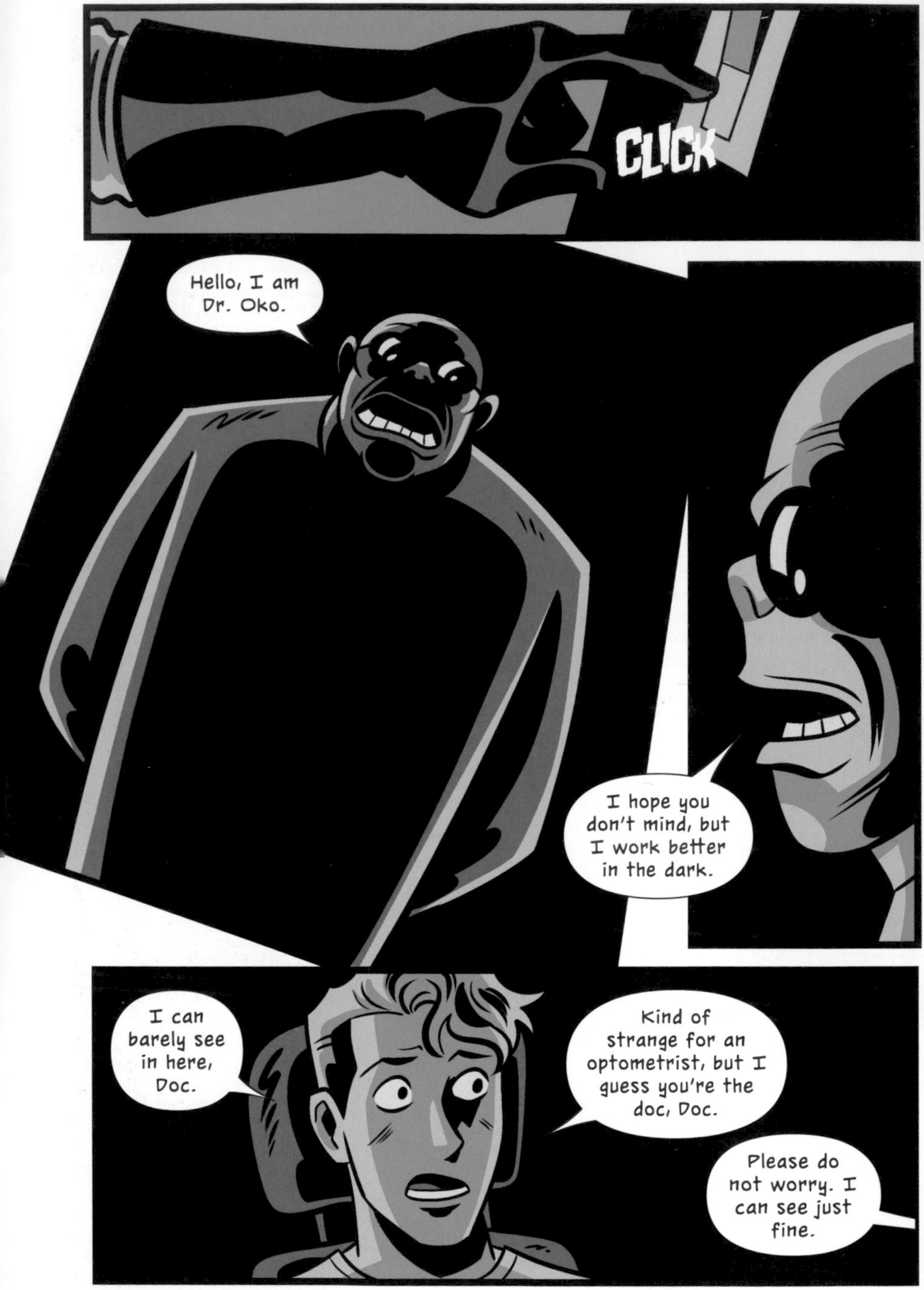
CLICK
Hello, I am Dr. Oko.
I hope you don't mind, but I work better in the dark.
I can barely see in here, Doc.
Kind of strange for an optometrist, but I guess you're the doc, Doc.
Please do not worry. I can see just fine.

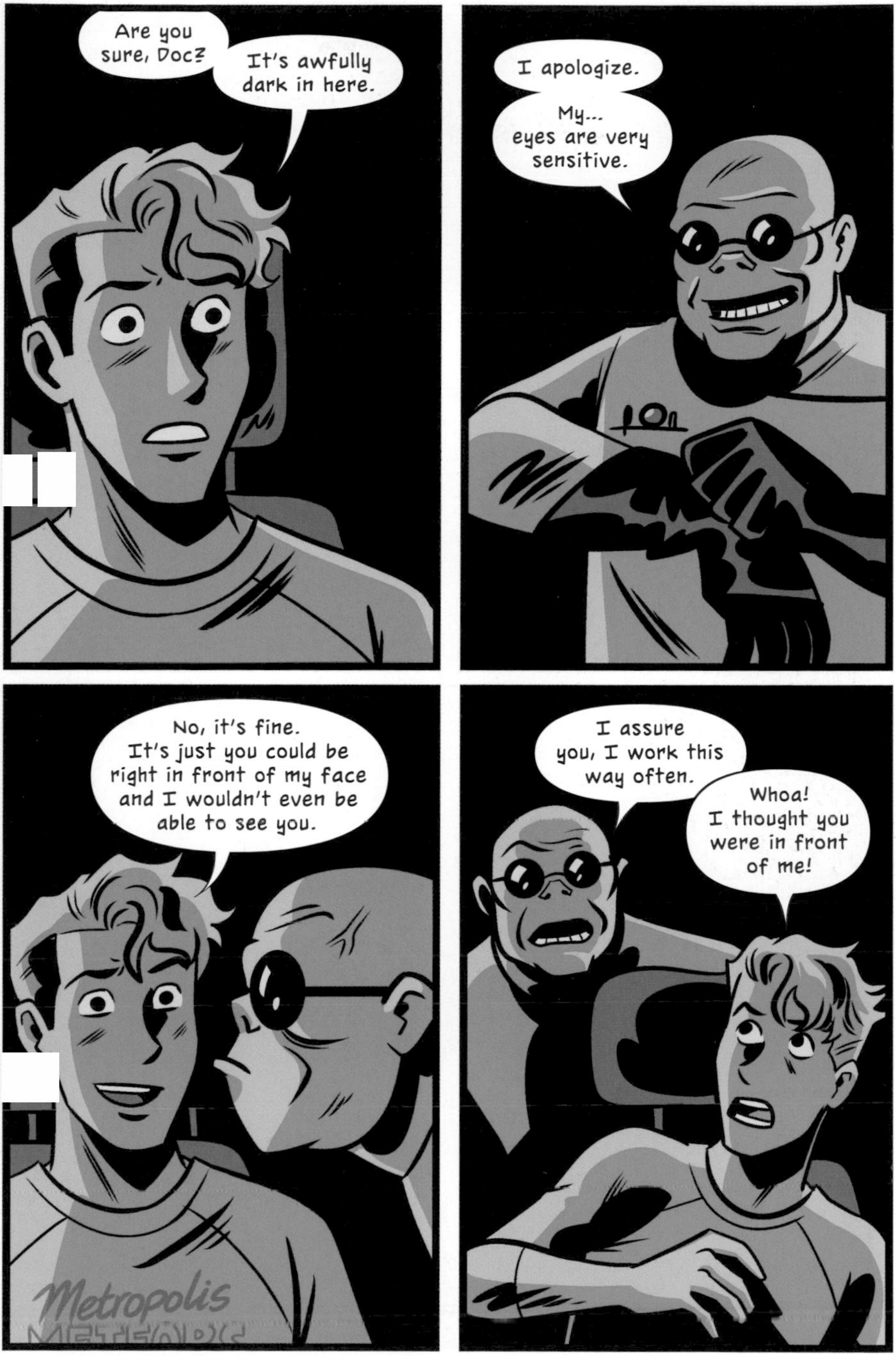
Are you sure, Doc?
It's awfully dark in here.
I apologize.
My... eyes are very sensitive.
No, it's fine. It's just you could be right in front of my face and I wouldn't even be able to see you.
I assure you, I work this way often.
Whoa! I thought you were in front of me!

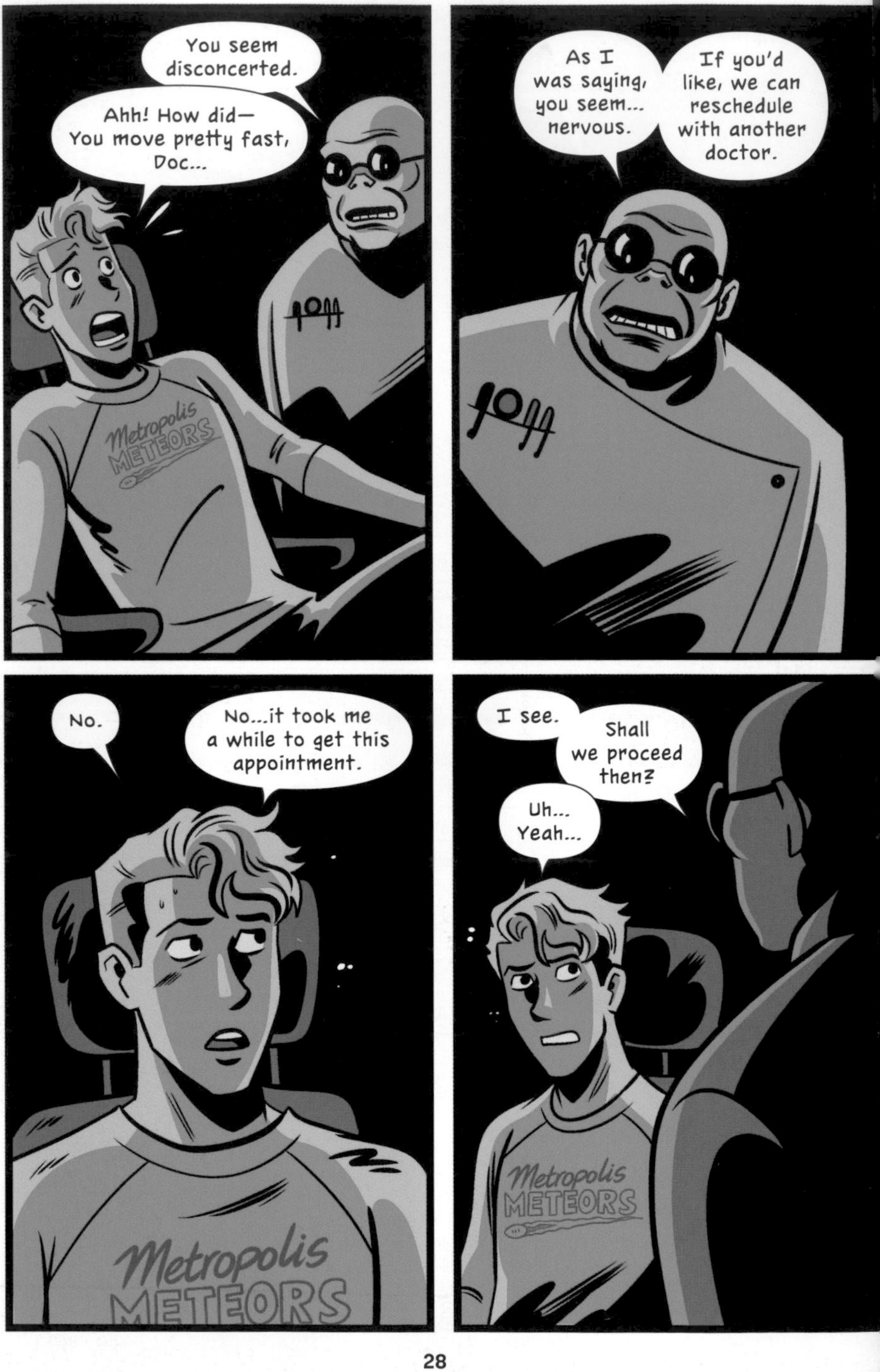
You seem disconcerted.
Ahh! How did— You move pretty fast, Doc...
As I was saying, you seem... nervous.
If you'd like, we can reschedule with another doctor.
No.
No...it took me a while to get this appointment.
I see.
Shall we proceed then?
Uh... Yeah...

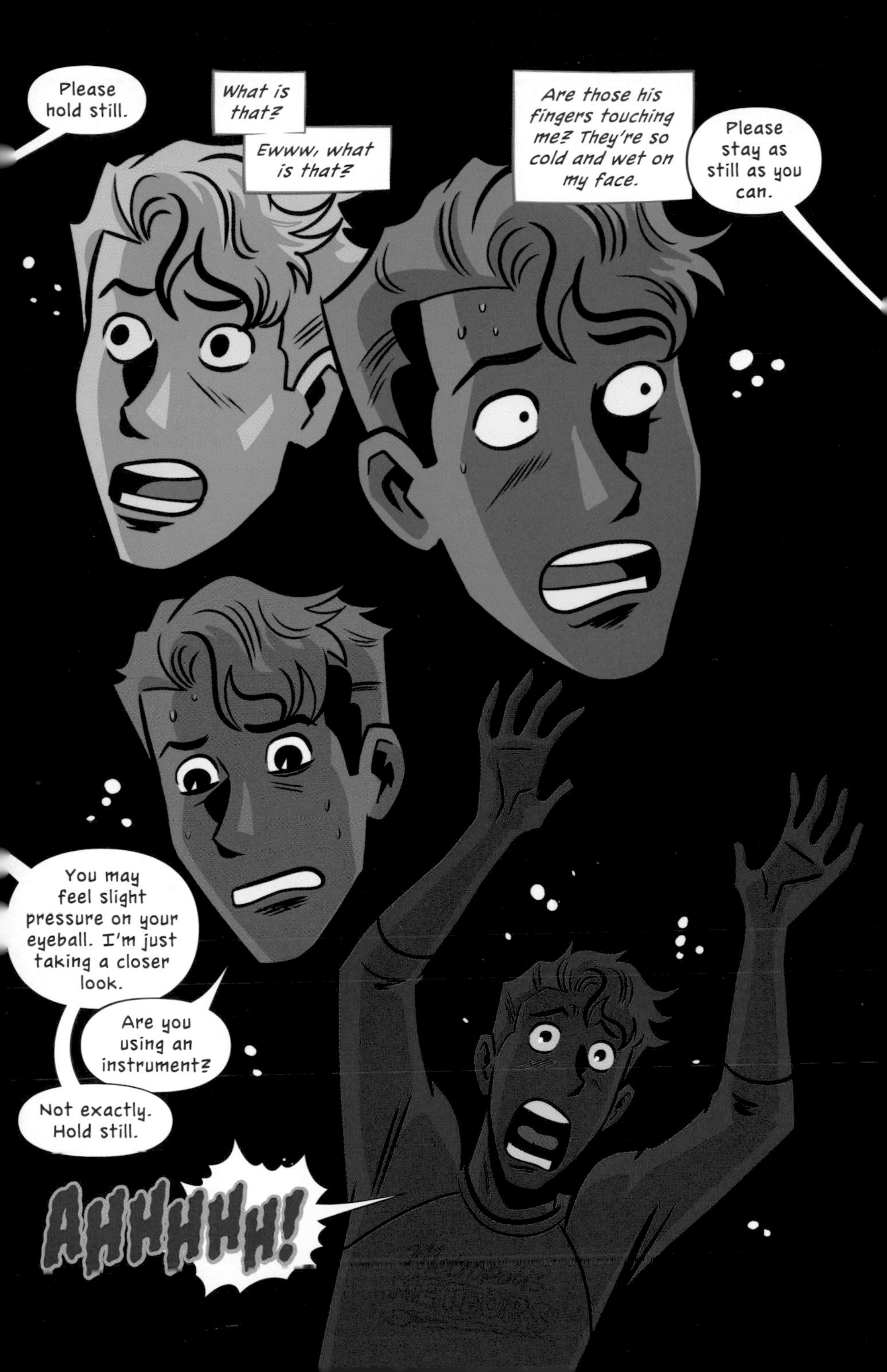
Please hold still.
What is that?
Ewww, what is that?
Are those his fingers touching me? They're so cold and wet on my face.
Please stay as still as you can.
You may feel slight pressure on your eyeball. I'm just taking a closer look.
Are you using an instrument?
Not exactly. Hold still.
AHHHHHH!

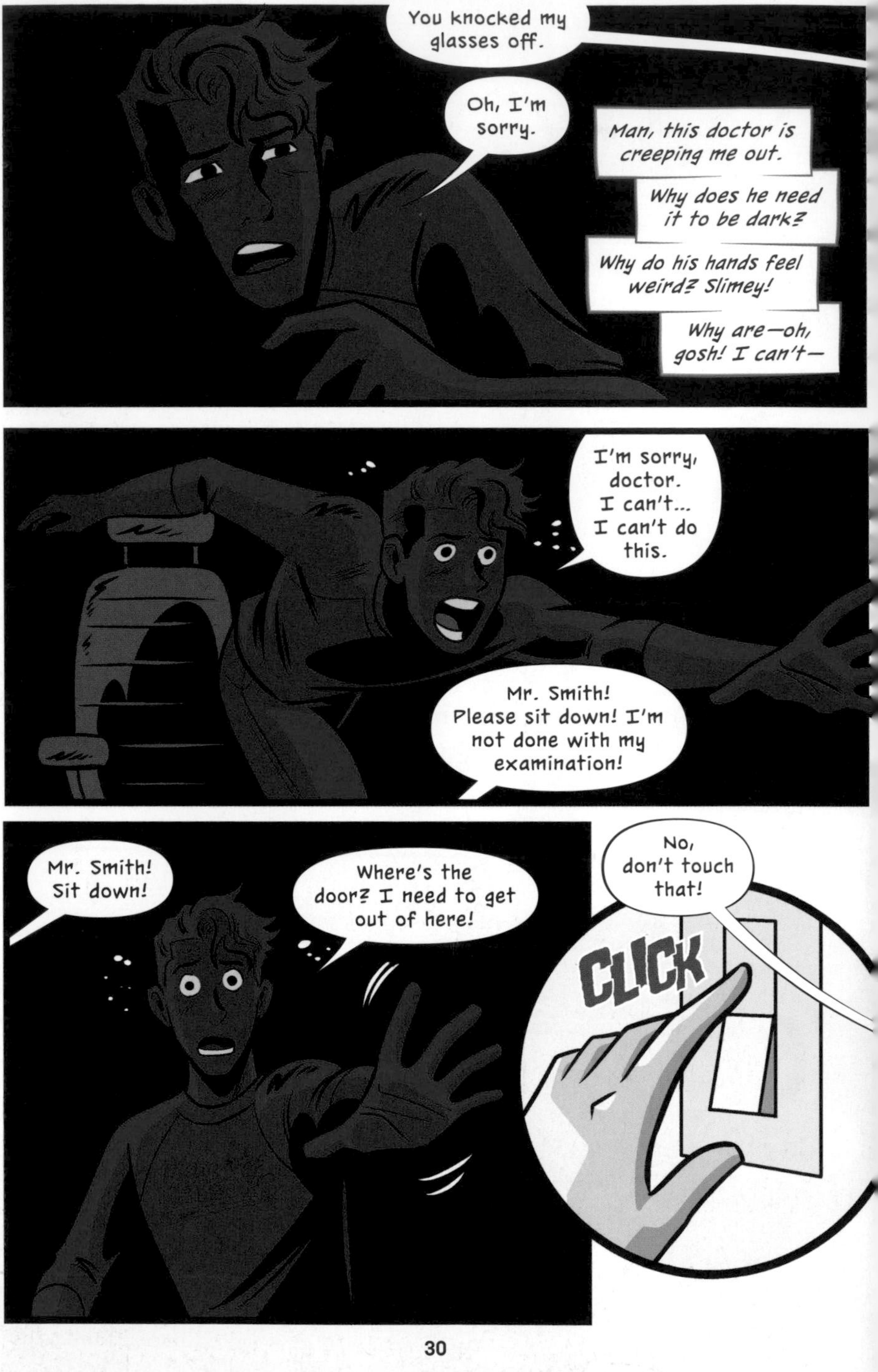
You knocked my glasses off.
Oh, I'm sorry.
Man, this doctor is creeping me out.
Why does he need it to be dark?
Why do his hands feel weird? Slimey!
Why are—oh, gosh! I can't—
I'm sorry, doctor. I can't... I can't do this.
Mr. Smith! Please sit down! I'm not done with my examination!
Mr. Smith! Sit down!
Where's the door? I need to get out of here!
No, don't touch that!
CLICK

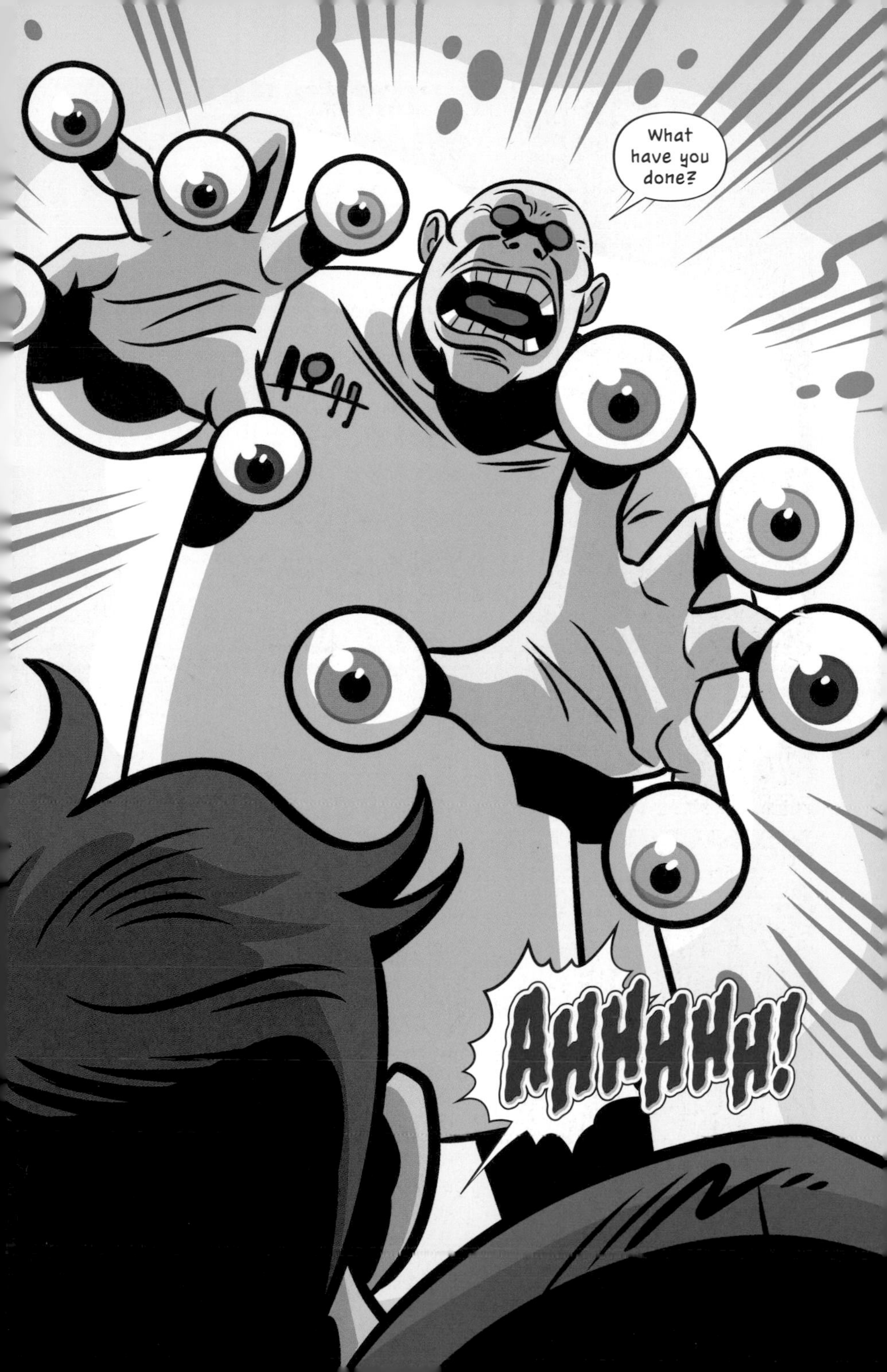
What have you done?
AHHHHH!

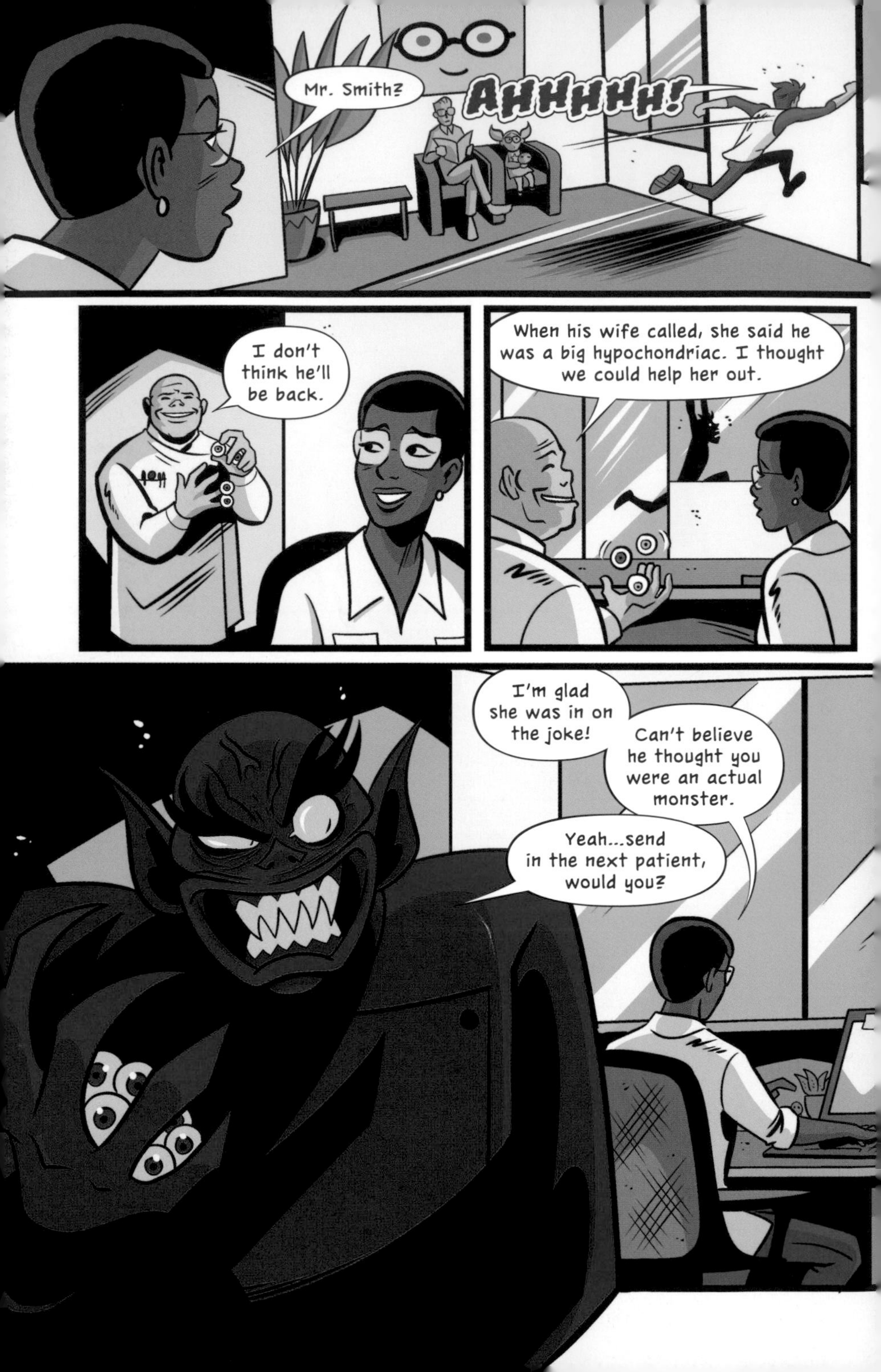
Mr. Smith?
AHHHHH!
I don't think he'll be back.
When his wife called, she said he was a big hypochondriac. I thought we could help her out.
I'm glad she was in on the joke!
Can't believe he thought you were an actual monster.
Yeah...send in the next patient, would you?

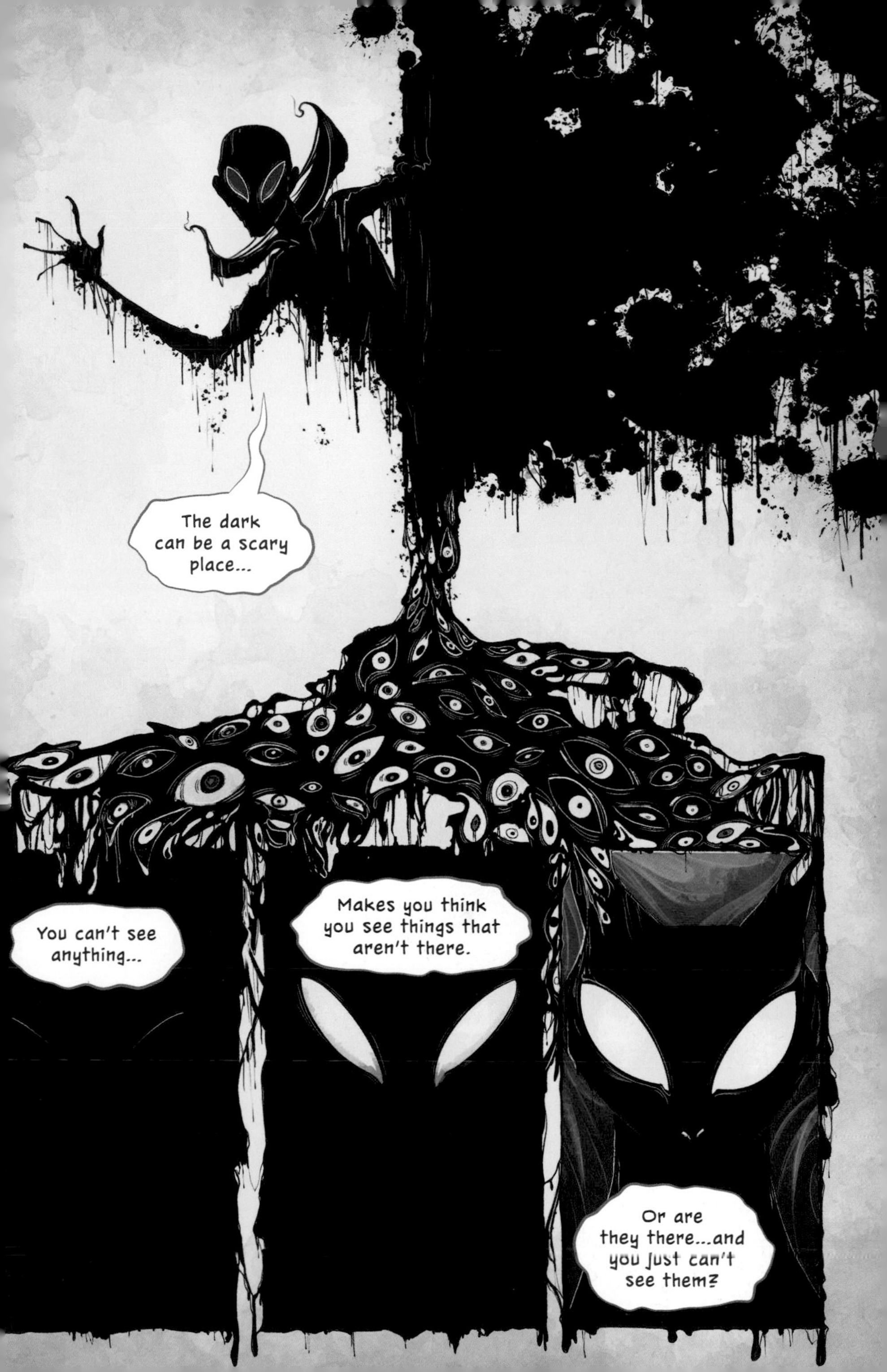
The dark can be a scary place...
You can't see anything...
Makes you think you see things that aren't there.
Or are they there...and you just can't see them?

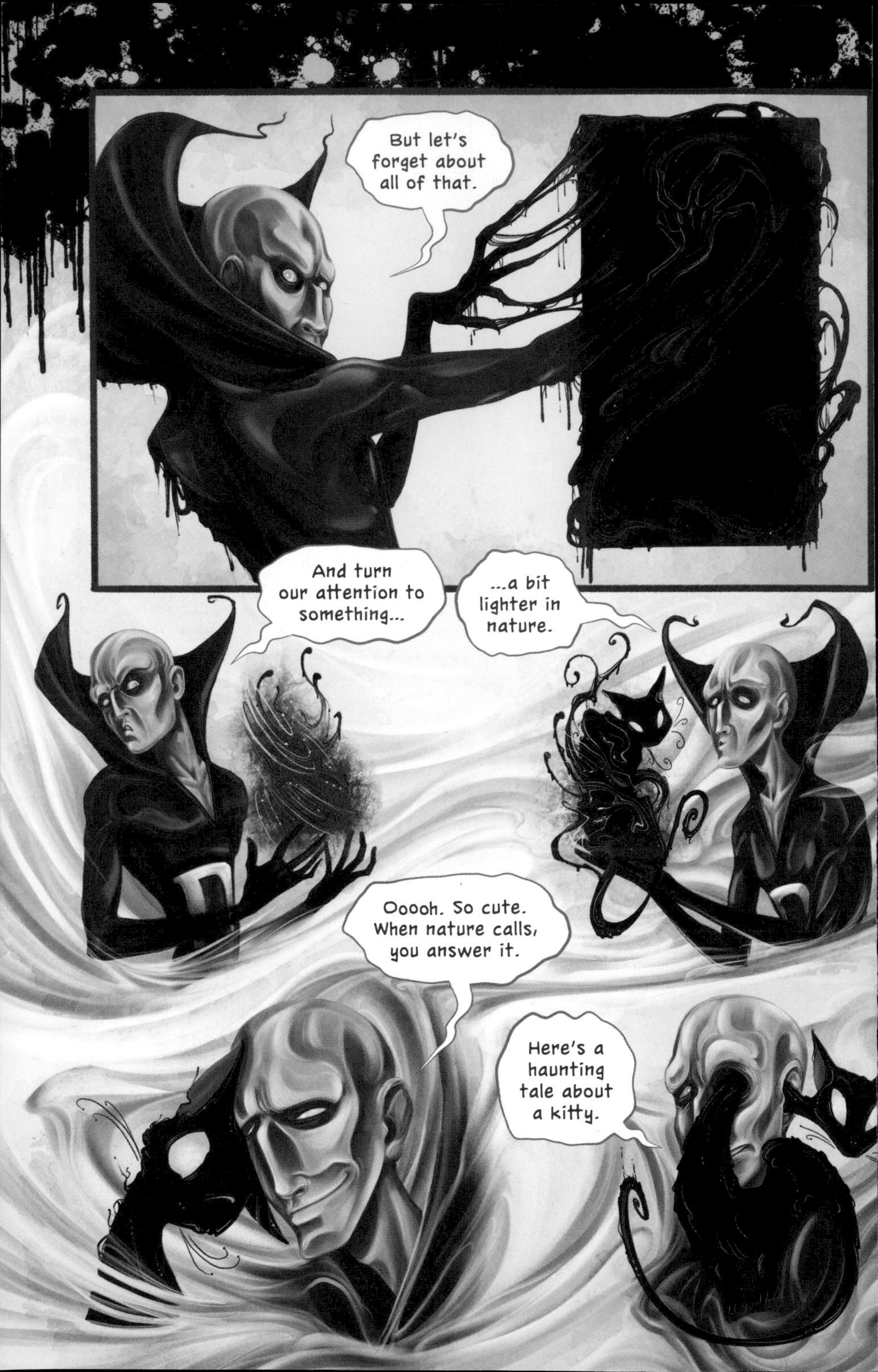
But let's forget about all of that.
And turn our attention to something...
...a bit lighter in nature.
Ooooh. So cute. When nature calls, you answer it.
Here's a haunting tale about a kitty.

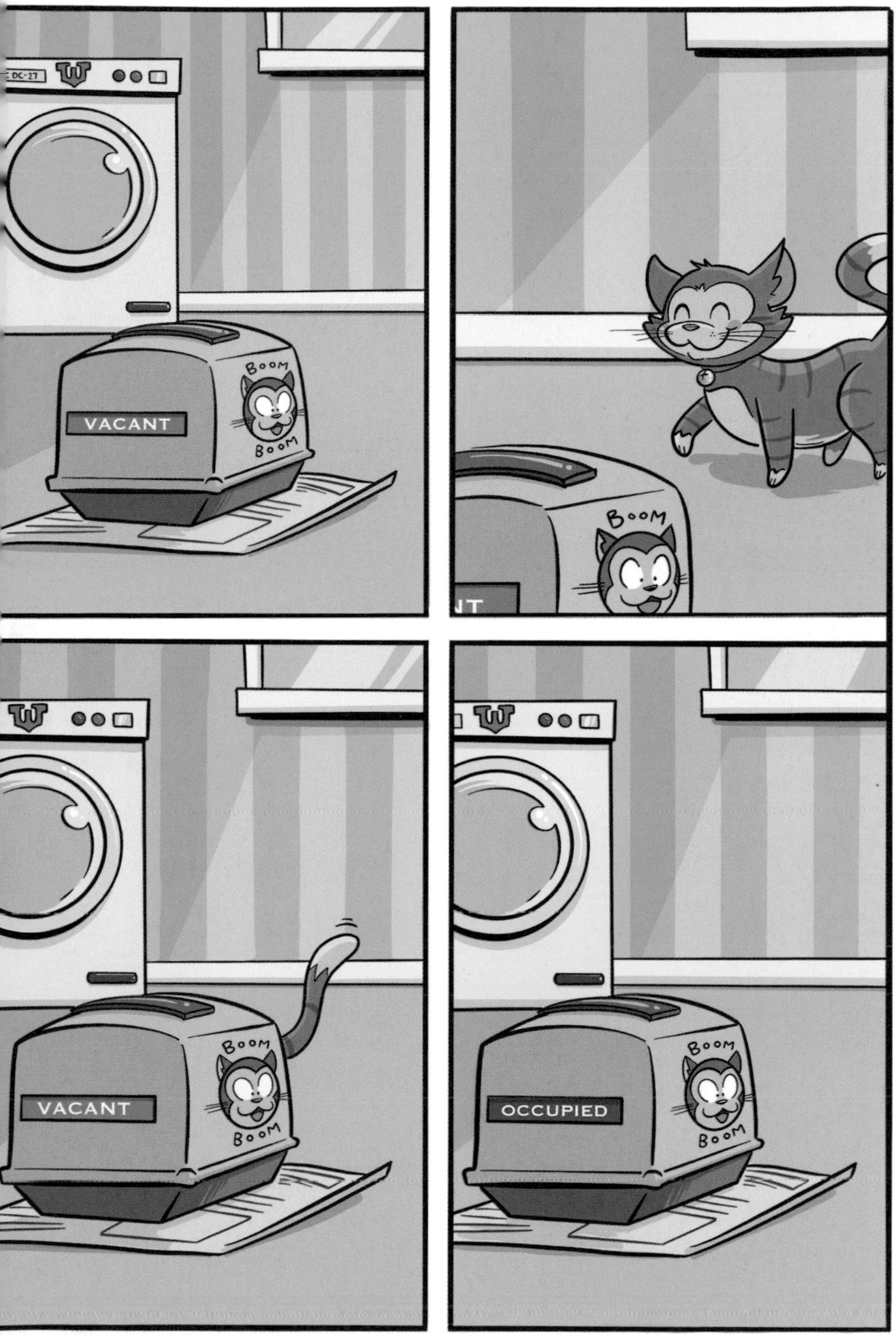
DC-27
BOOM
VACANT
BOOM
BOOM
BOOM
VACANT
BOOM
BOOM
OCCUPIED
BOOM

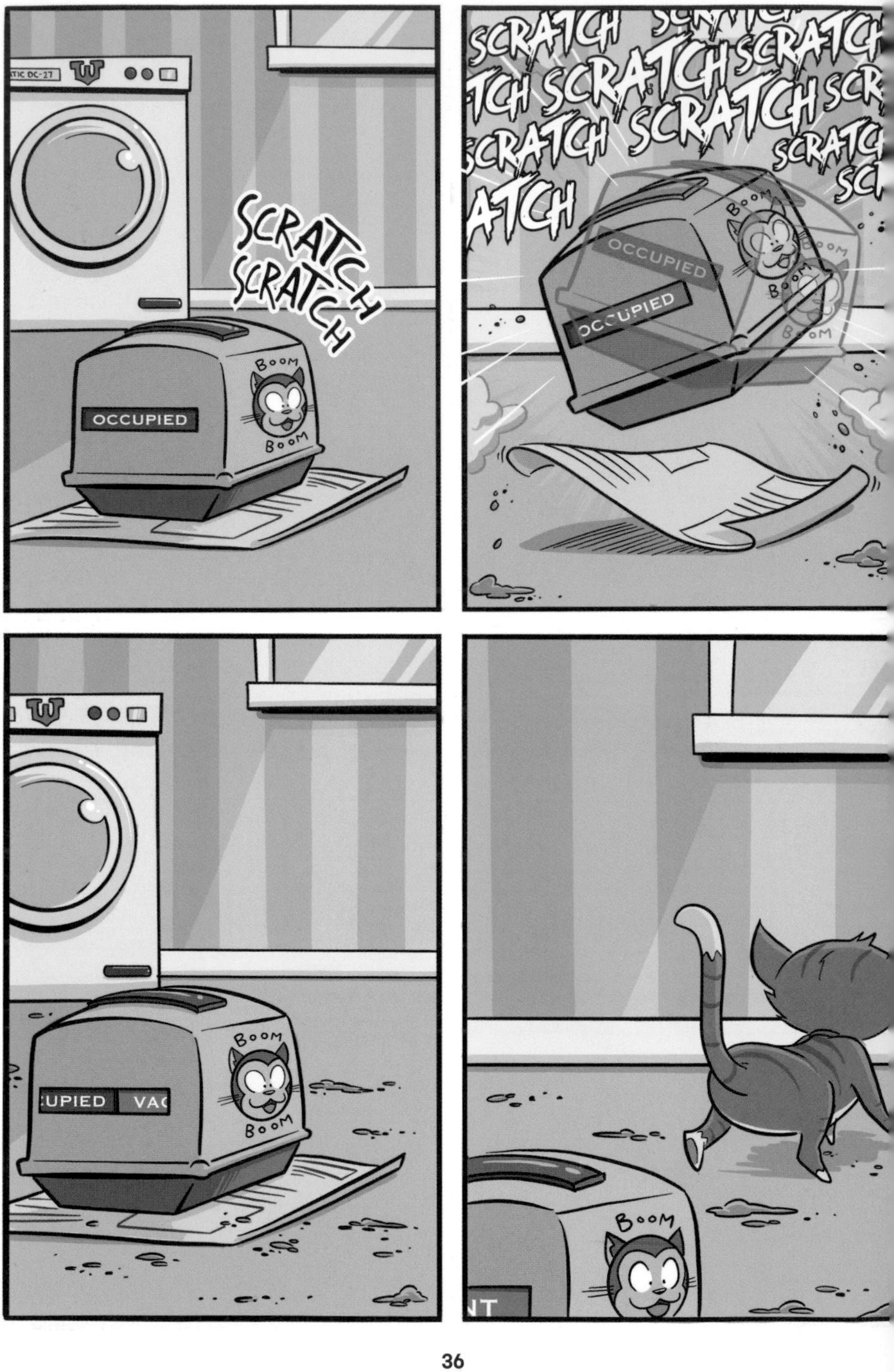
SCRATCH
SCRATCH
OCCUPIED
BOOM
BOOM
SCRATCH SCRATCH SCRATCH SCRATCH SCRATCH SCRATCH SCRATCH
OCCUPIED
OCCUPIED
BOOM
BOOM
BOOM
BOOM
BOOM

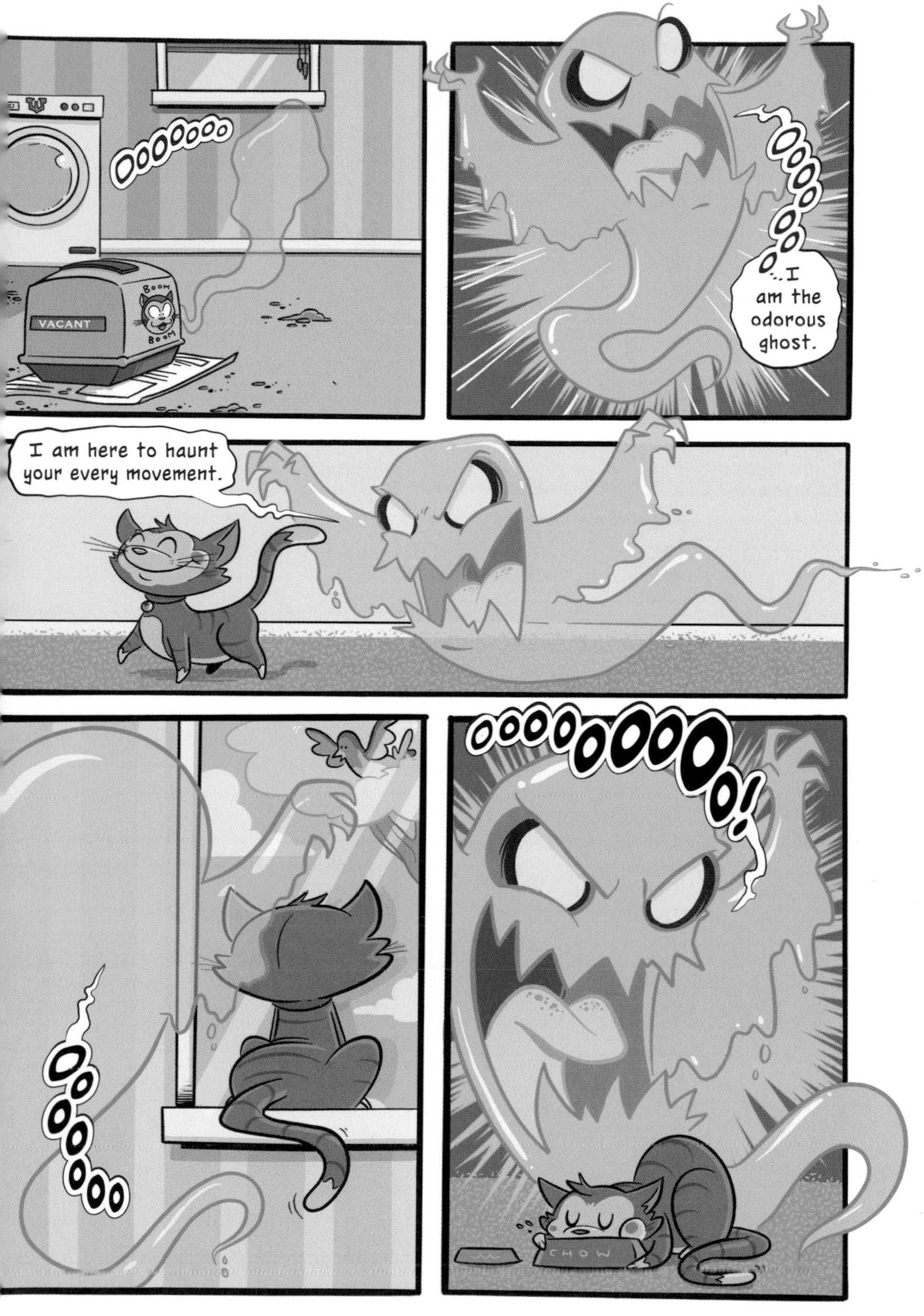

OOOOooo
VACANT
BOOM BOOM
OOOOOOOO...I am the odorous ghost.
I am here to haunt your every movement.
OOOOOOOO
OOOOOOOOOOOOO!
CHOW

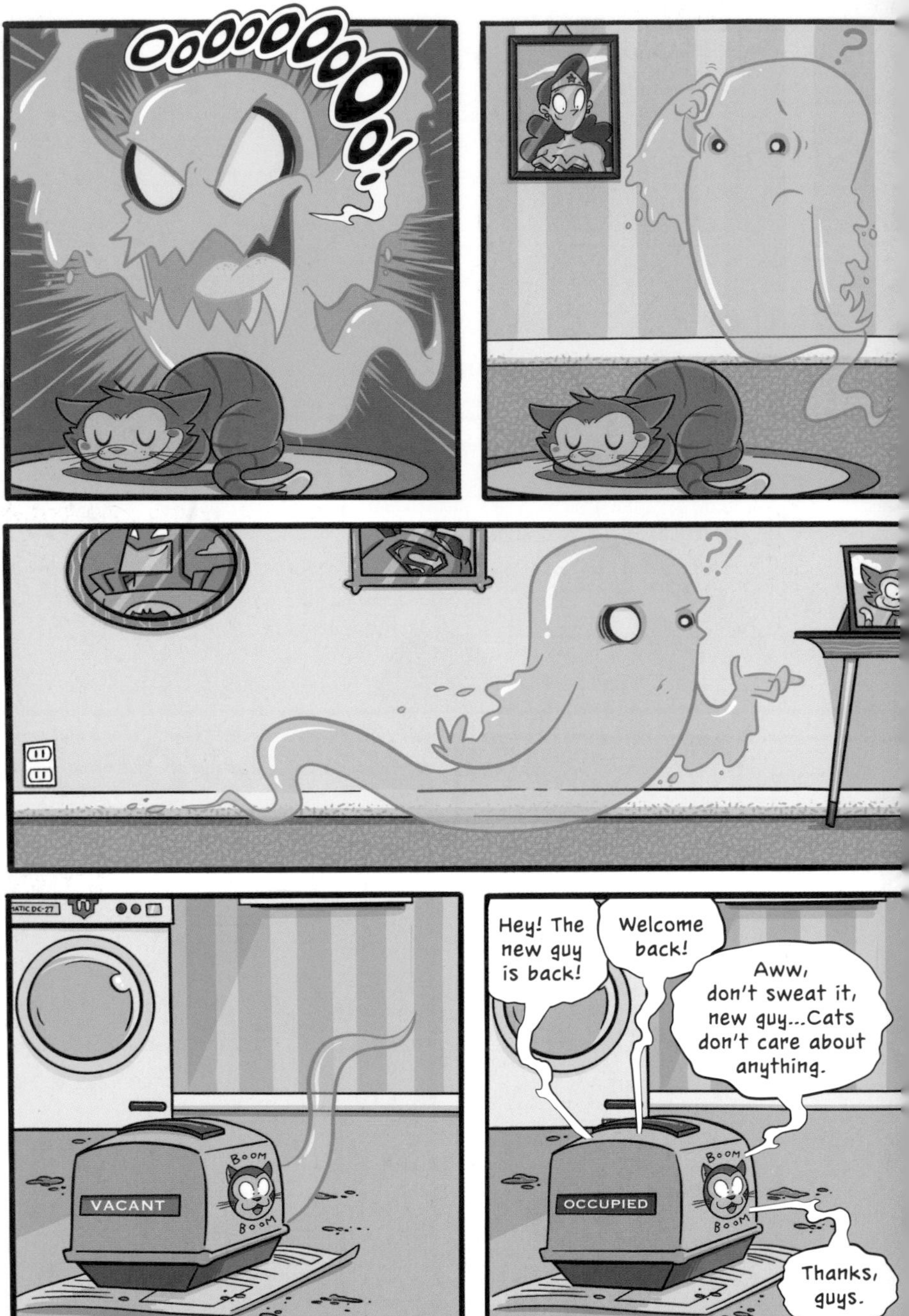

OoooooOOOo!
?
?!
VACANT
OCCUPIED
Hey! The new guy is back!
Welcome back!
Aww, don't sweat it, new guy...Cats don't care about anything.
Thanks, guys.

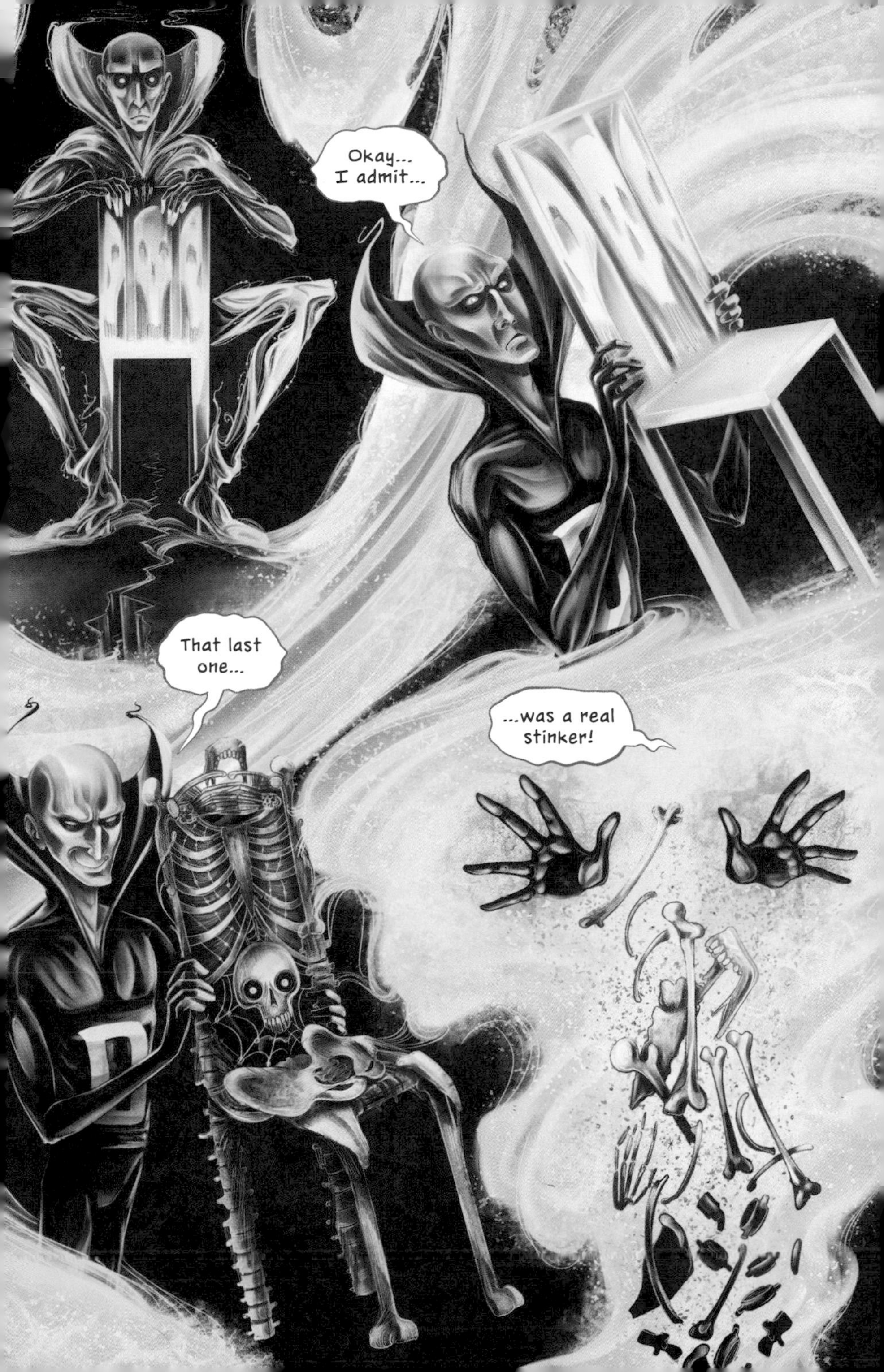
Okay... I admit...
That last one...
...was a real stinker!

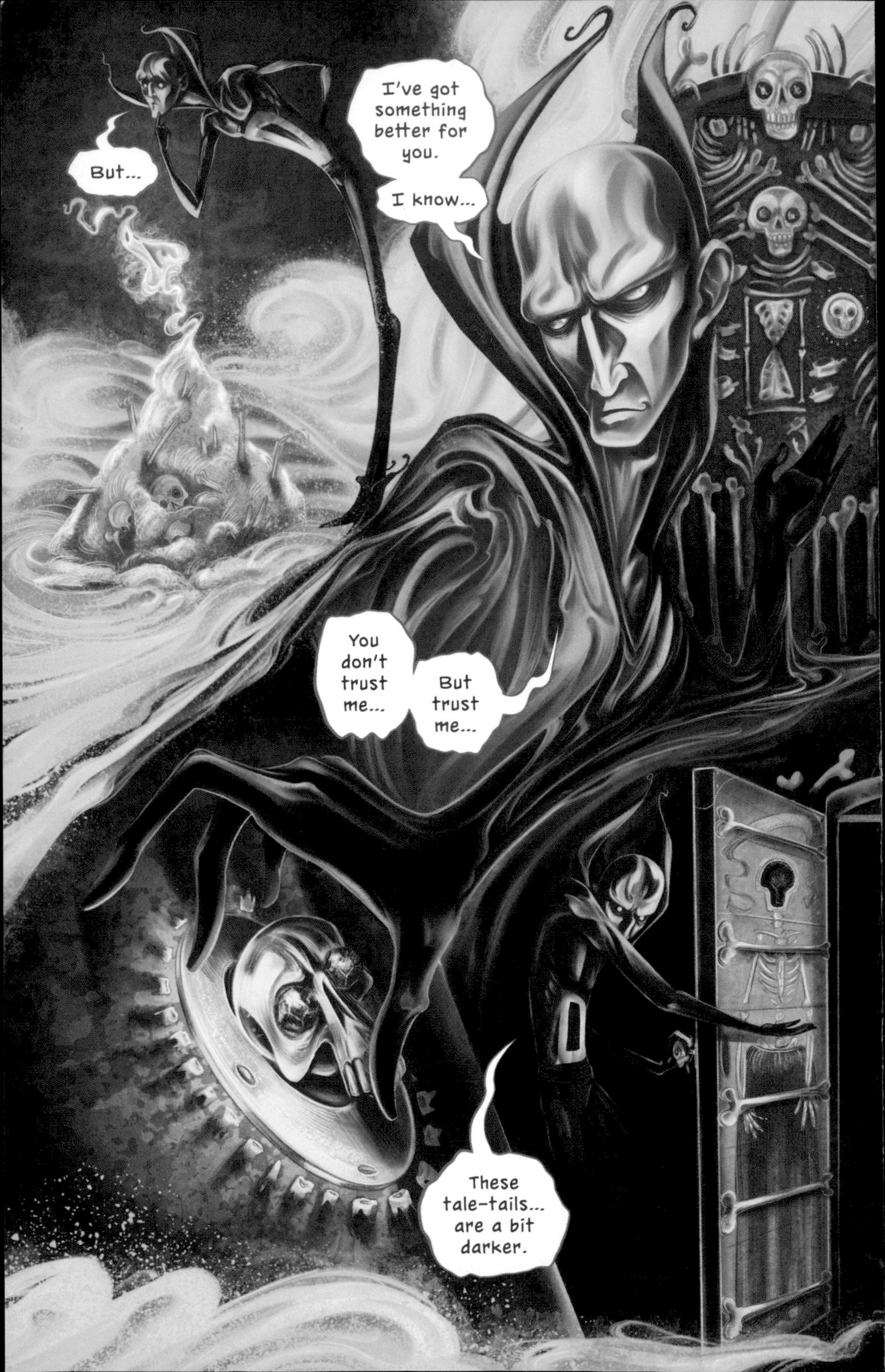

But...
I've got something better for you.
I know...
You don't trust me...
But trust me...
These tale-tails... are a bit darker.

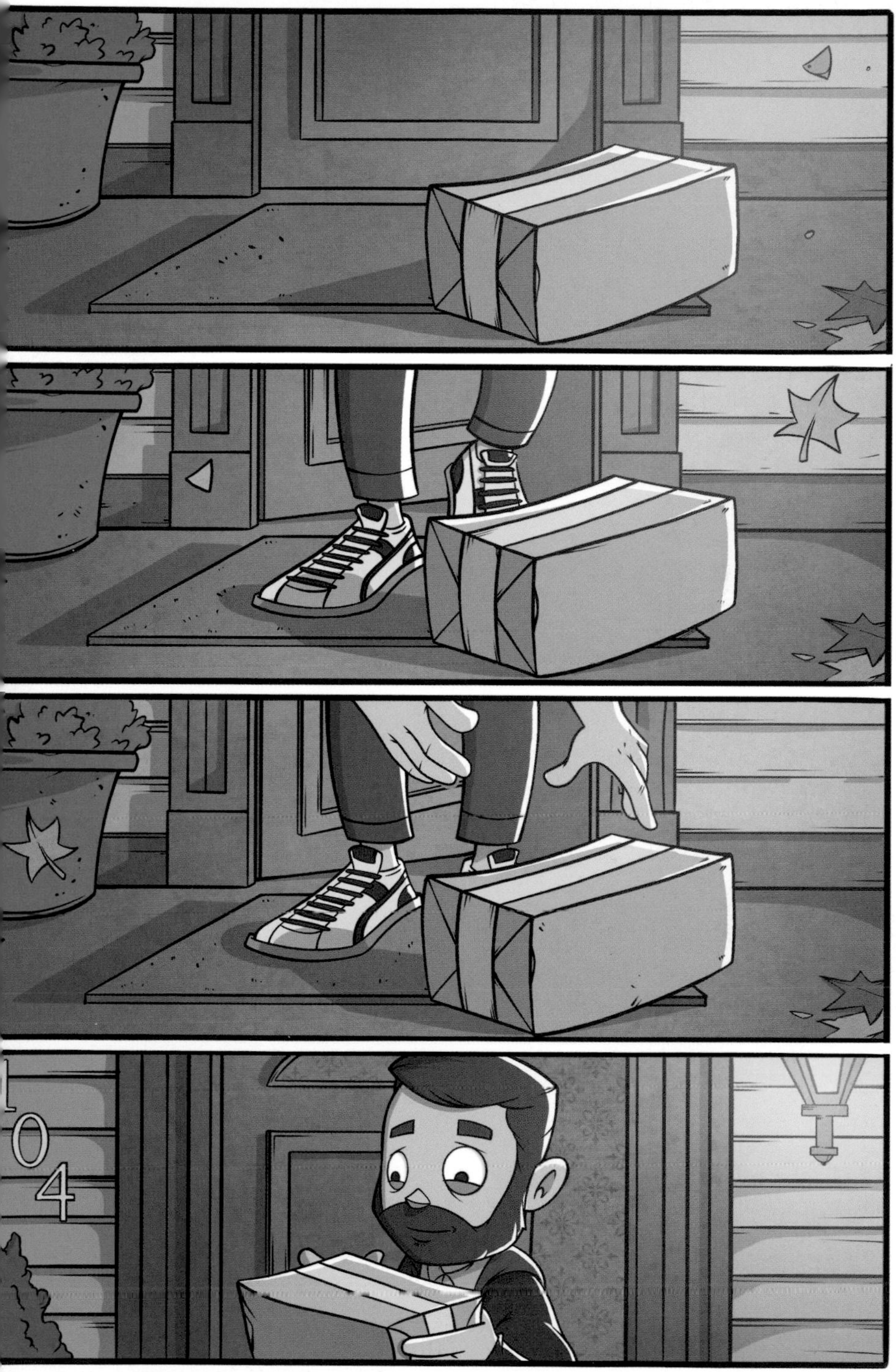
104

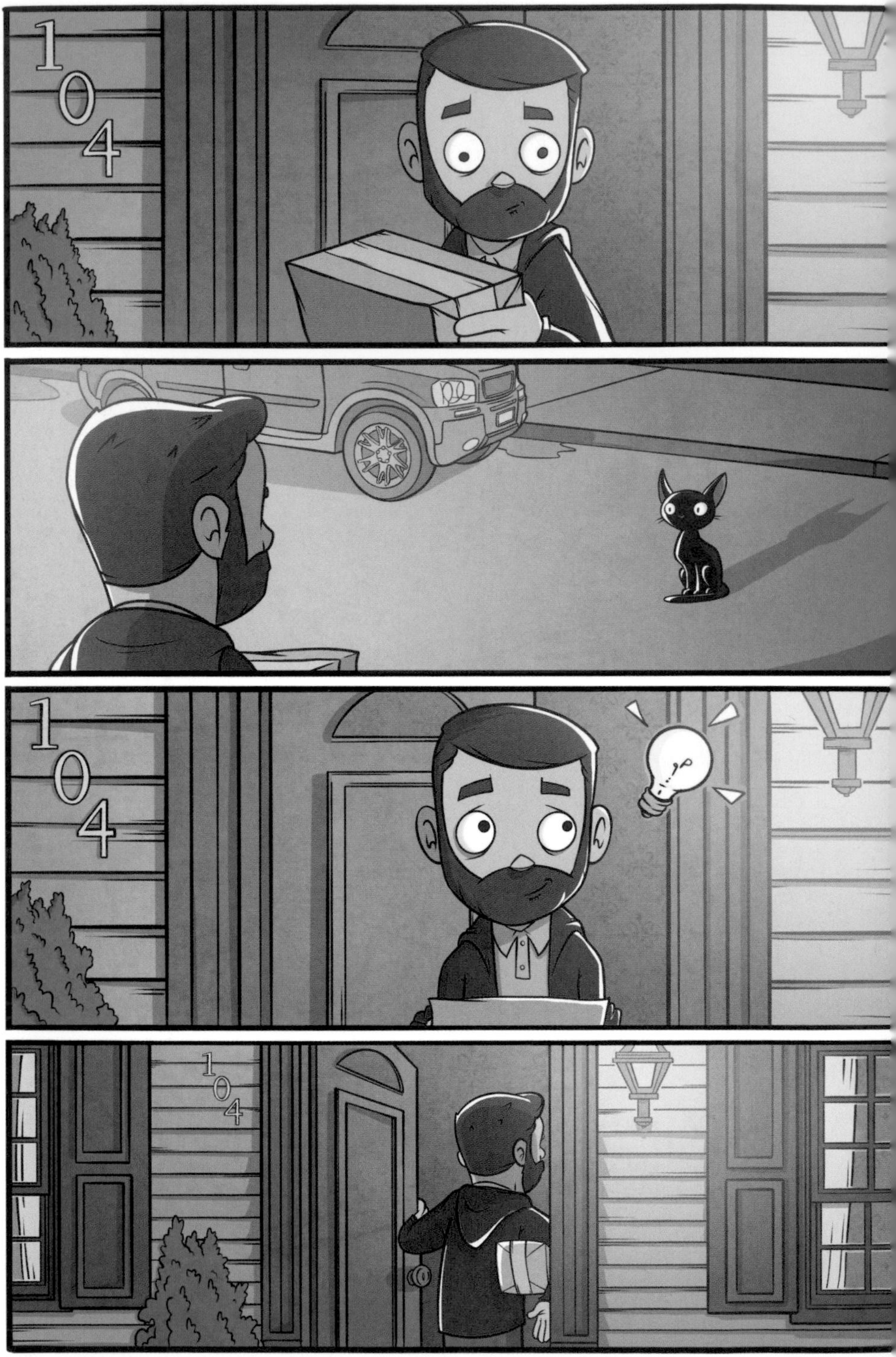
104
104
104

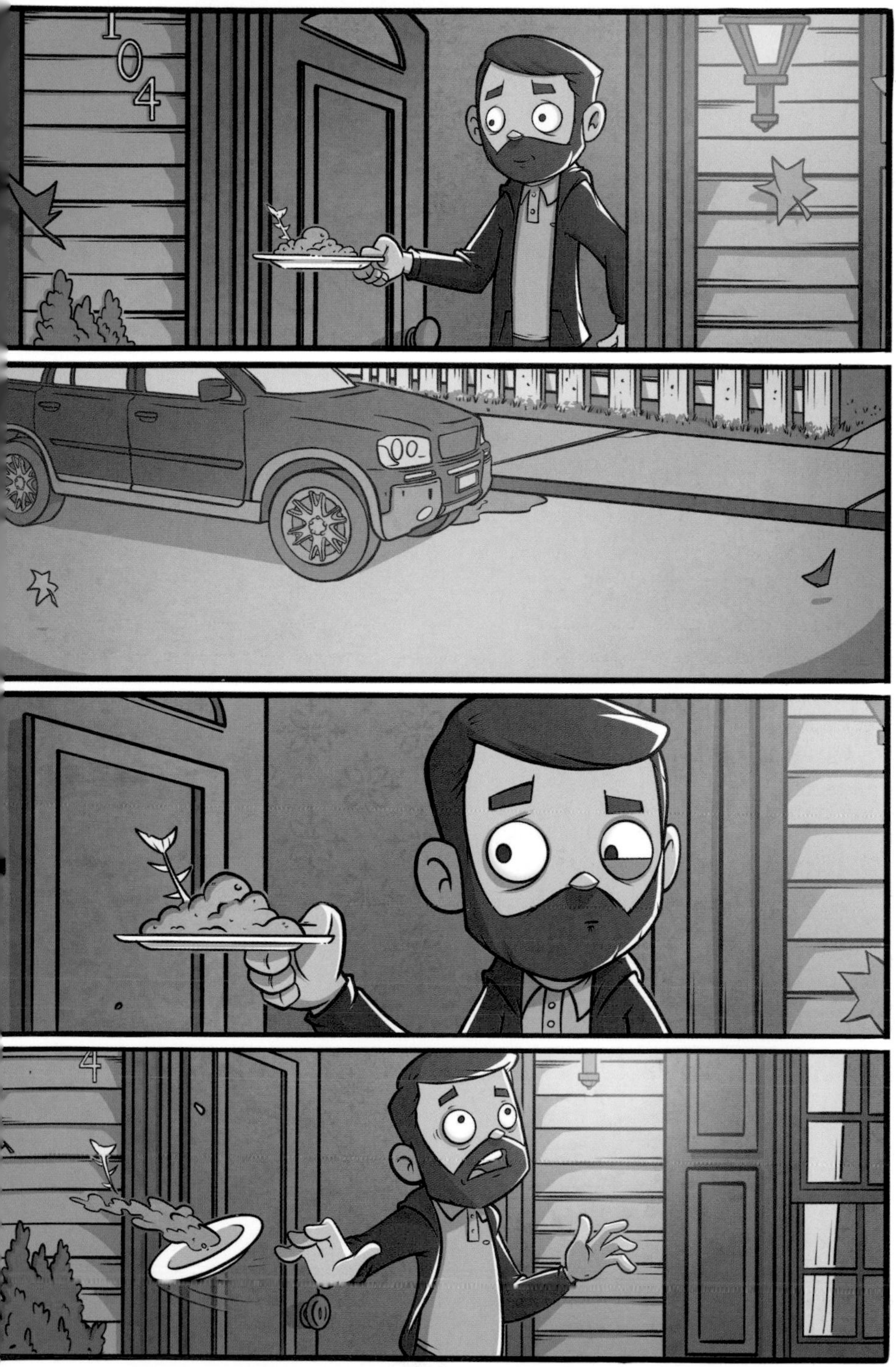
104
4

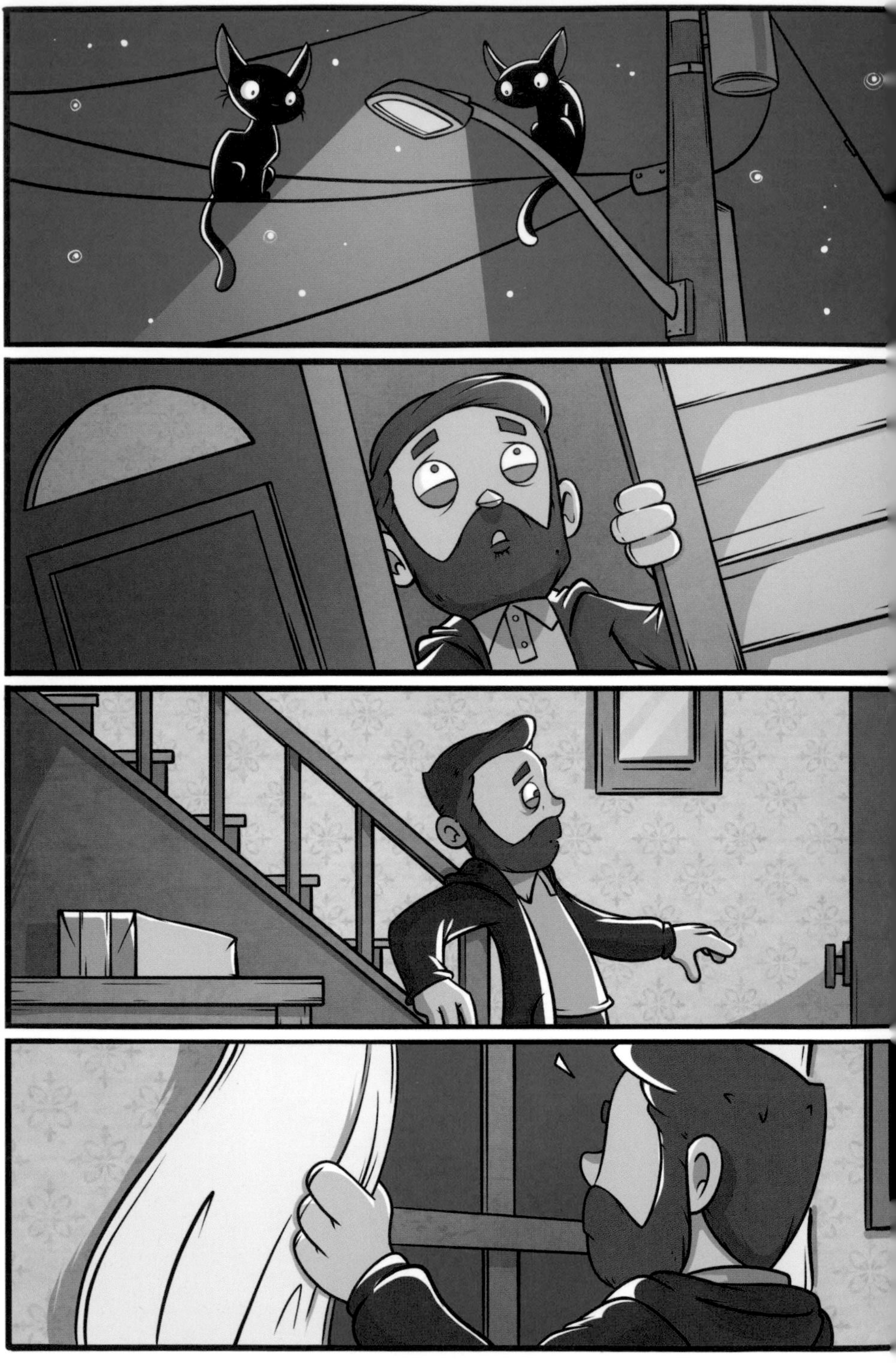

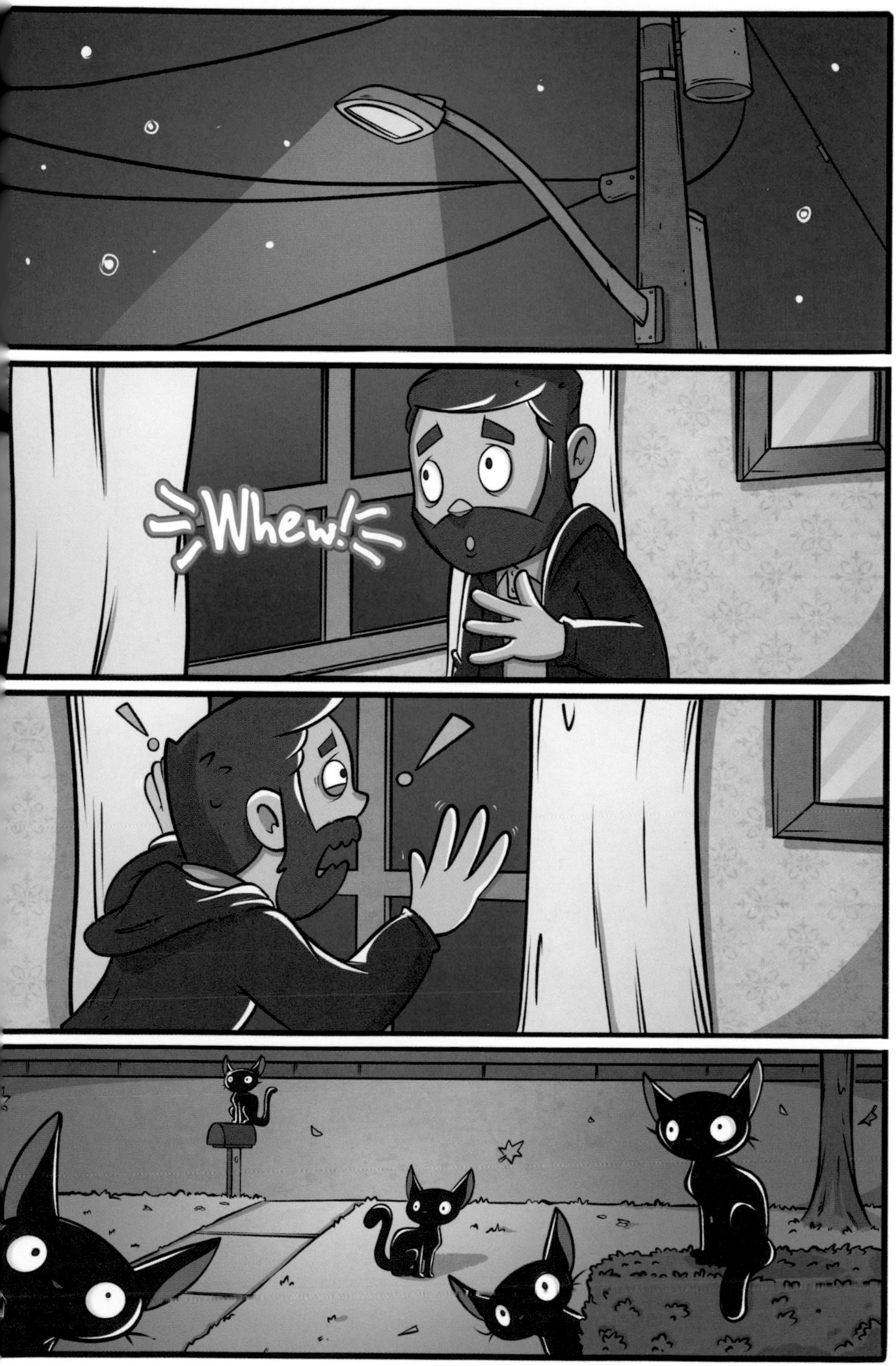
Whew!

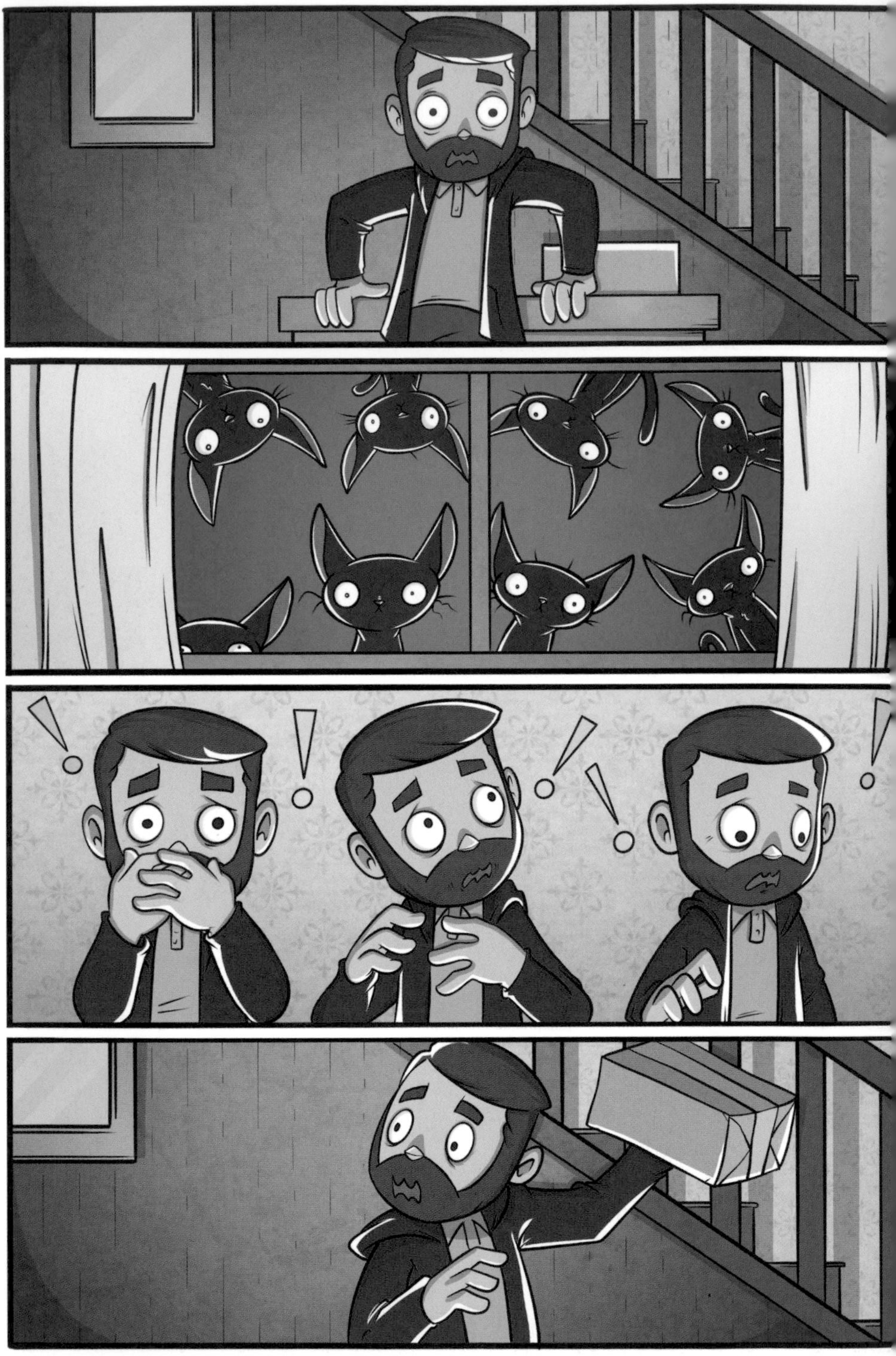

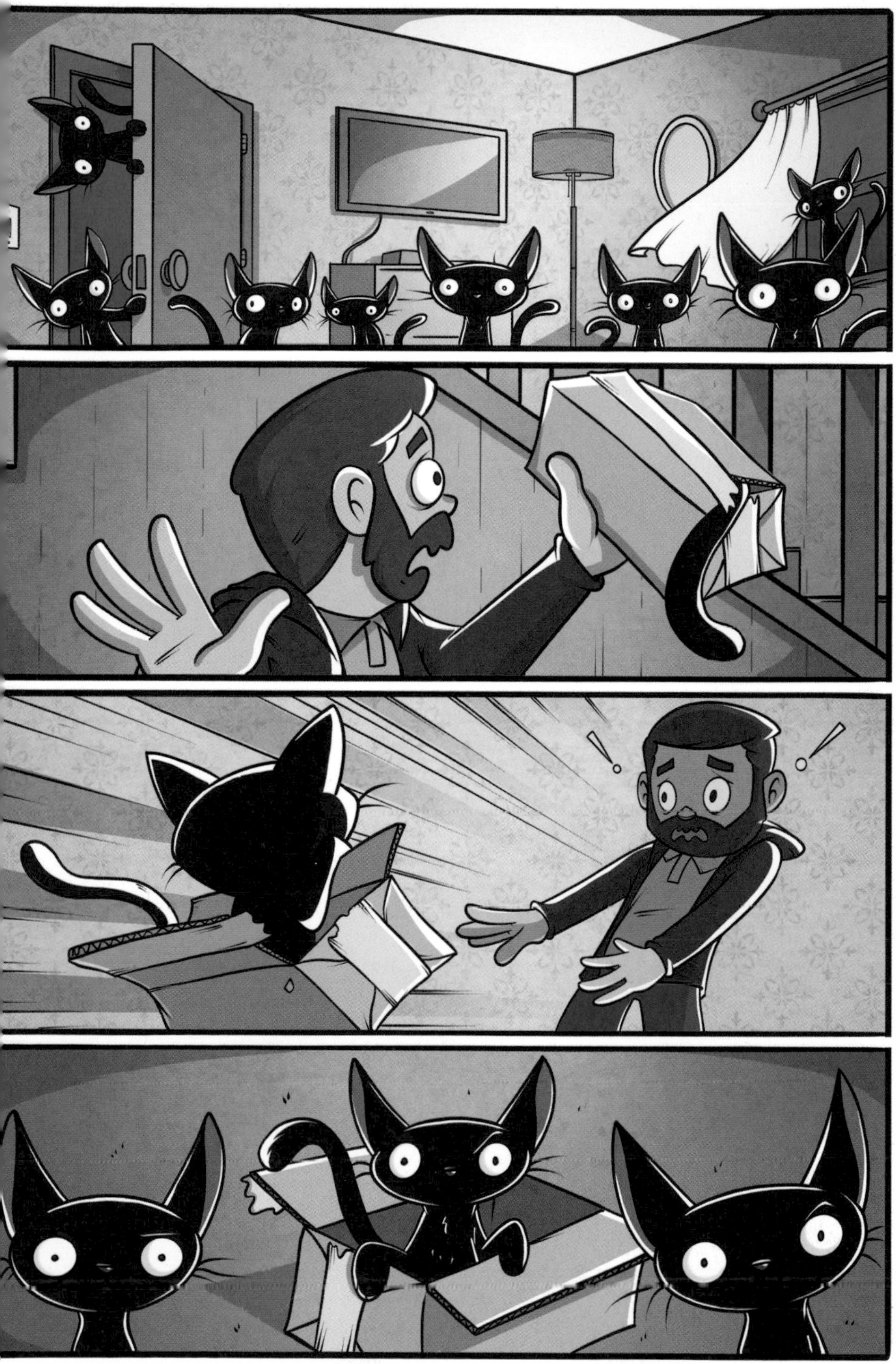

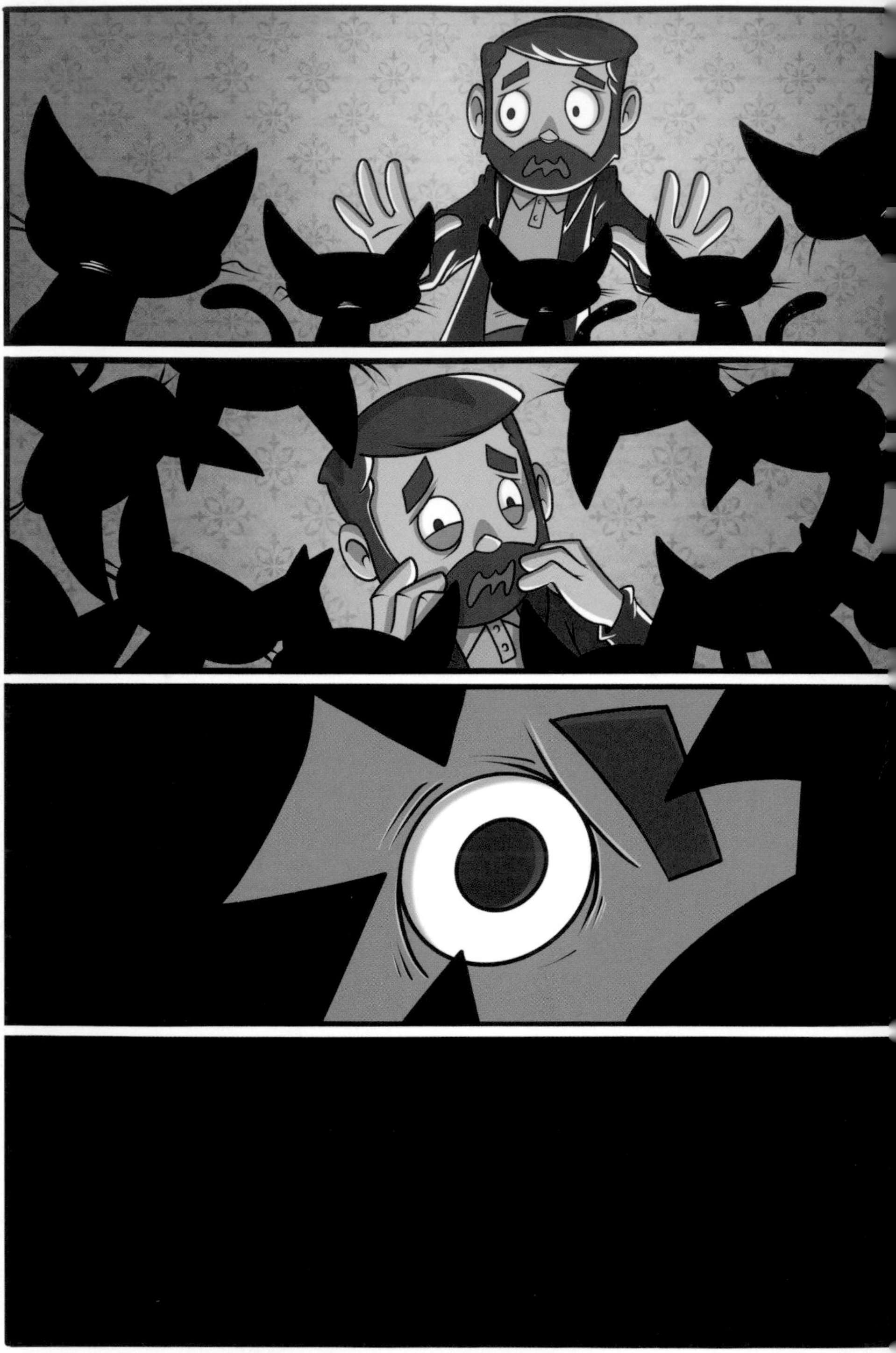

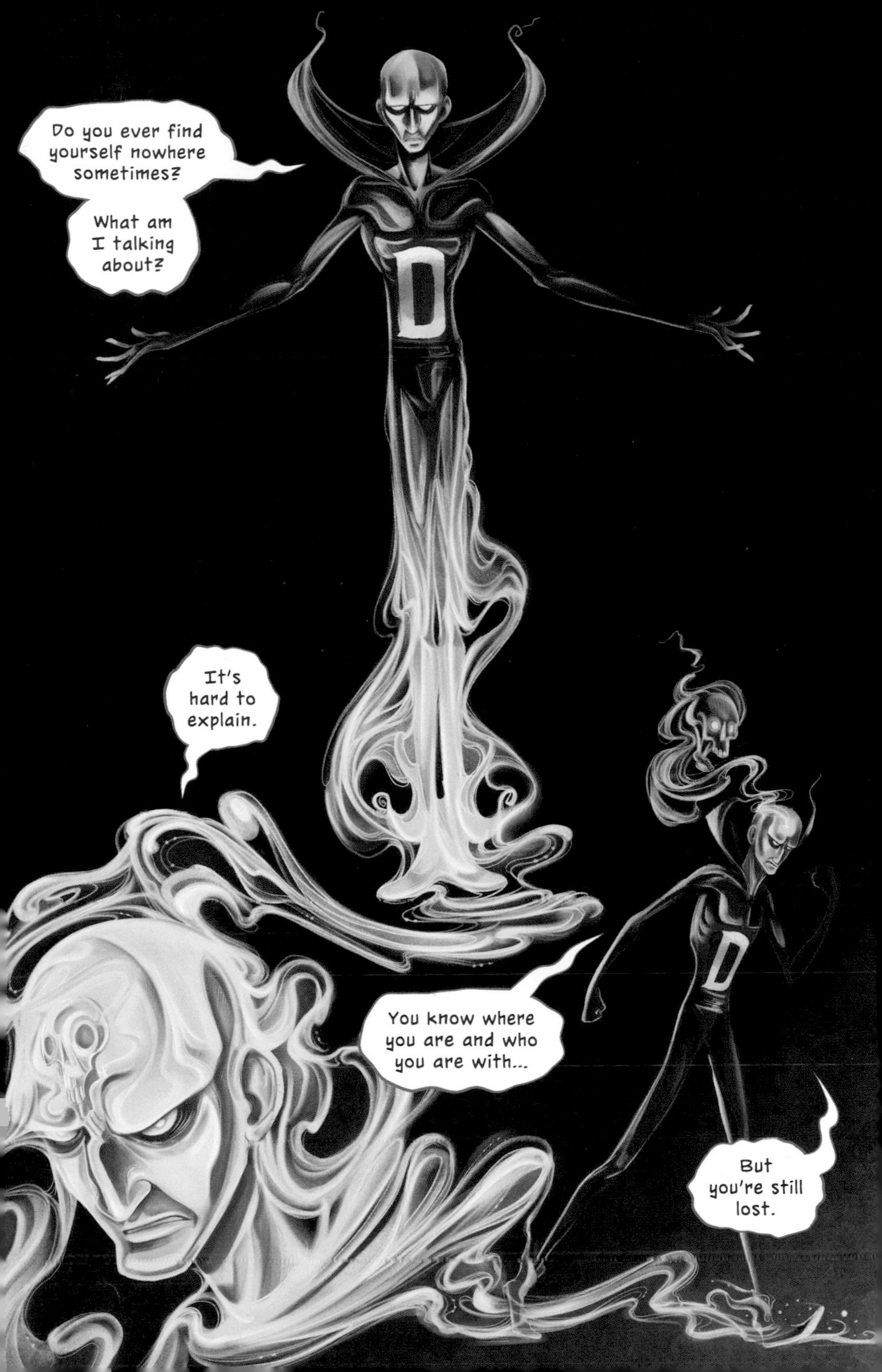

Do you ever find yourself nowhere sometimes?
What am I talking about?
It's hard to explain.
You know where you are and who you are with...
But you're still lost.

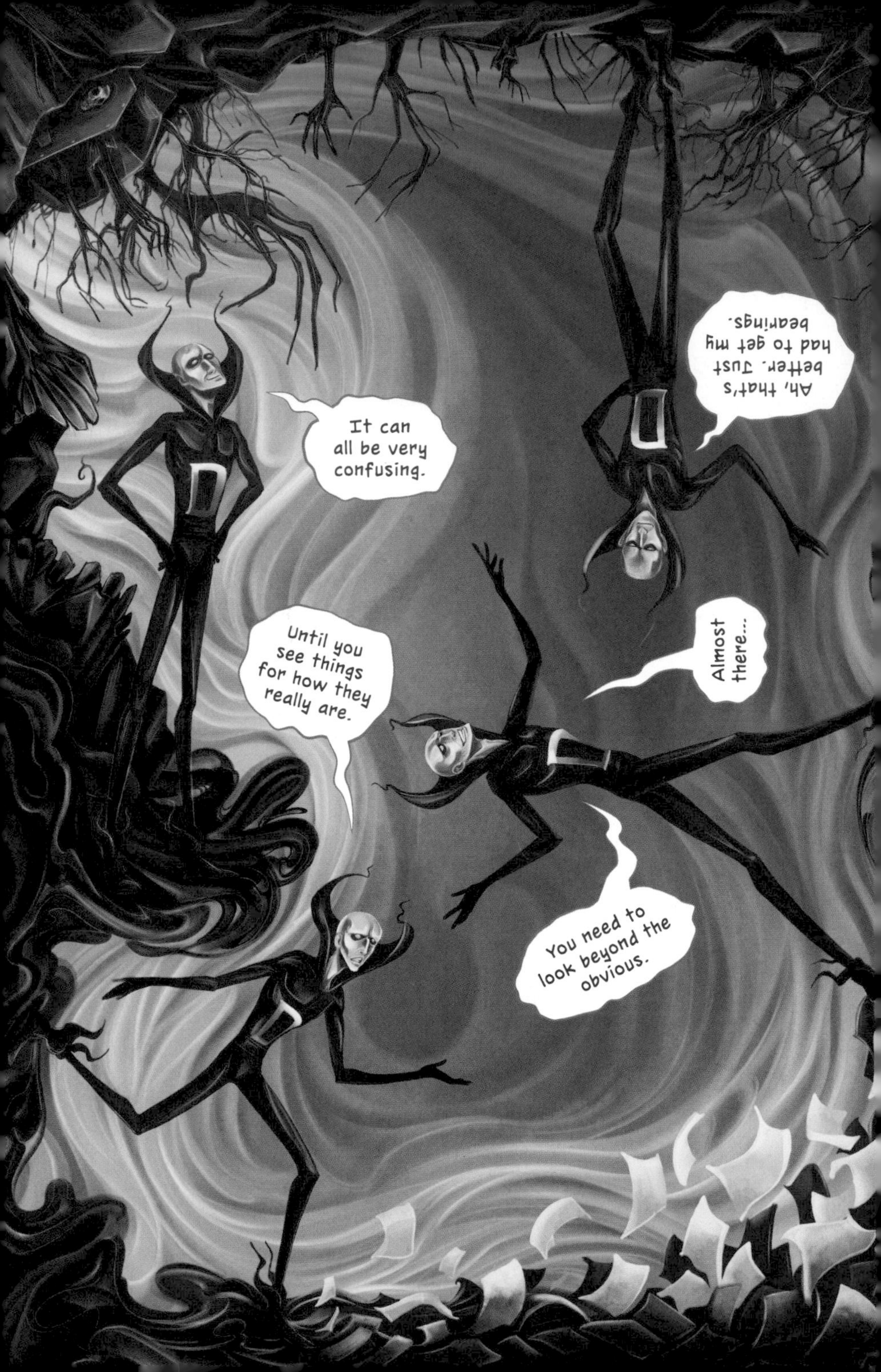
Ah, that's better. Just had to get my bearings.
It can all be very confusing.
Almost there...
Until you see things for how they really are.
You need to look beyond the obvious.

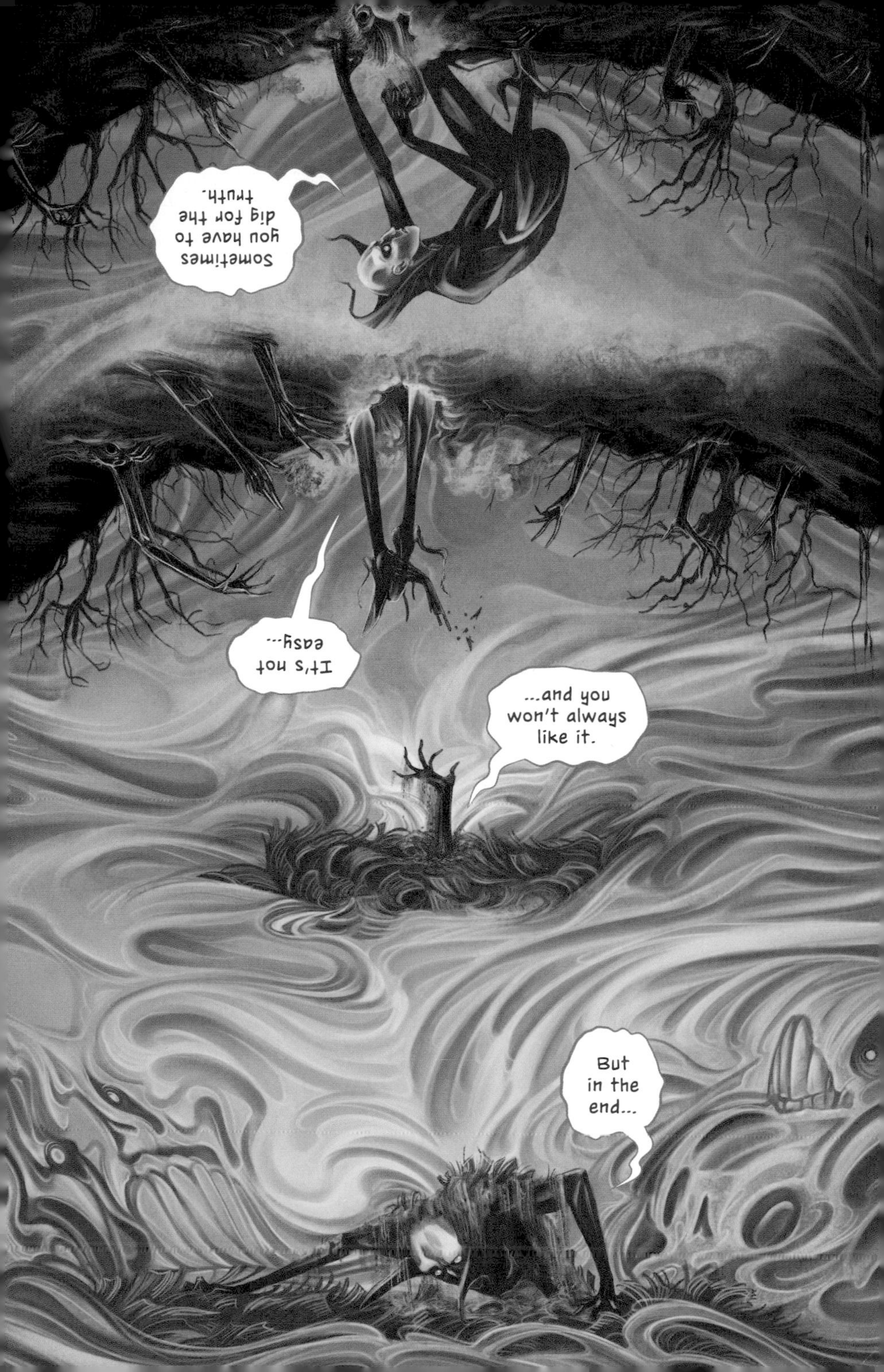
Sometimes you have to dig for the truth.
It's not easy...
...and you won't always like it.
But in the end...

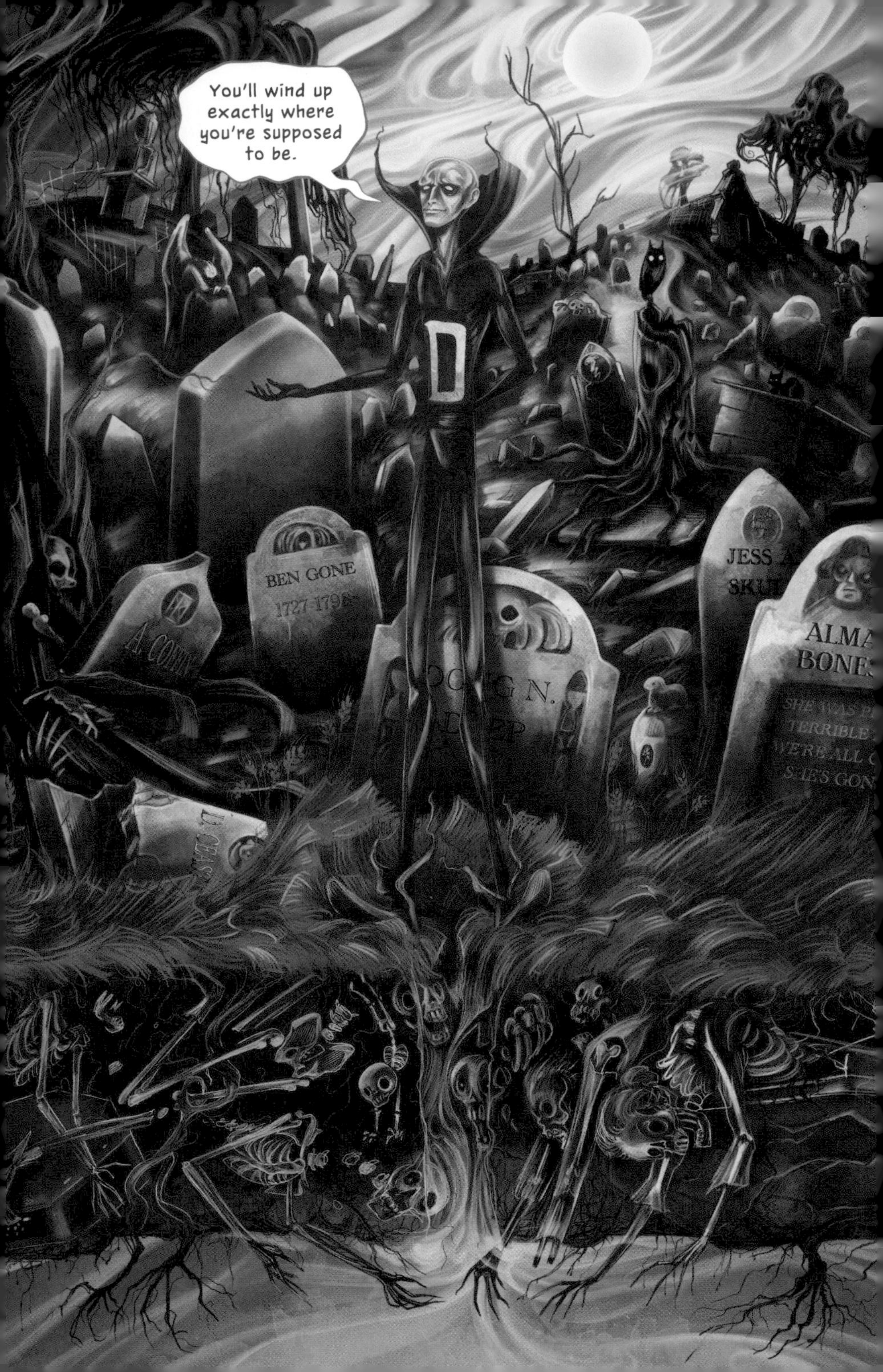
You'll wind up exactly where you're supposed to be.
BEN GONE

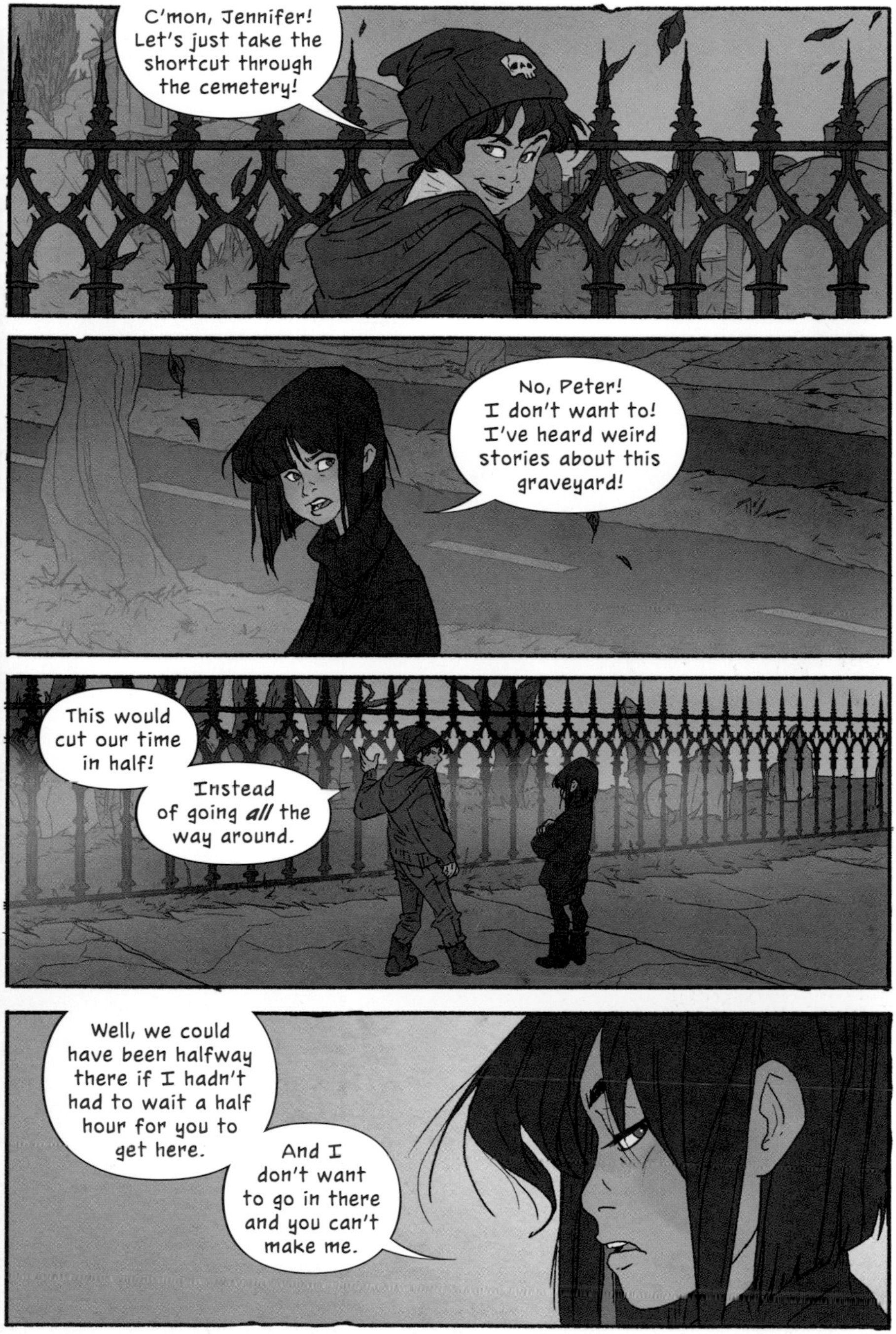
C'mon, Jennifer! Let's just take the shortcut through the cemetery!
No, Peter! I don't want to! I've heard weird stories about this graveyard!
This would cut our time in half!
Instead of going *all* the way around.
Well, we could have been halfway there if I hadn't had to wait a half hour for you to get here.
And I don't want to go in there and you can't make me.

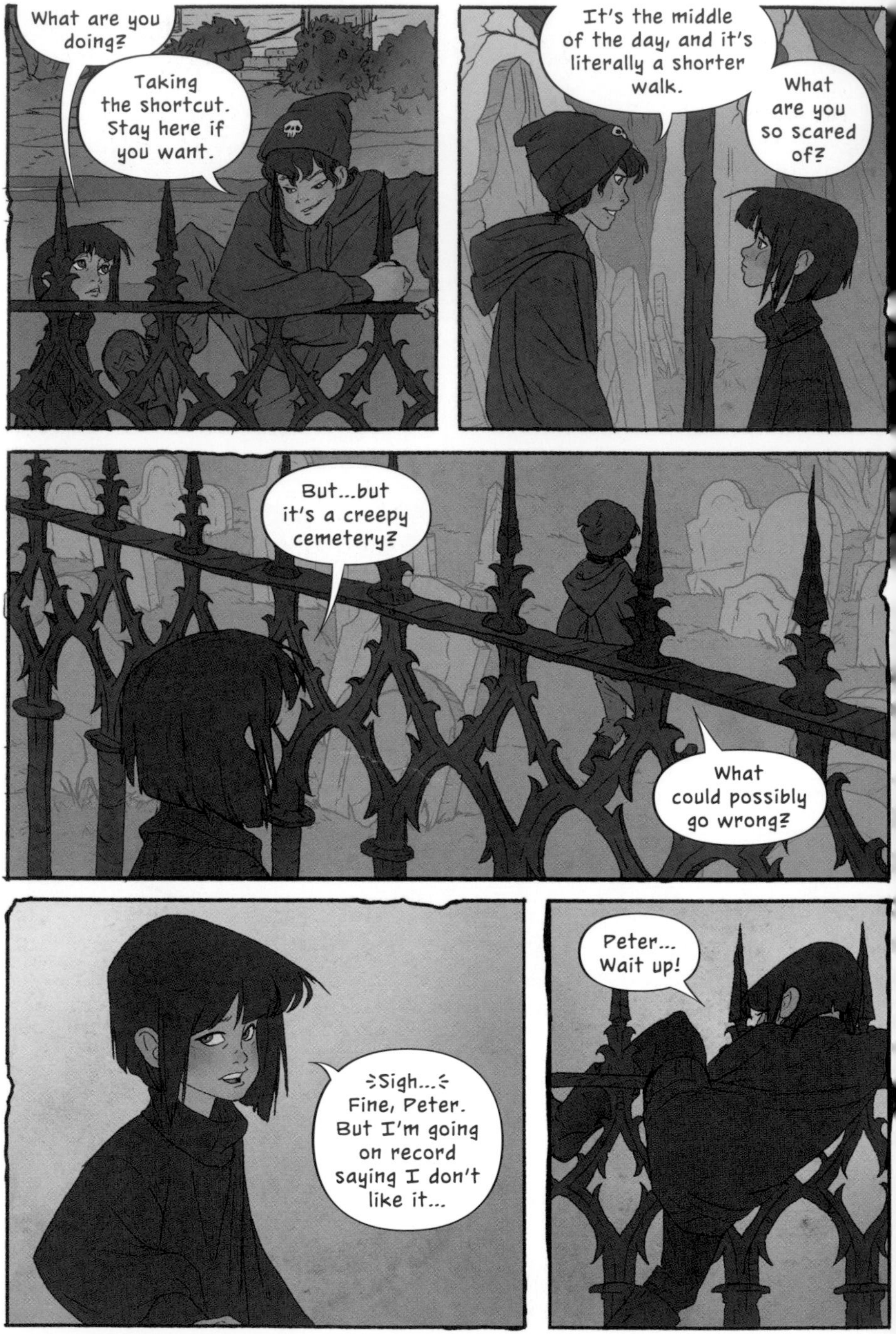
What are you doing?
Taking the shortcut. Stay here if you want.
It's the middle of the day, and it's literally a shorter walk.
What are you so scared of?
But...but it's a creepy cemetery?
What could possibly go wrong?
Sigh...
Fine, Peter. But I'm going on record saying I don't like it...
Peter... Wait up!

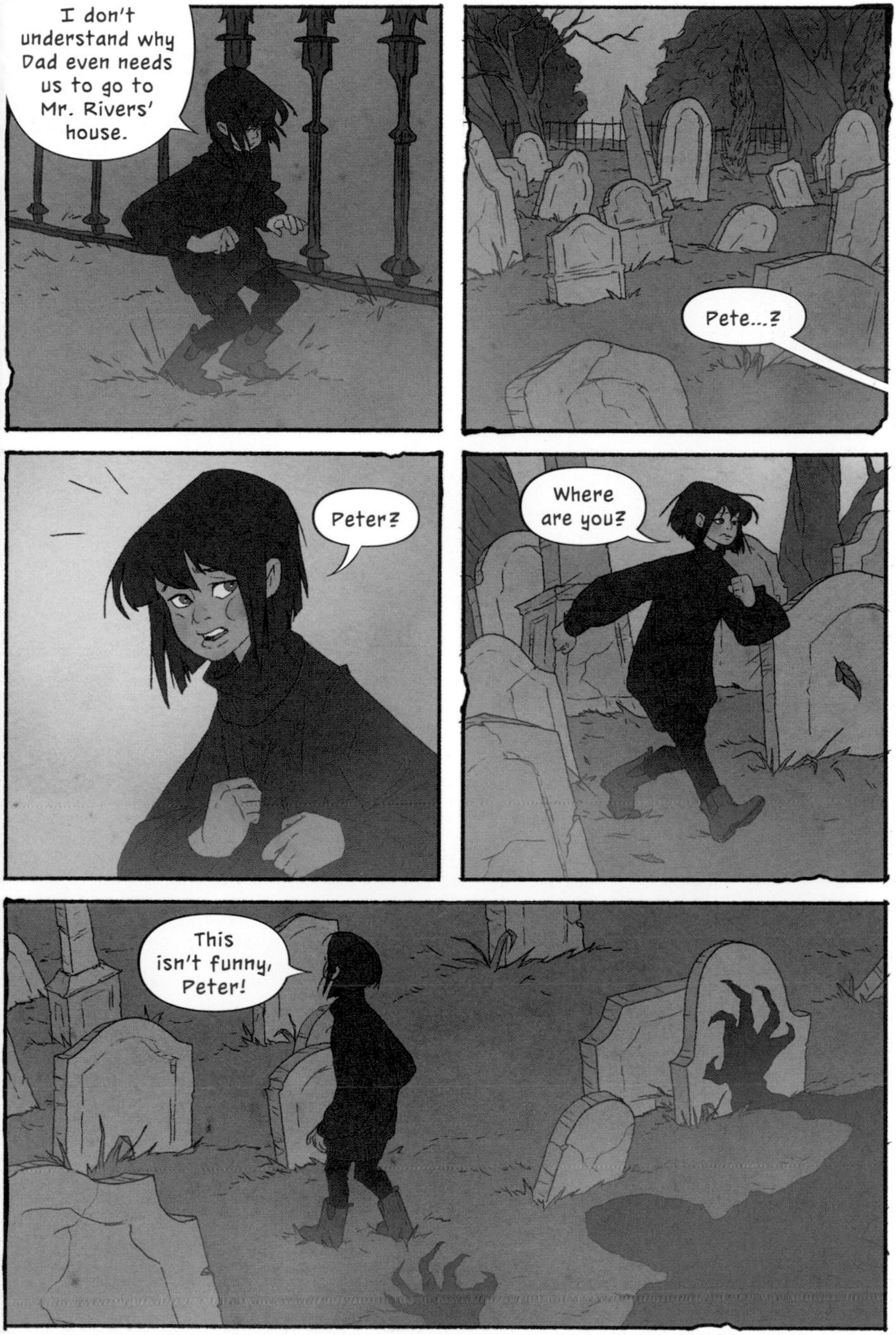
I don't understand why Dad even needs us to go to Mr. Rivers' house.
Pete...?
Peter?
Where are you?
This isn't funny, Peter!

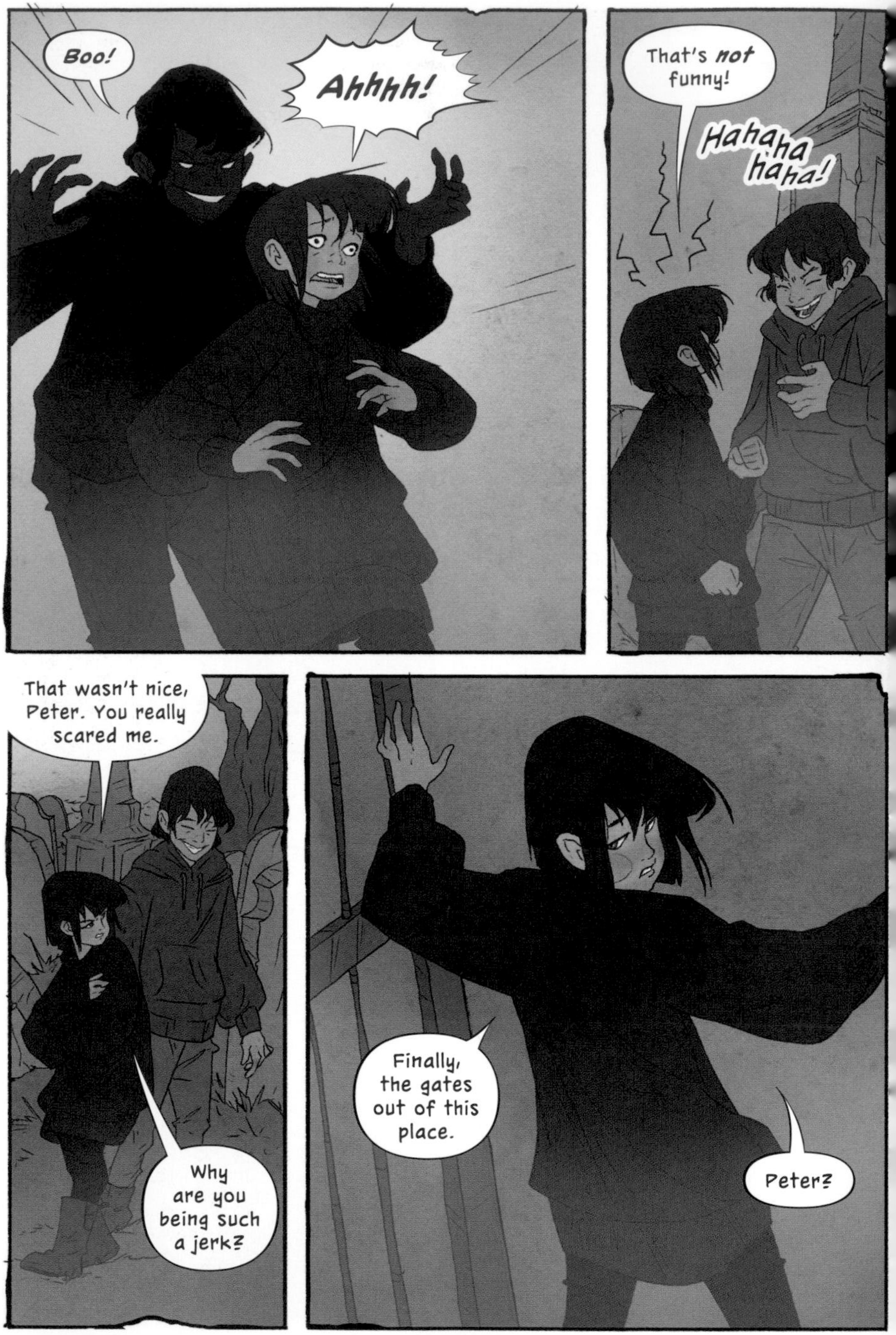
Boo!
Ahhhh!
That's *not* funny!
Hahaha haha!
That wasn't nice, Peter. You really scared me.
Why are you being such a jerk?
Finally, the gates out of this place.
Peter?

What? How did you—?

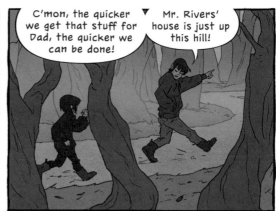

C'mon, the quicker we get that stuff for Dad, the quicker we can be done!

Mr. Rivers' house is just up this hill!

There it is!

Why...why does it look abandoned?

Maybe he's a hermit.

But I just saw Mr. Rivers at the store the other day.

Doesn't matter, I guess. These must be what Dad wanted.

Let's see what's so important that Dad told you he needed it urgently.

Wait! There's nothing but blank pages here!

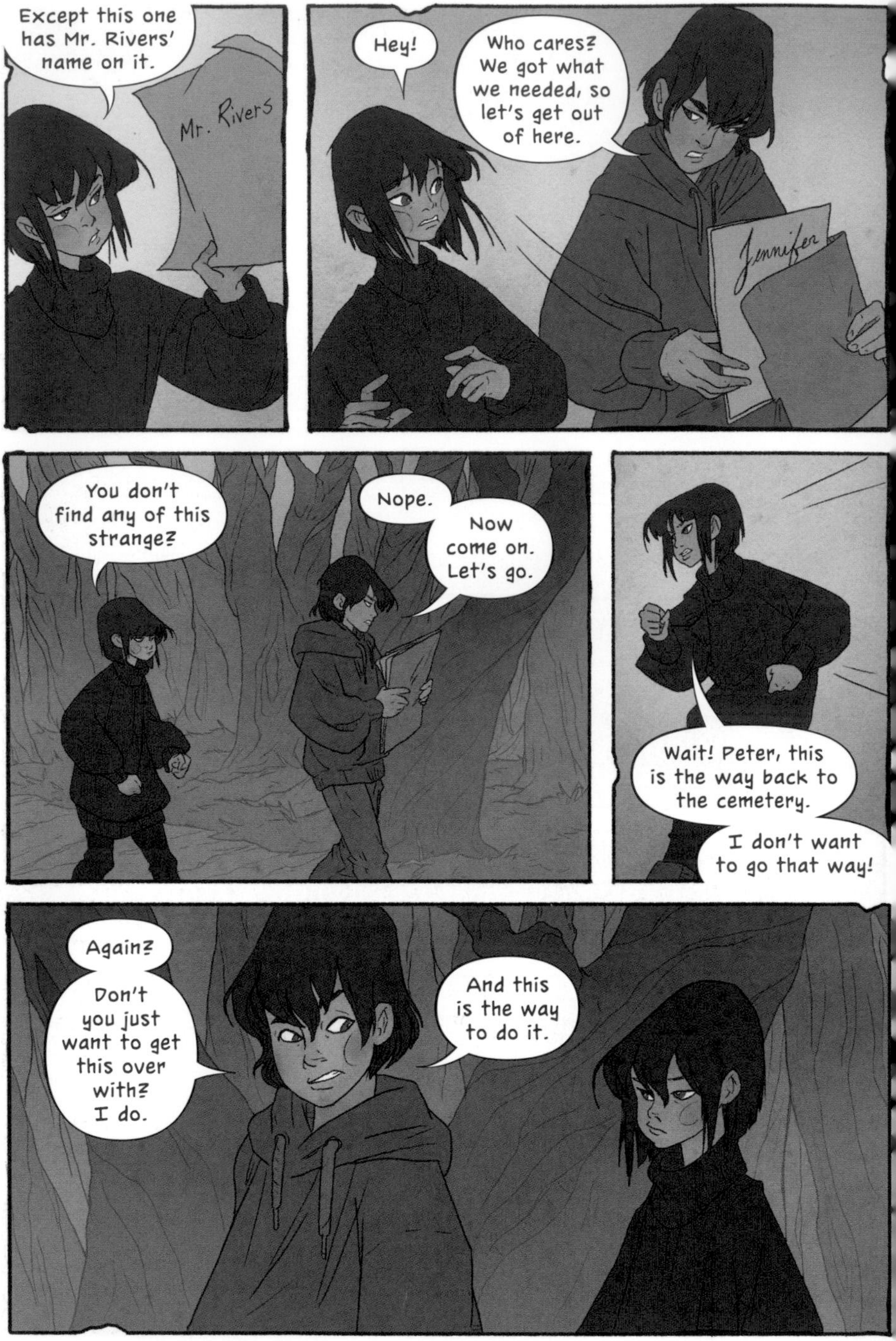
Except this one has Mr. Rivers' name on it.
Mr. Rivers
Hey!
Who cares? We got what we needed, so let's get out of here.
Jennifer
You don't find any of this strange?
Nope.
Now come on. Let's go.
Wait! Peter, this is the way back to the cemetery.
I don't want to go that way!
Again?
Don't you just want to get this over with? I do.
And this is the way to do it.

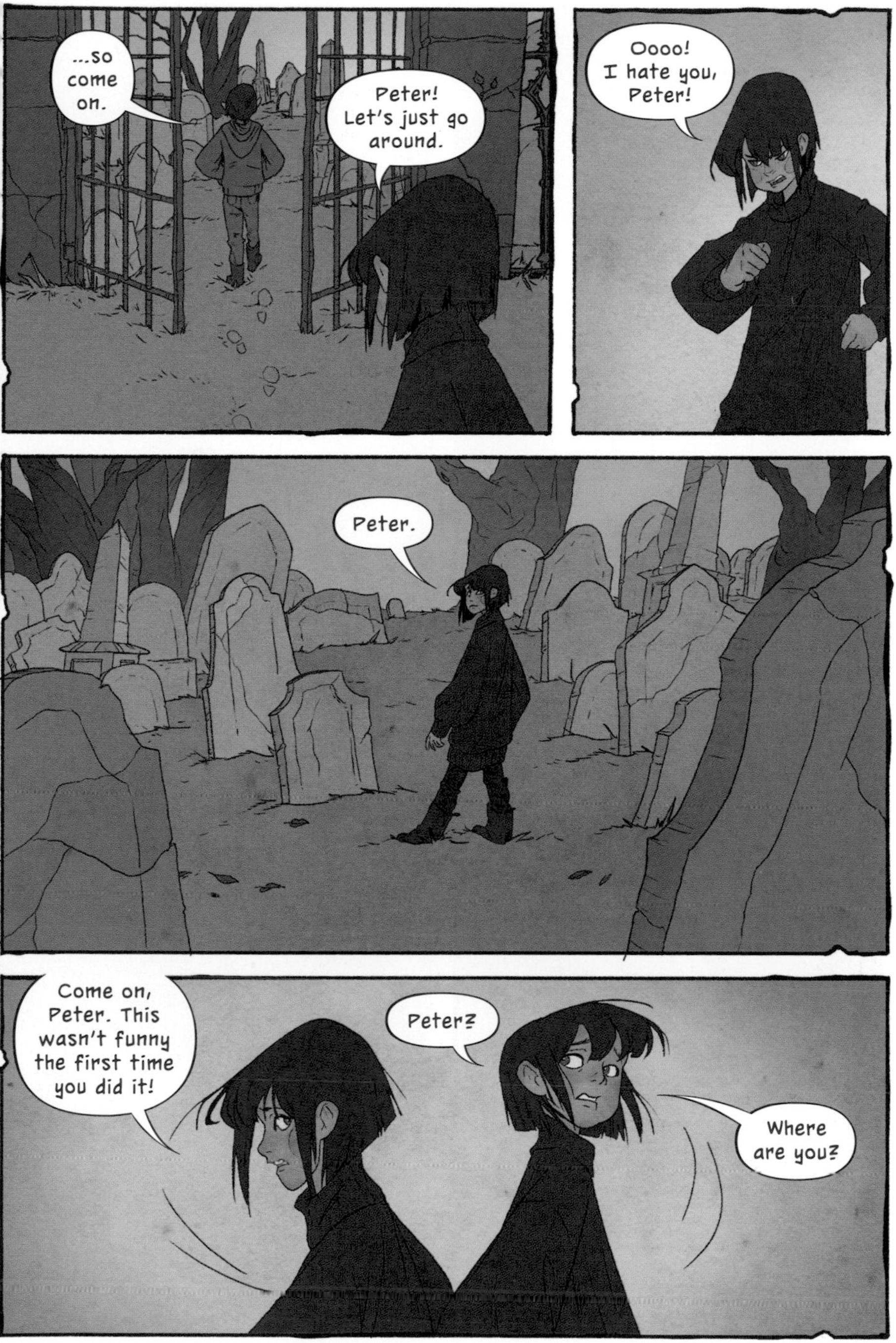
...so come on.
Peter! Let's just go around.
Oooo! I hate you, Peter!
Peter.
Come on, Peter. This wasn't funny the first time you did it!
Peter?
Where are you?

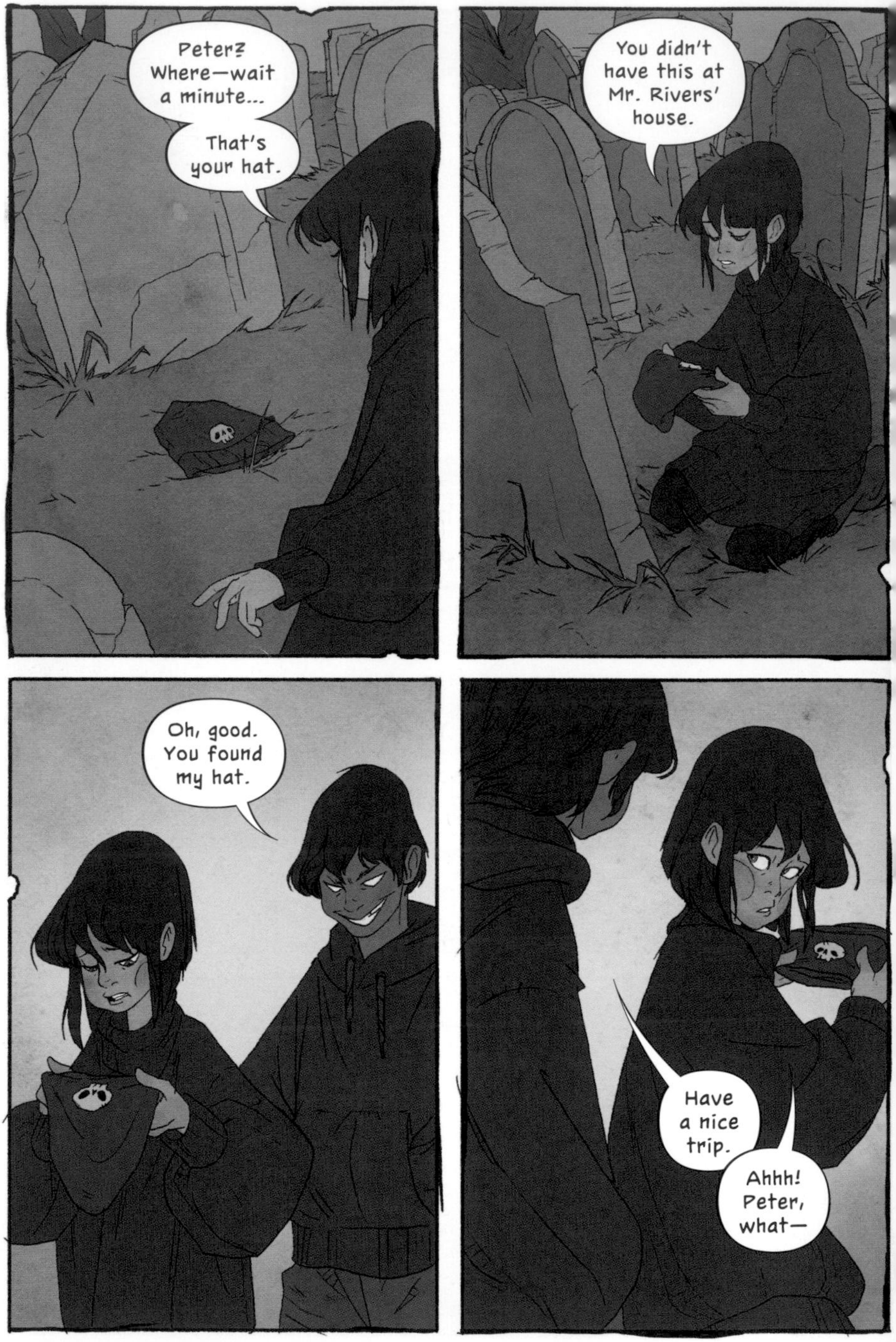
Peter? Where—wait a minute...
That's your hat.
You didn't have this at Mr. Rivers' house.
Oh, good. You found my hat.
Have a nice trip.
Ahhh! Peter, what—

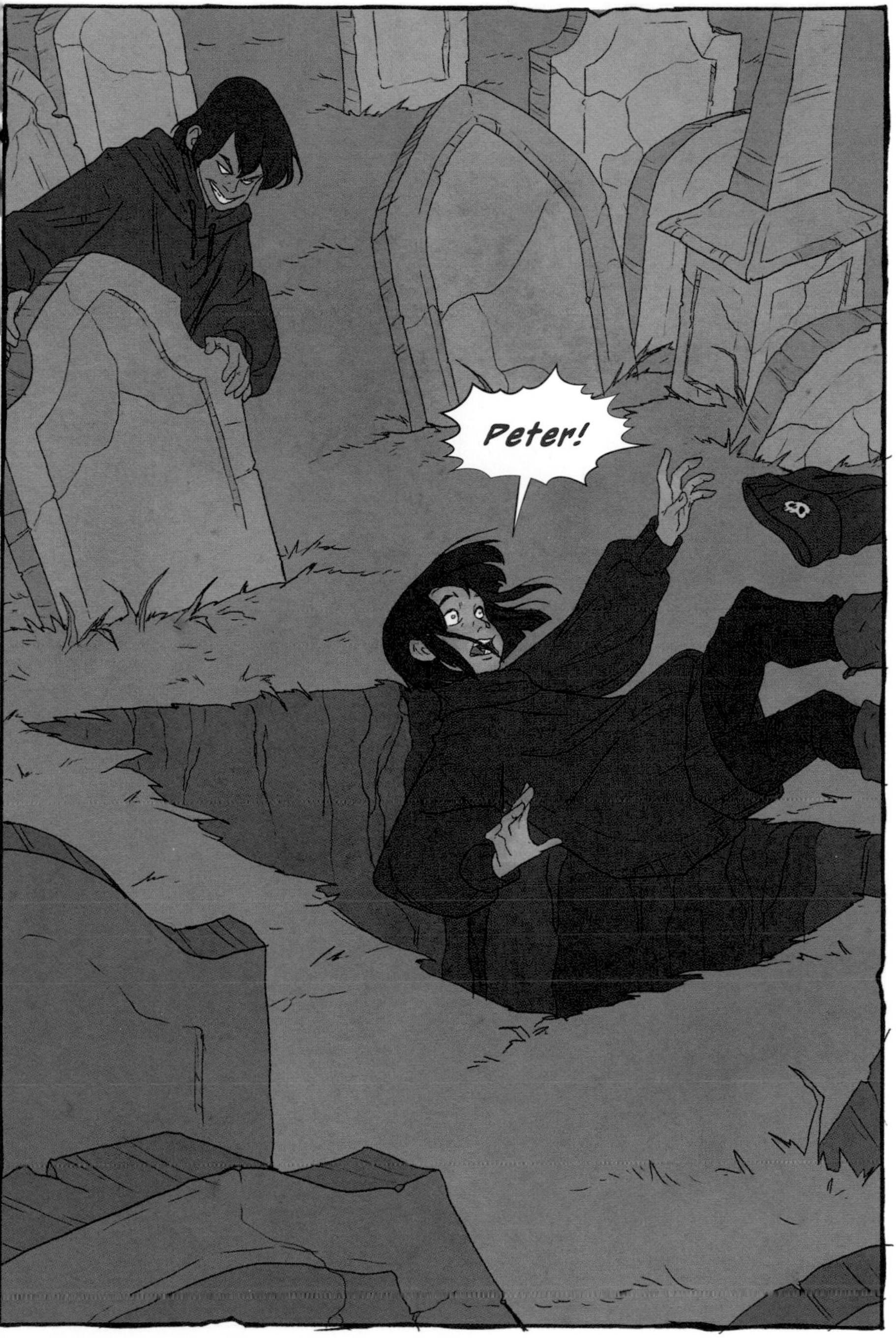
Peter!

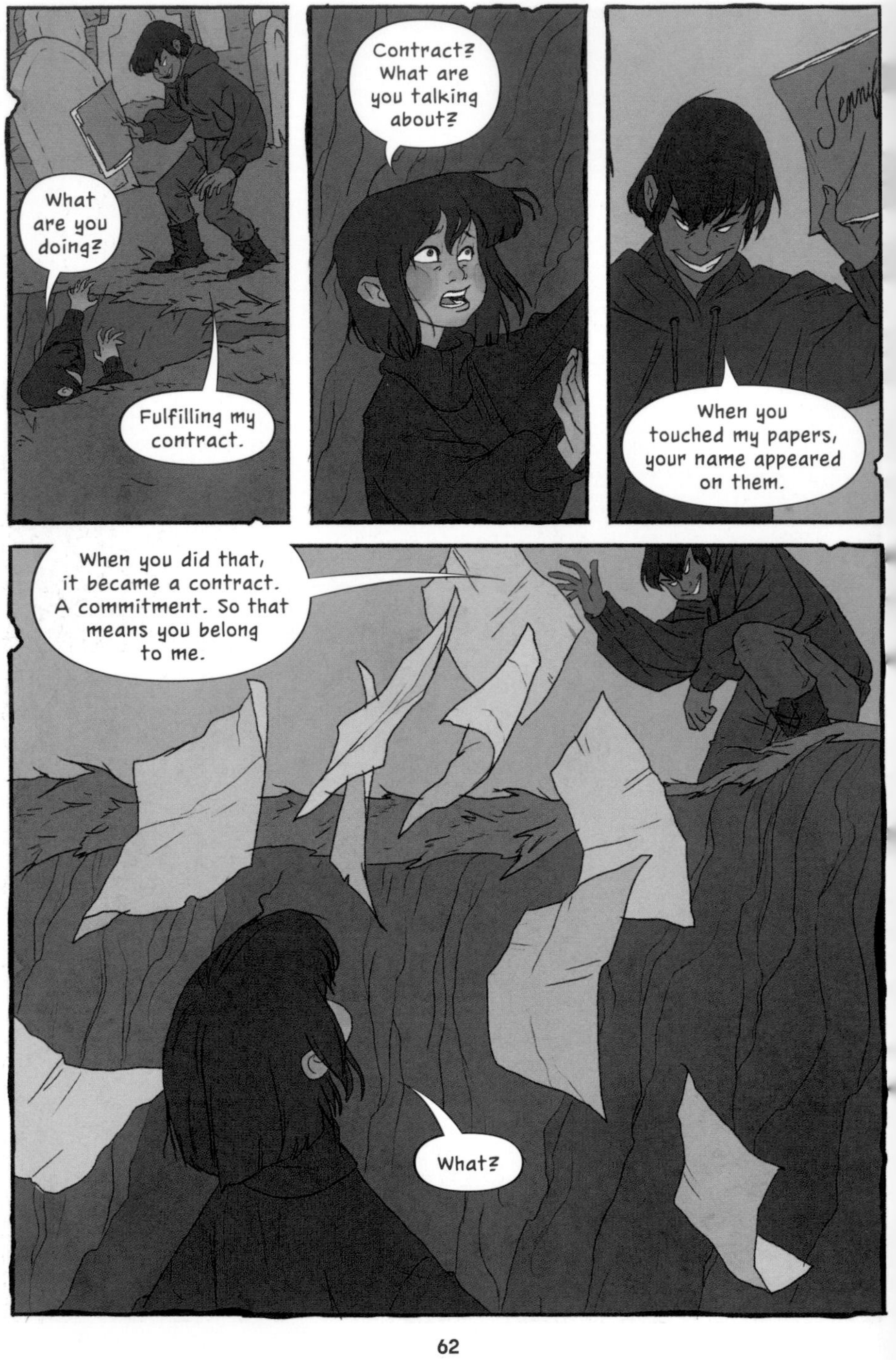
What are you doing?
Fulfilling my contract.
Contract? What are you talking about?
When you touched my papers, your name appeared on them.
When you did that, it became a contract. A commitment. So that means you belong to me.
What?

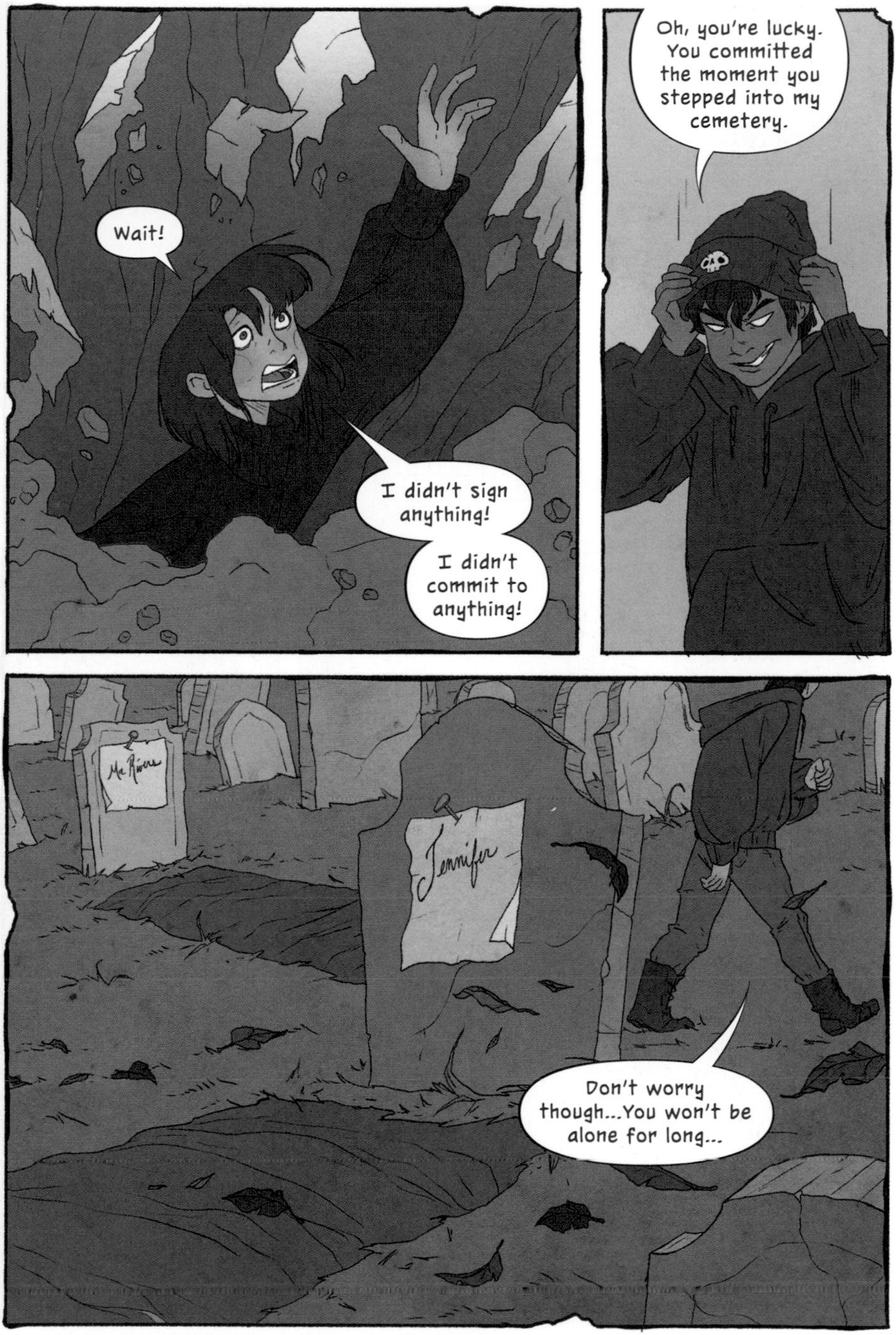
Wait!
I didn't sign anything!
I didn't commit to anything!
Oh, you're lucky. You committed the moment you stepped into my cemetery.
Mr. Rivers
Jennifer
Don't worry though...You won't be alone for long...

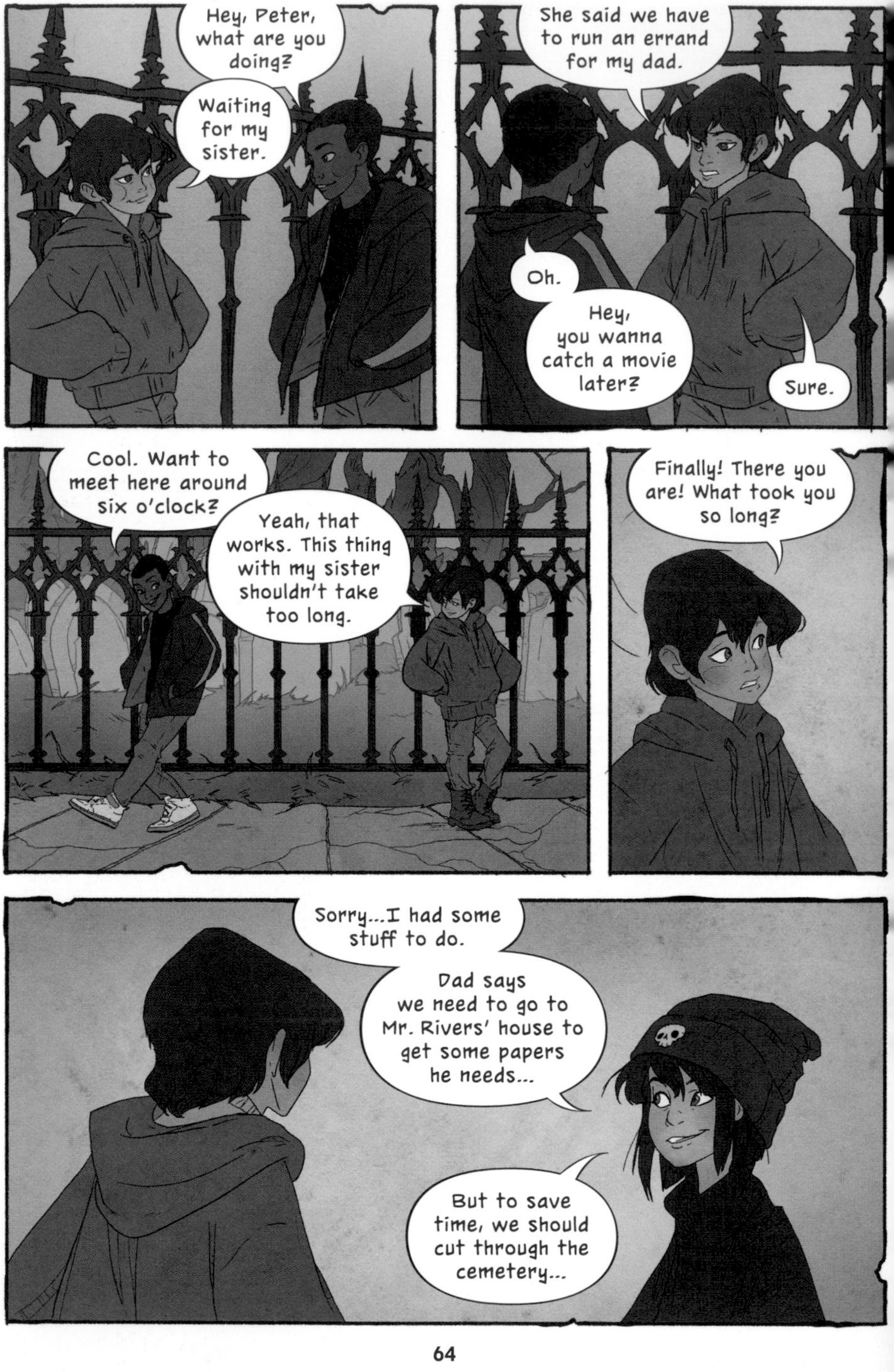
Hey, Peter, what are you doing?
Waiting for my sister.
She said we have to run an errand for my dad.
Oh.
Hey, you wanna catch a movie later?
Sure.
Cool. Want to meet here around six o'clock?
Yeah, that works. This thing with my sister shouldn't take too long.
Finally! There you are! What took you so long?
Sorry...I had some stuff to do.
Dad says we need to go to Mr. Rivers' house to get some papers he needs...
But to save time, we should cut through the cemetery...

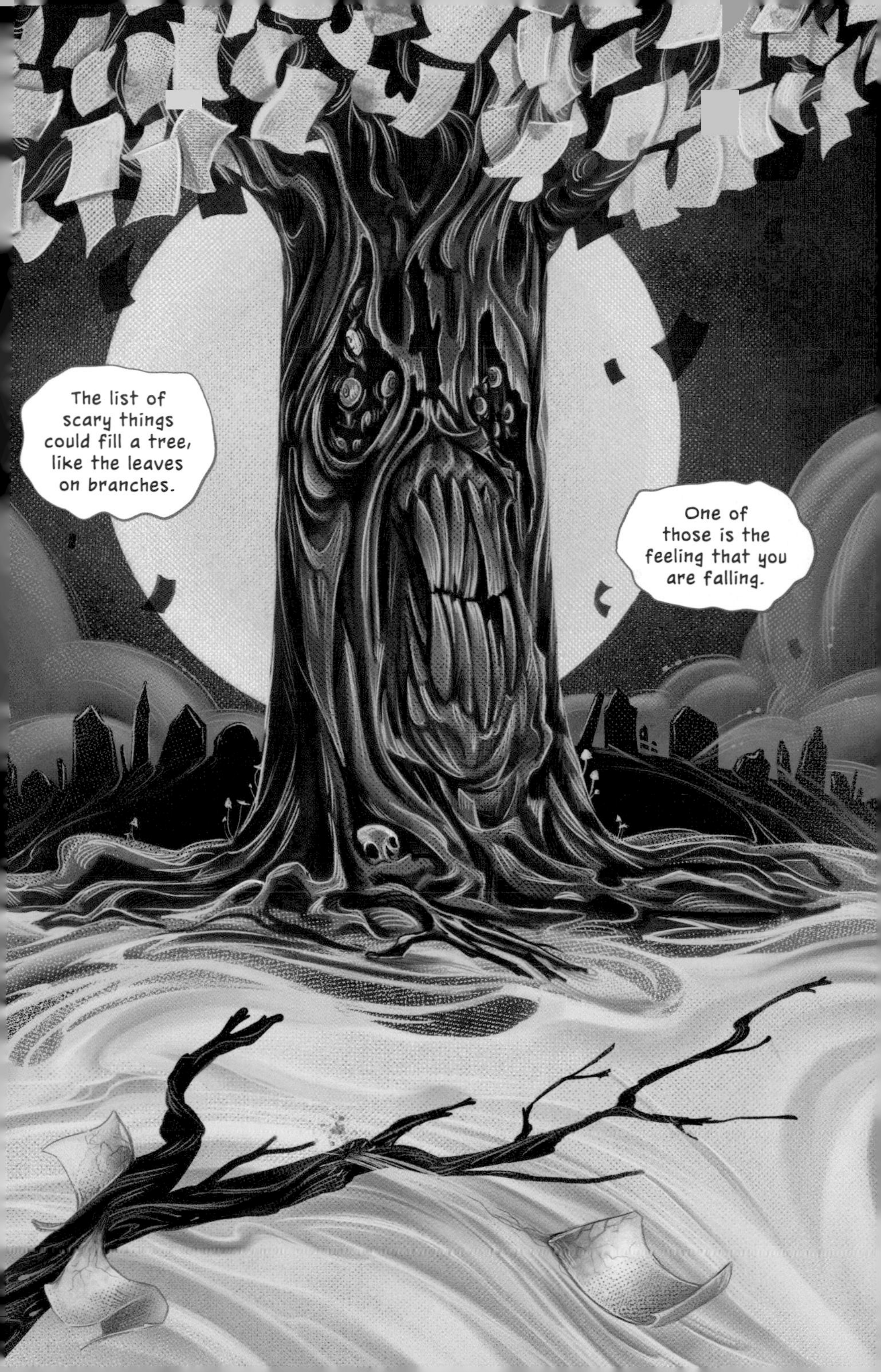
The list of scary things could fill a tree, like the leaves on branches.
One of those is the feeling that you are falling.

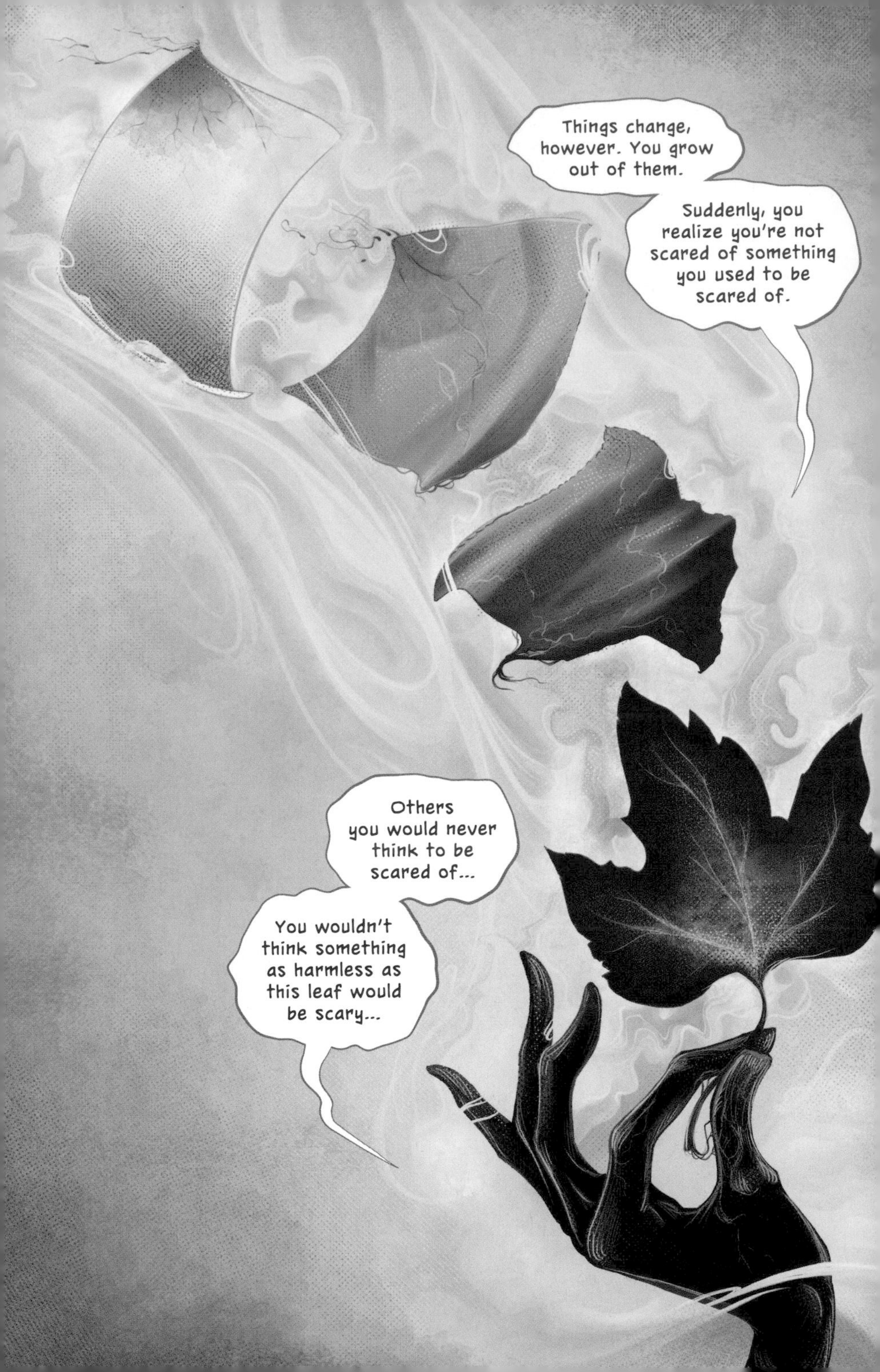
Things change, however. You grow out of them.
Suddenly, you realize you're not scared of something you used to be scared of.
Others you would never think to be scared of...
You wouldn't think something as harmless as this leaf would be scary...

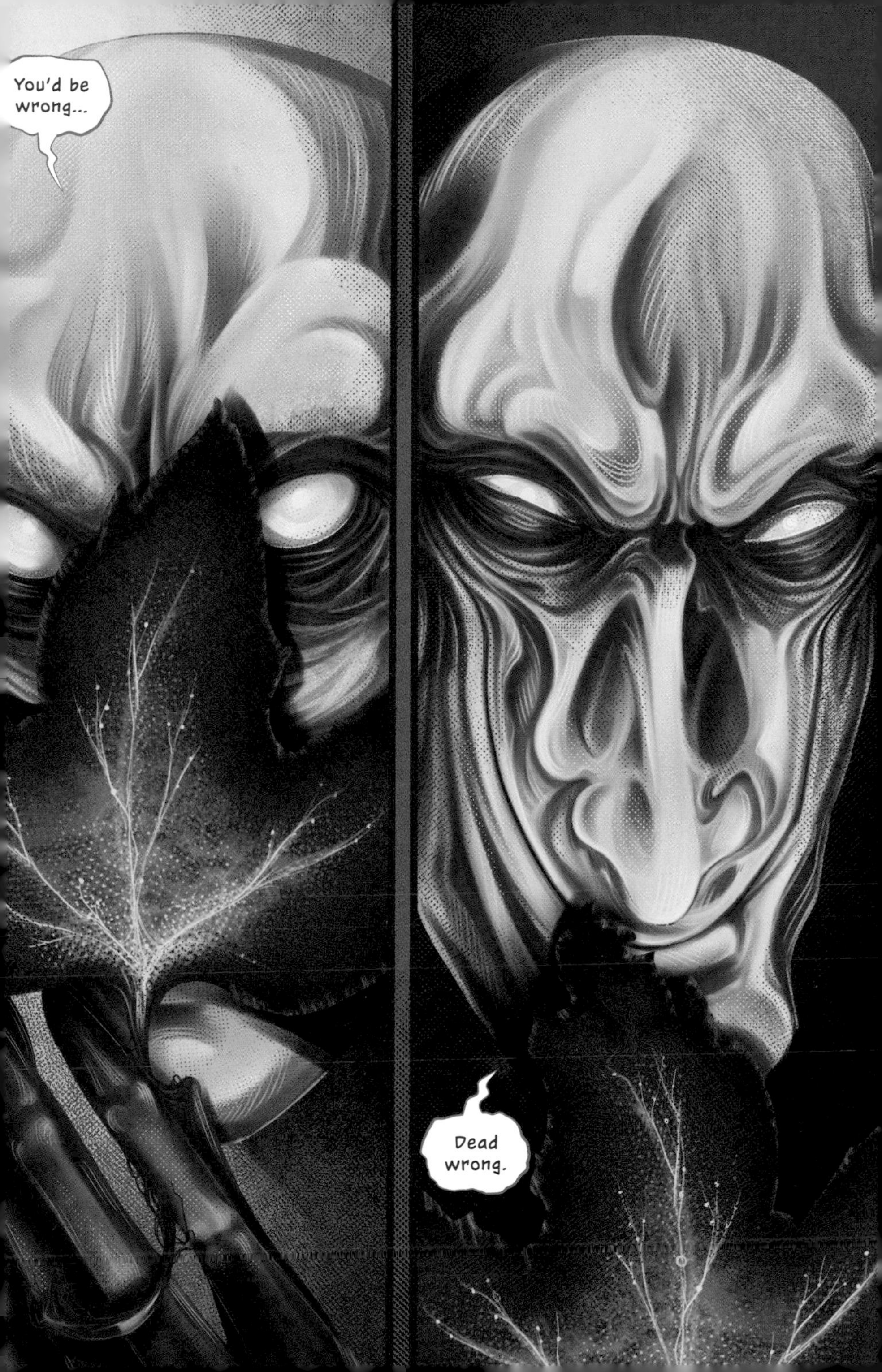
You'd be wrong...
Dead wrong.

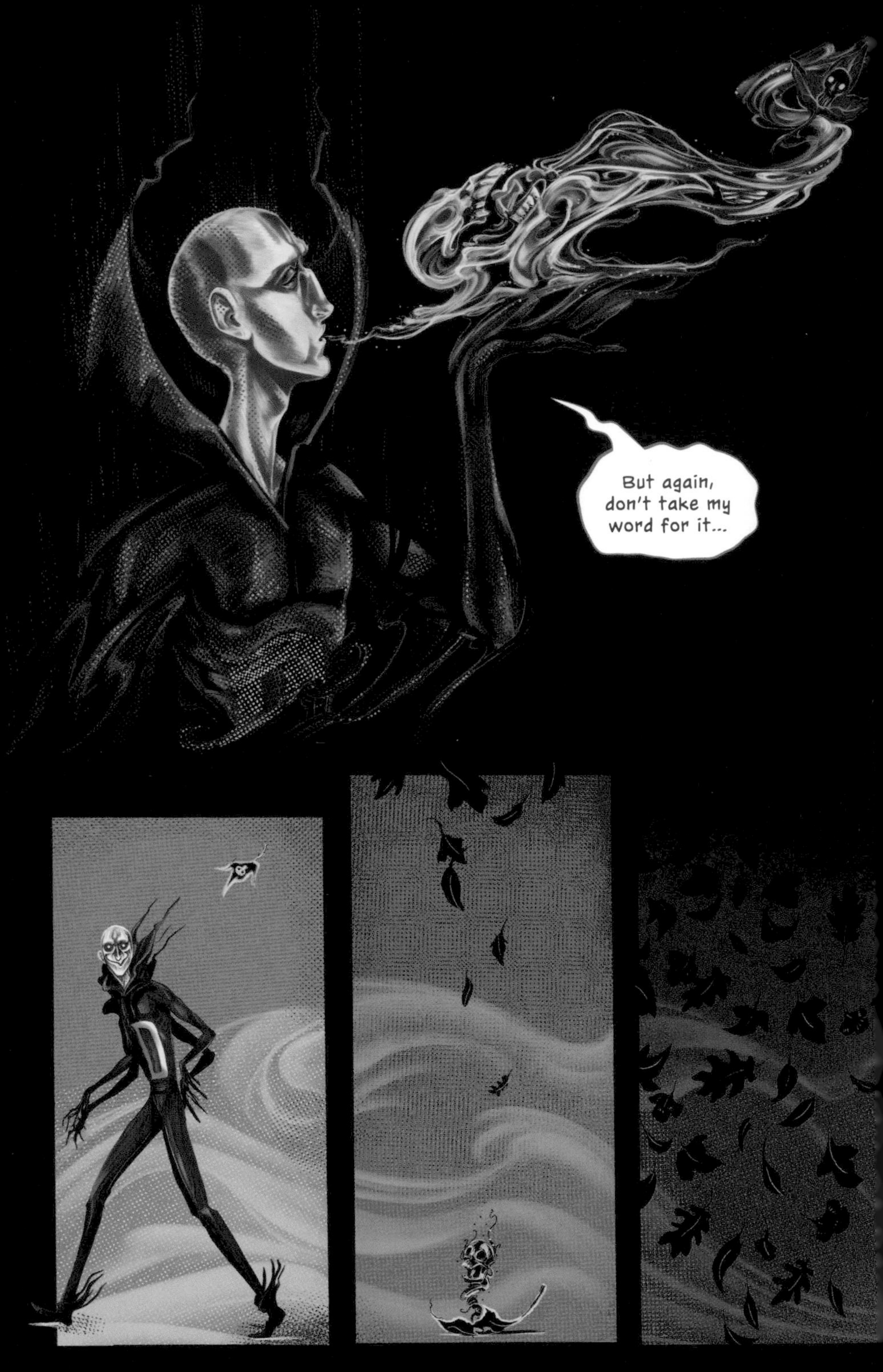
But again, don't take my word for it...

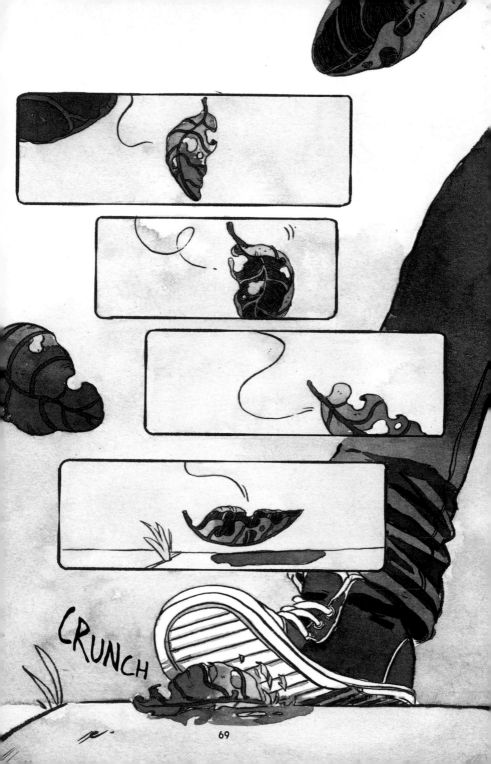

CRUNCH

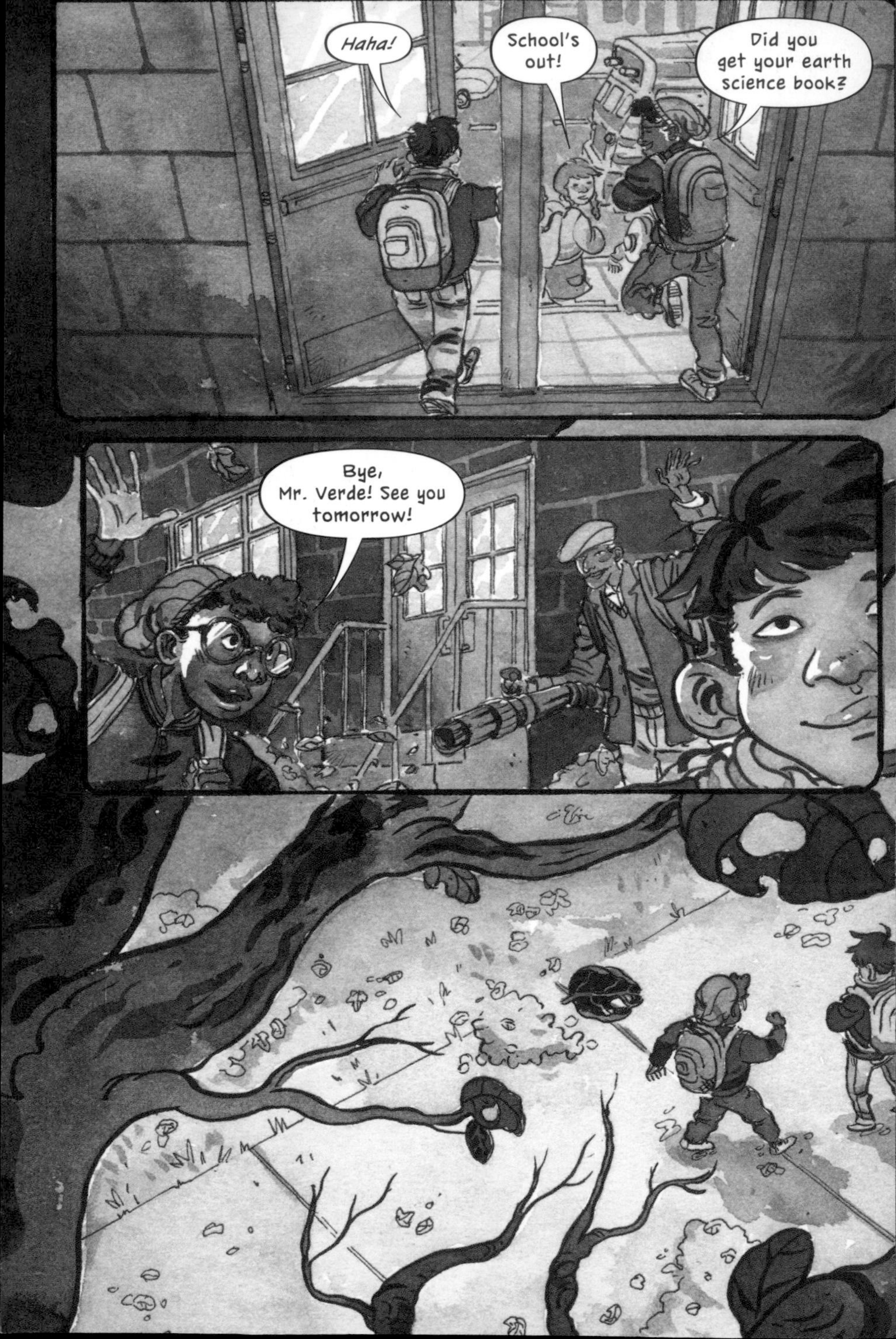
Haha!
School's out!
Did you get your earth science book?
Bye, Mr. Verde! See you tomorrow!

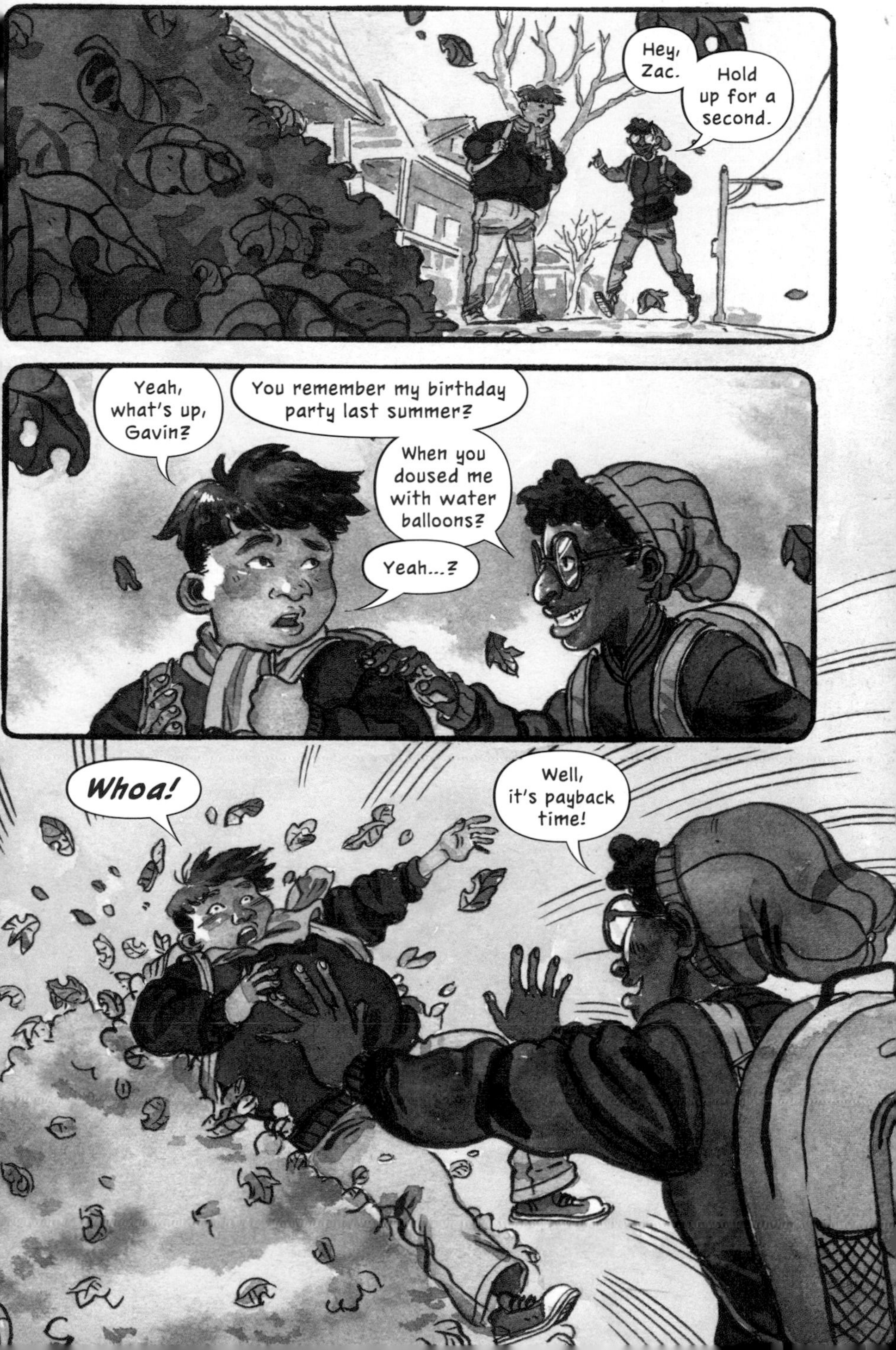
Hey, Zac.
Hold up for a second.
Yeah, what's up, Gavin?
You remember my birthday party last summer?
When you doused me with water balloons?
Yeah...?
Whoa!
Well, it's payback time!

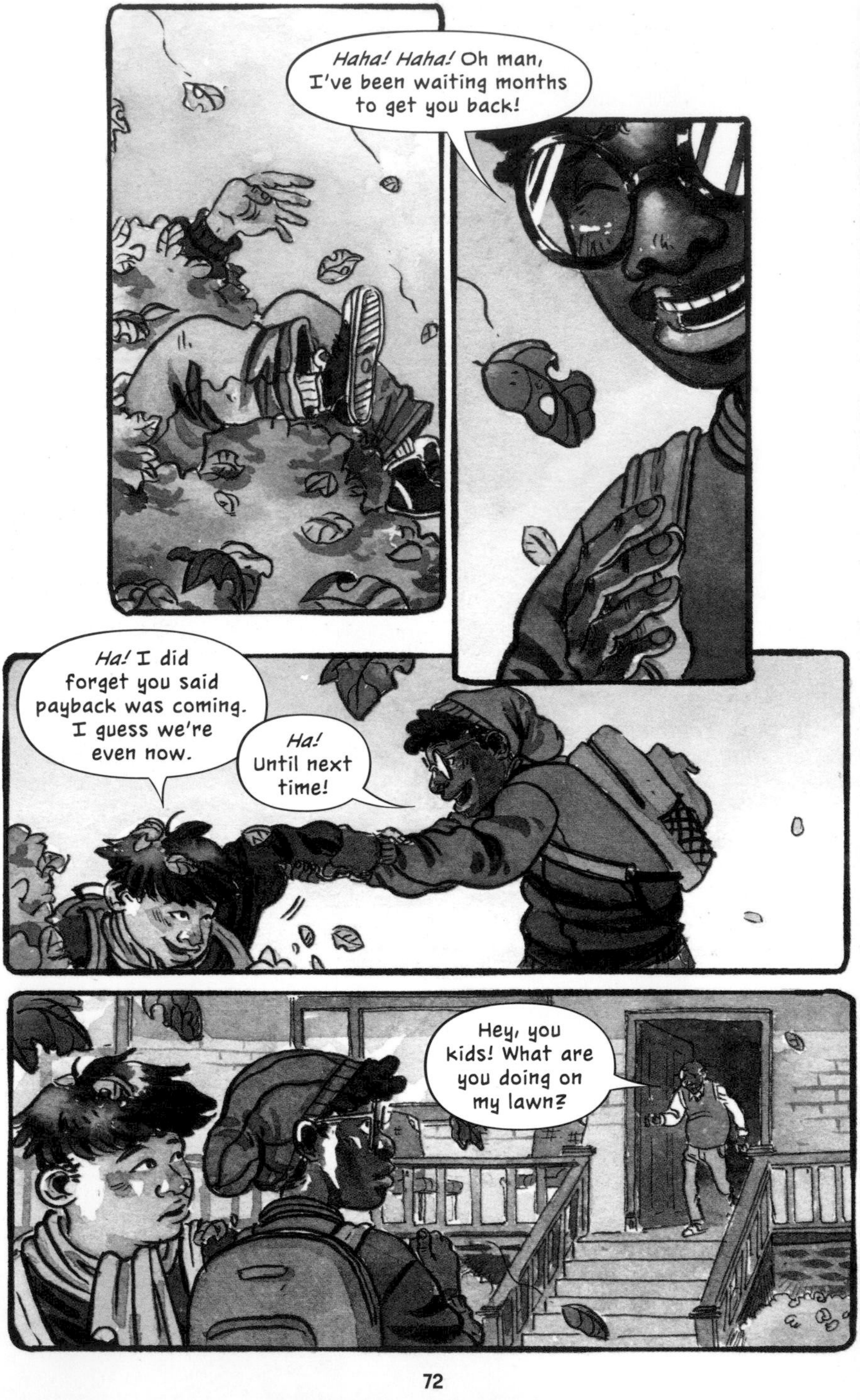
Haha! Haha! Oh man, I've been waiting months to get you back!
Ha! I did forget you said payback was coming. I guess we're even now.
Ha! Until next time!
Hey, you kids! What are you doing on my lawn?

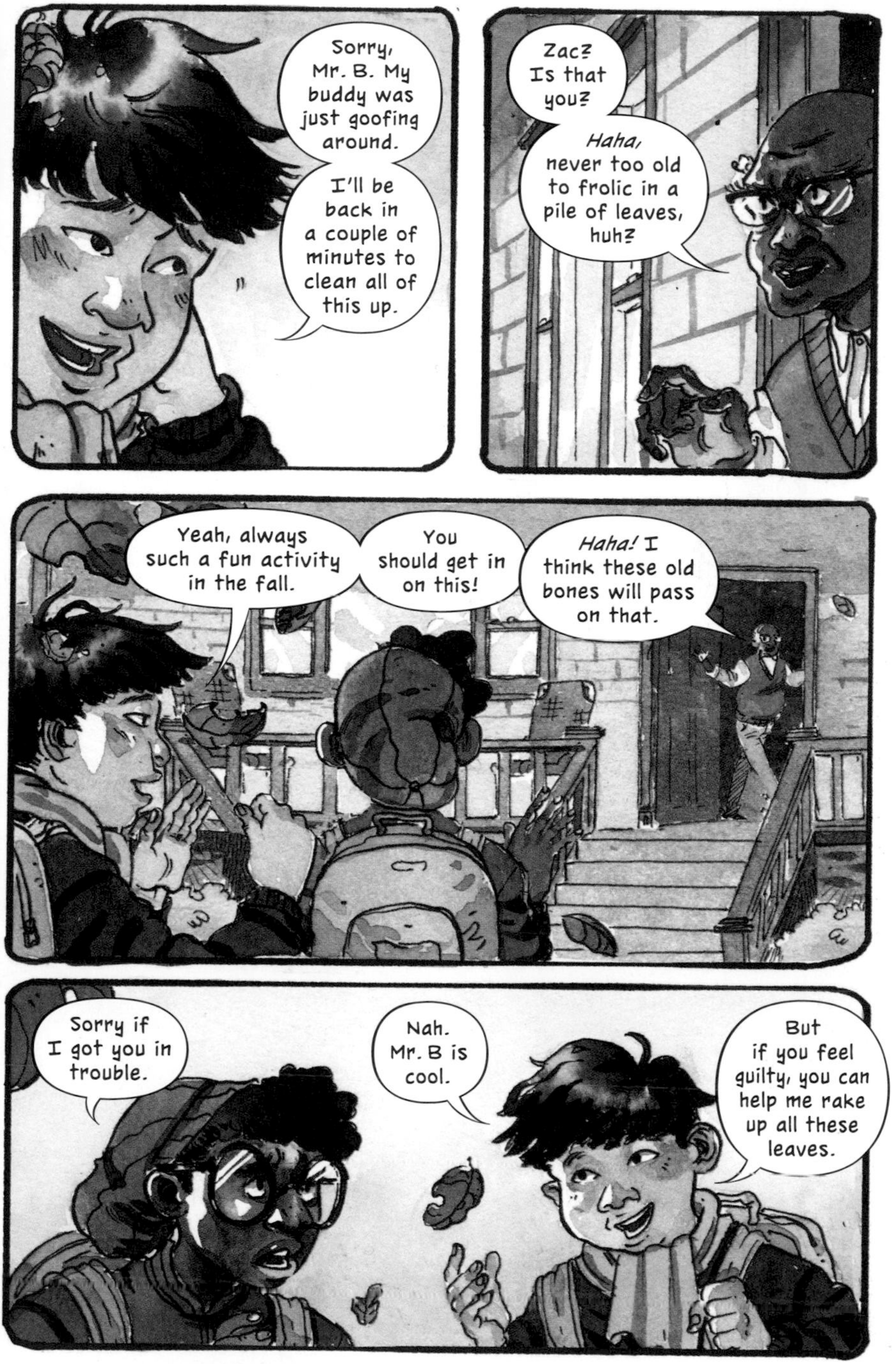

Sorry, Mr. B. My buddy was just goofing around.
I'll be back in a couple of minutes to clean all of this up.
Zac? Is that you?
Haha, never too old to frolic in a pile of leaves, huh?
Yeah, always such a fun activity in the fall.
You should get in on this!
Haha! I think these old bones will pass on that.
Sorry if I got you in trouble.
Nah. Mr. B is cool.
But if you feel guilty, you can help me rake up all these leaves.

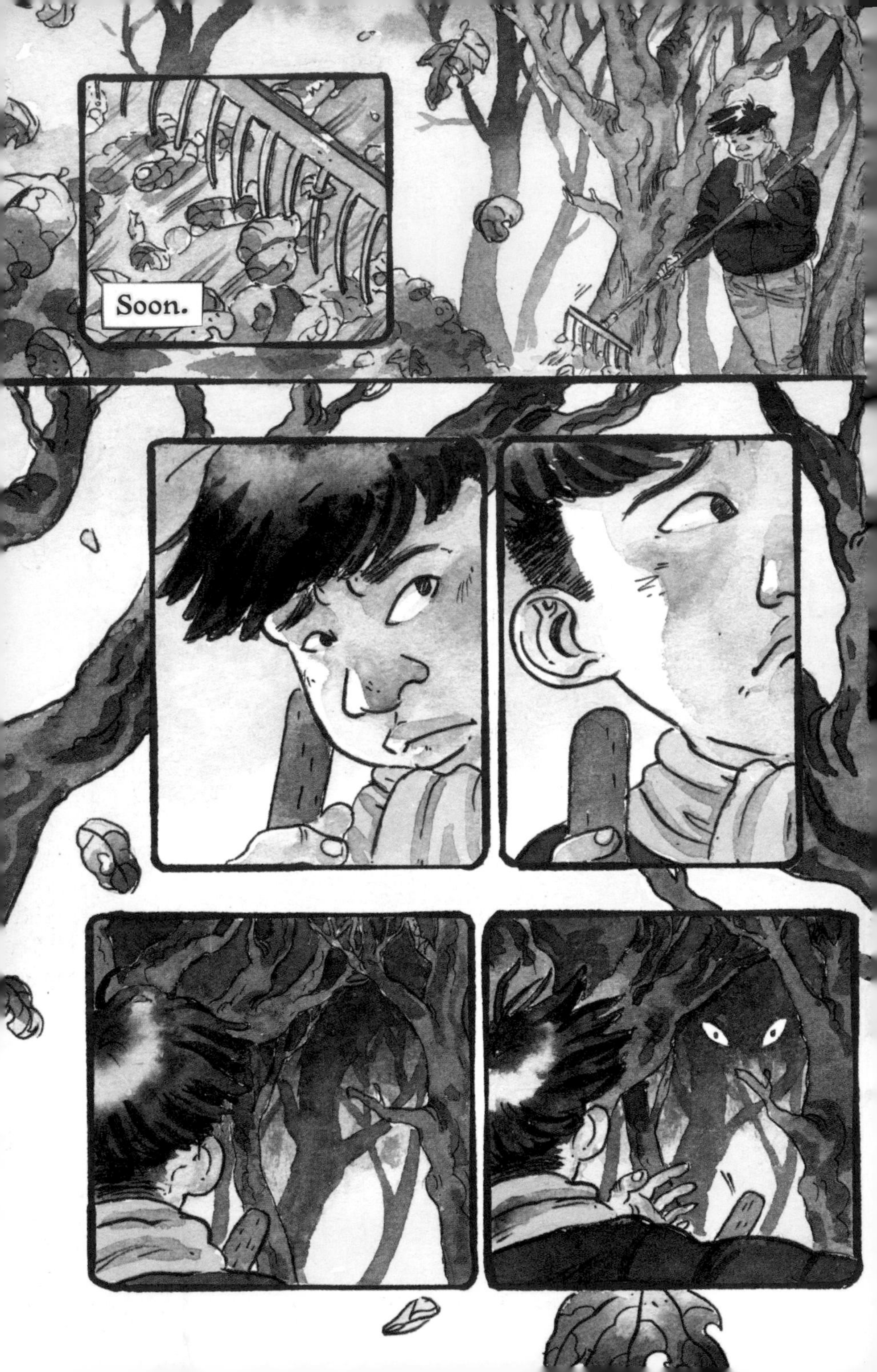
Soon.

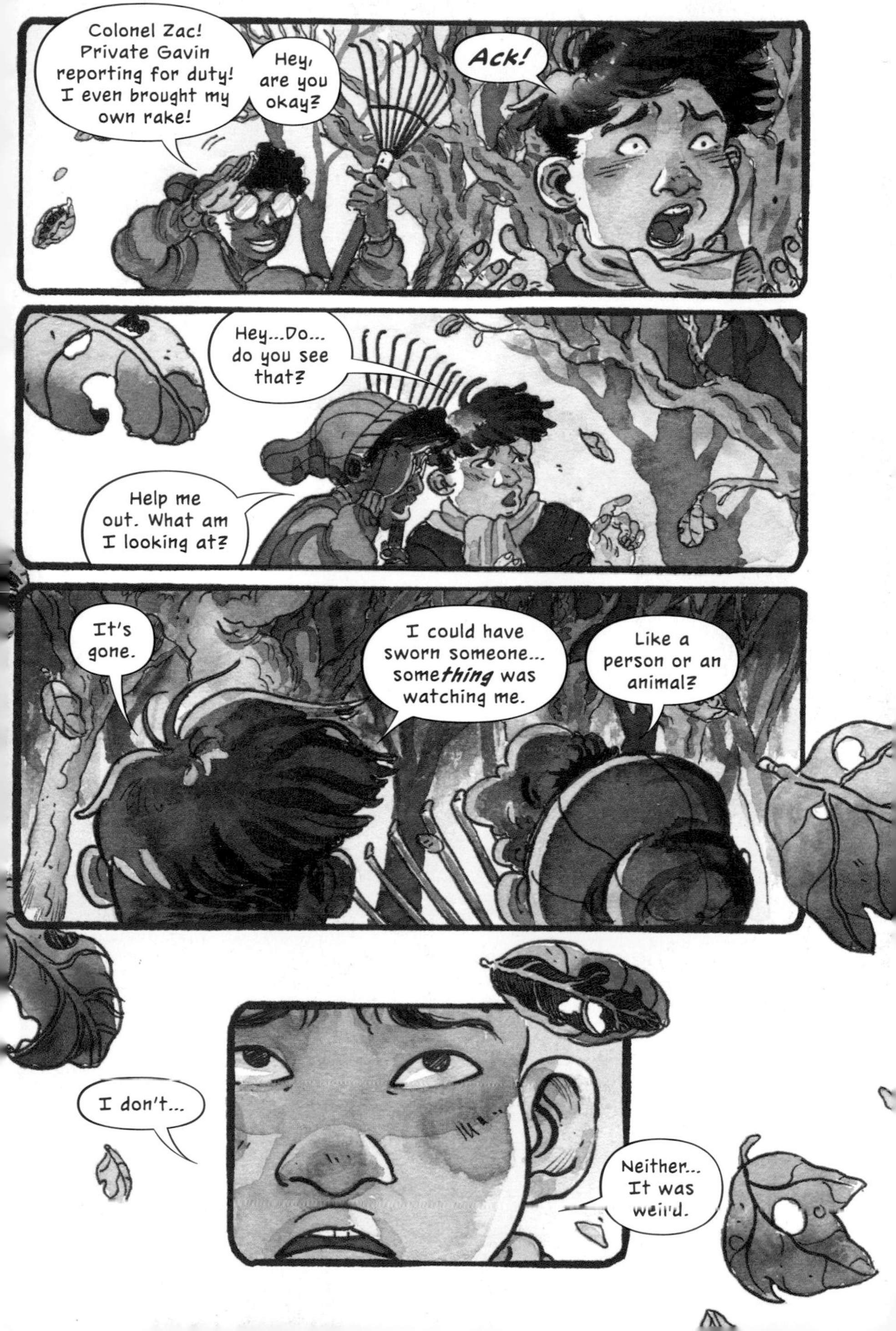
Colonel Zac! Private Gavin reporting for duty! I even brought my own rake!
Hey, are you okay?
Ack!
Hey...Do... do you see that?
Help me out. What am I looking at?
It's gone.
I could have sworn someone... some*thing* was watching me.
Like a person or an animal?
I don't...
Neither... It was weird.

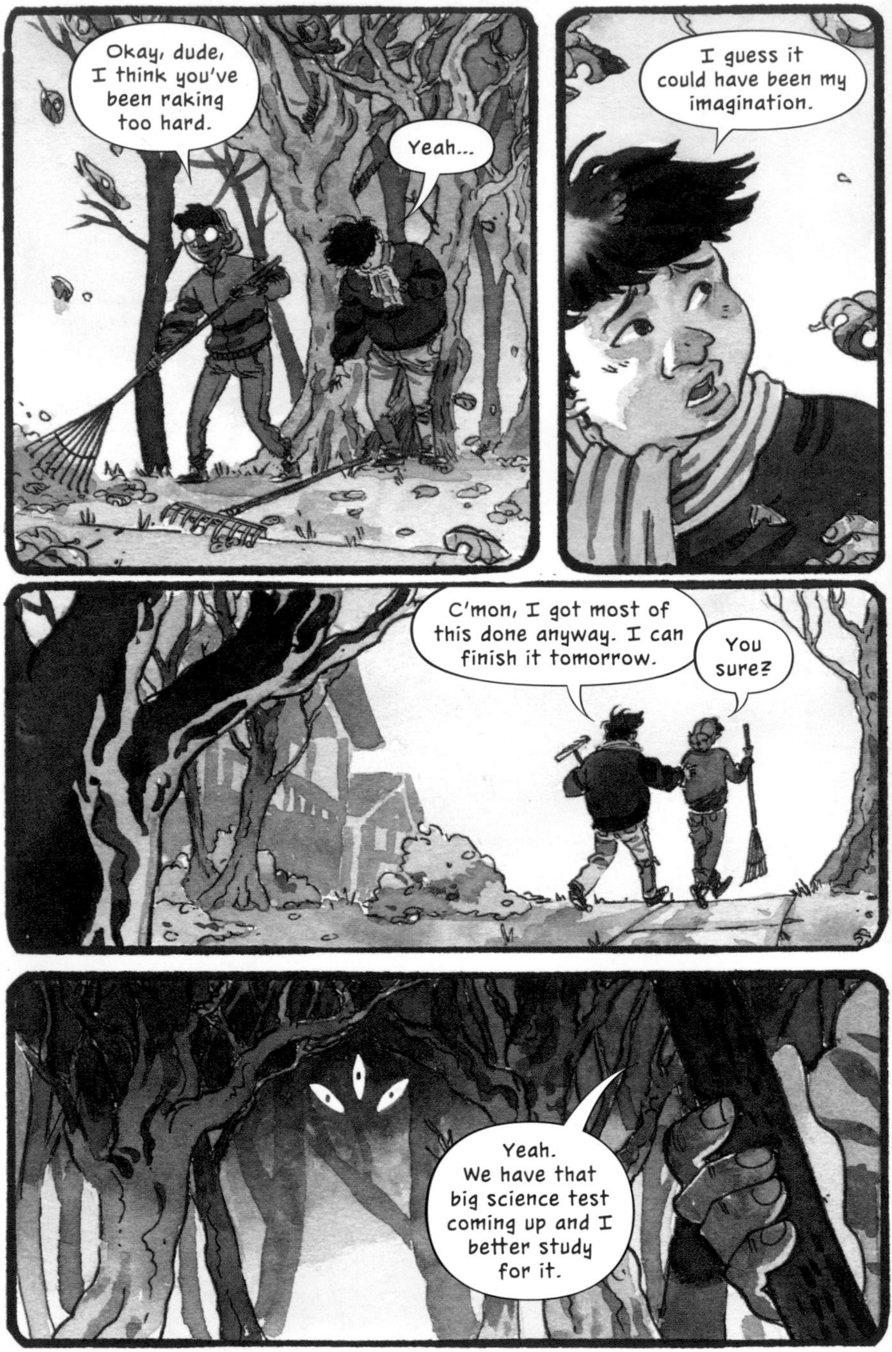
Okay, dude, I think you've been raking too hard.
Yeah...
I guess it could have been my imagination.
C'mon, I got most of this done anyway. I can finish it tomorrow.
You sure?
Yeah. We have that big science test coming up and I better study for it.

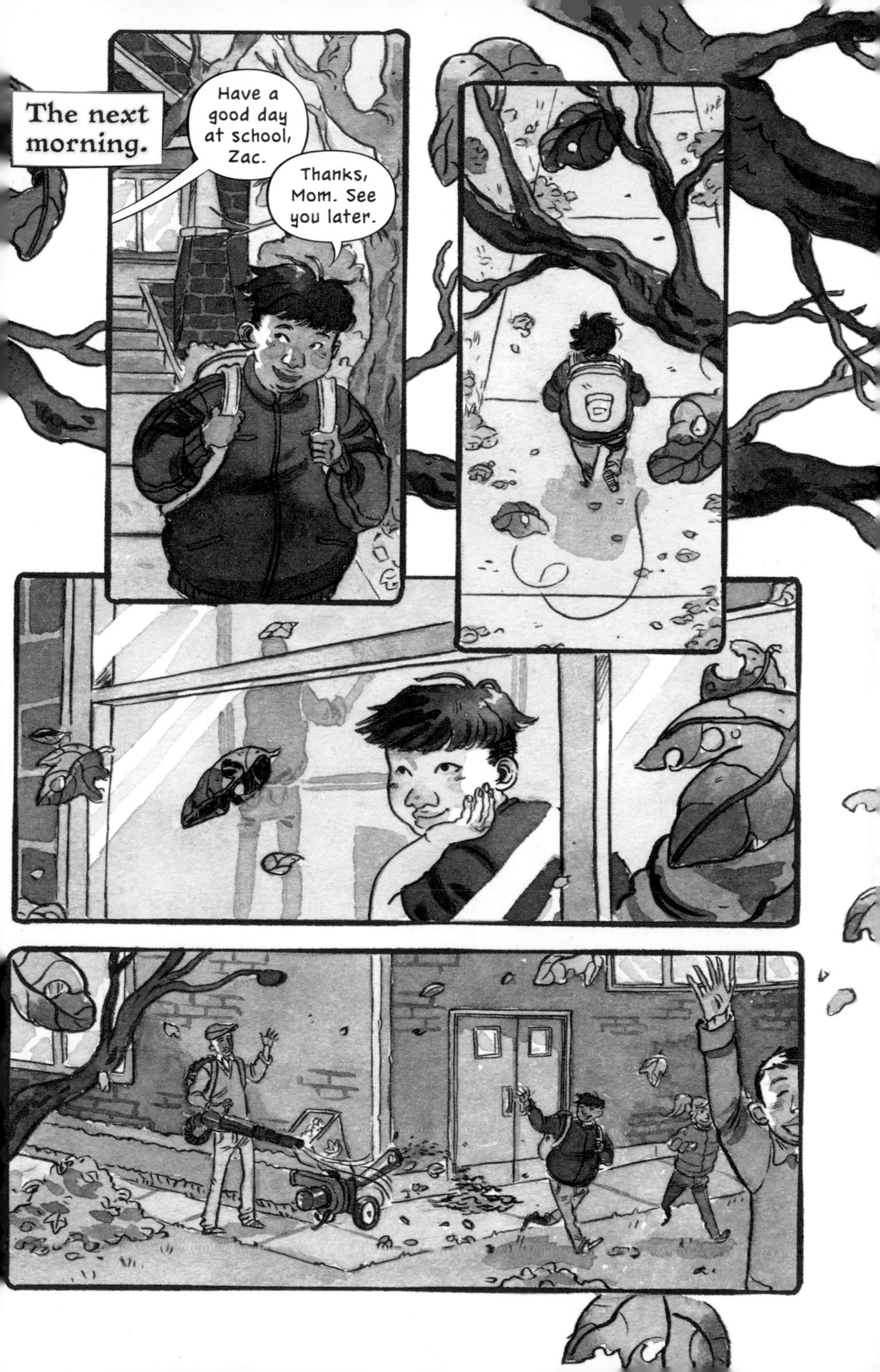
The next morning.
Have a good day at school, Zac.
Thanks, Mom. See you later.

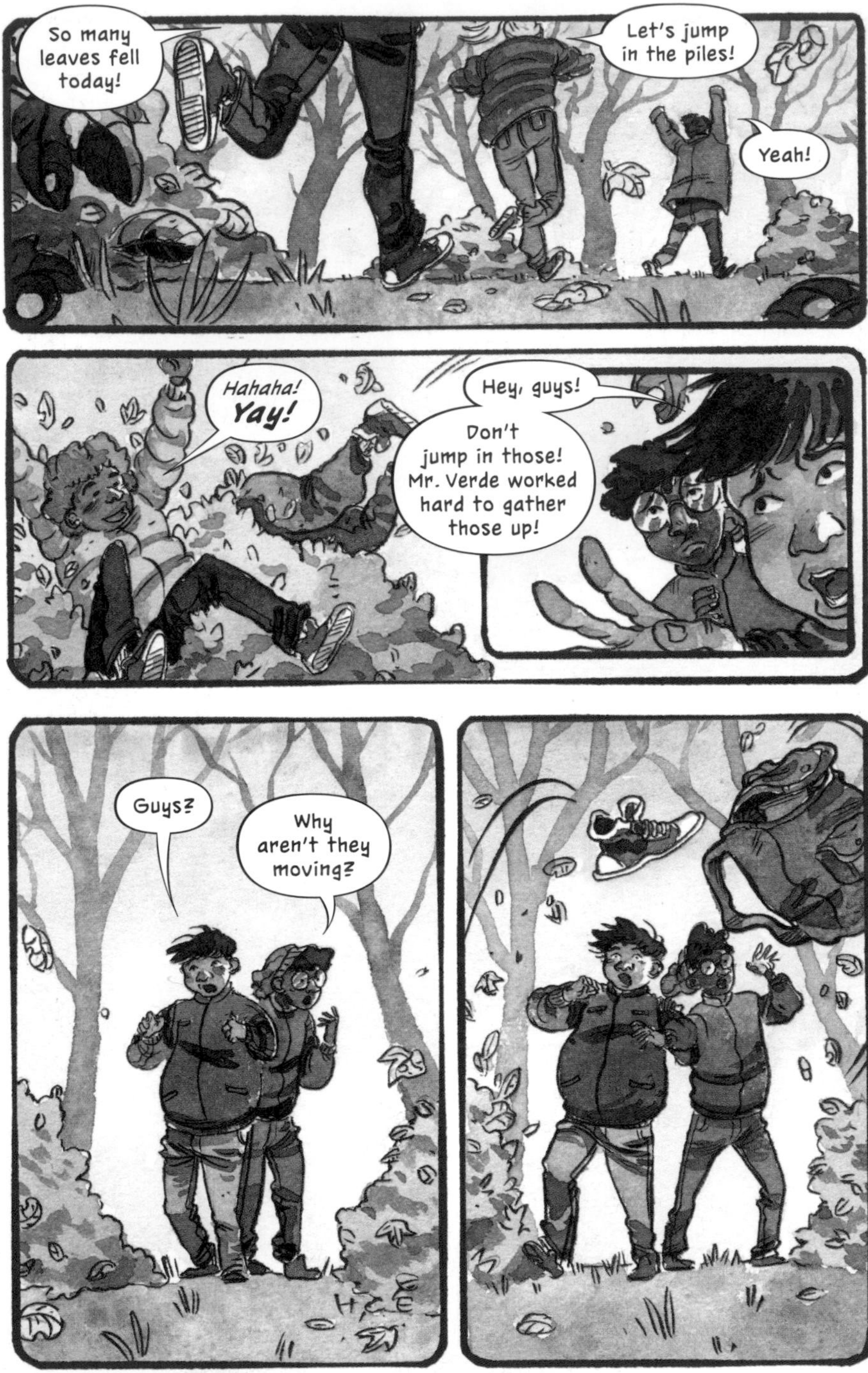
So many leaves fell today!
Let's jump in the piles!
Yeah!
Hahaha! **Yay!**
Hey, guys!
Don't jump in those! Mr. Verde worked hard to gather those up!
Guys?
Why aren't they moving?

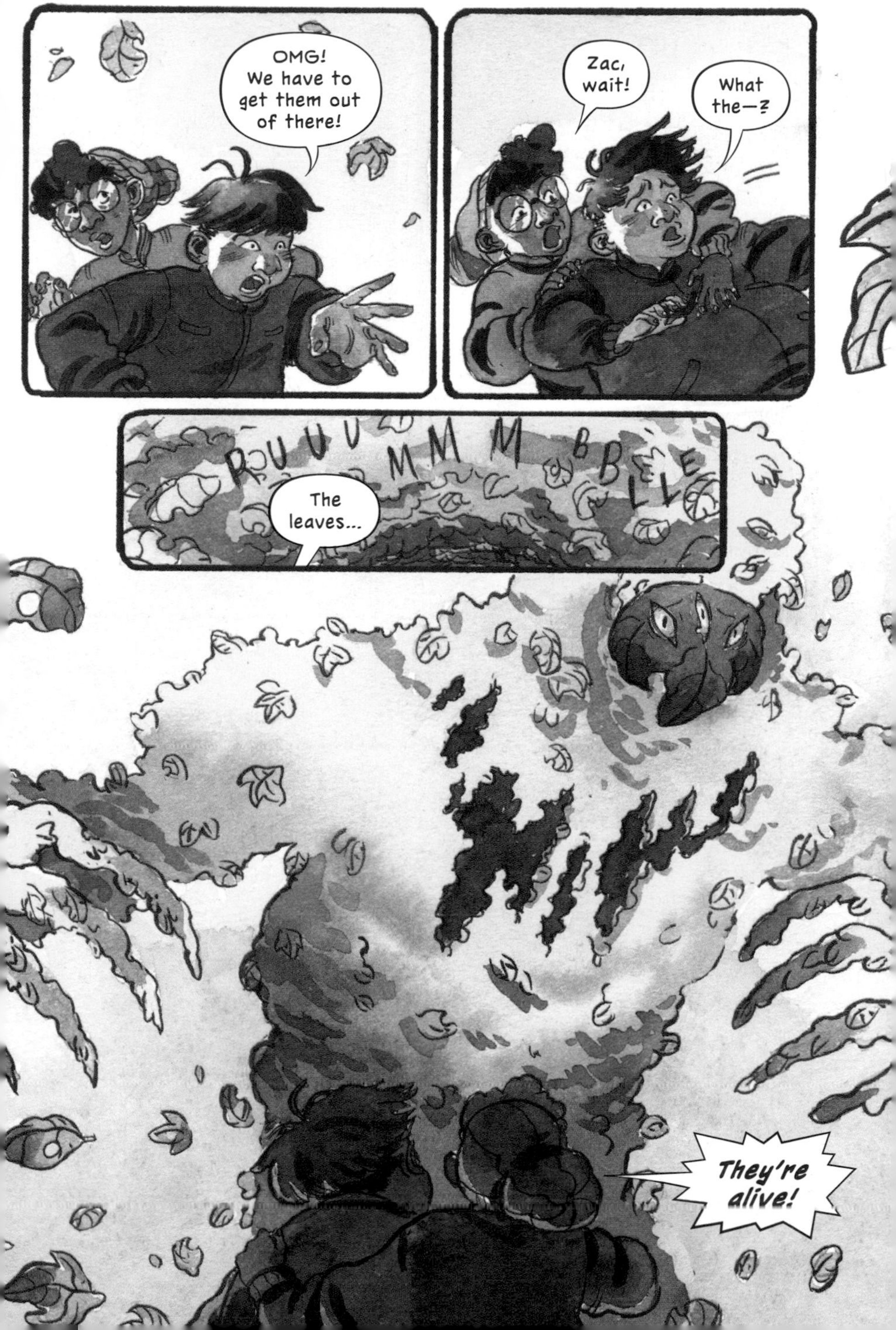
OMG! We have to get them out of there!
Zac, wait!
What the—?
RUUUMMMBBLLE
The leaves...
They're alive!

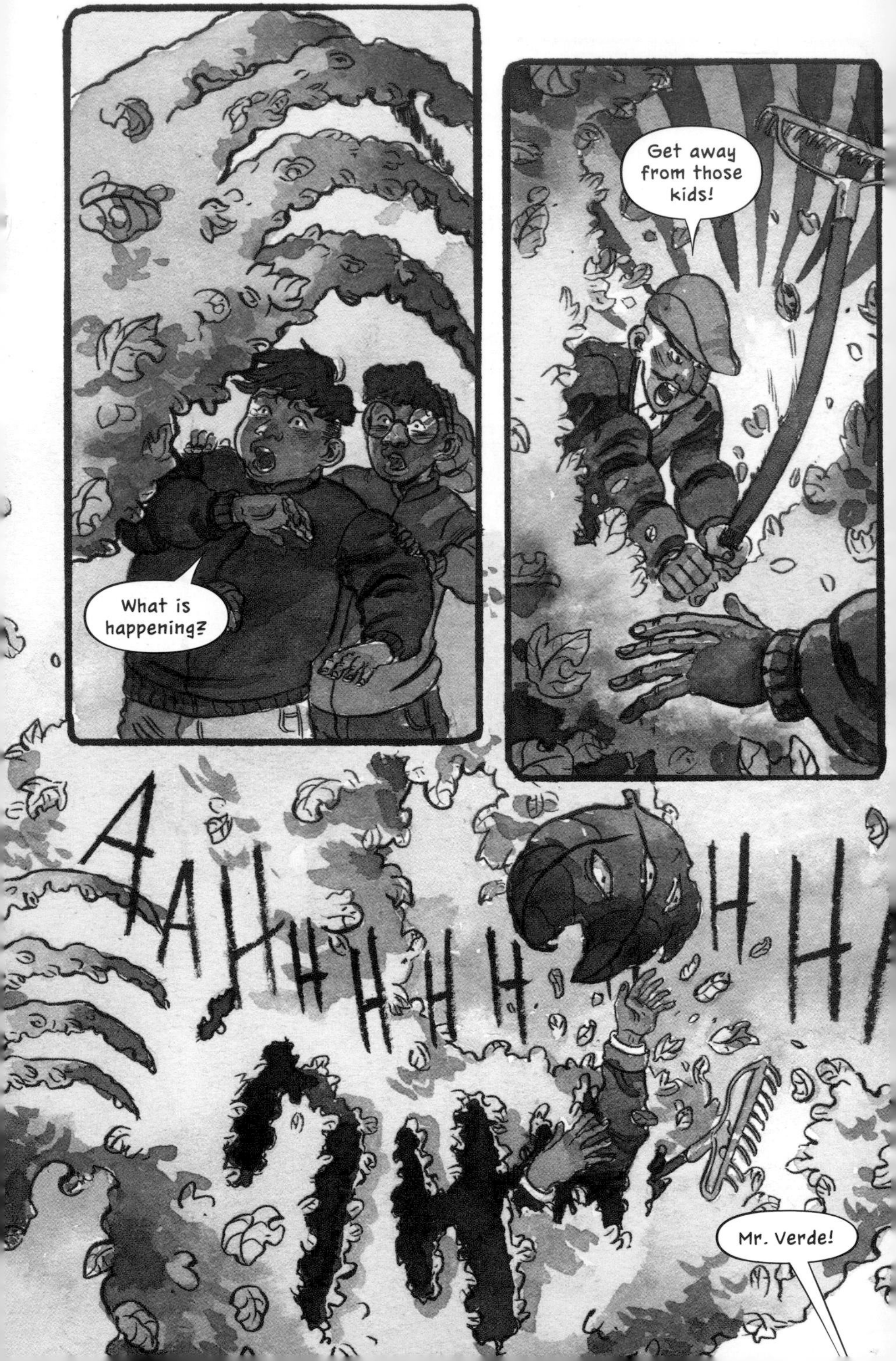
What is happening?
Get away from those kids!
AAHHHHHHHHHHH
Mr. Verde!

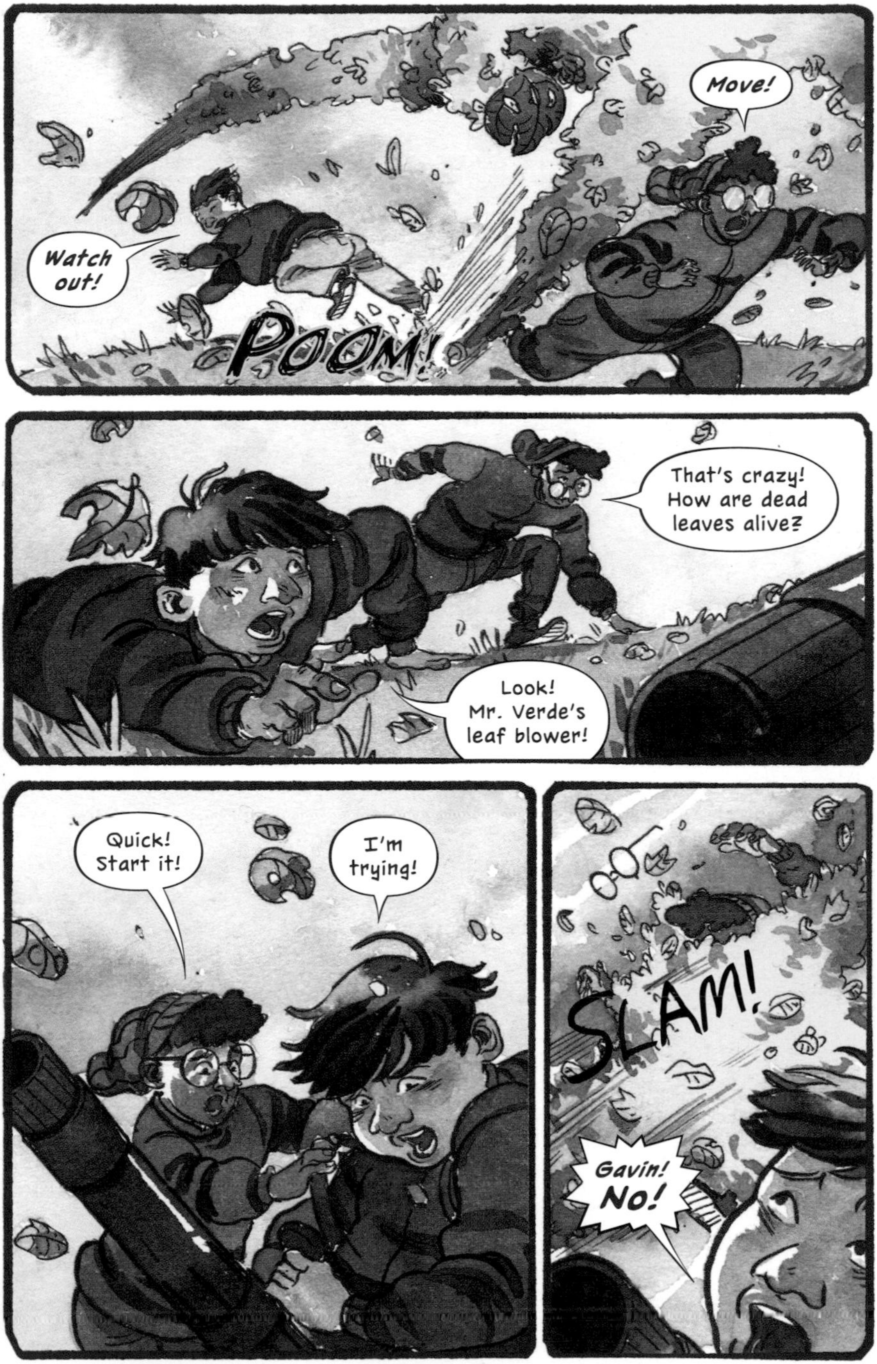
Move!
Watch out!
POOM!
That's crazy! How are dead leaves alive?
Look! Mr. Verde's leaf blower!
Quick! Start it!
I'm trying!
SLAM!
Gavin! No!

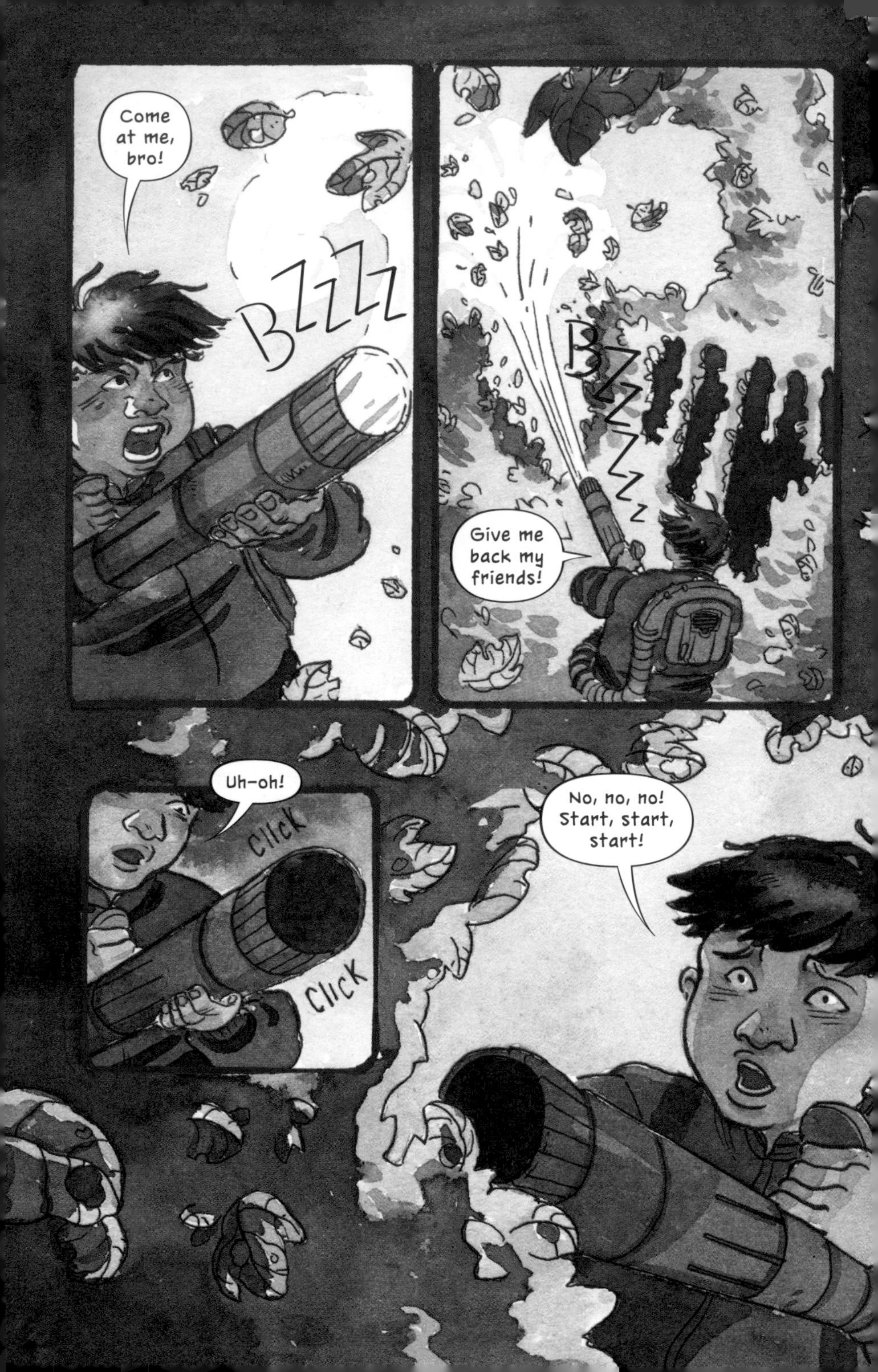
Come at me, bro!
BZZZZ
BZZZZZ
Give me back my friends!
Uh-oh!
CLICK
CLICK
No, no, no! Start, start, start!

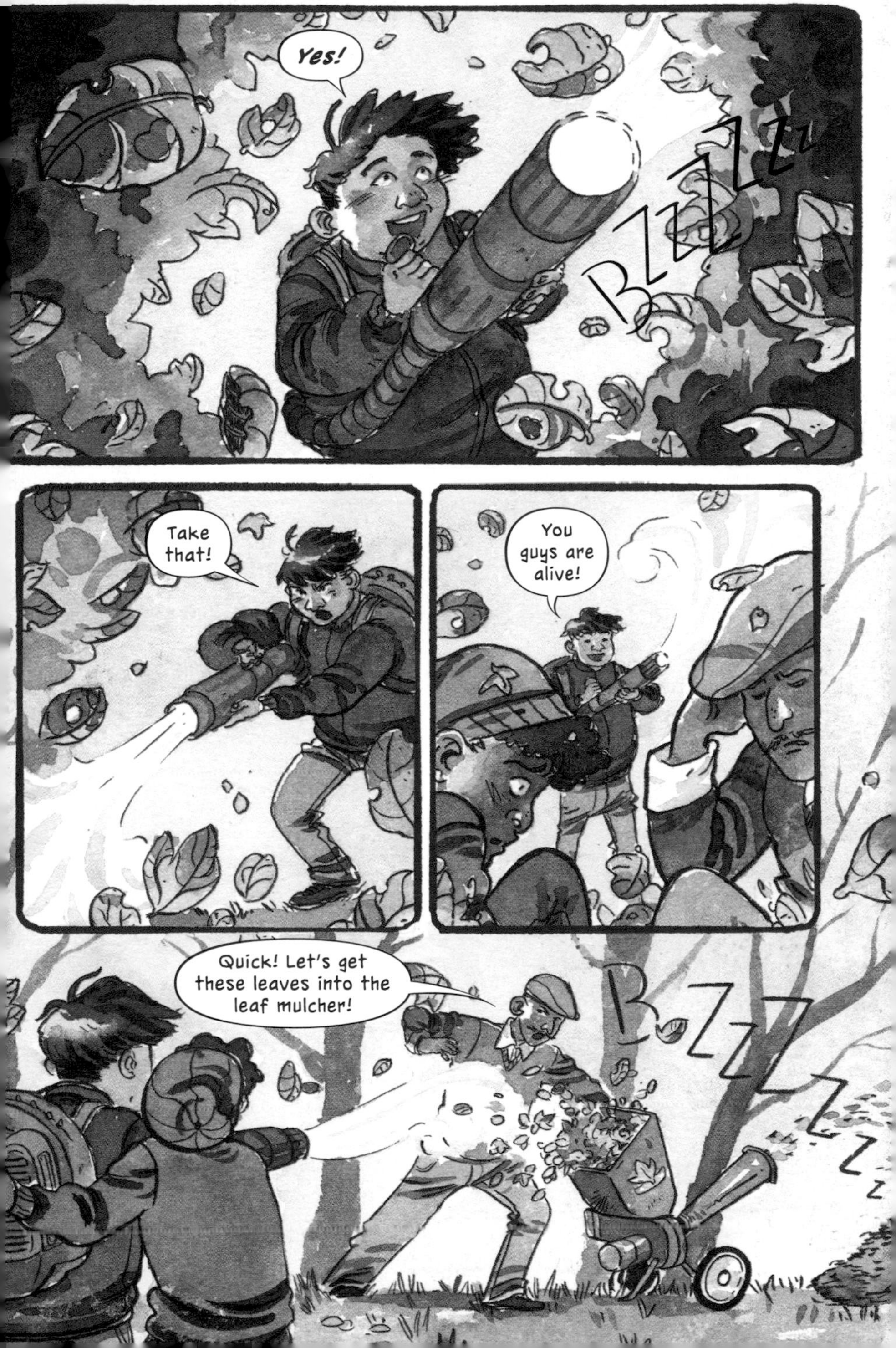
Yes!
BZZZZZzz
Take that!
You guys are alive!
Quick! Let's get these leaves into the leaf mulcher!
BZZZZZ

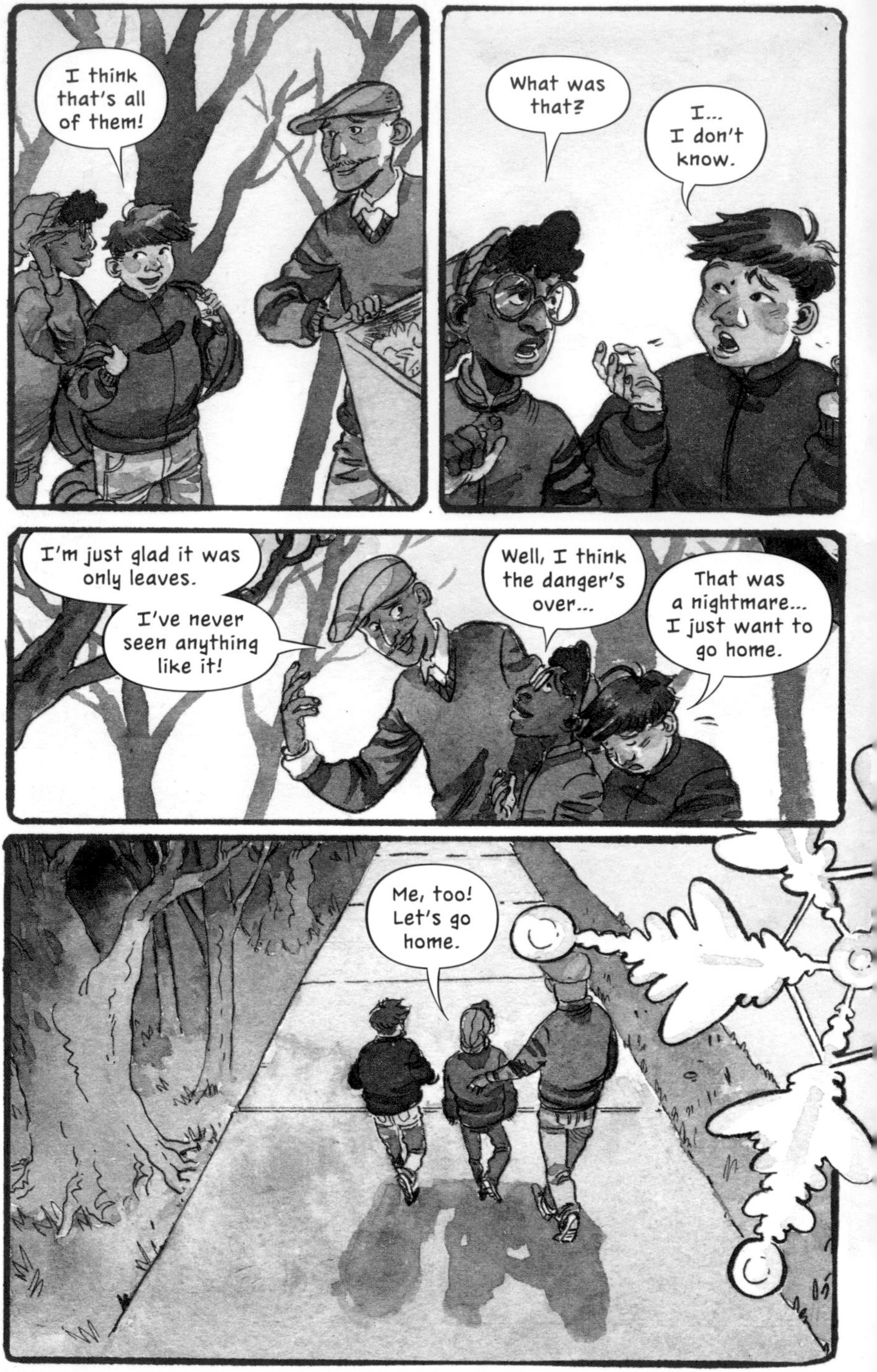
I think that's all of them!
What was that?
I... I don't know.
I'm just glad it was only leaves.
I've never seen anything like it!
Well, I think the danger's over...
That was a nightmare... I just want to go home.
Me, too! Let's go home.

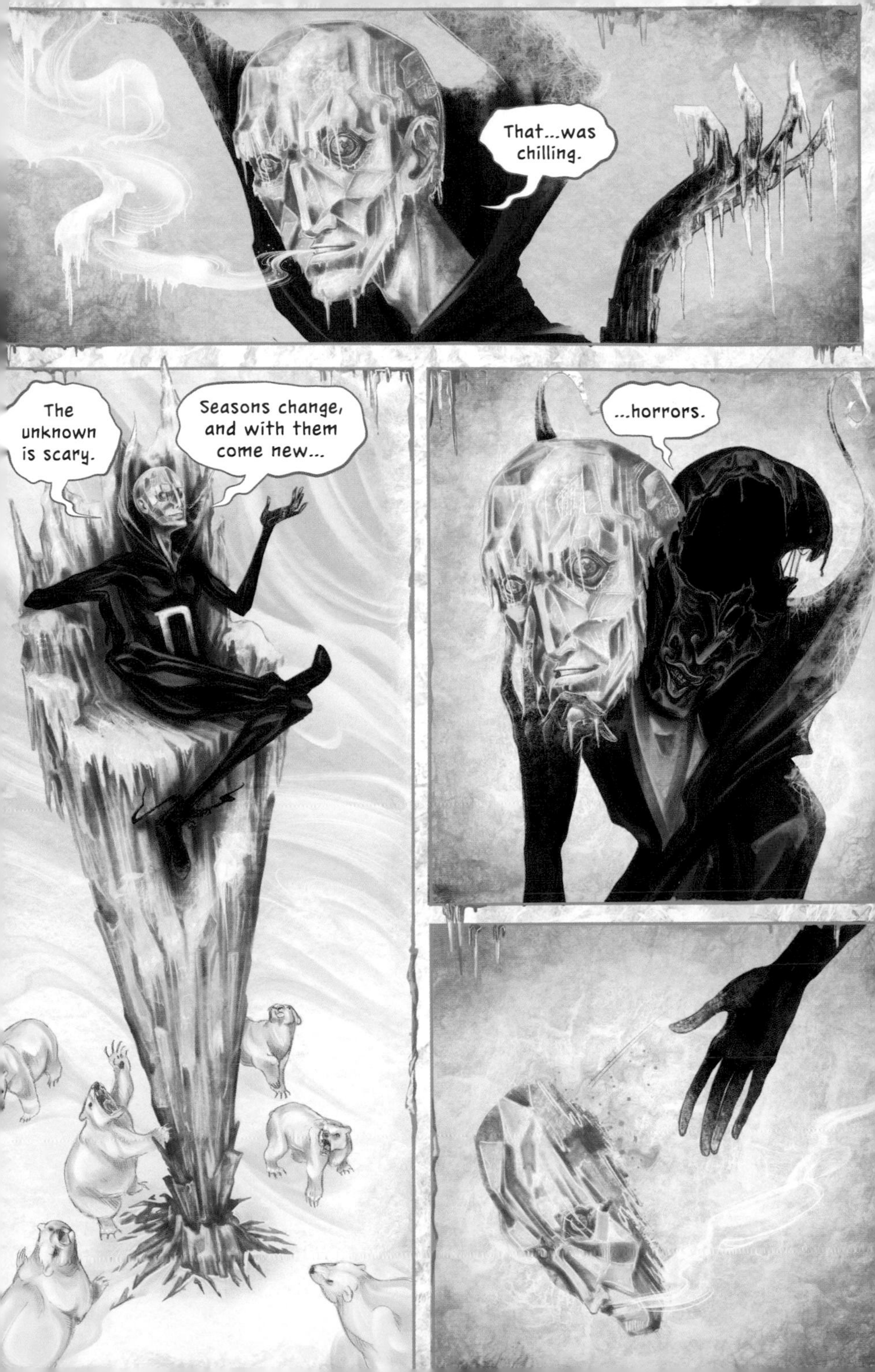
That...was chilling.
The unknown is scary.
Seasons change, and with them come new...
...horrors.

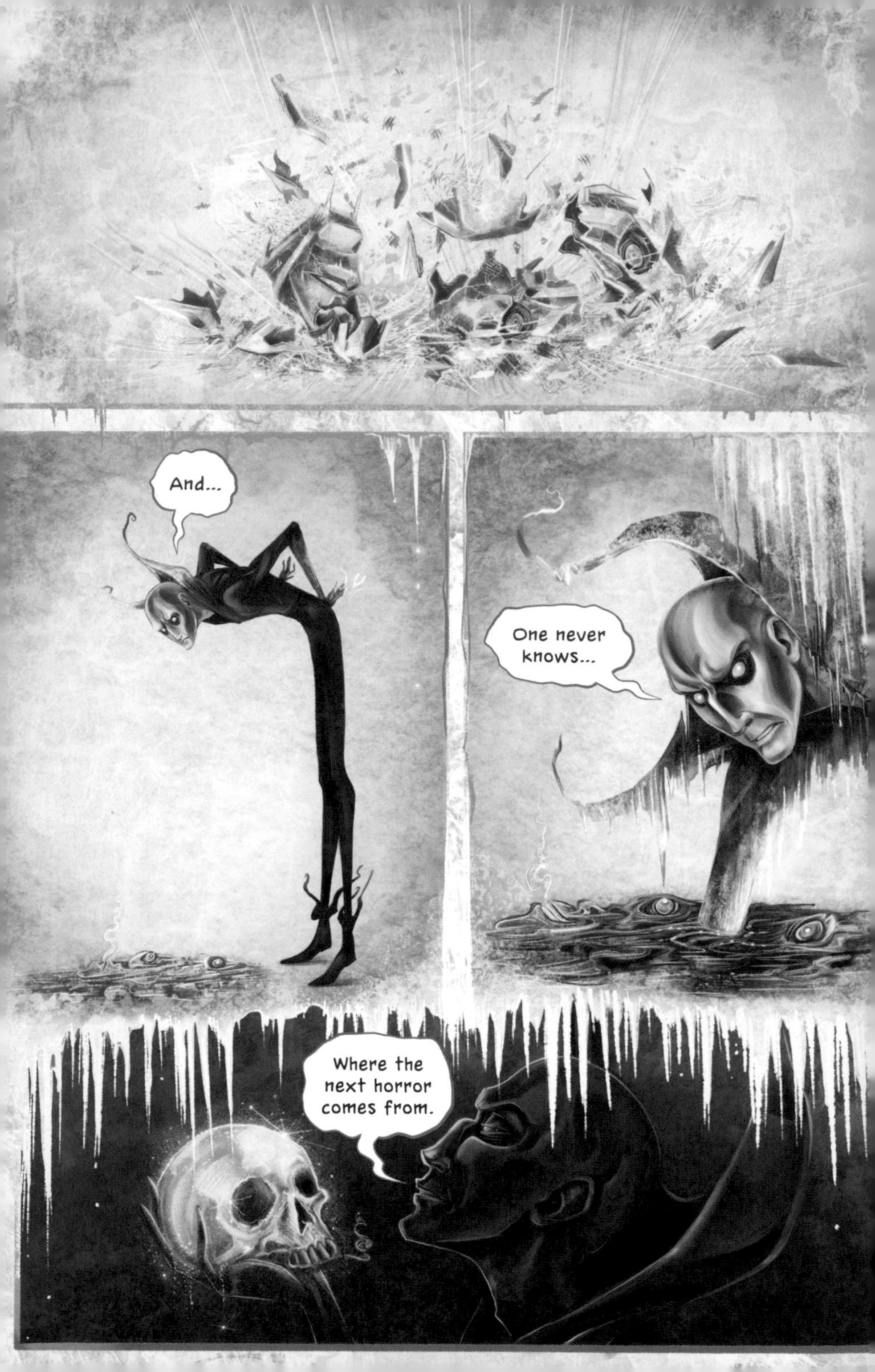
And...
One never knows...
Where the next horror comes from.

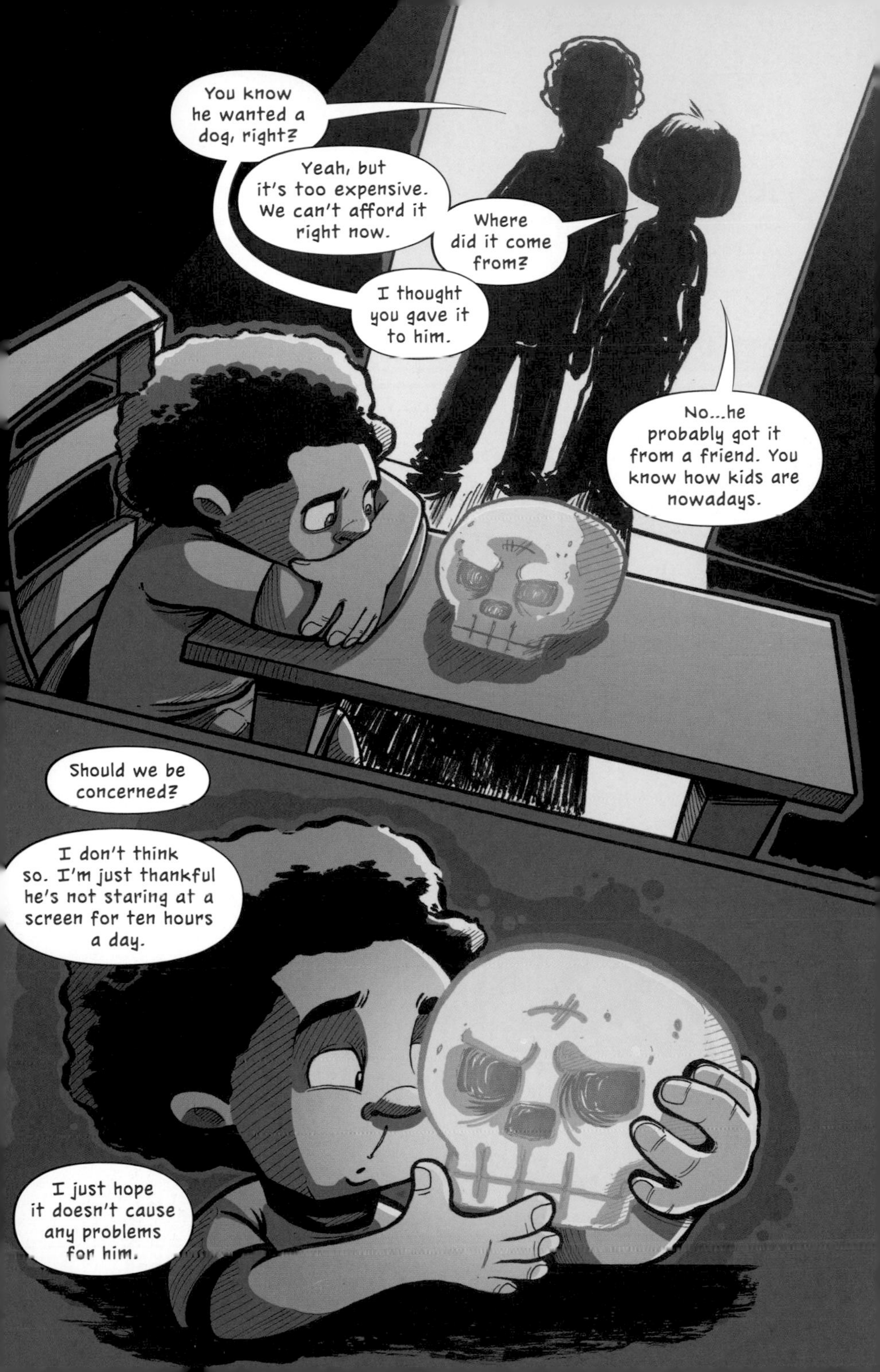

You know he wanted a dog, right?
Yeah, but it's too expensive. We can't afford it right now.
Where did it come from?
I thought you gave it to him.
No...he probably got it from a friend. You know how kids are nowadays.
Should we be concerned?
I don't think so. I'm just thankful he's not staring at a screen for ten hours a day.
I just hope it doesn't cause any problems for him.

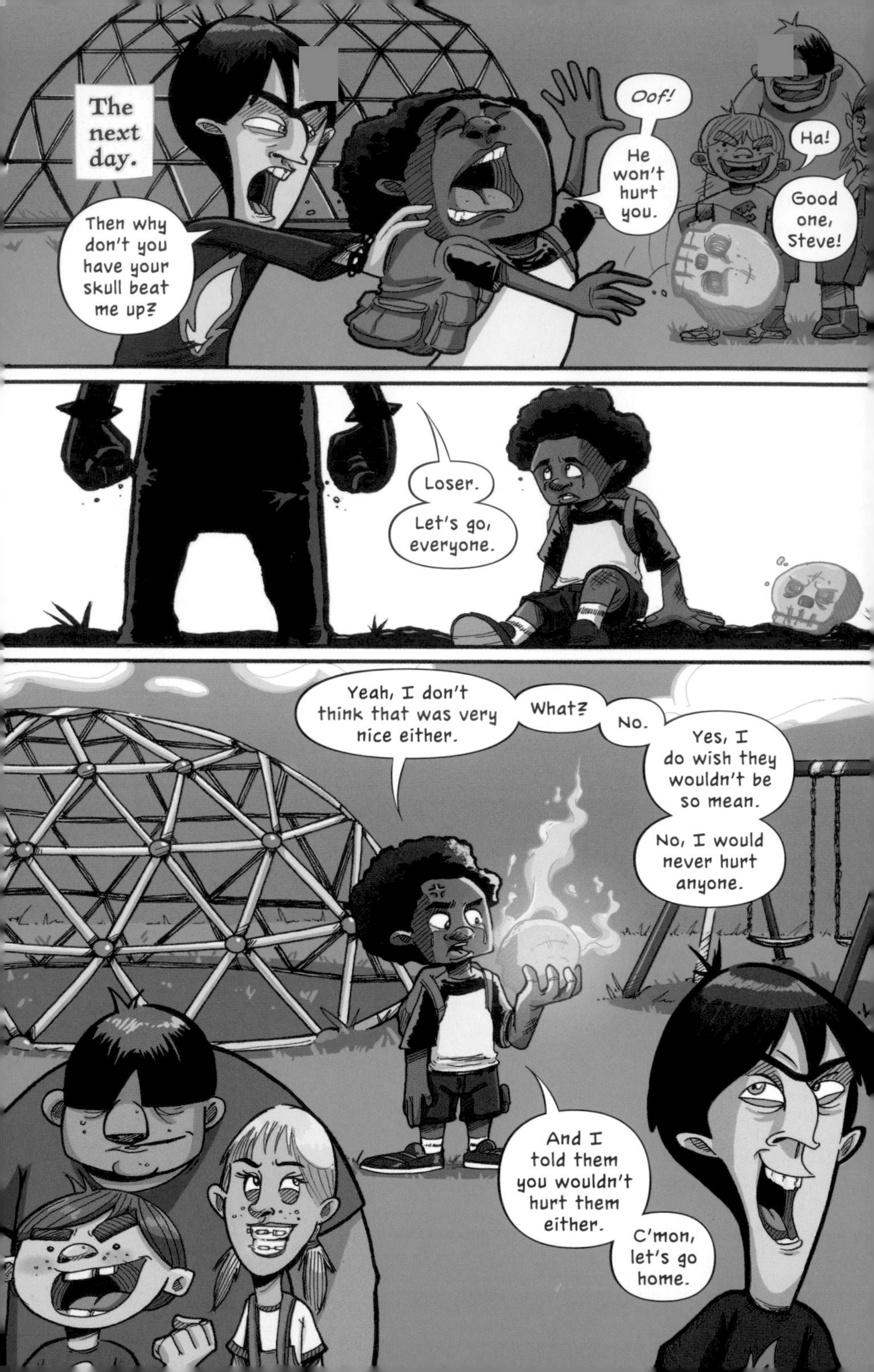
The next day.
Then why don't you have your skull beat me up?
Oof!
He won't hurt you.
Ha!
Good one, Steve!
Loser.
Let's go, everyone.
Yeah, I don't think that was very nice either.
What?
No.
Yes, I do wish they wouldn't be so mean.
No, I would never hurt anyone.
And I told them you wouldn't hurt them either.
C'mon, let's go home.

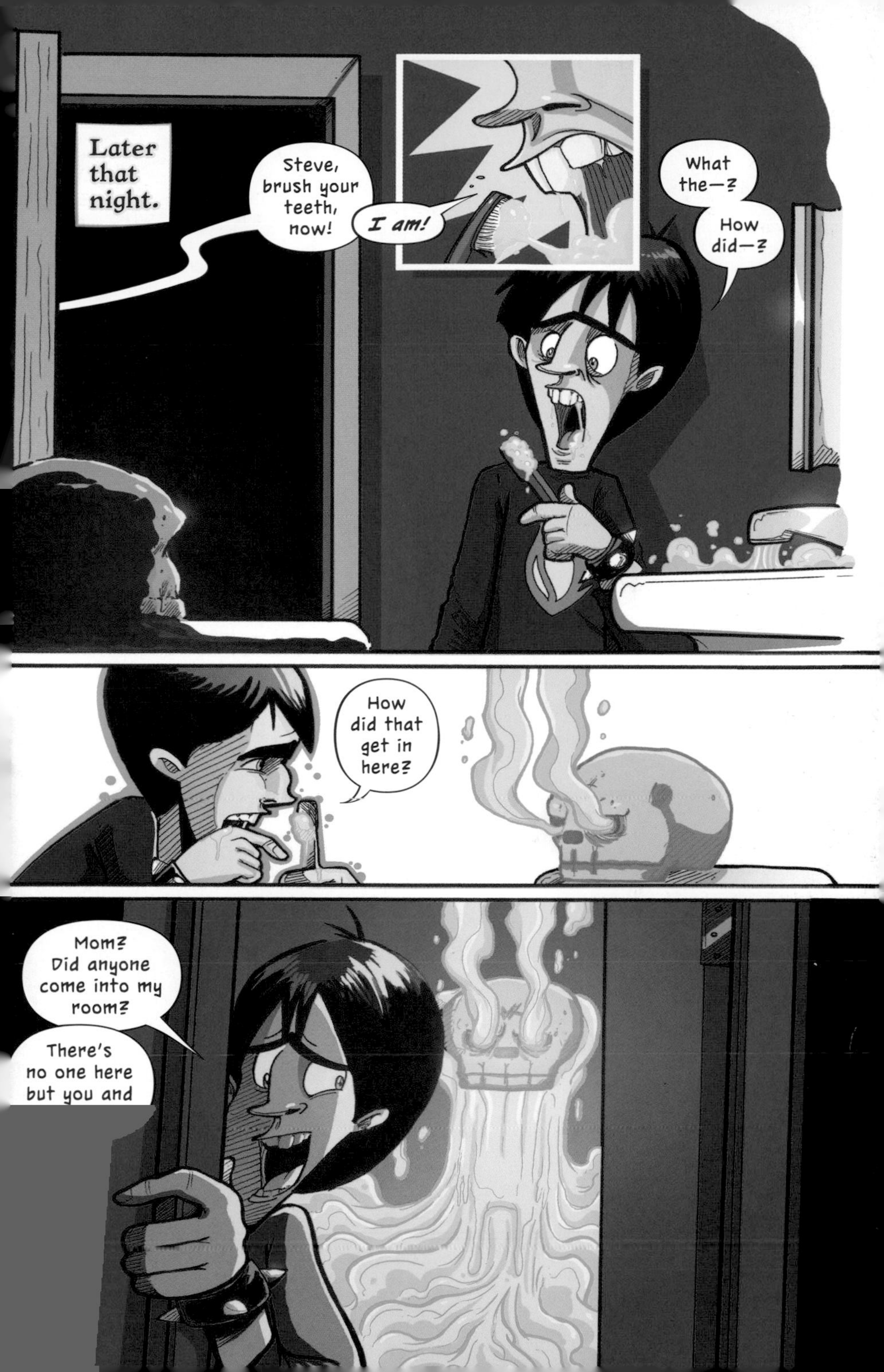
Later that night.
Steve, brush your teeth, now!
I am!
What the—?
How did—?
How did that get in here?
Mom? Did anyone come into my room?
There's no one here but you and

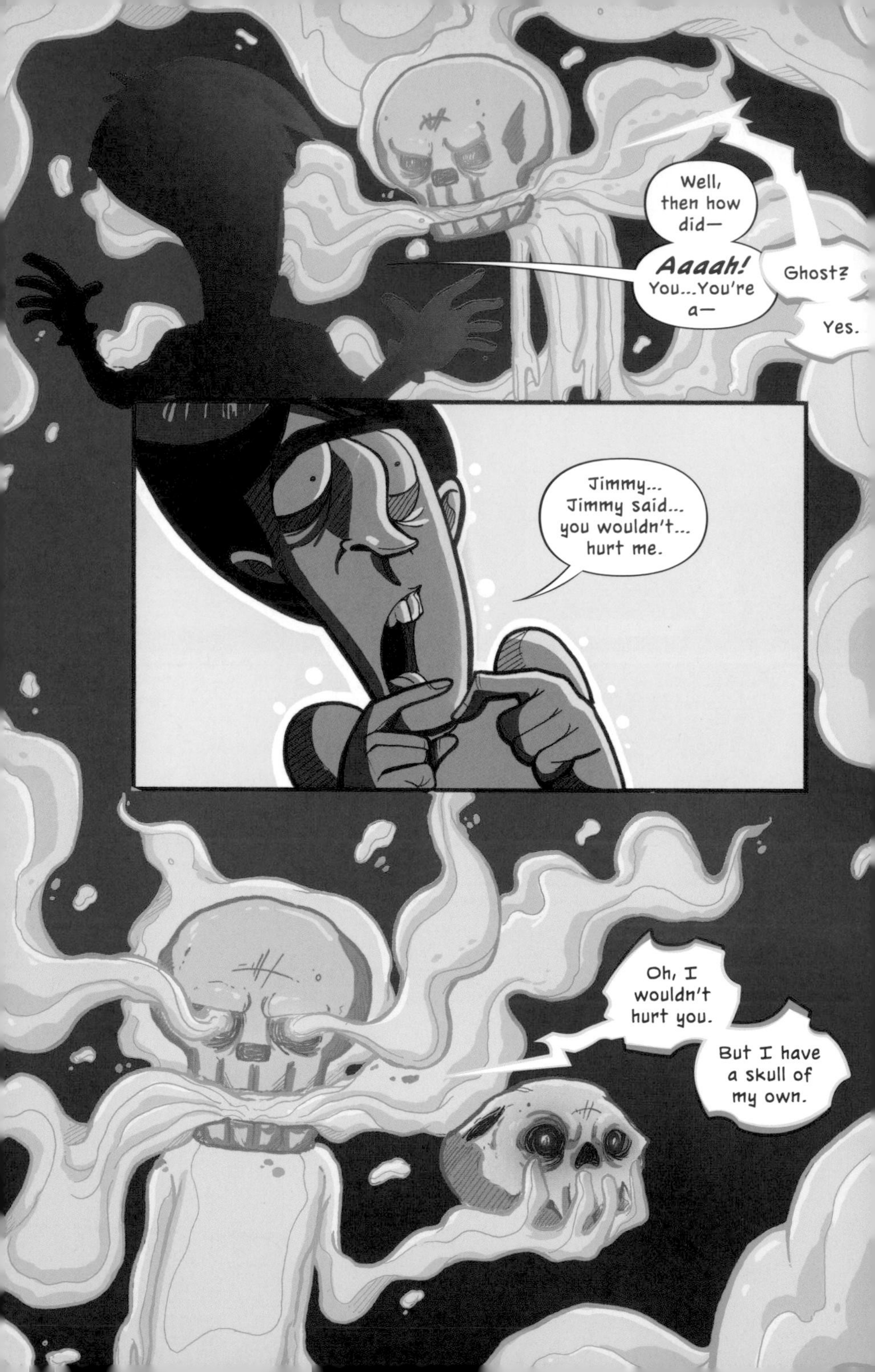
Well, then how did—
Aaaah! You...You're a—
Ghost?
Yes.
Jimmy... Jimmy said... you wouldn't... hurt me.
Oh, I wouldn't hurt you.
But I have a skull of my own.

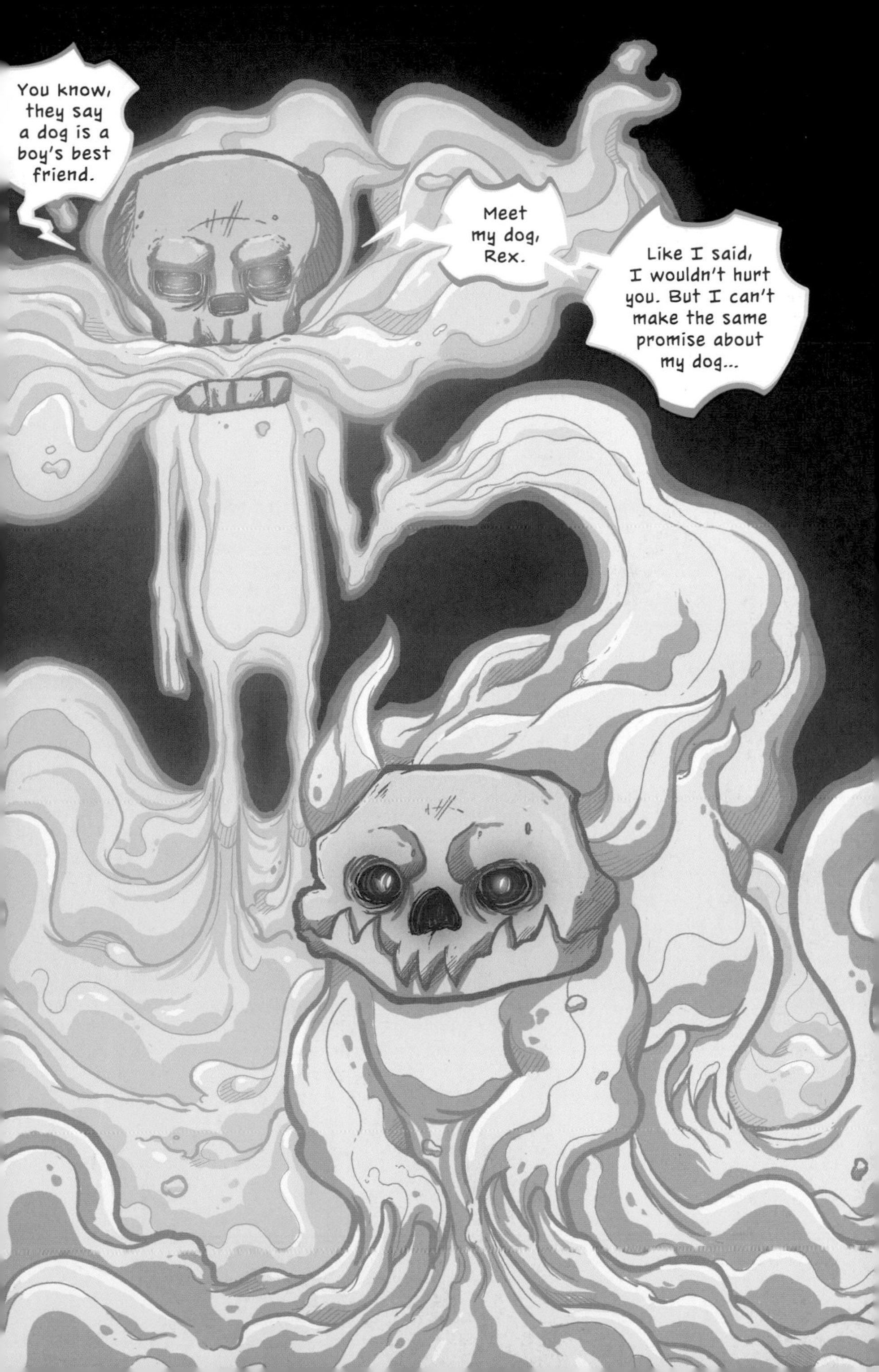
You know, they say a dog is a boy's best friend.
Meet my dog, Rex.
Like I said, I wouldn't hurt you. But I can't make the same promise about my dog...

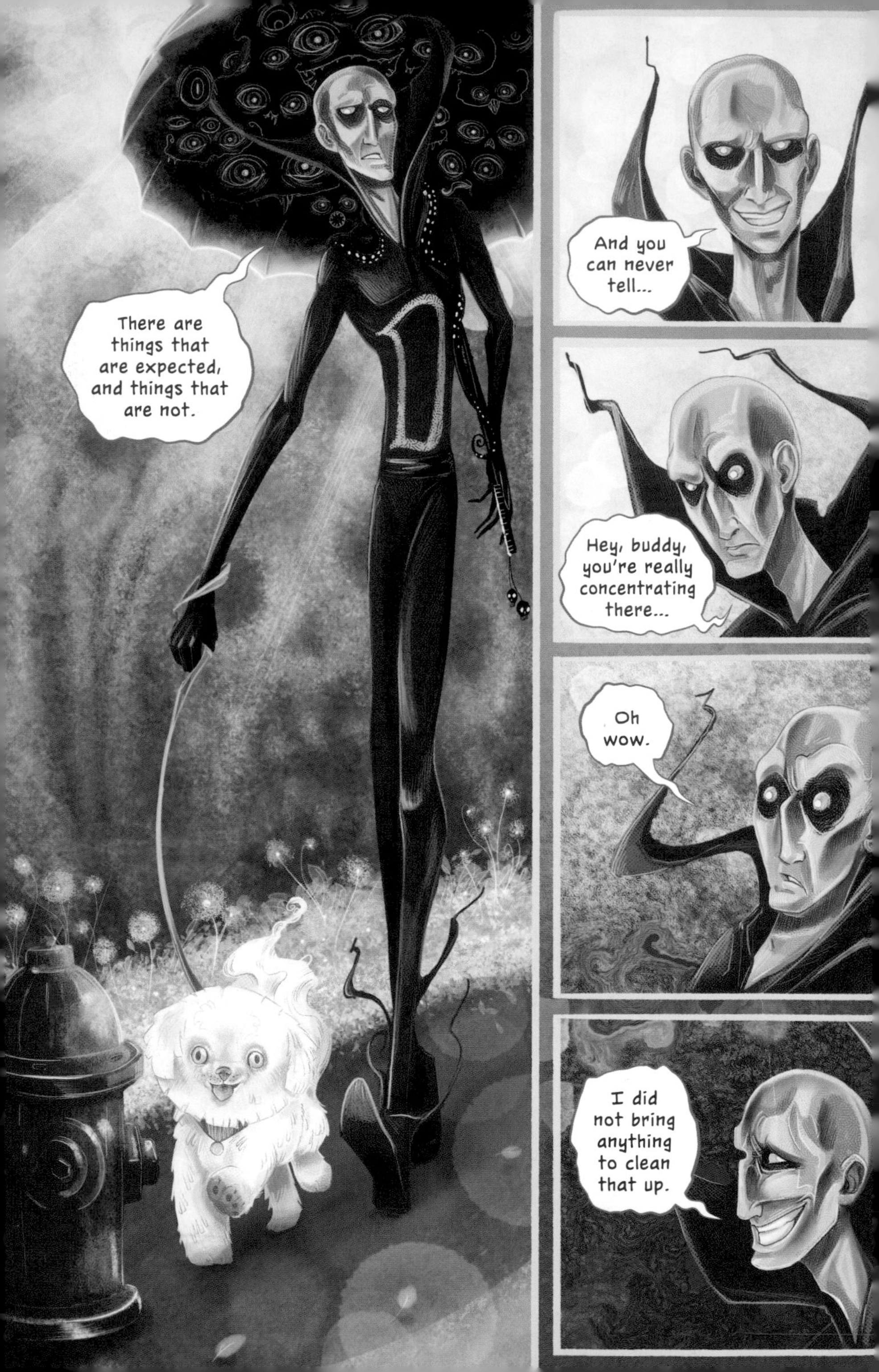
There are things that are expected, and things that are not.
And you can never tell...
Hey, buddy, you're really concentrating there...
Oh wow.
I did not bring anything to clean that up.

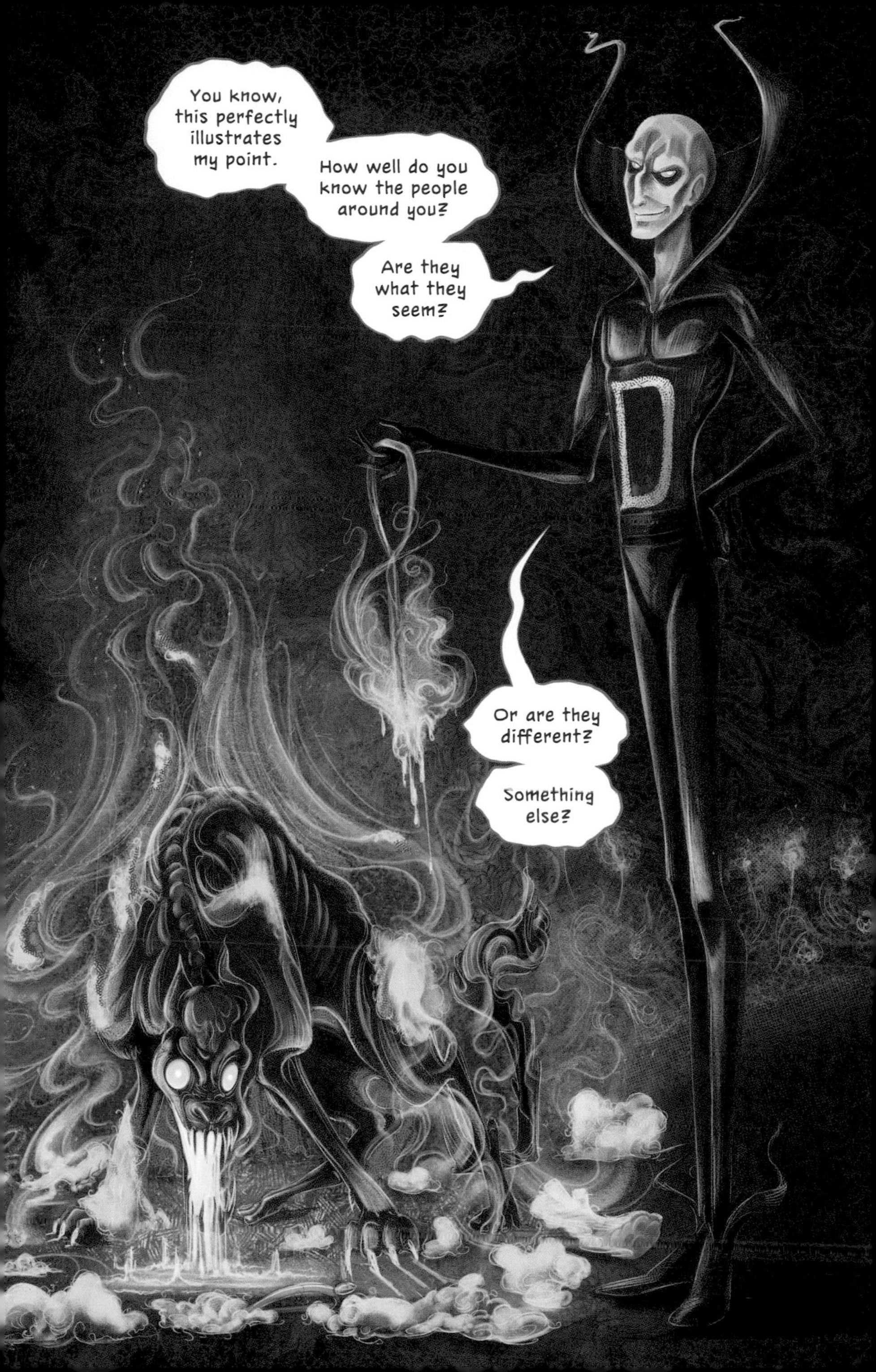
You know, this perfectly illustrates my point.
How well do you know the people around you?
Are they what they seem?
Or are they different?
Something else?

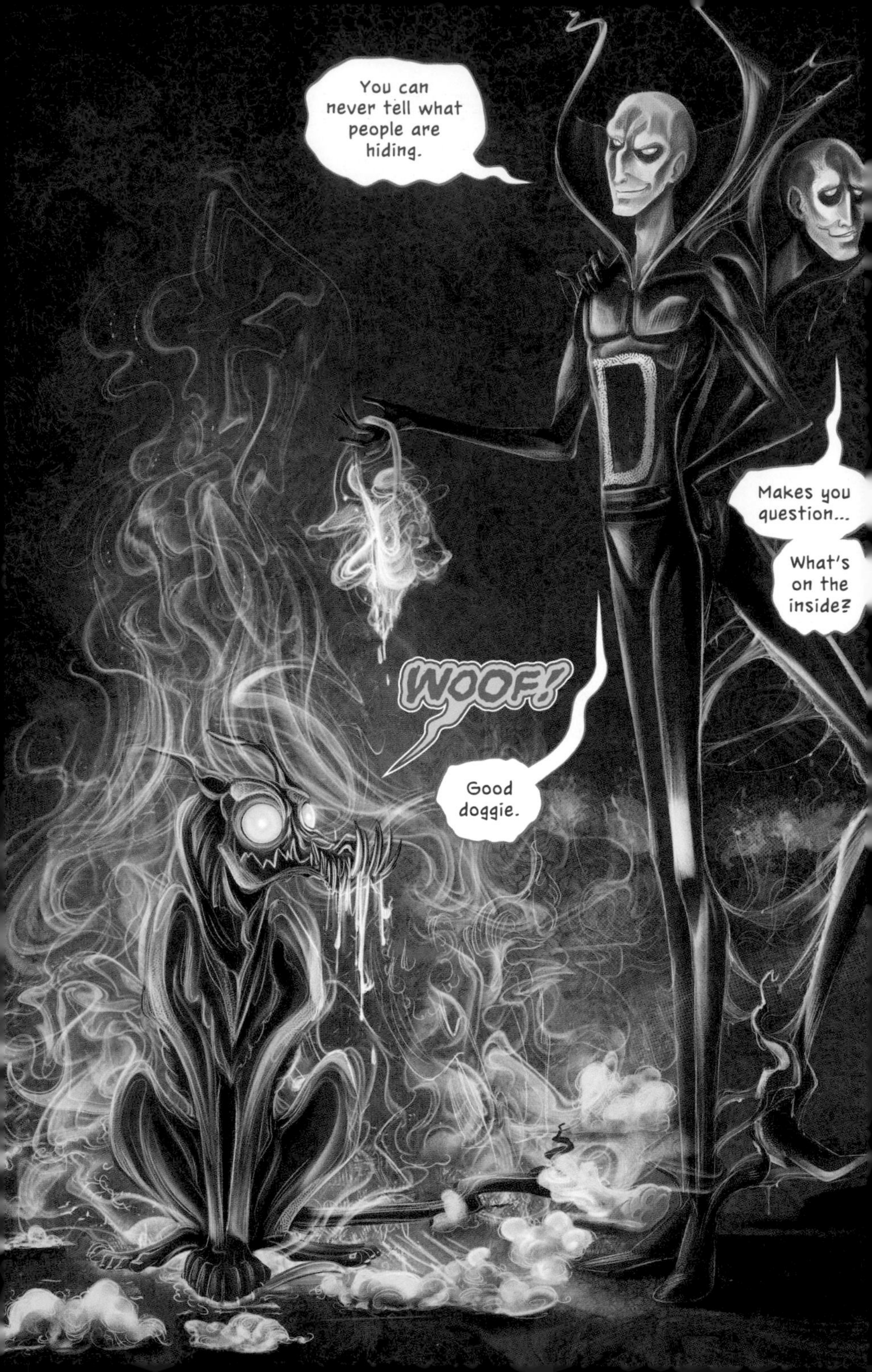
You can never tell what people are hiding.
Makes you question...
What's on the inside?
WOOF!
Good doggie.

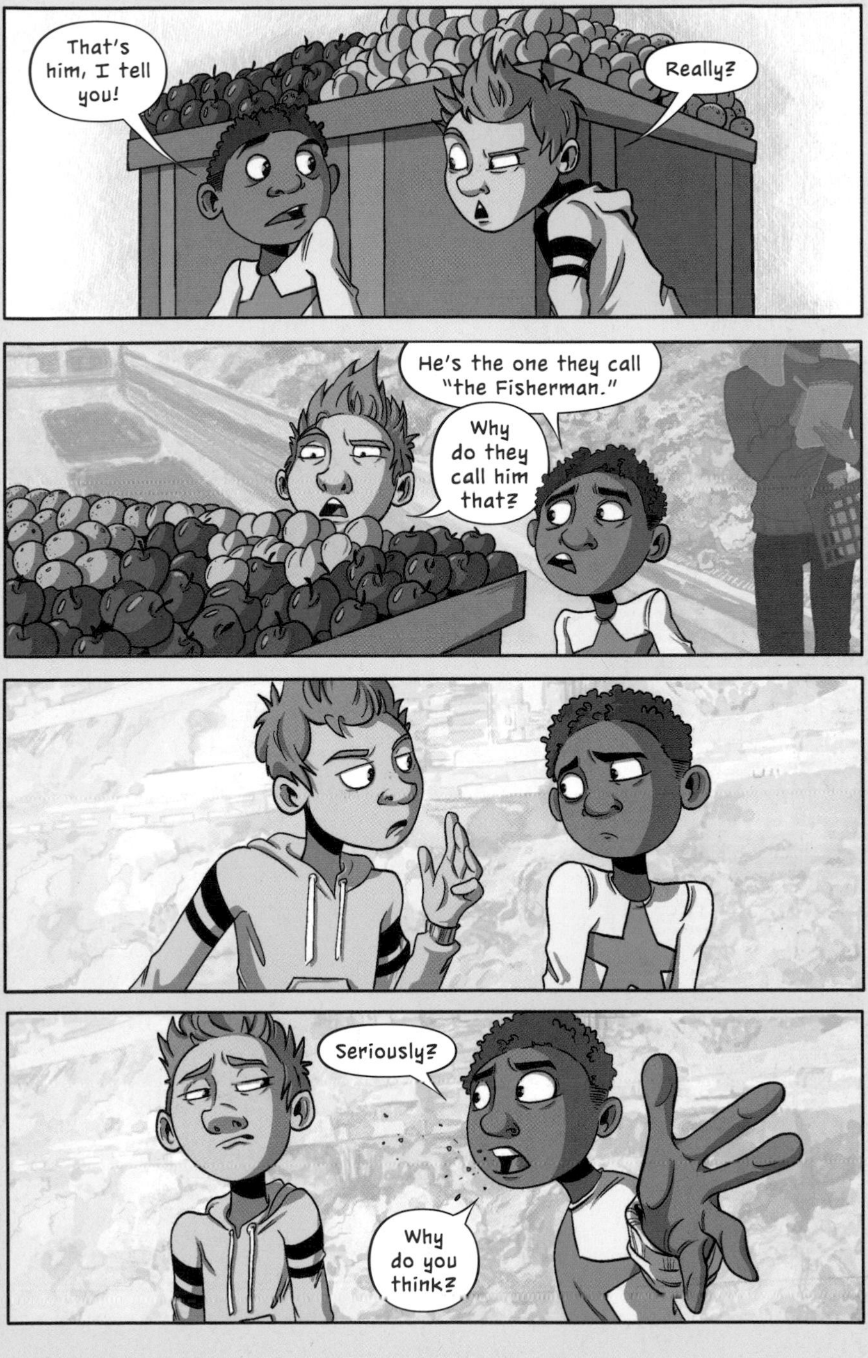
That's him, I tell you!
Really?
He's the one they call "the Fisherman."
Why do they call him that?
Seriously?
Why do you think?

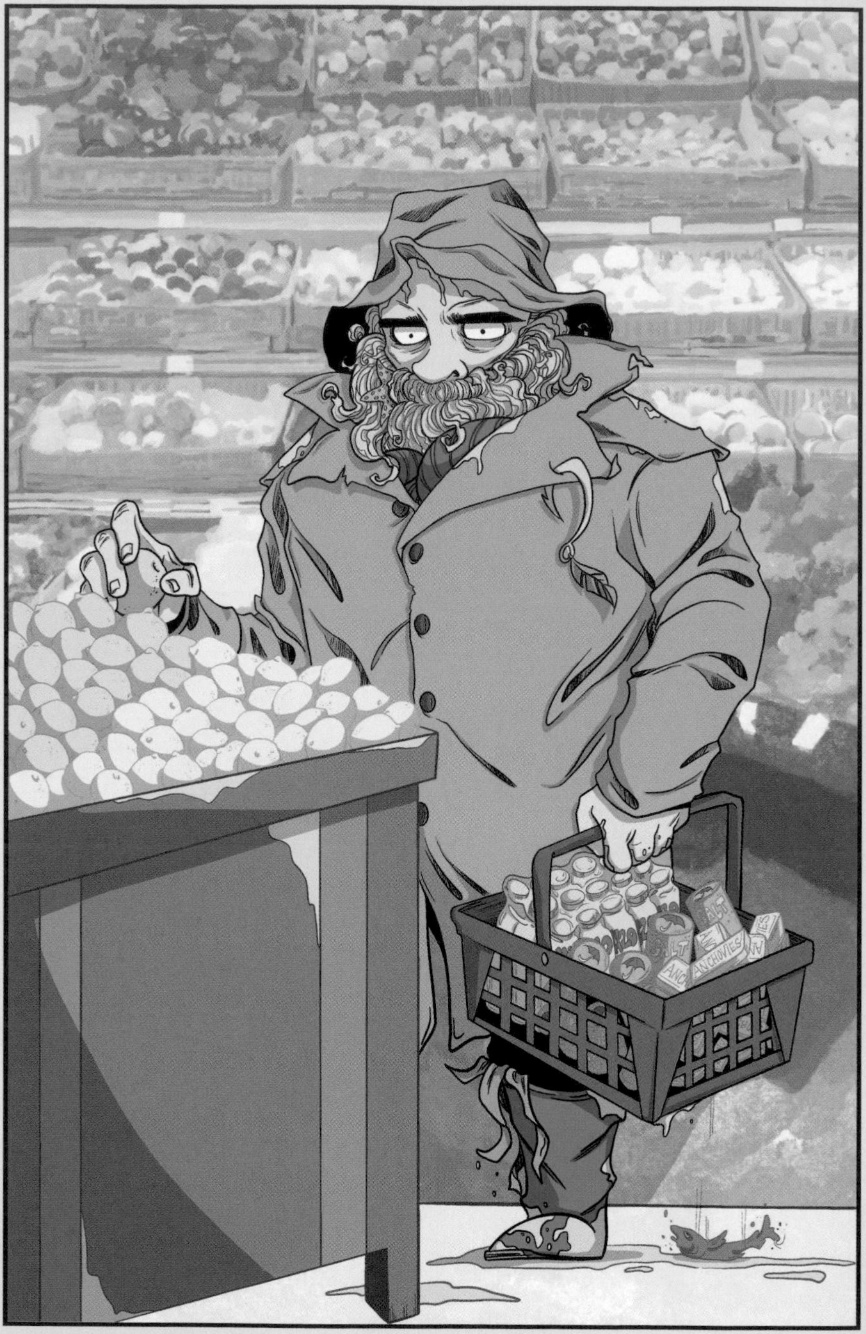
ANCHOVIES

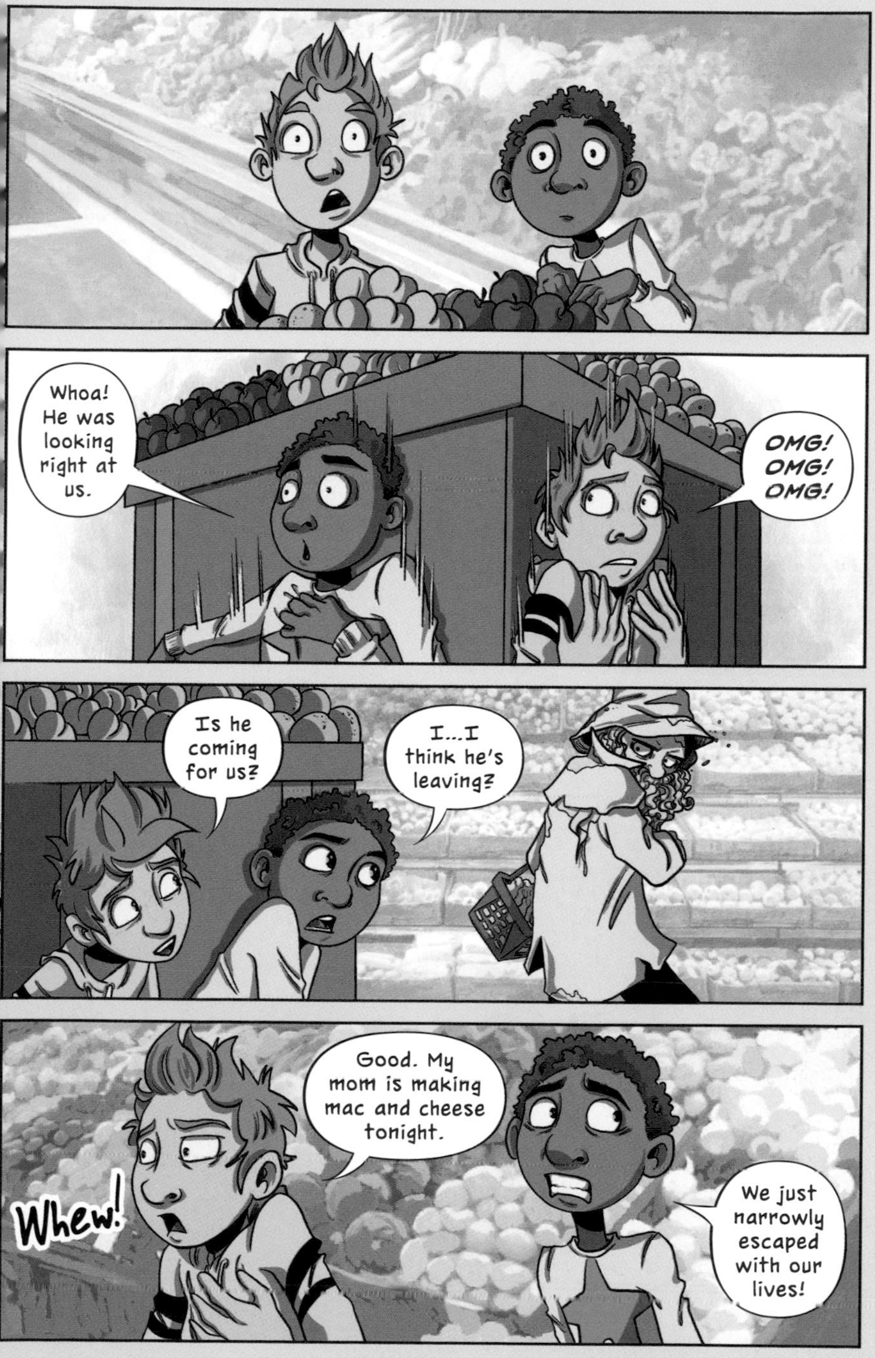

Whoa! He was looking right at us.
OMG! OMG! OMG!
Is he coming for us?
I...I think he's leaving?
Good. My mom is making mac and cheese tonight.
Whew!
We just narrowly escaped with our lives!

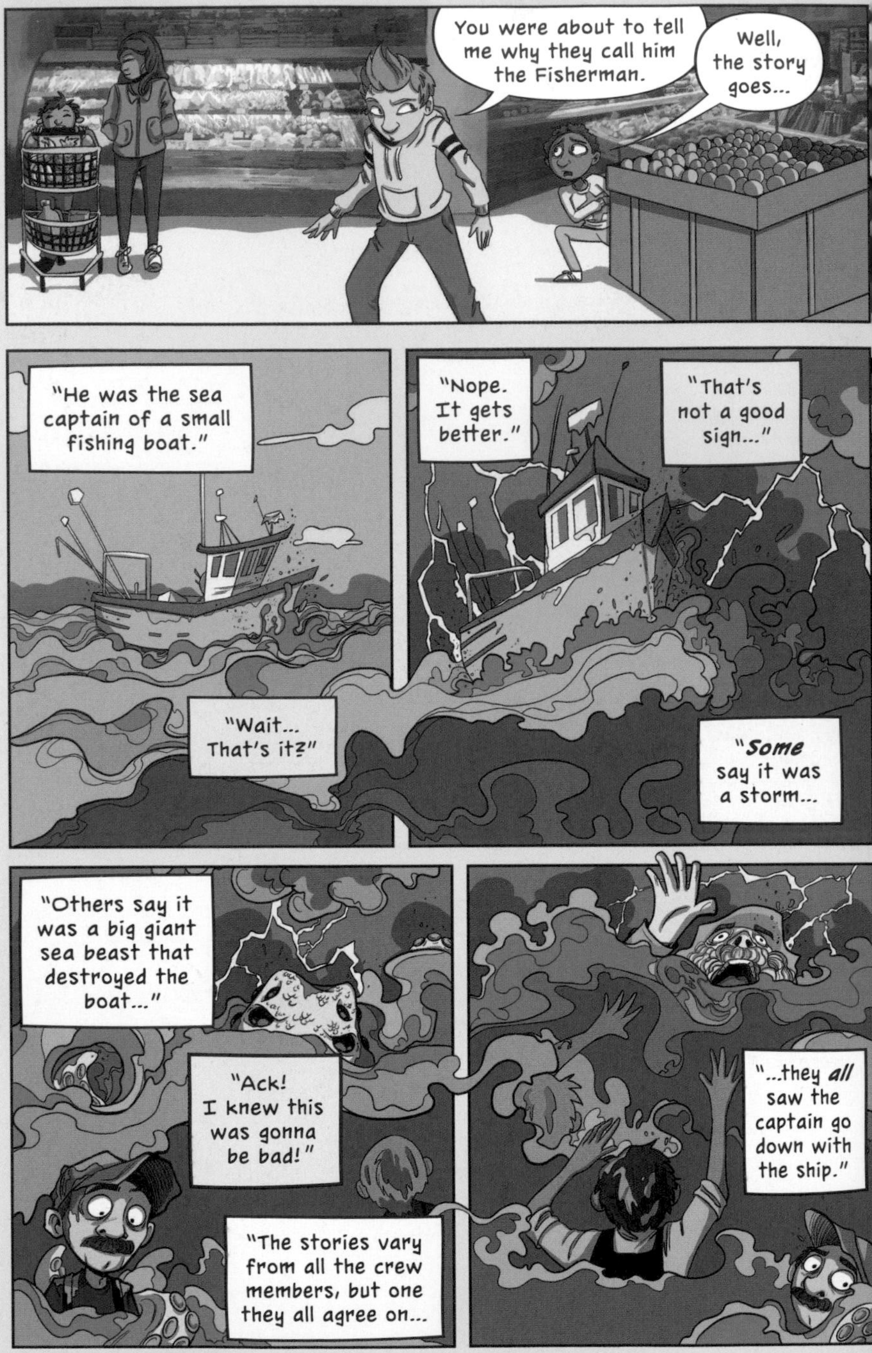
You were about to tell me why they call him the Fisherman.
Well, the story goes...
"He was the sea captain of a small fishing boat."
"Wait... That's it?"
"Nope. It gets better."
"That's not a good sign..."
"*Some* say it was a storm...
"Others say it was a big giant sea beast that destroyed the boat..."
"Ack! I knew this was gonna be bad!"
"The stories vary from all the crew members, but one they all agree on...
"...they *all* saw the captain go down with the ship."

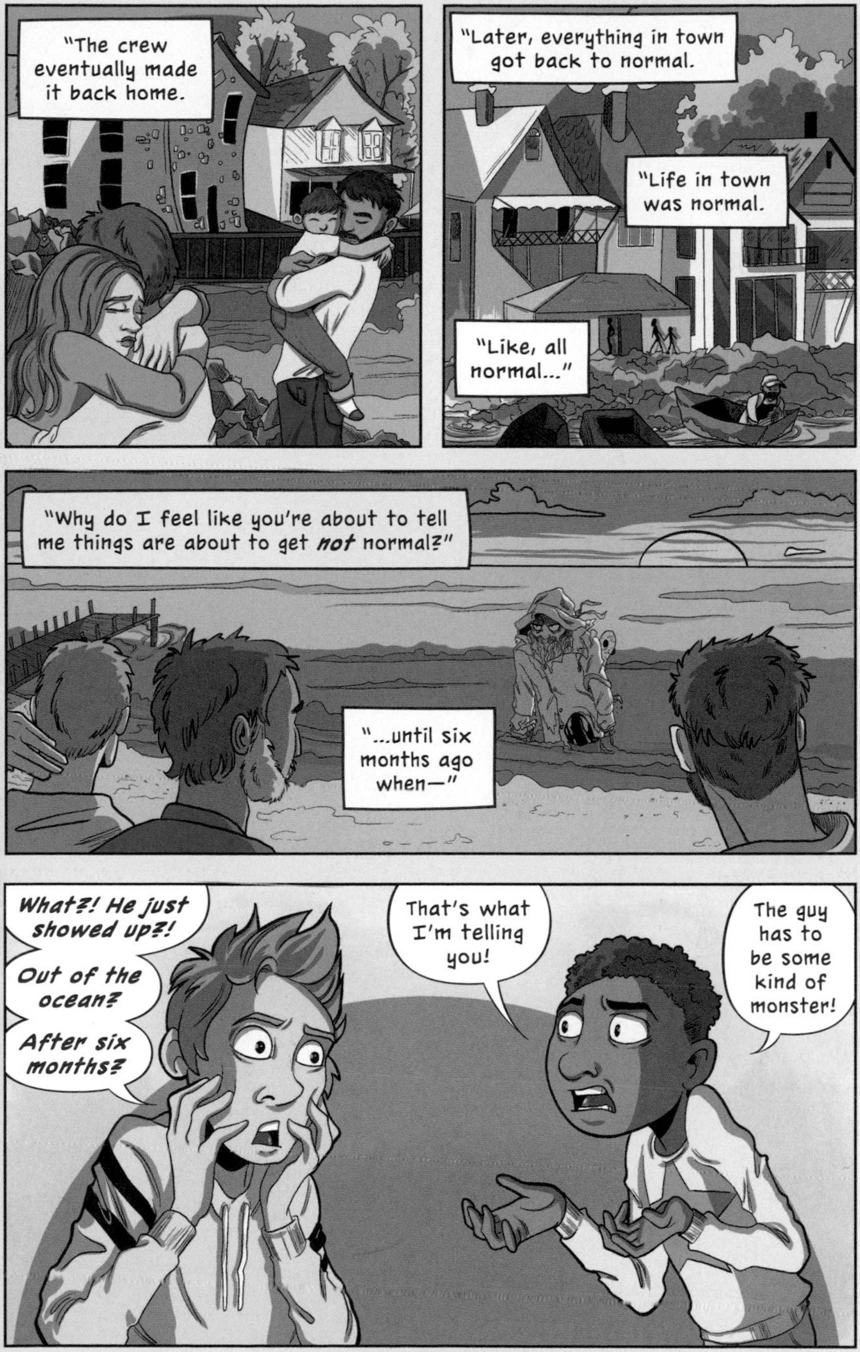
"The crew eventually made it back home.
"Later, everything in town got back to normal.
"Life in town was normal.
"Like, all normal..."
"Why do I feel like you're about to tell me things are about to get *not* normal?"
"...until six months ago when—"
What?! He just showed up?!
Out of the ocean?
After six months?
That's what I'm telling you!
The guy has to be some kind of monster!

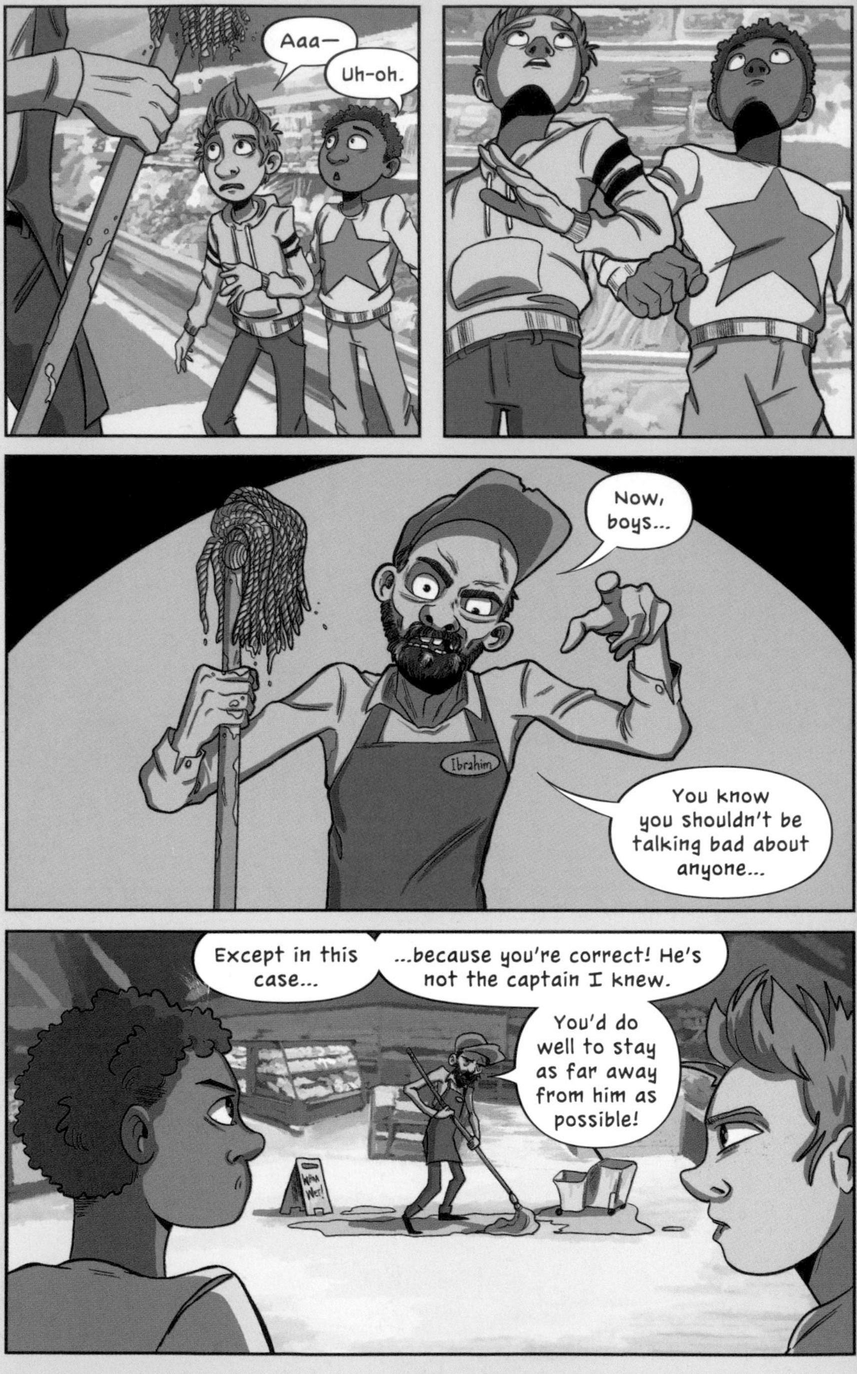

Aaa—
Uh-oh.
Now, boys...
Ibrahim
You know you shouldn't be talking bad about anyone...
Except in this case...
...because you're correct! He's not the captain I knew.
You'd do well to stay as far away from him as possible!

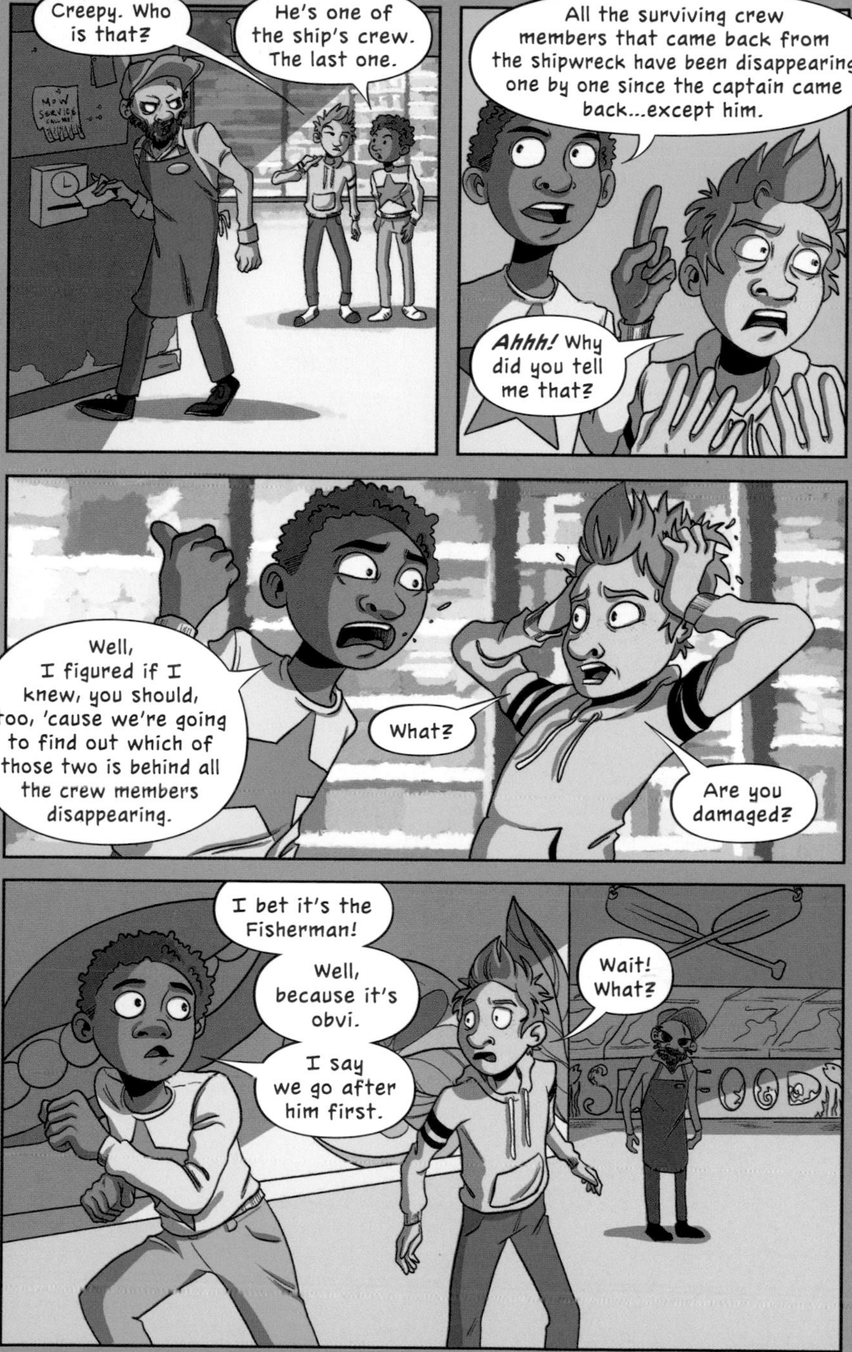
Creepy. Who is that?
He's one of the ship's crew. The last one.
All the surviving crew members that came back from the shipwreck have been disappearing one by one since the captain came back...except him.
Ahhh! Why did you tell me that?
Well, I figured if I knew, you should, too, 'cause we're going to find out which of those two is behind all the crew members disappearing.
What?
Are you damaged?
I bet it's the Fisherman!
Well, because it's obvi.
I say we go after him first.
Wait! What?

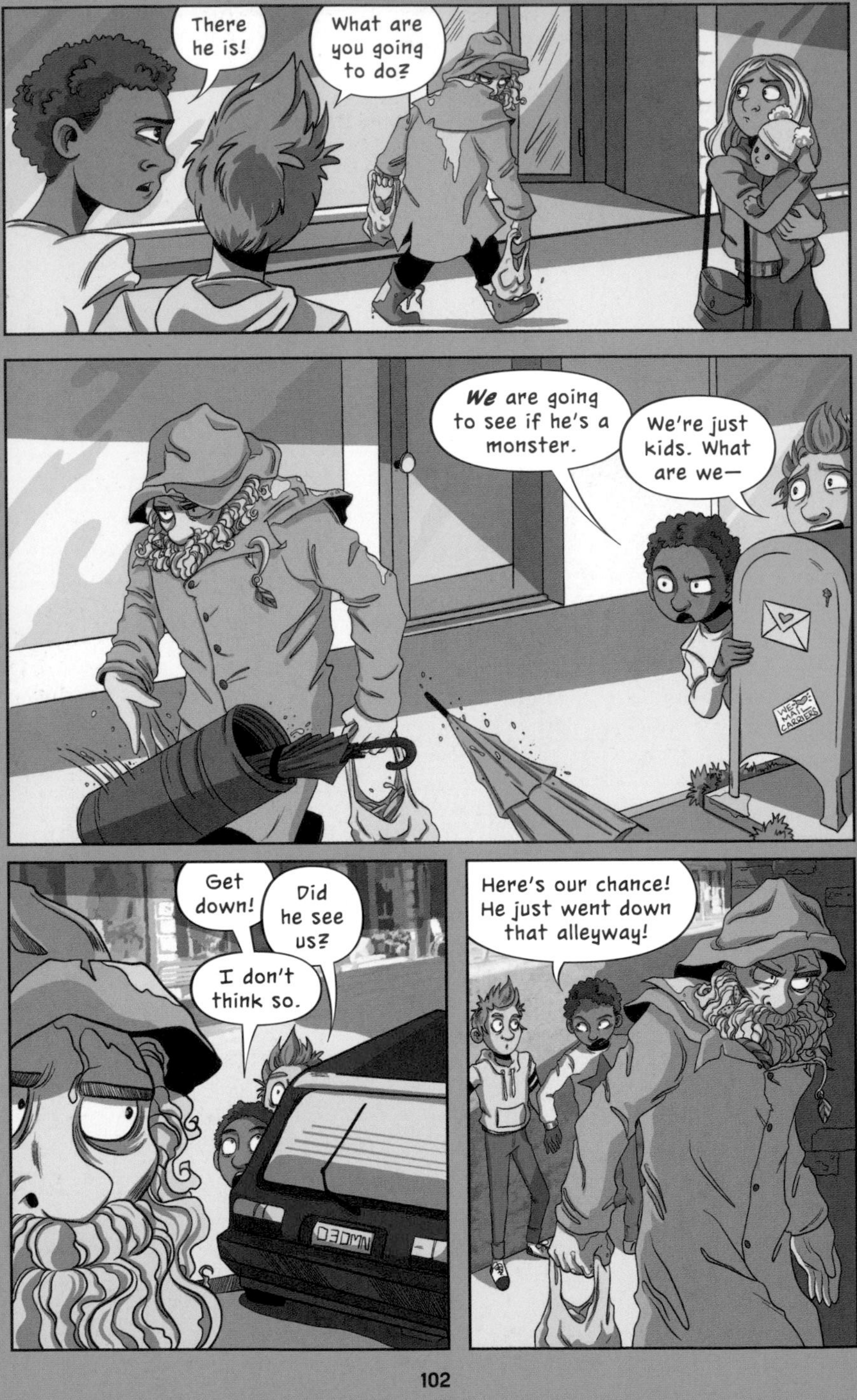
There he is!
What are you going to do?
We are going to see if he's a monster.
We're just kids. What are we—
WE ♥ MAIL CARRIERS
Get down!
Did he see us?
I don't think so.
D3DMN
Here's our chance! He just went down that alleyway!

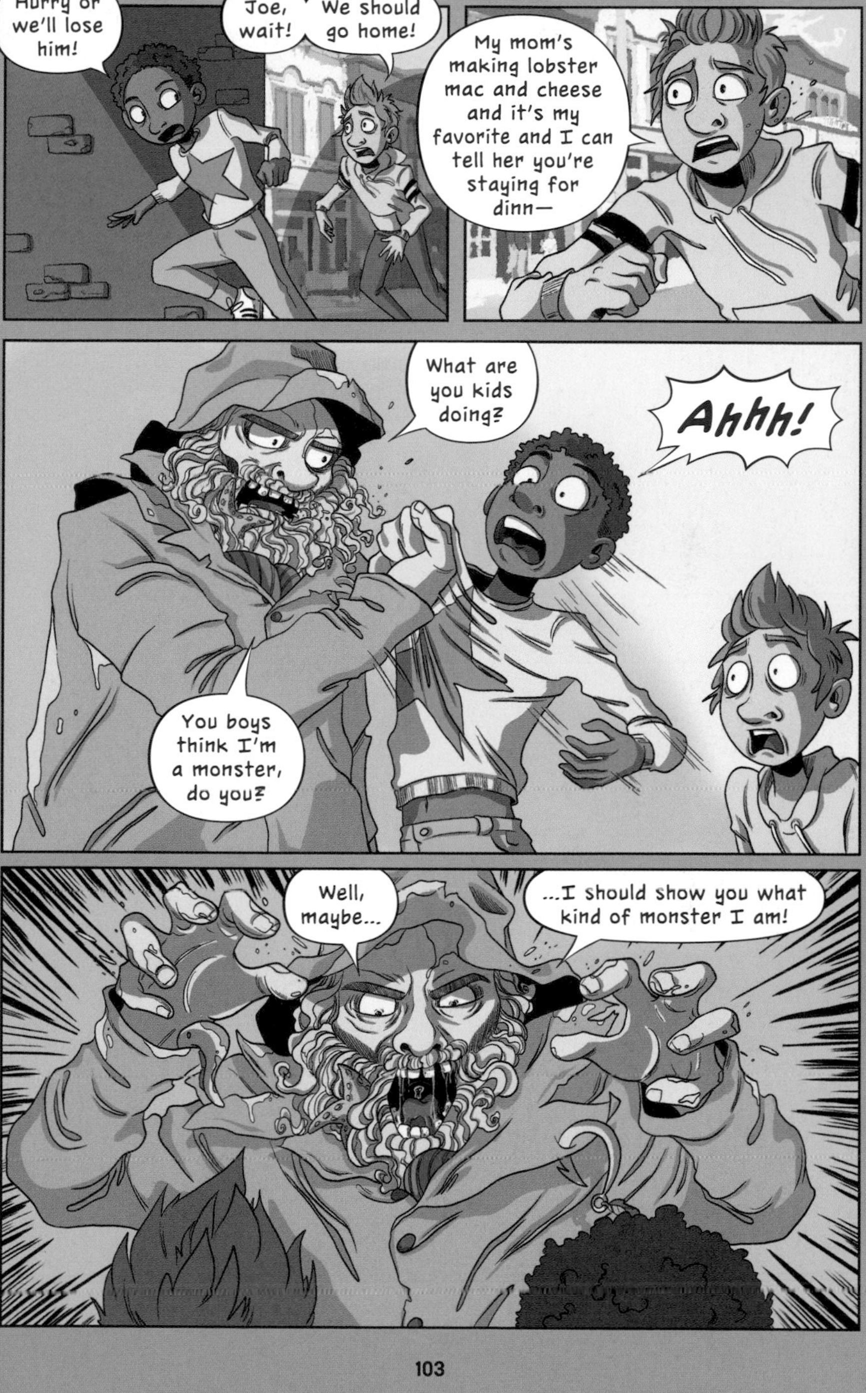
Hurry or we'll lose him!
Joe, wait!
We should go home!
My mom's making lobster mac and cheese and it's my favorite and I can tell her you're staying for dinn—
What are you kids doing?
Ahhh!
You boys think I'm a monster, do you?
Well, maybe...
...I should show you what kind of monster I am!

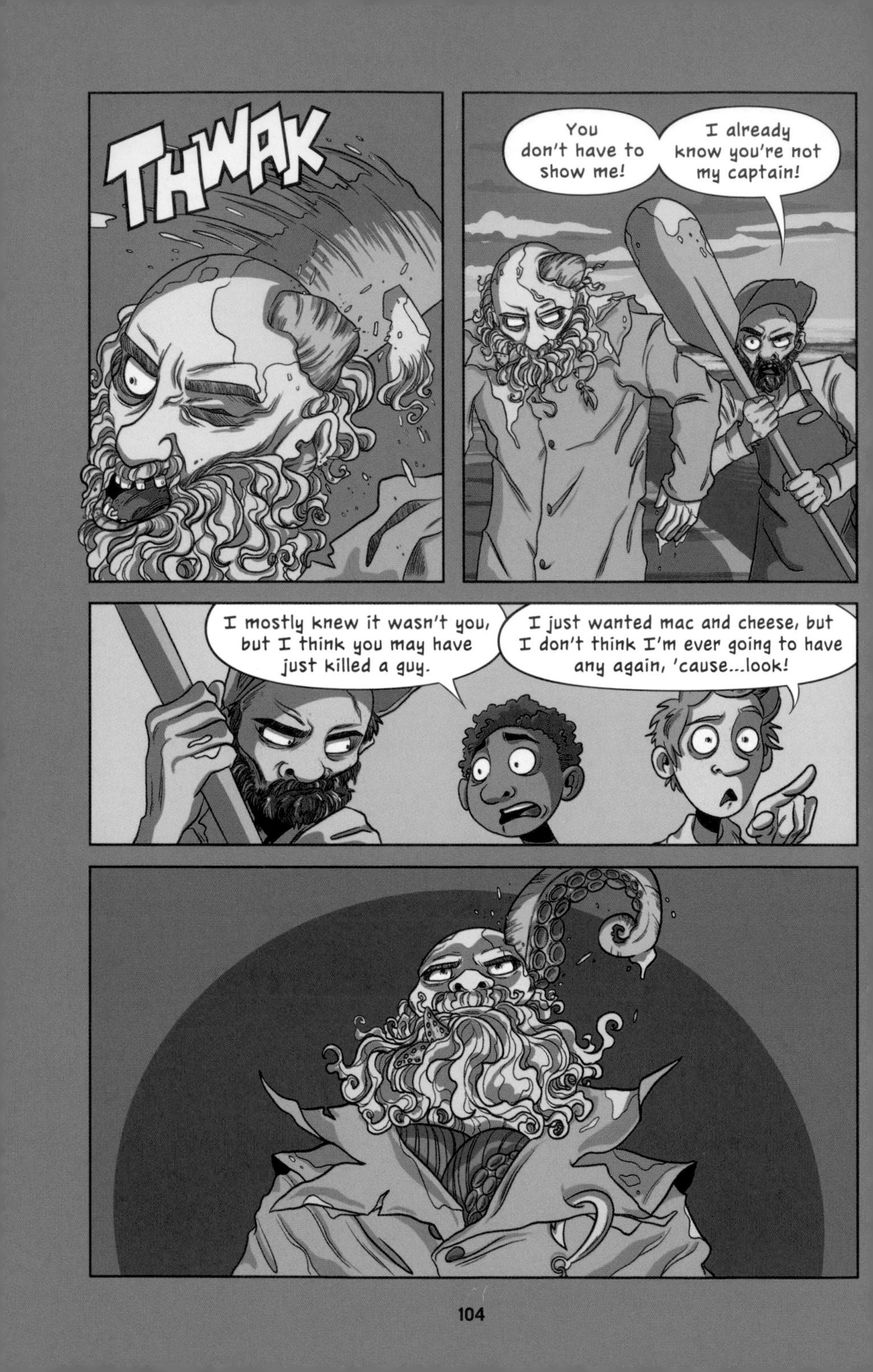
THWAK
You don't have to show me!
I already know you're not my captain!
I mostly knew it wasn't you, but I think you may have just killed a guy.
I just wanted mac and cheese, but I don't think I'm ever going to have any again, 'cause...look!

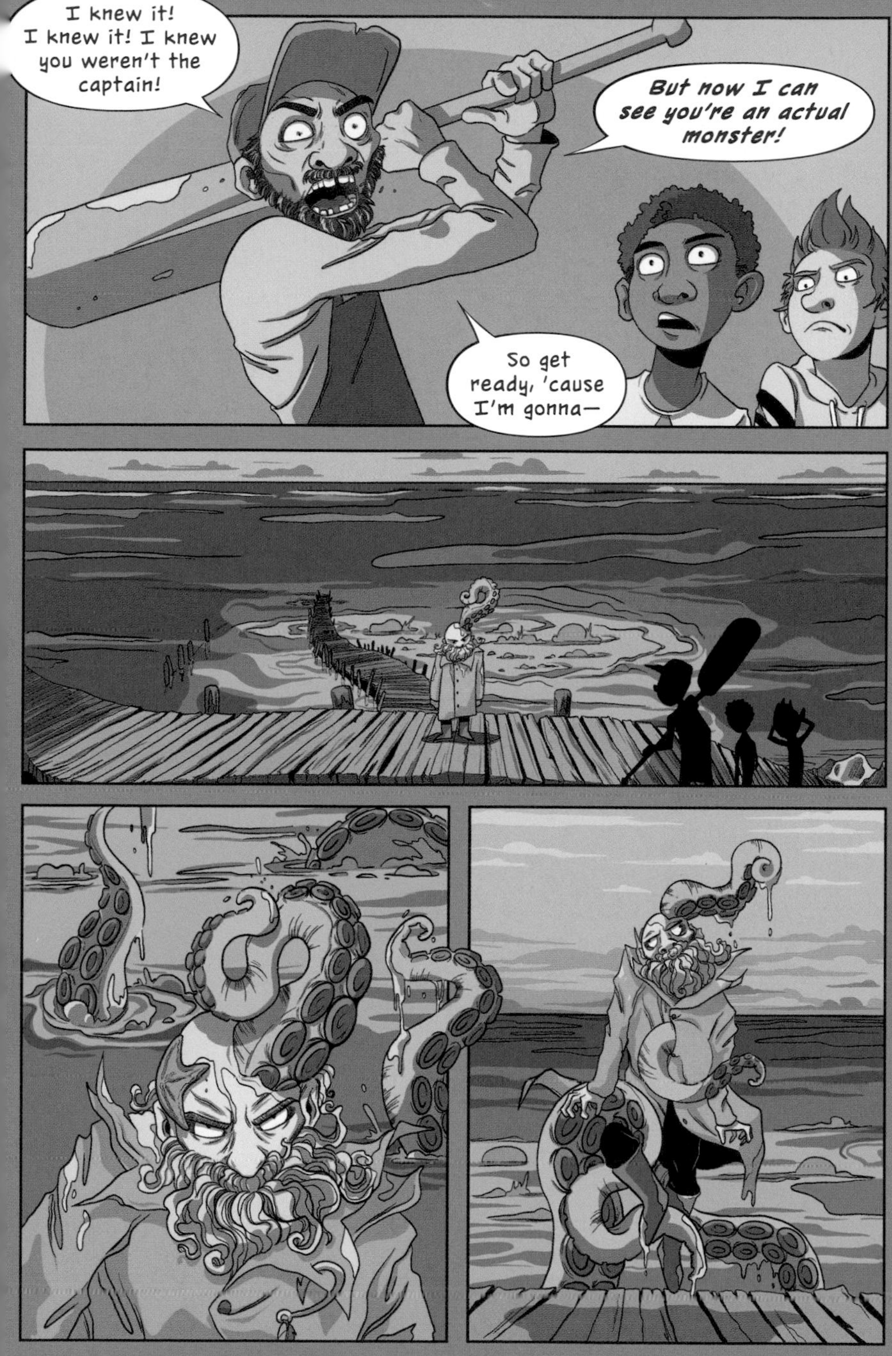

I knew it! I knew it! I knew you weren't the captain!
But now I can see you're an actual monster!
So get ready, 'cause I'm gonna—

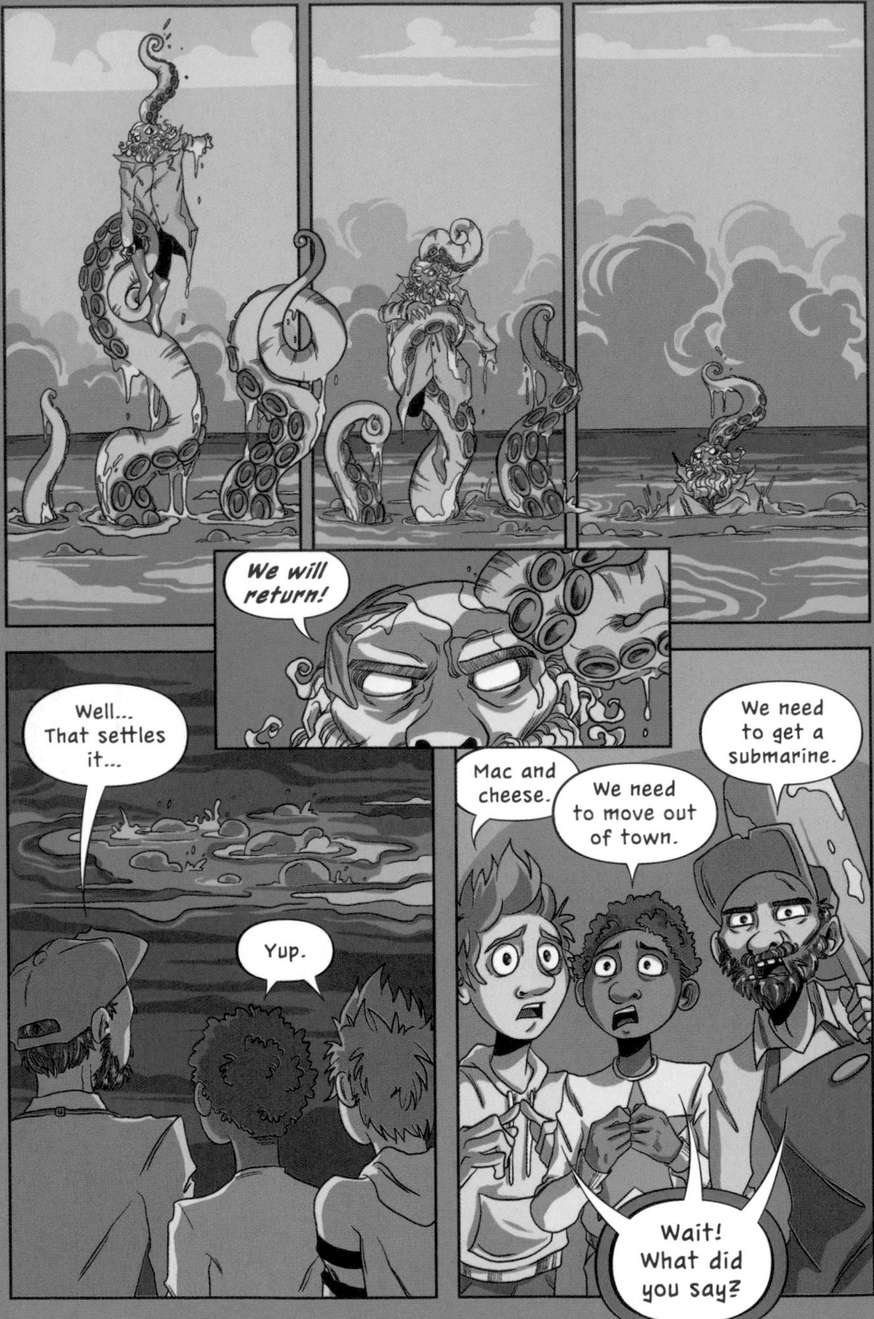
We will return!
Well... That settles it...
Yup.
Mac and cheese.
We need to move out of town.
We need to get a submarine.
Wait! What did you say?

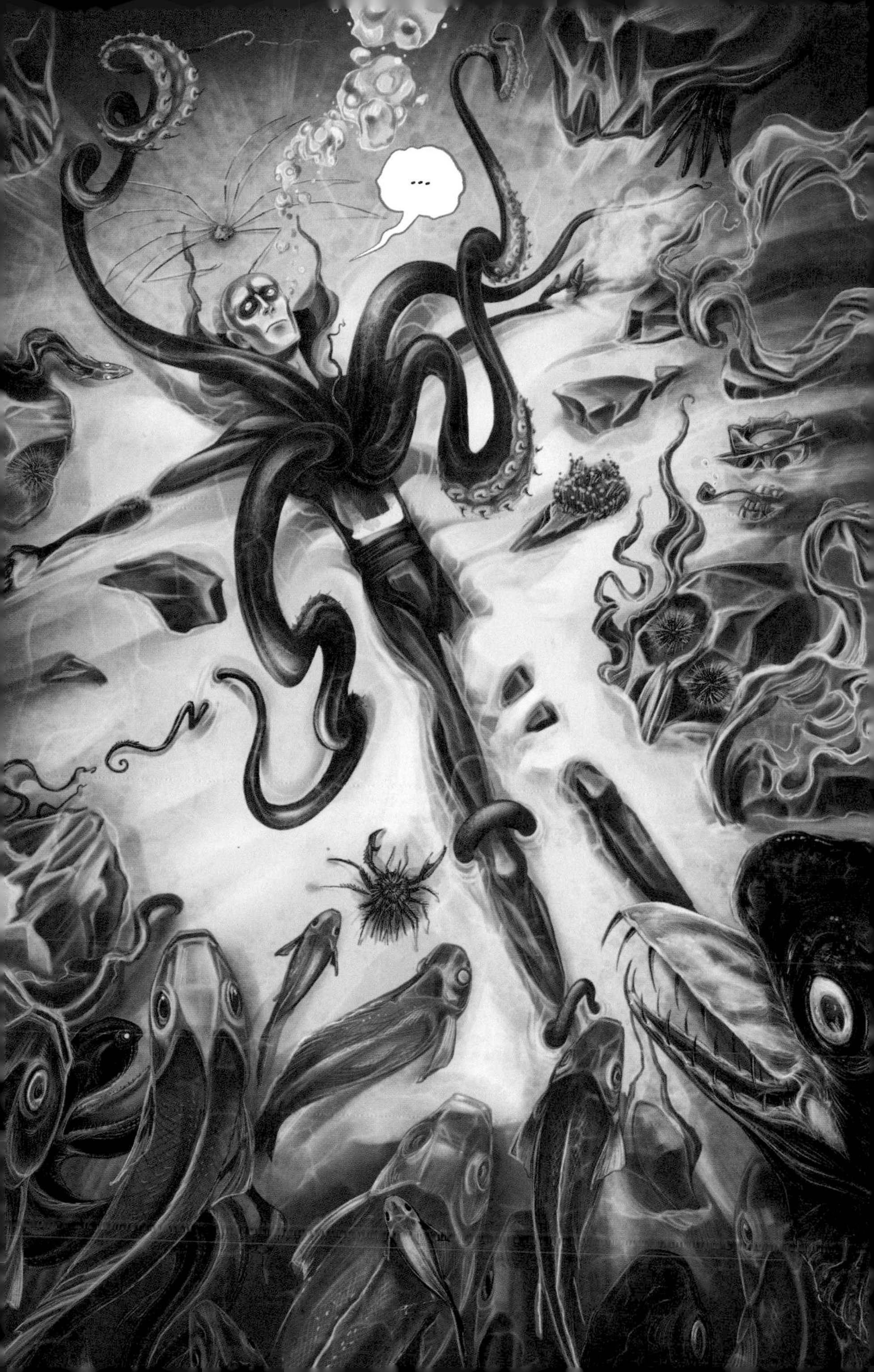
...

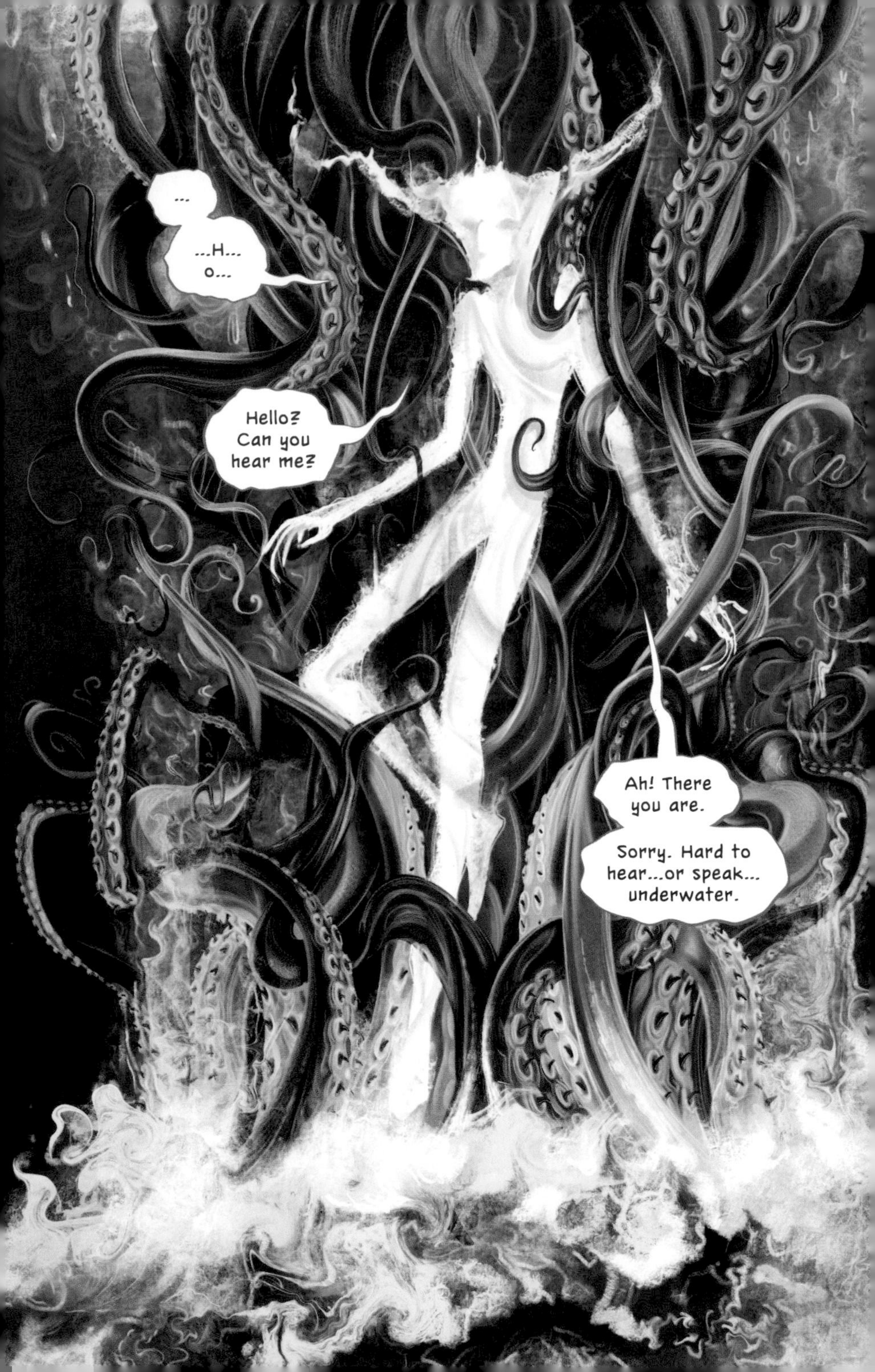
...
...H...
o...
Hello? Can you hear me?
Ah! There you are.
Sorry. Hard to hear...or speak... underwater.

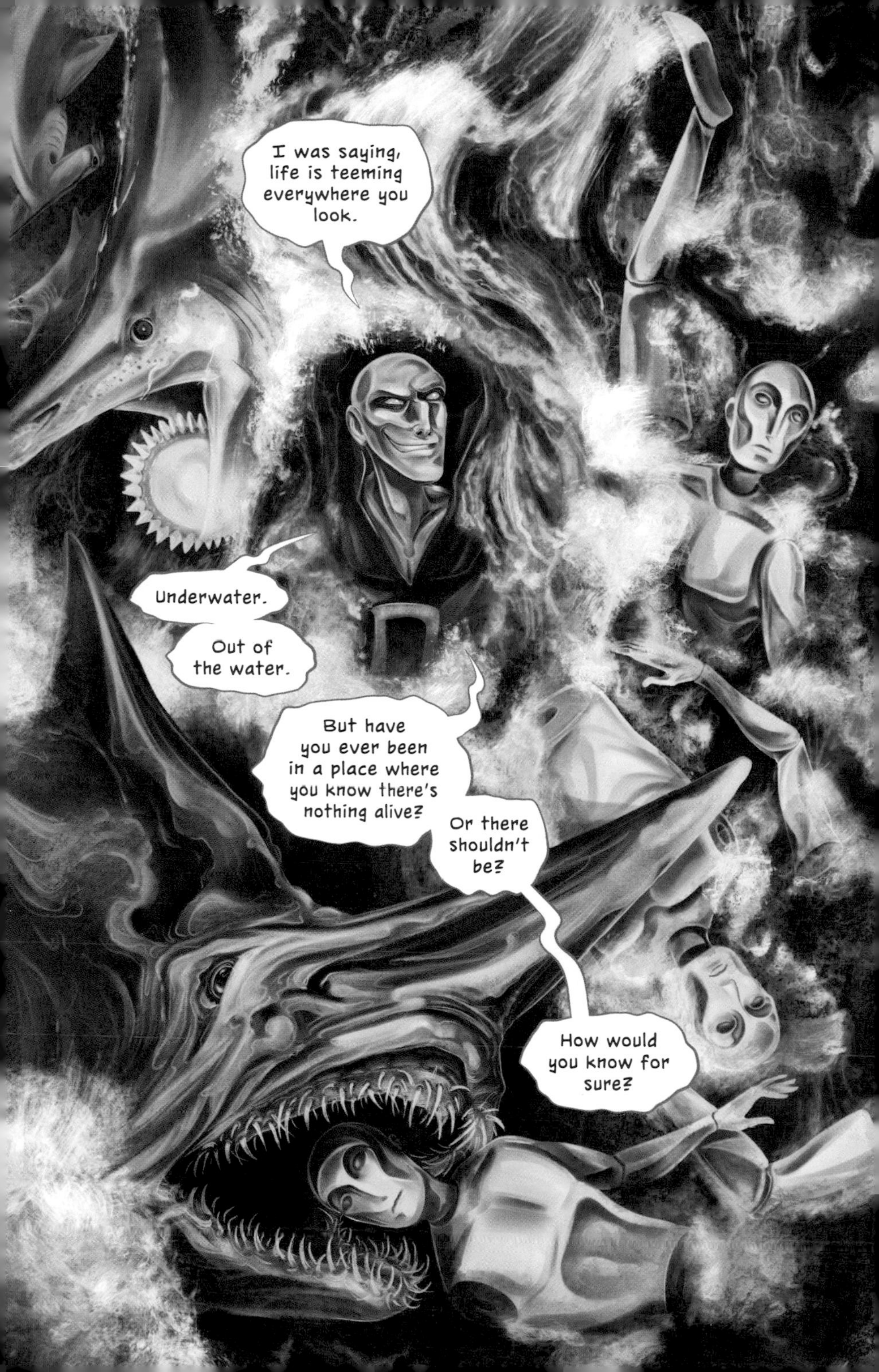
I was saying, life is teeming everywhere you look.
Underwater.
Out of the water.
But have you ever been in a place where you know there's nothing alive?
Or there shouldn't be?
How would you know for sure?

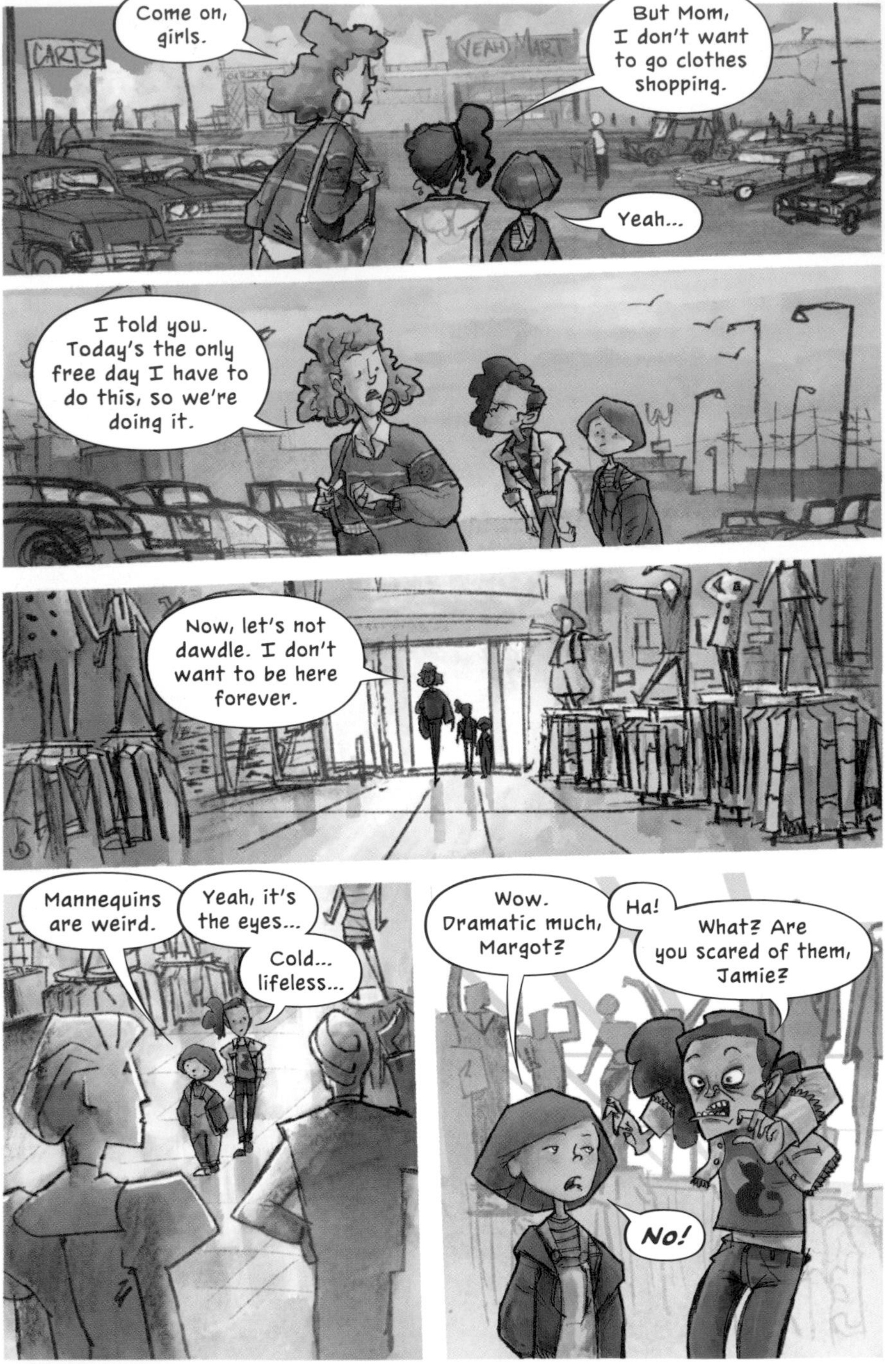
CARTS
YEAH MART
Come on, girls.
But Mom, I don't want to go clothes shopping.
Yeah...
I told you. Today's the only free day I have to do this, so we're doing it.
Now, let's not dawdle. I don't want to be here forever.
Mannequins are weird.
Yeah, it's the eyes...
Cold... lifeless...
Wow. Dramatic much, Margot?
Ha!
What? Are you scared of them, Jamie?
No!

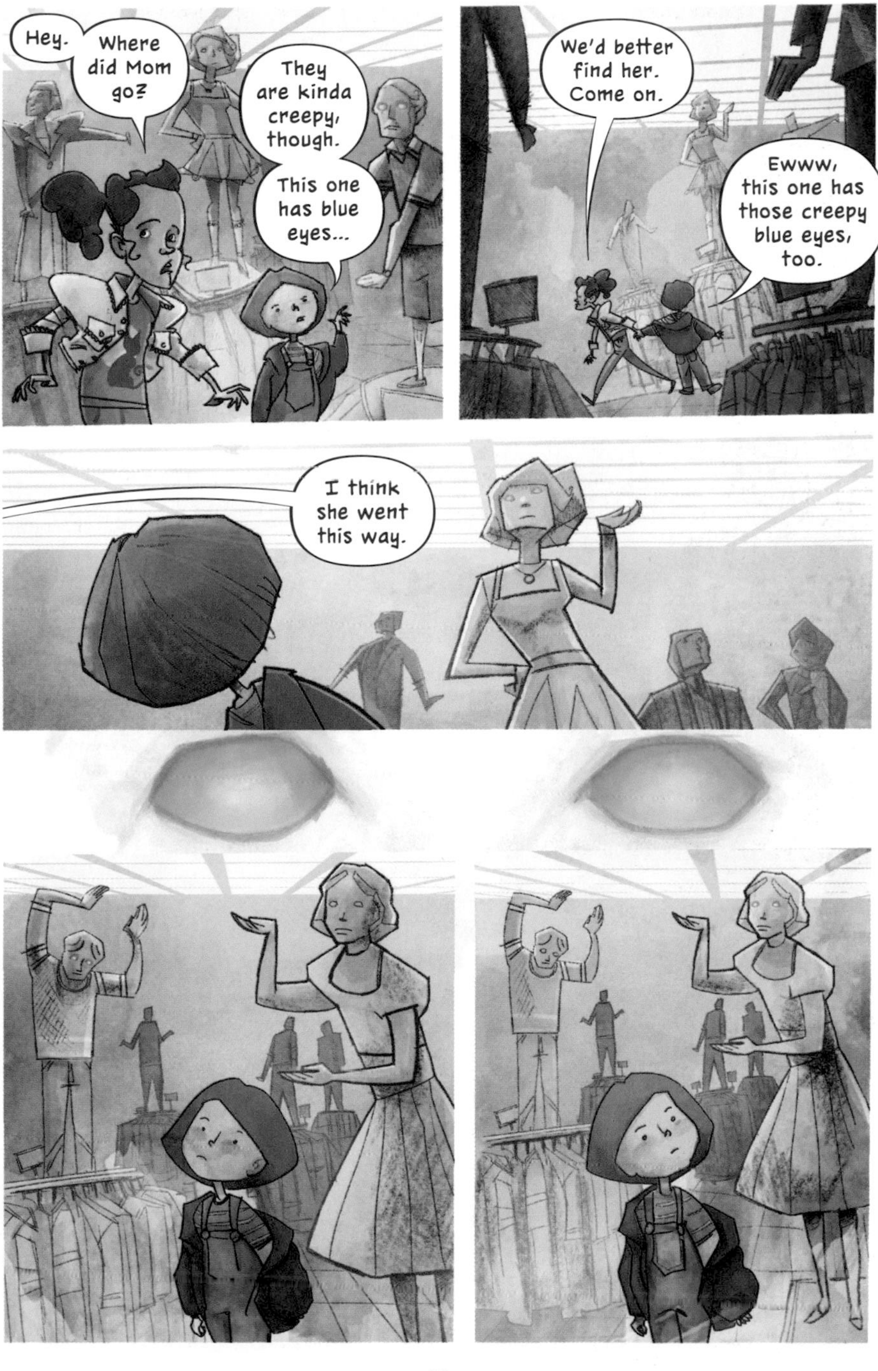
Hey.
Where did Mom go?
They are kinda creepy, though.
This one has blue eyes...
We'd better find her. Come on.
Ewww, this one has those creepy blue eyes, too.
I think she went this way.

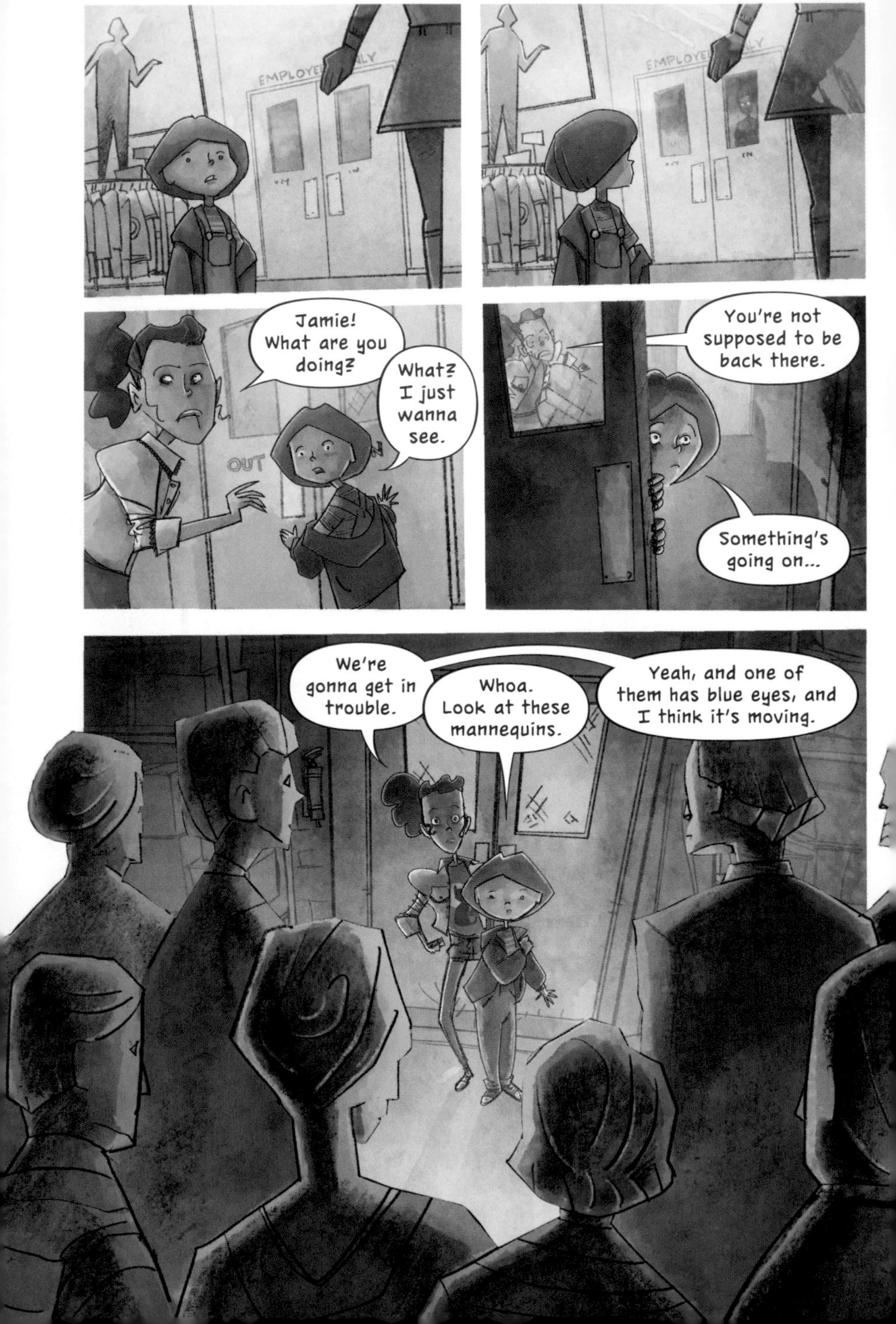

EMPLOYEES ONLY
Jamie! What are you doing?
What? I just wanna see.
OUT
You're not supposed to be back there.
Something's going on...
We're gonna get in trouble.
Whoa. Look at these mannequins.
Yeah, and one of them has blue eyes, and I think it's moving.

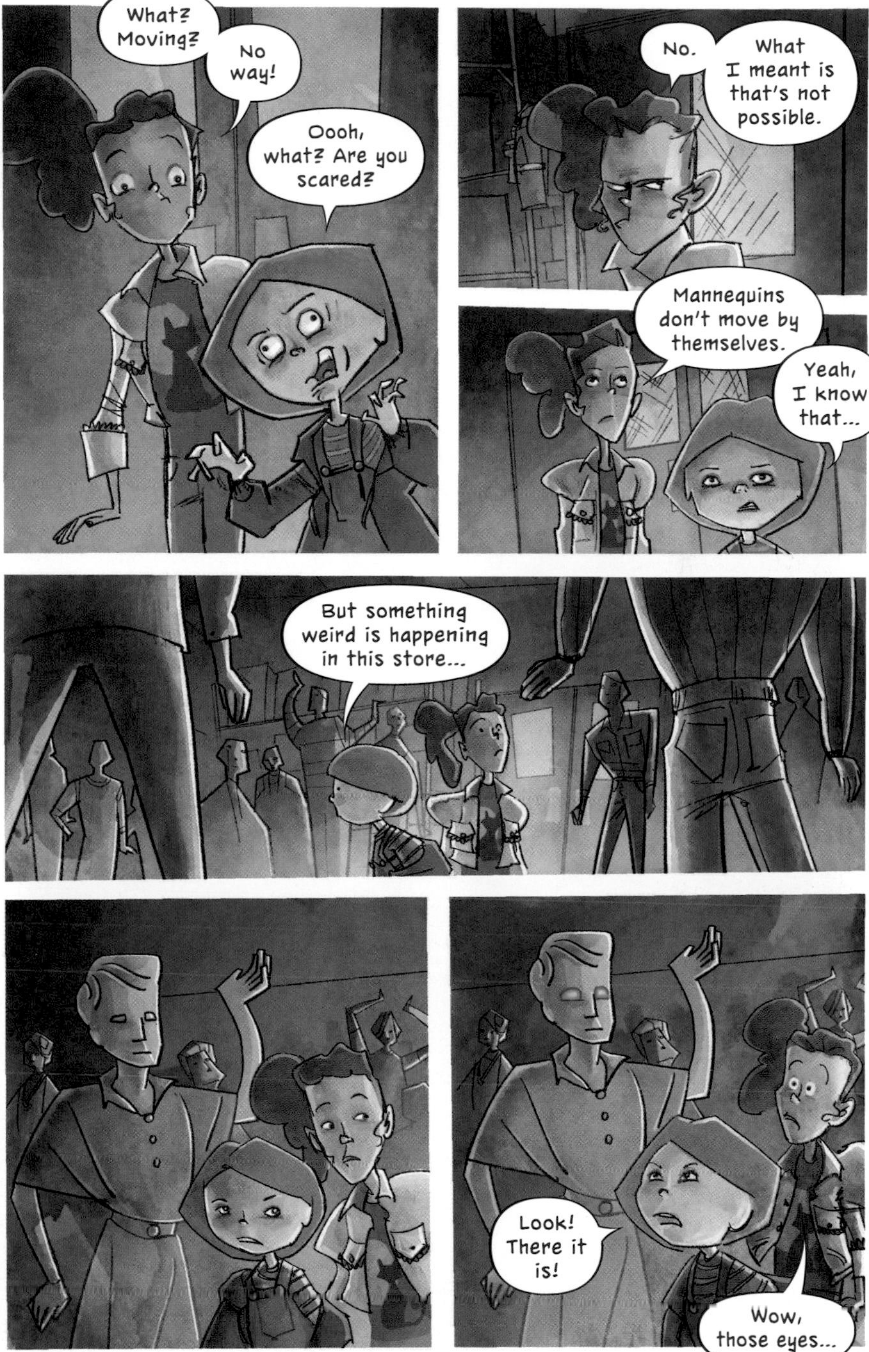
What? Moving?
No way!
Oooh, what? Are you scared?
No.
What I meant is that's not possible.
Mannequins don't move by themselves.
Yeah, I know that...
But something weird is happening in this store...
Look! There it is!
Wow, those eyes...

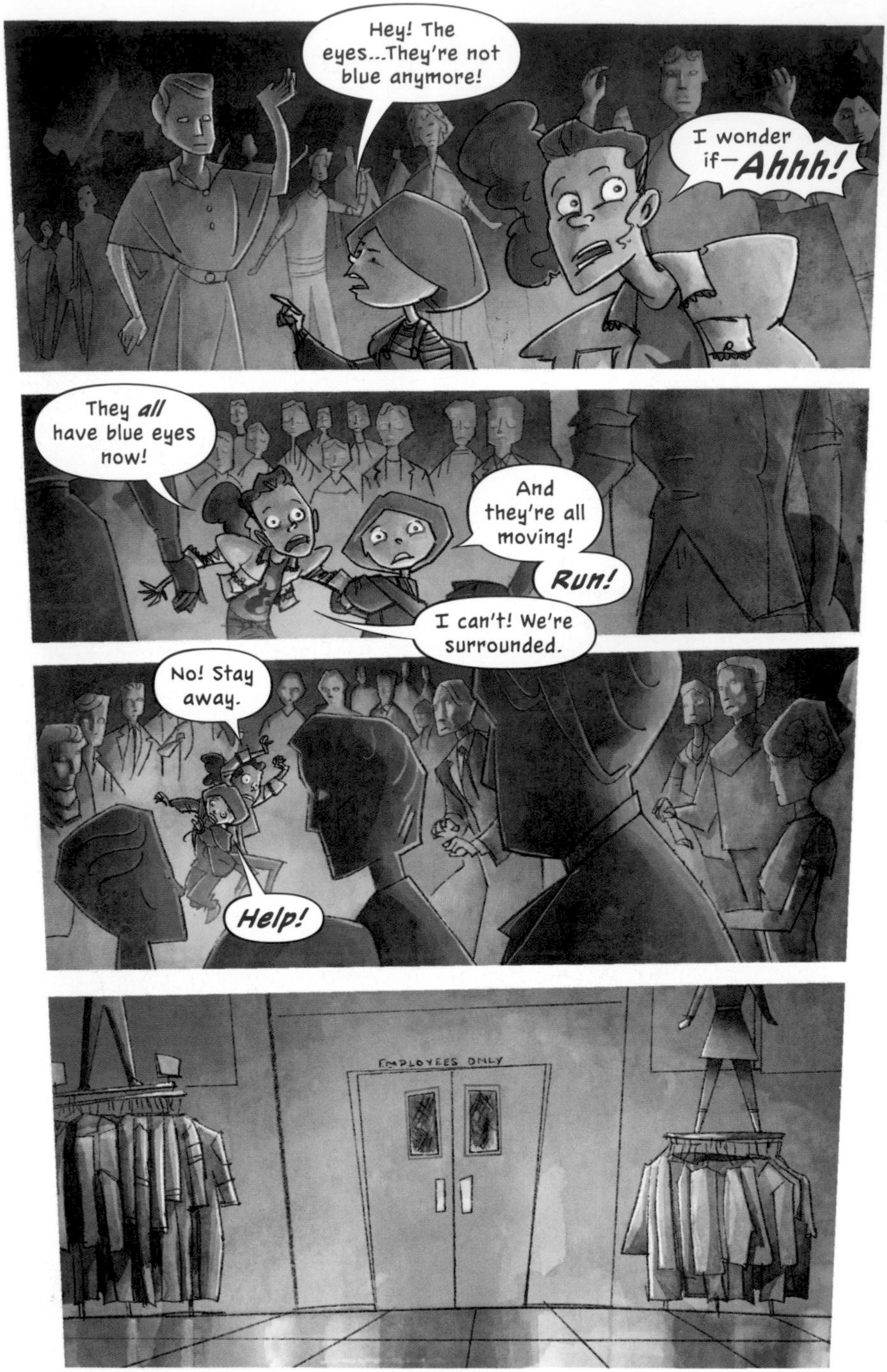
Hey! The eyes...They're not blue anymore!
I wonder if—Ahhh!
They *all* have blue eyes now!
And they're all moving!
Run!
I can't! We're surrounded.
No! Stay away.
Help!
EMPLOYEES ONLY

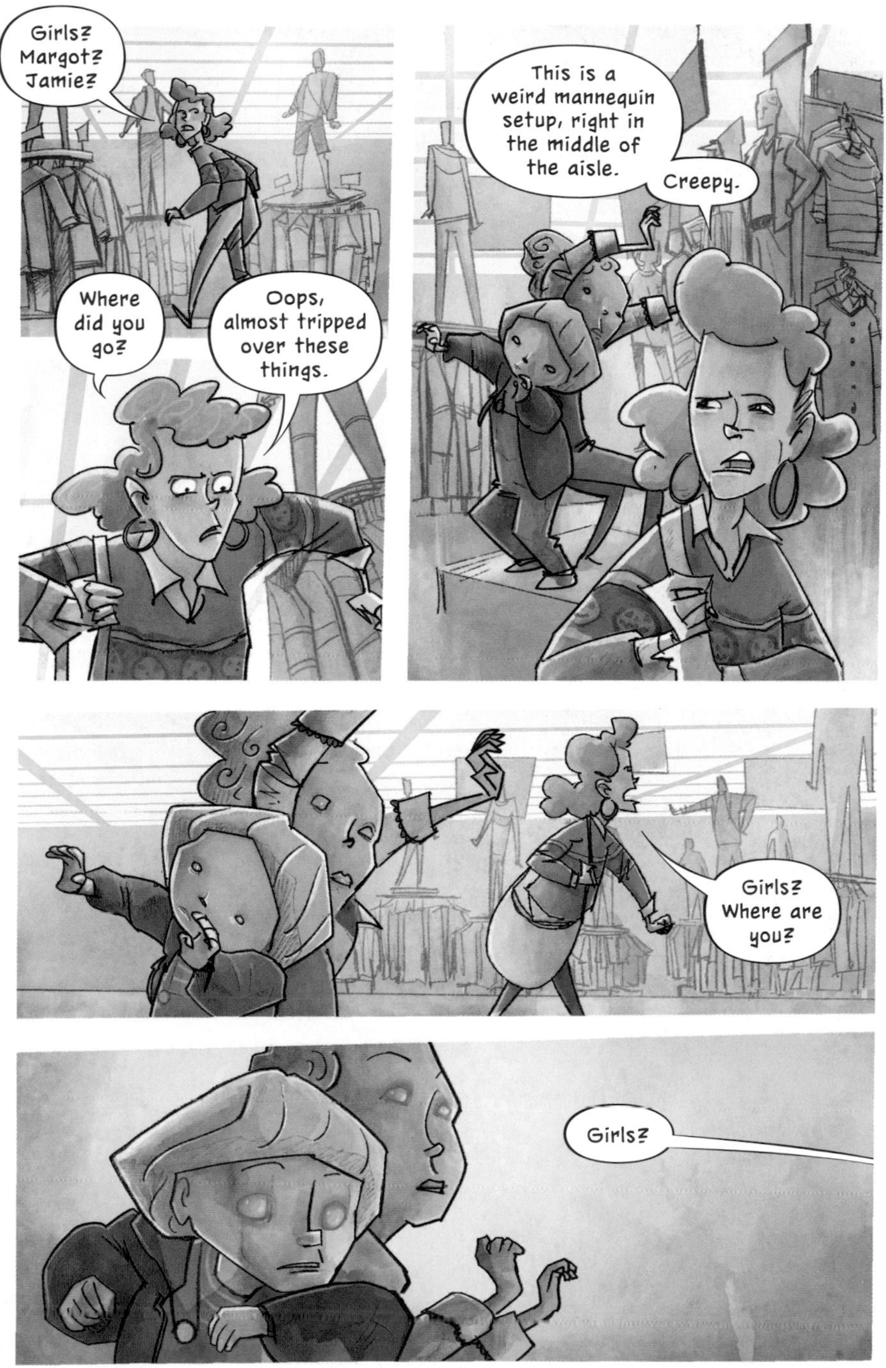
Girls?
Margot?
Jamie?
Where did you go?
Oops, almost tripped over these things.
This is a weird mannequin setup, right in the middle of the aisle.
Creepy.
Girls? Where are you?
Girls?

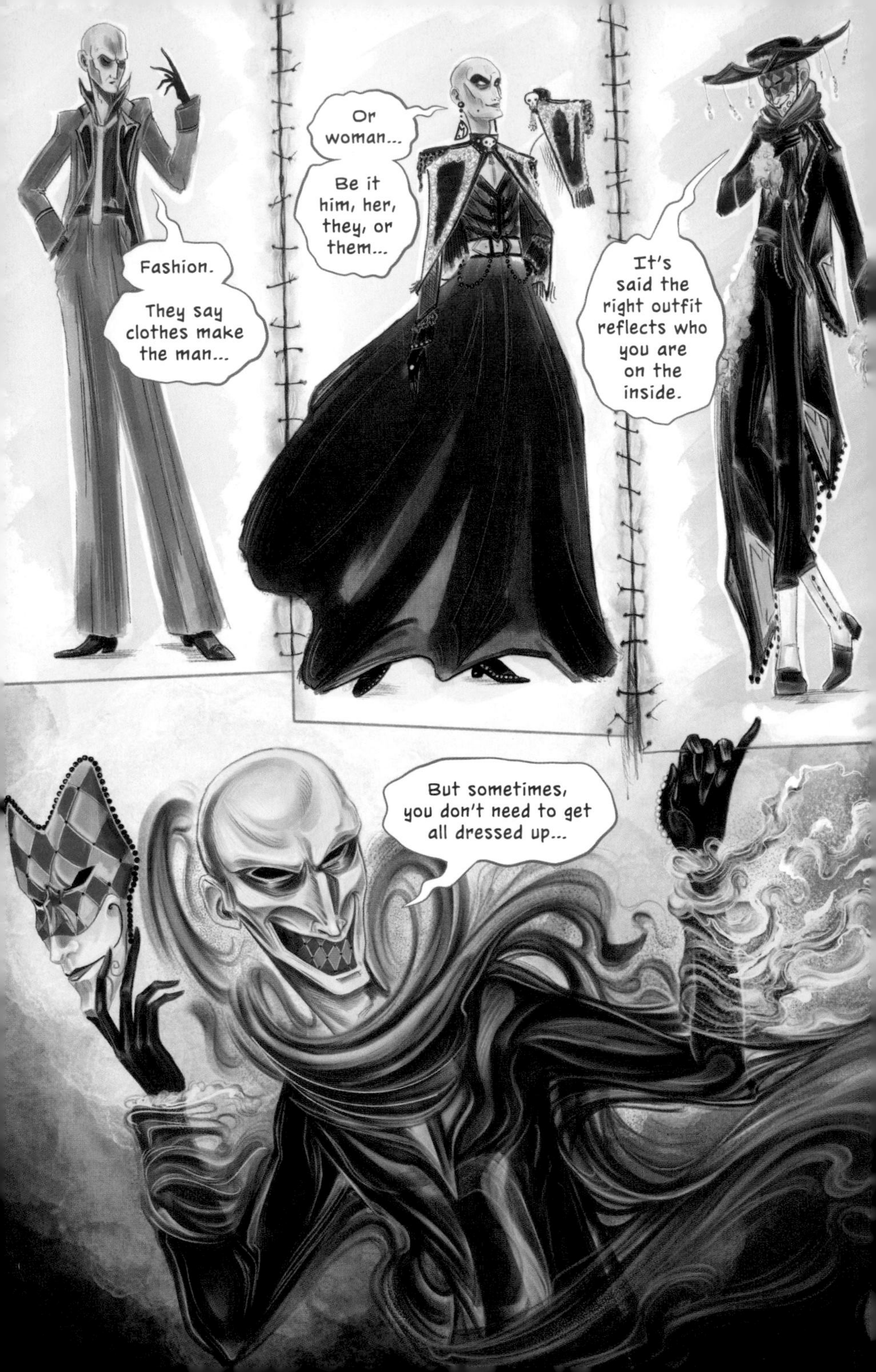
Fashion.
They say clothes make the man...
Or woman...
Be it him, her, they, or them...
It's said the right outfit reflects who you are on the inside.
But sometimes, you don't need to get all dressed up...

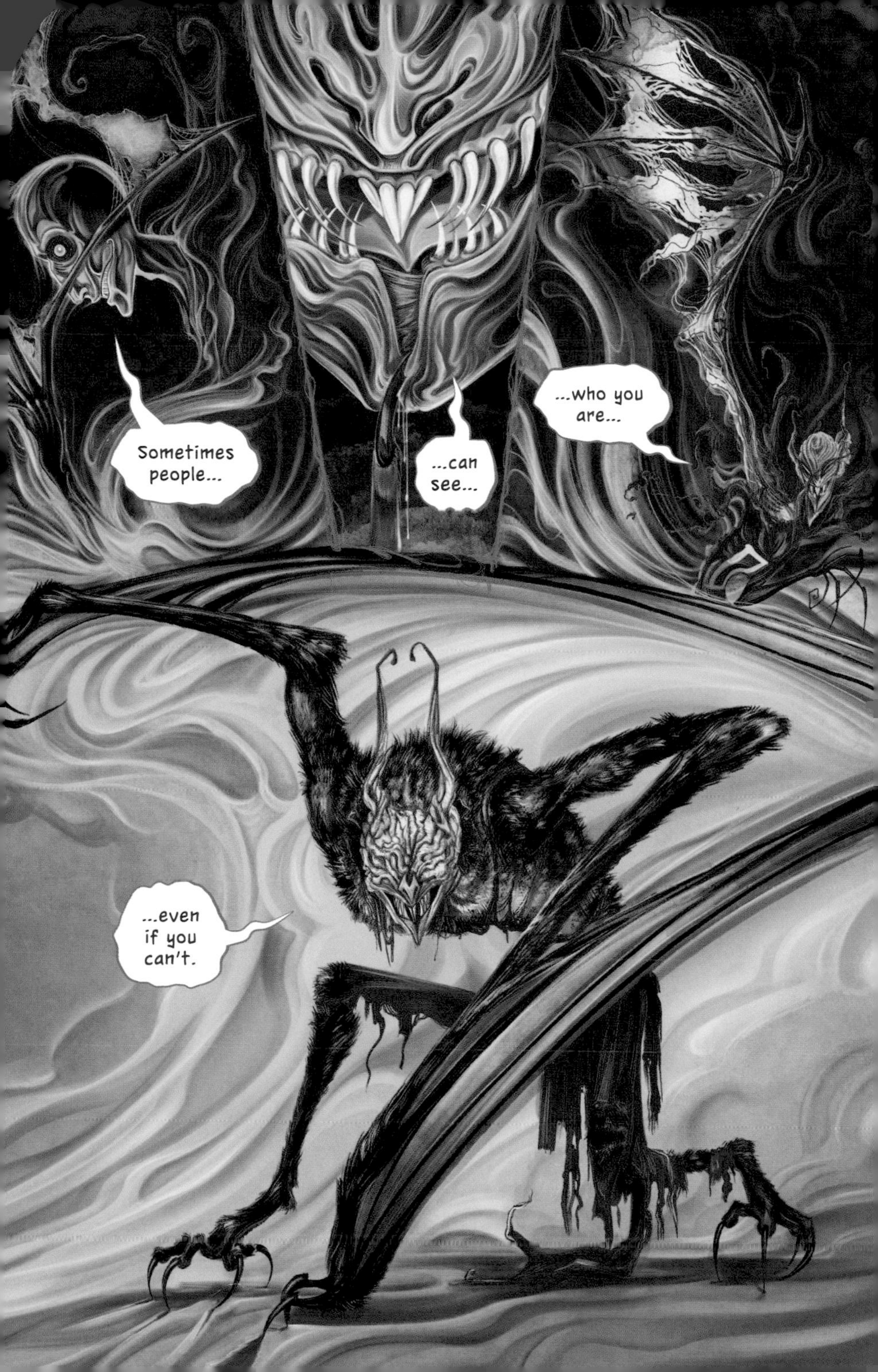
Sometimes people...
...can see...
...who you are...
...even if you can't.

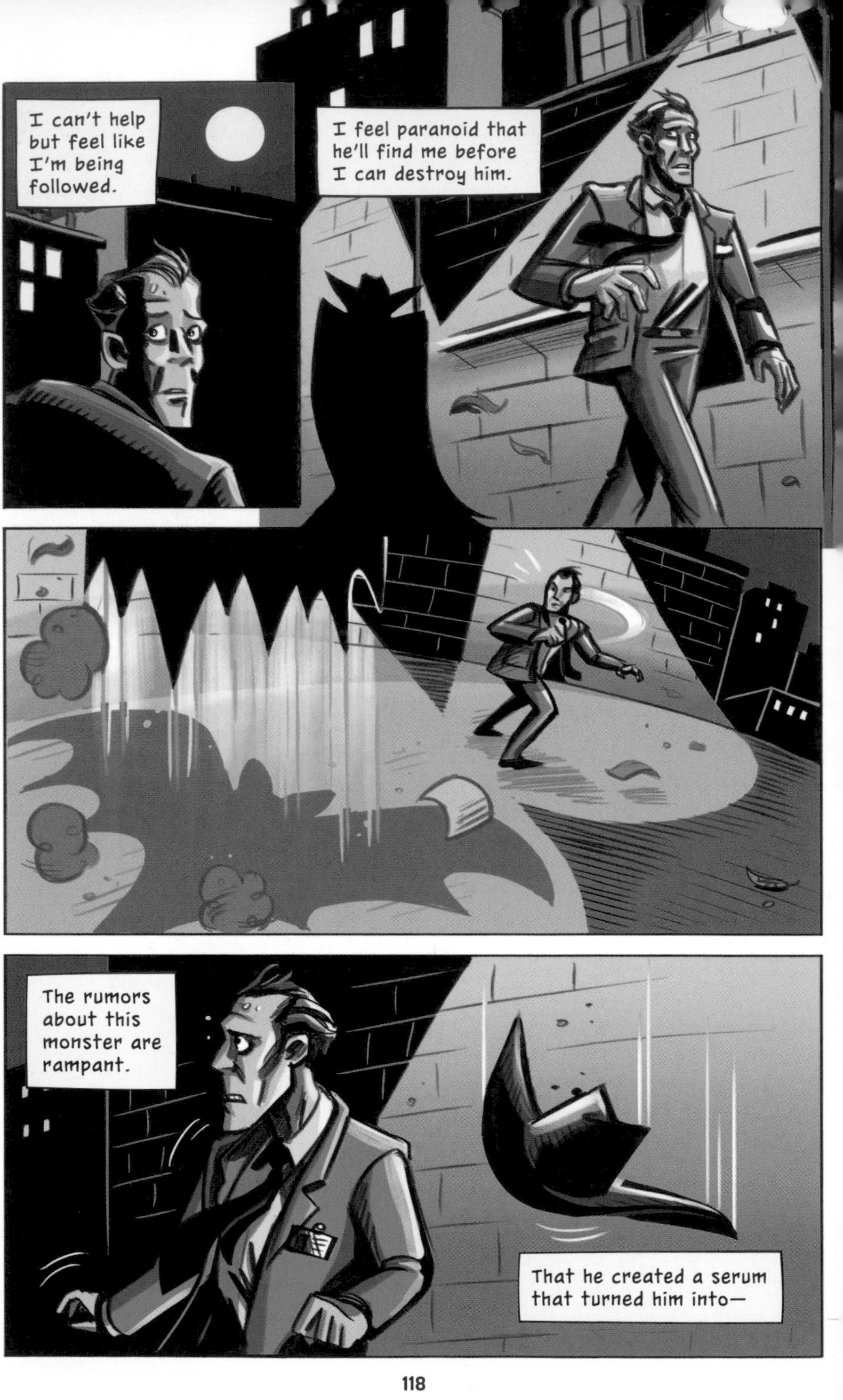
I can't help but feel like I'm being followed.
I feel paranoid that he'll find me before I can destroy him.
The rumors about this monster are rampant.
That he created a serum that turned him into—

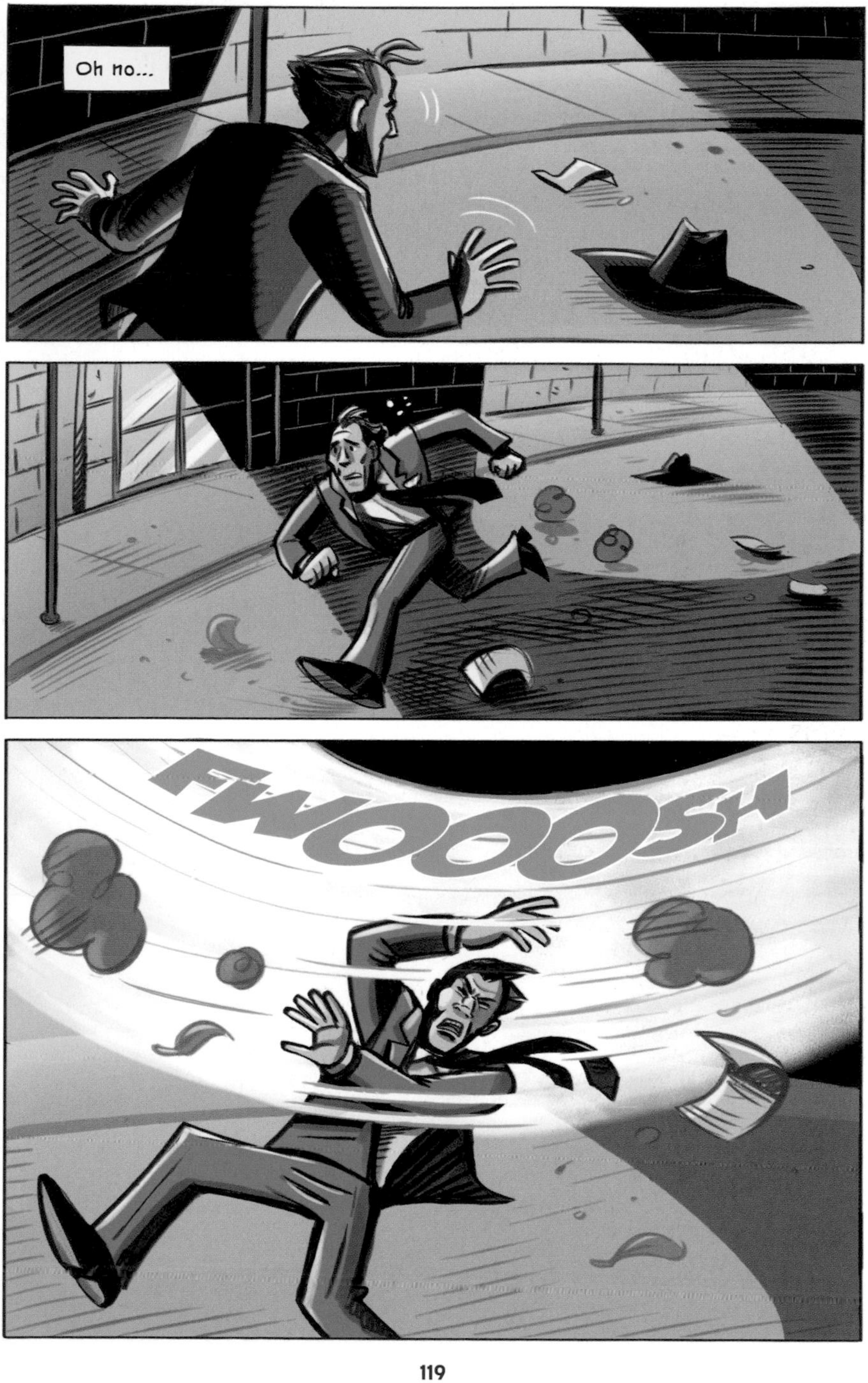
Oh no...
FWOOOSH

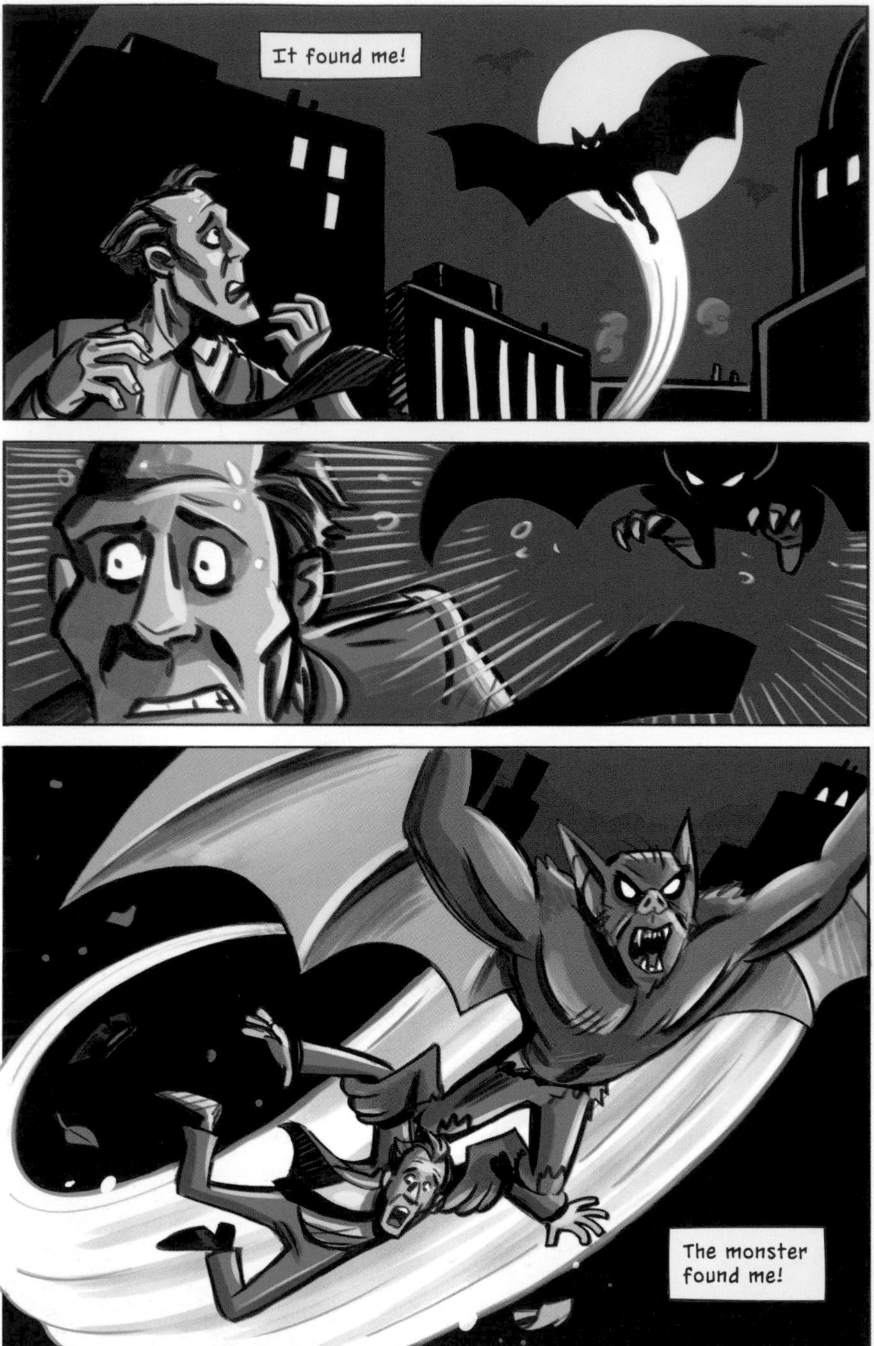
It found me!
The monster found me!

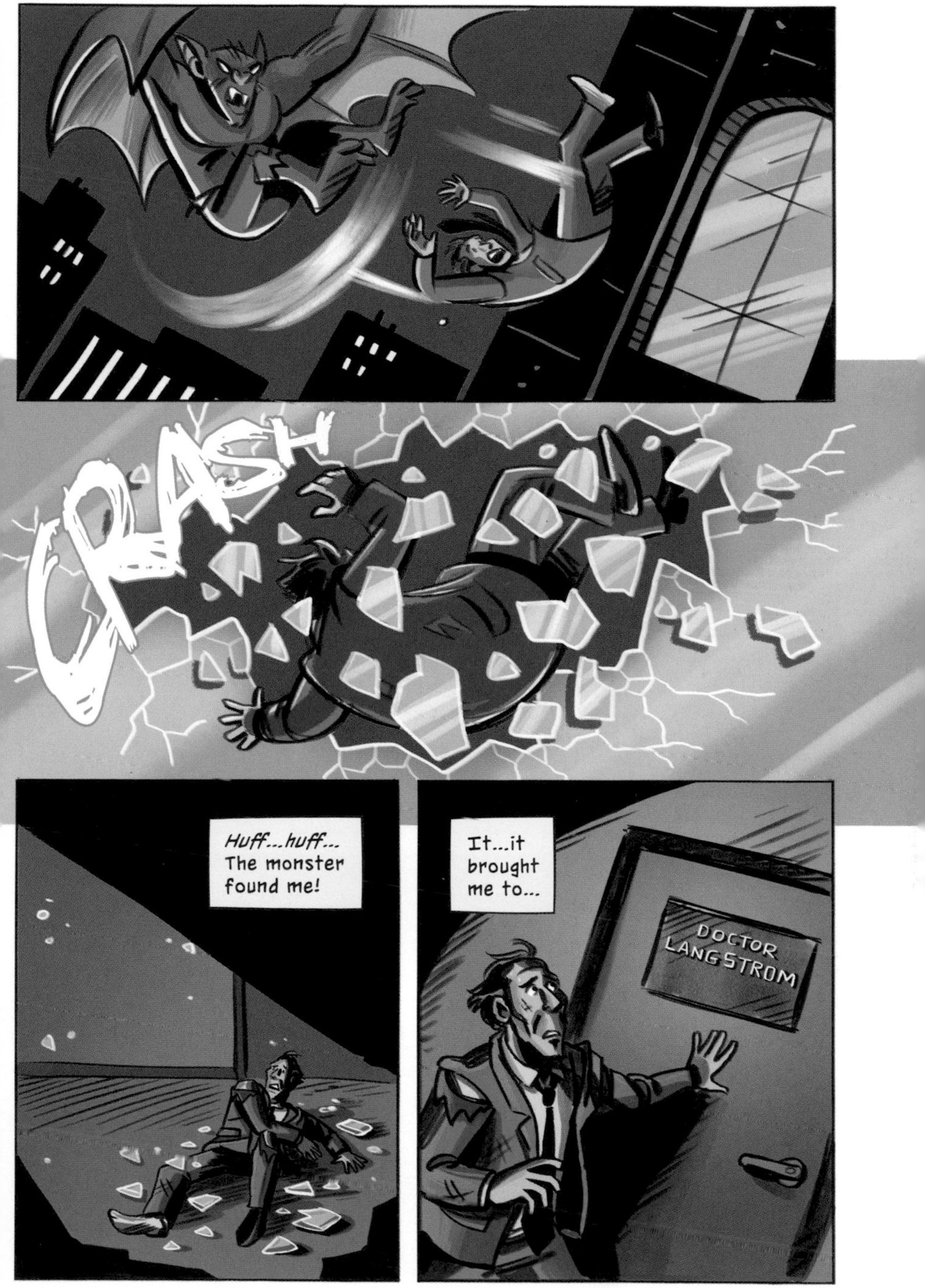
CRASH
Huff...huff... The monster found me!
It...it brought me to...
DOCTOR LANGSTROM

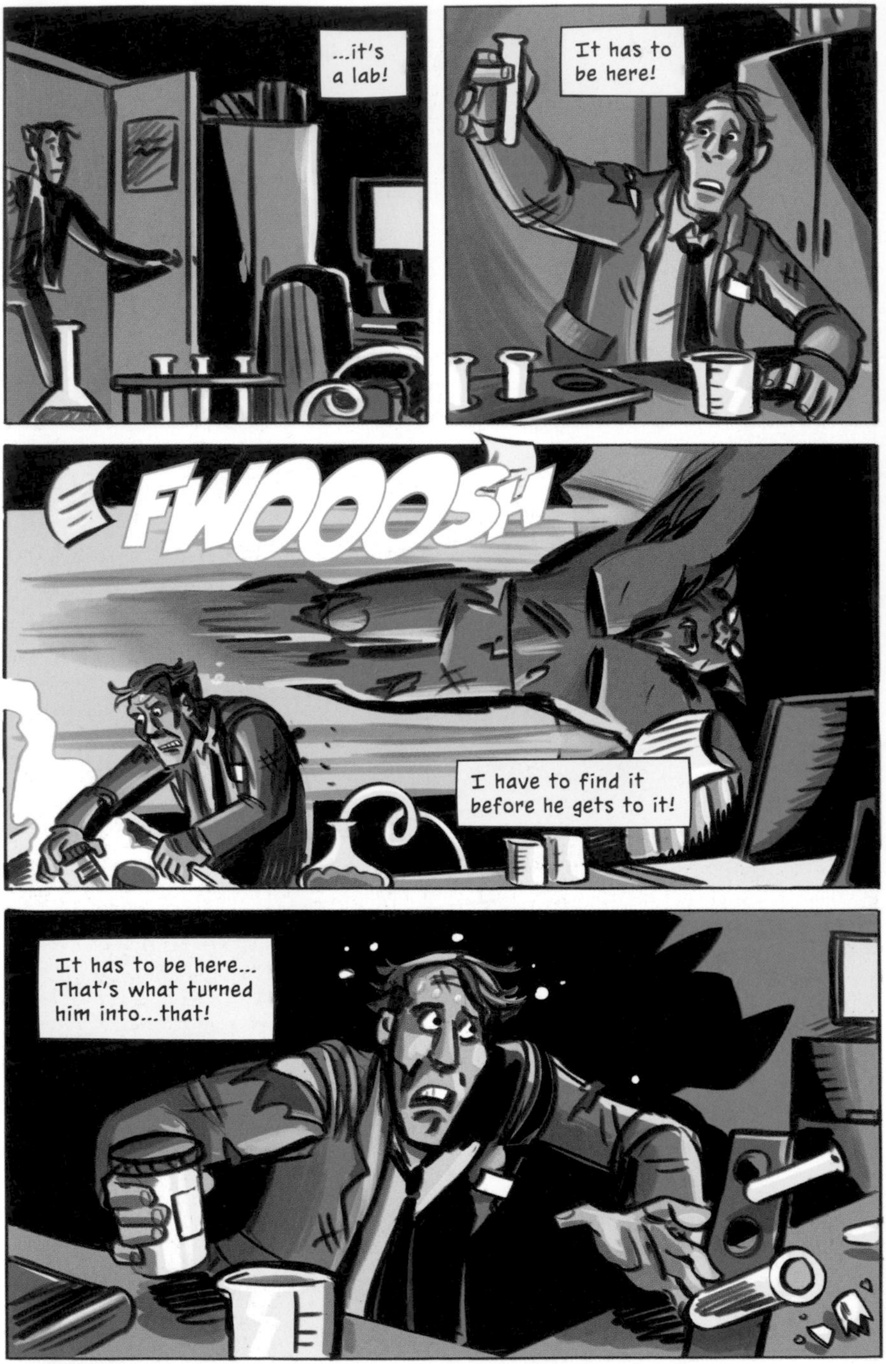
...it's a lab!
It has to be here!
FWOOOSH
I have to find it before he gets to it!
It has to be here... That's what turned him into...that!

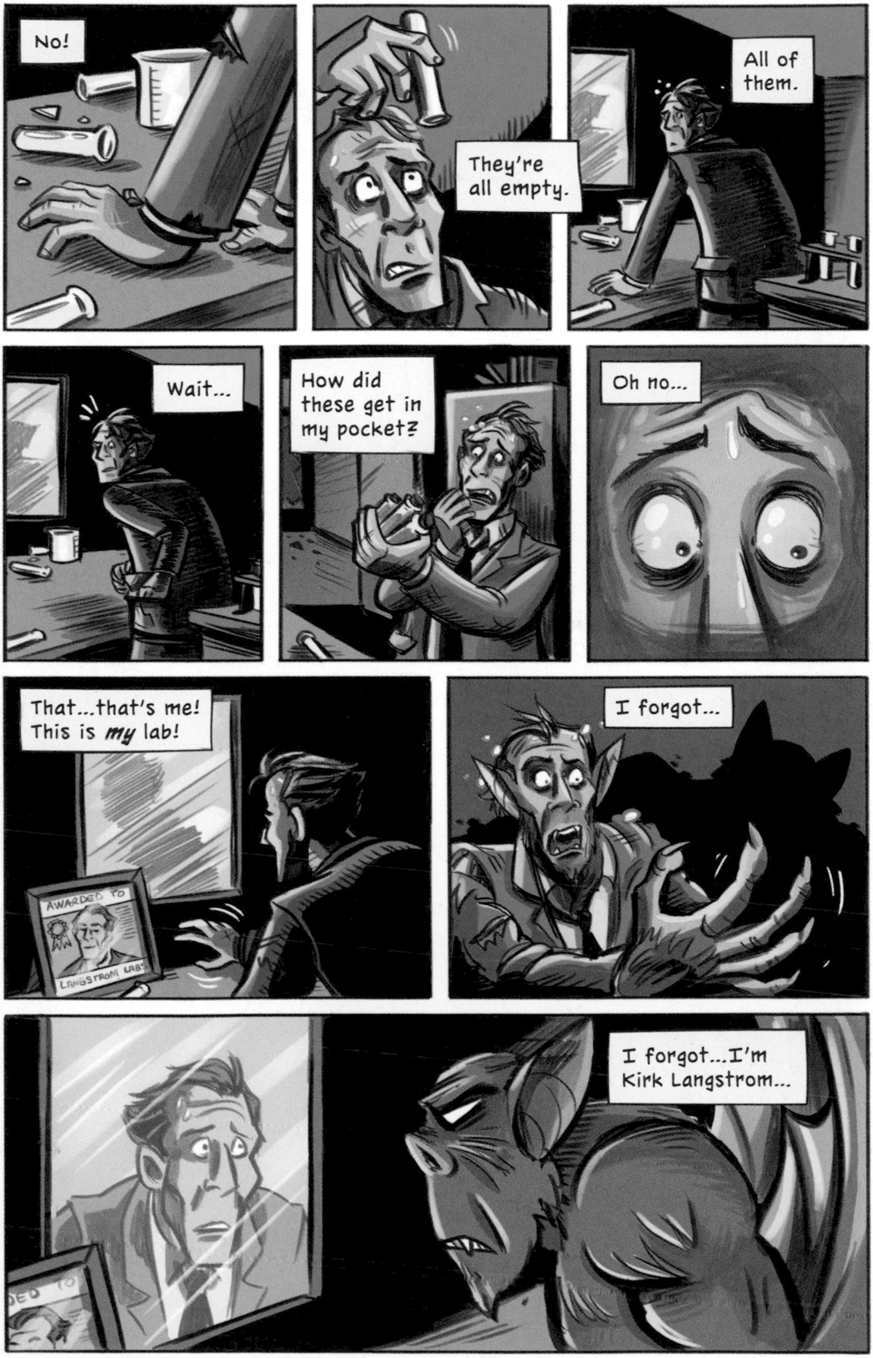
No!
They're all empty.
All of them.
Wait...
How did these get in my pocket?
Oh no...
That...that's me! This is *my* lab!
AWARDED TO
LANGSTROM LABS
I forgot...
I forgot...I'm Kirk Langstrom...

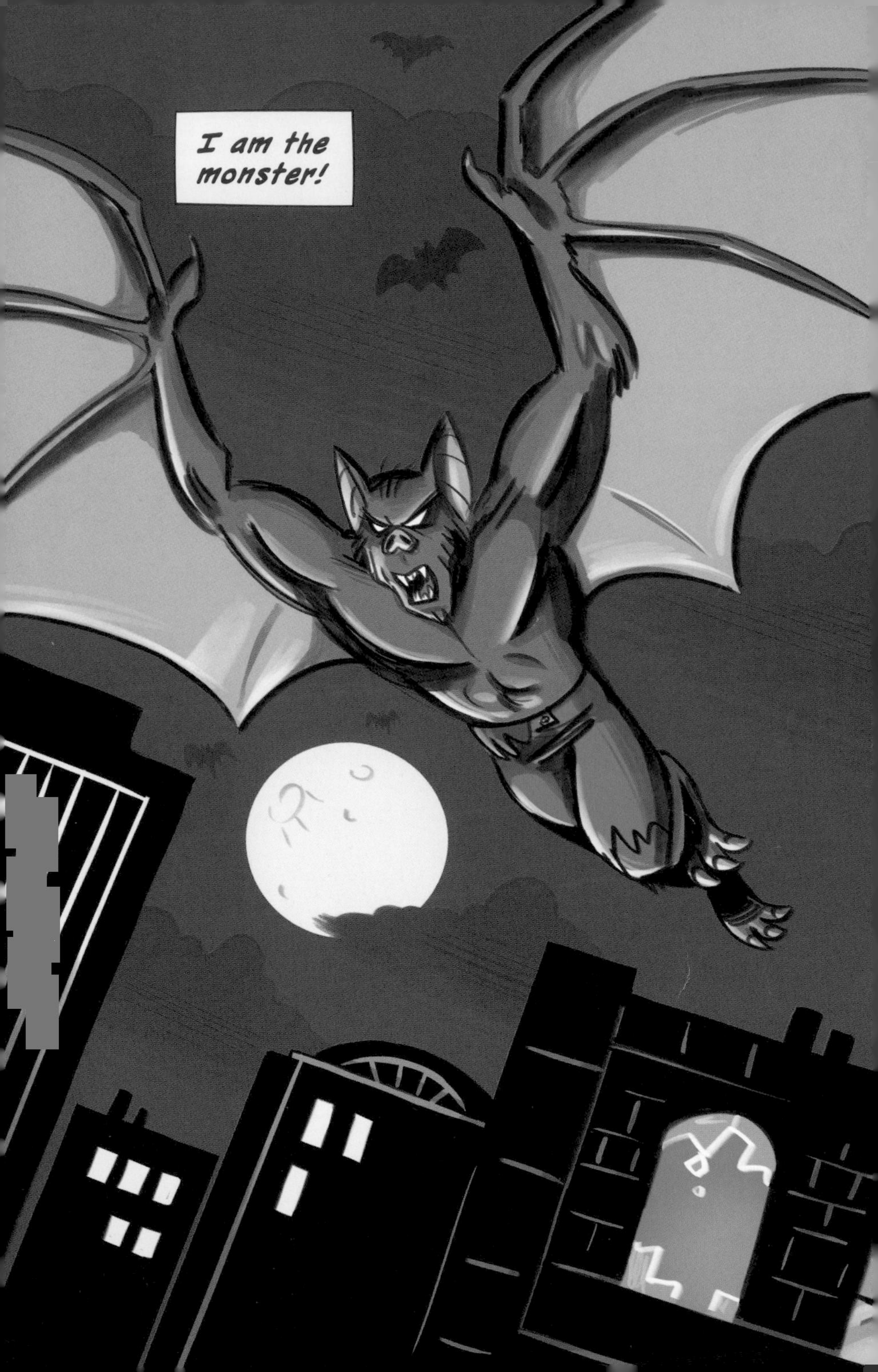
I am the monster!

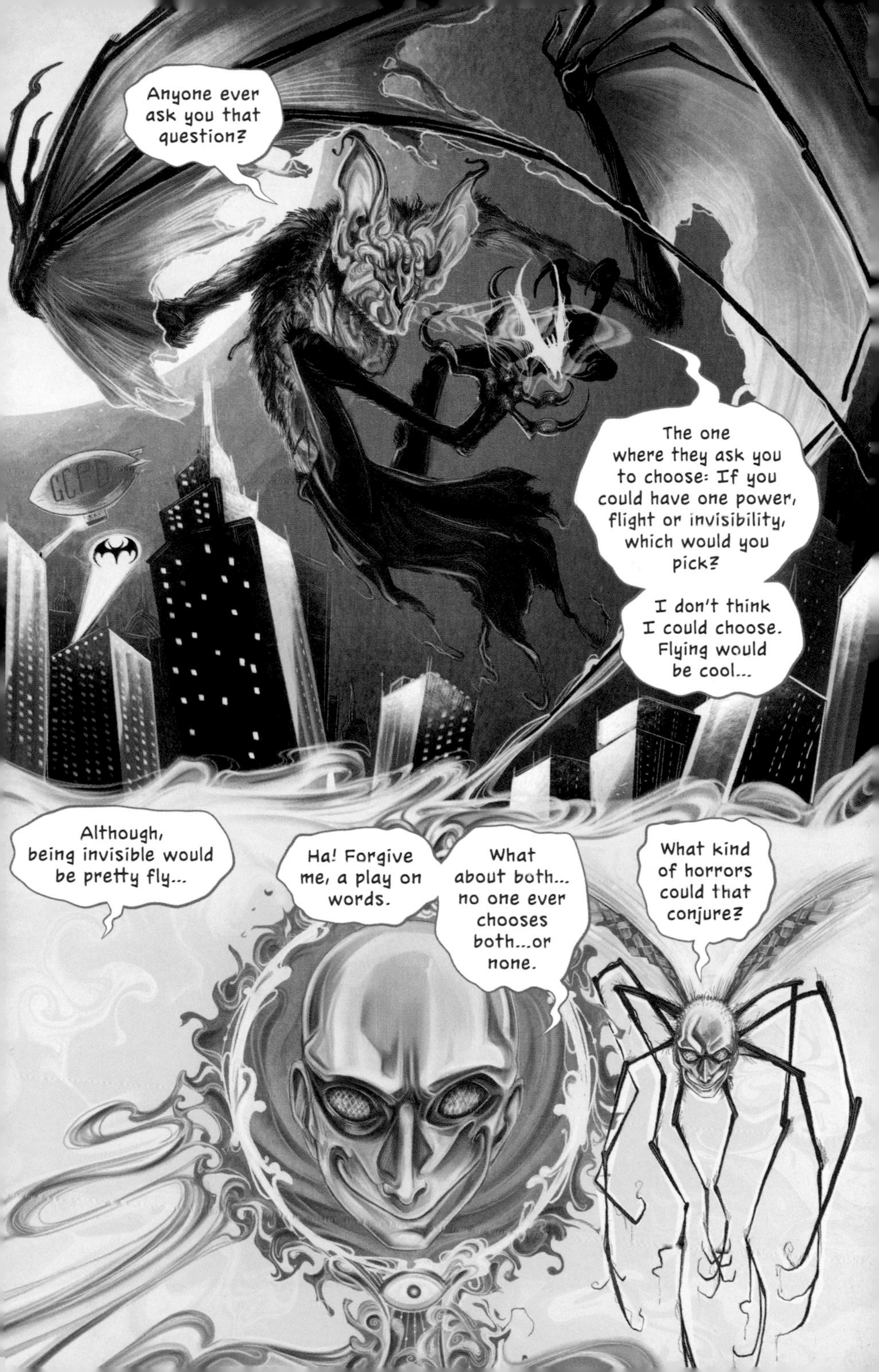
Anyone ever ask you that question?
The one where they ask you to choose: If you could have one power, flight or invisibility, which would you pick?
I don't think I could choose. Flying would be cool...
Although, being invisible would be pretty fly...
Ha! Forgive me, a play on words.
What about both... no one ever chooses both...or none.
What kind of horrors could that conjure?

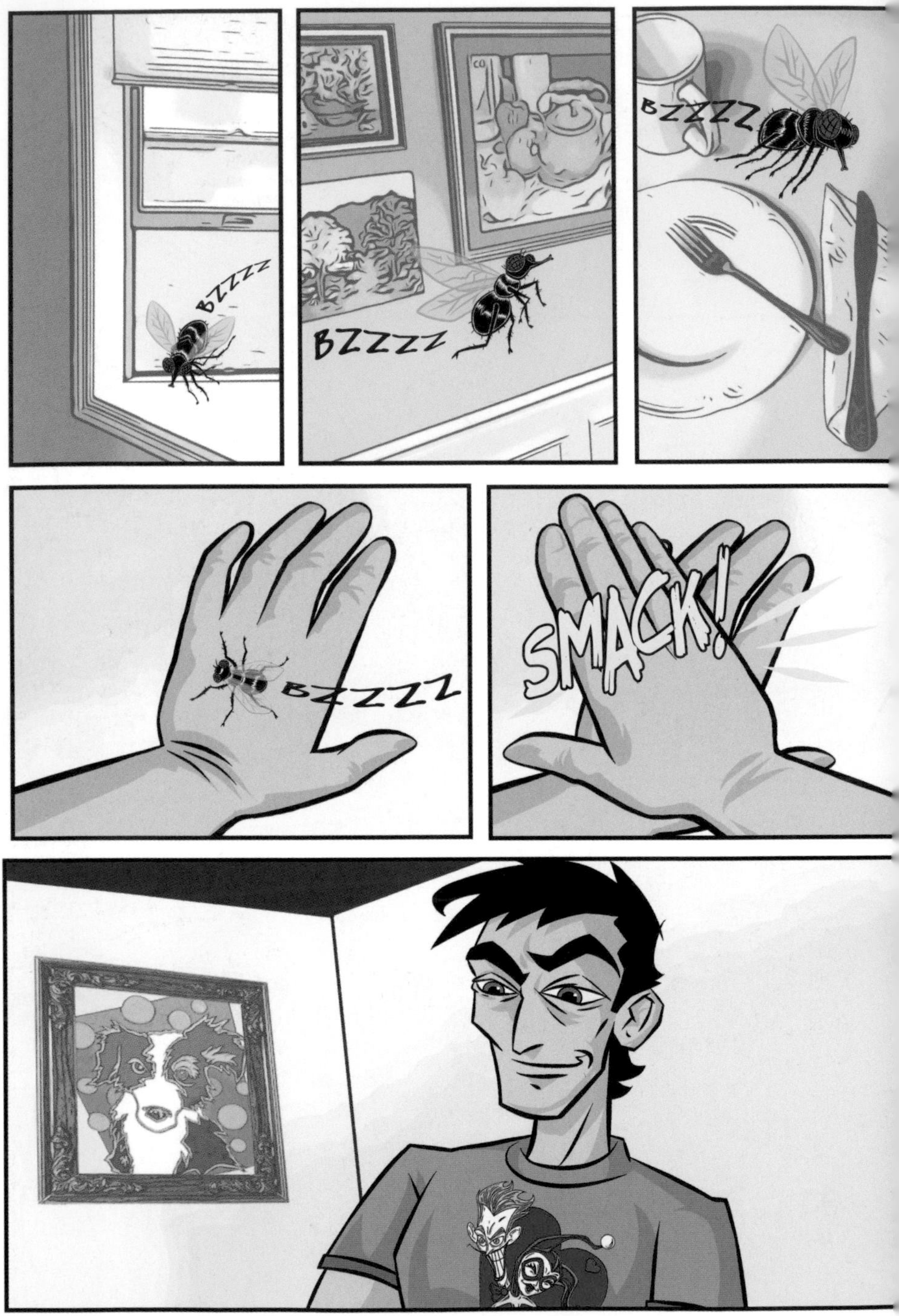
BZZZZ
BZZZZ
BZZZZZ
BZZZZZ
SMACK!

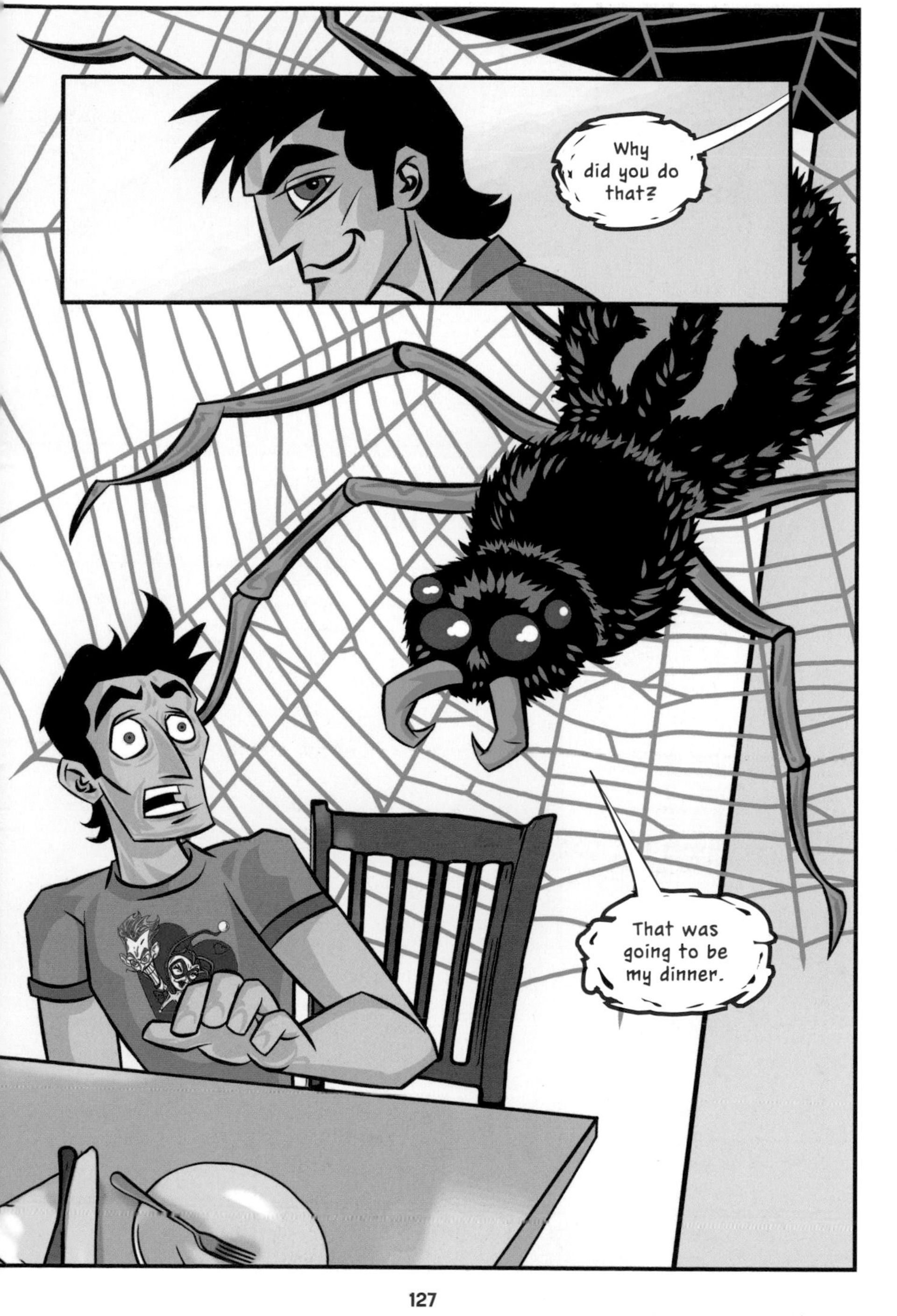
Why did you do that?
That was going to be my dinner.

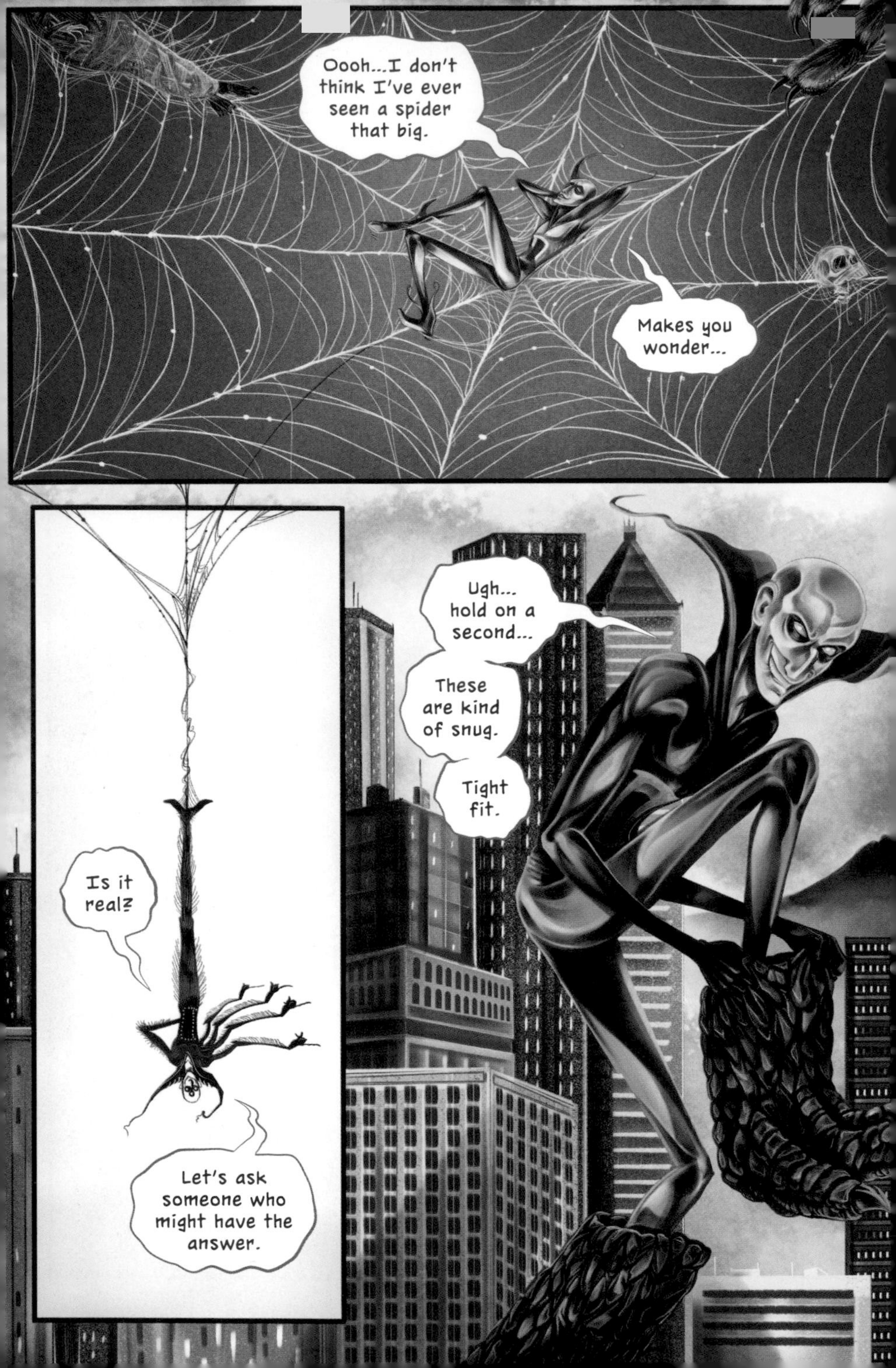
Oooh...I don't think I've ever seen a spider that big.
Makes you wonder...
Is it real?
Let's ask someone who might have the answer.
Ugh... hold on a second...
These are kind of snug.
Tight fit.

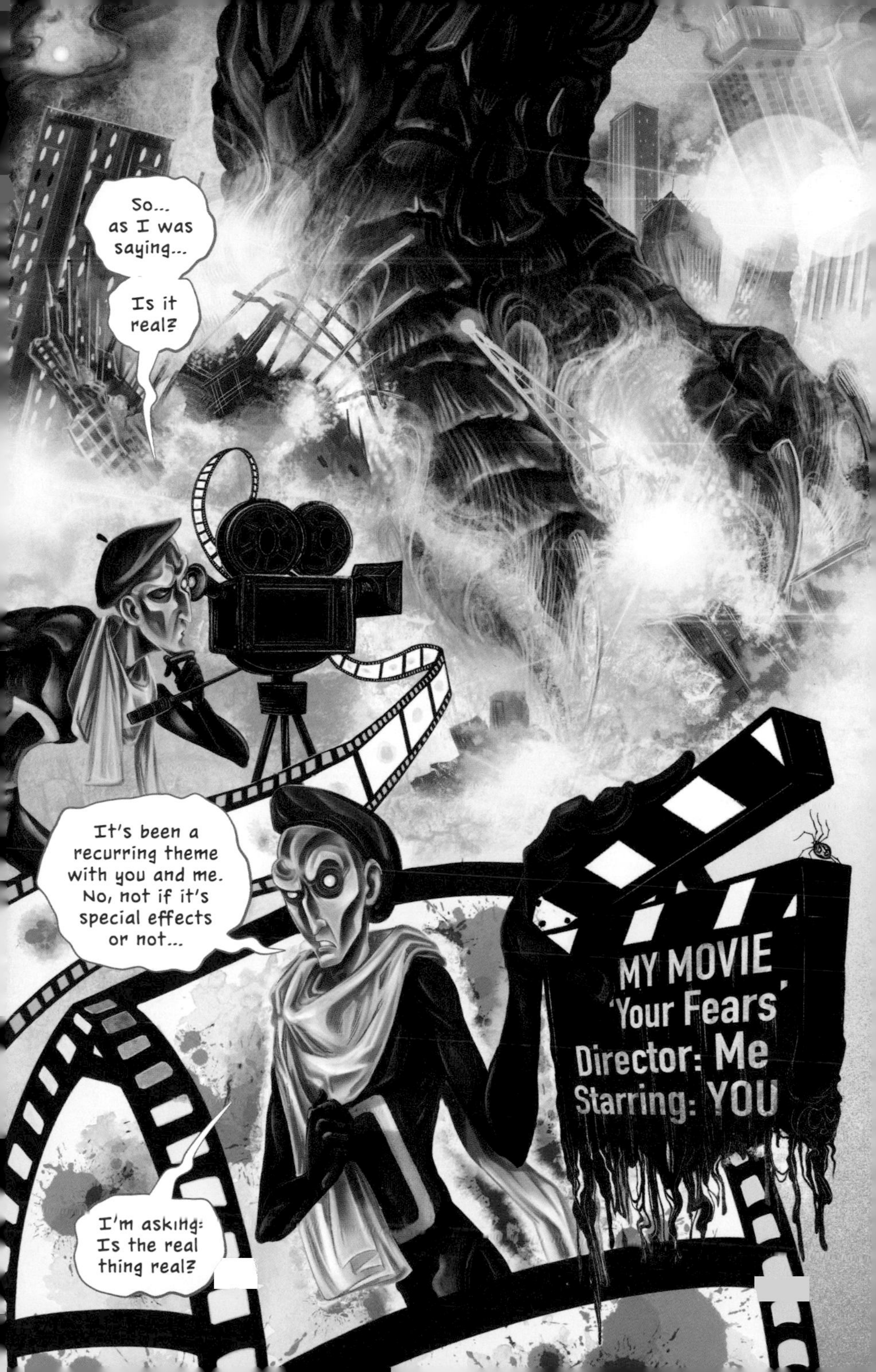
So... as I was saying...
Is it real?
It's been a recurring theme with you and me. No, not if it's special effects or not...
MY MOVIE
'Your Fears'
Director: Me
Starring: YOU
I'm asking: Is the real thing real?

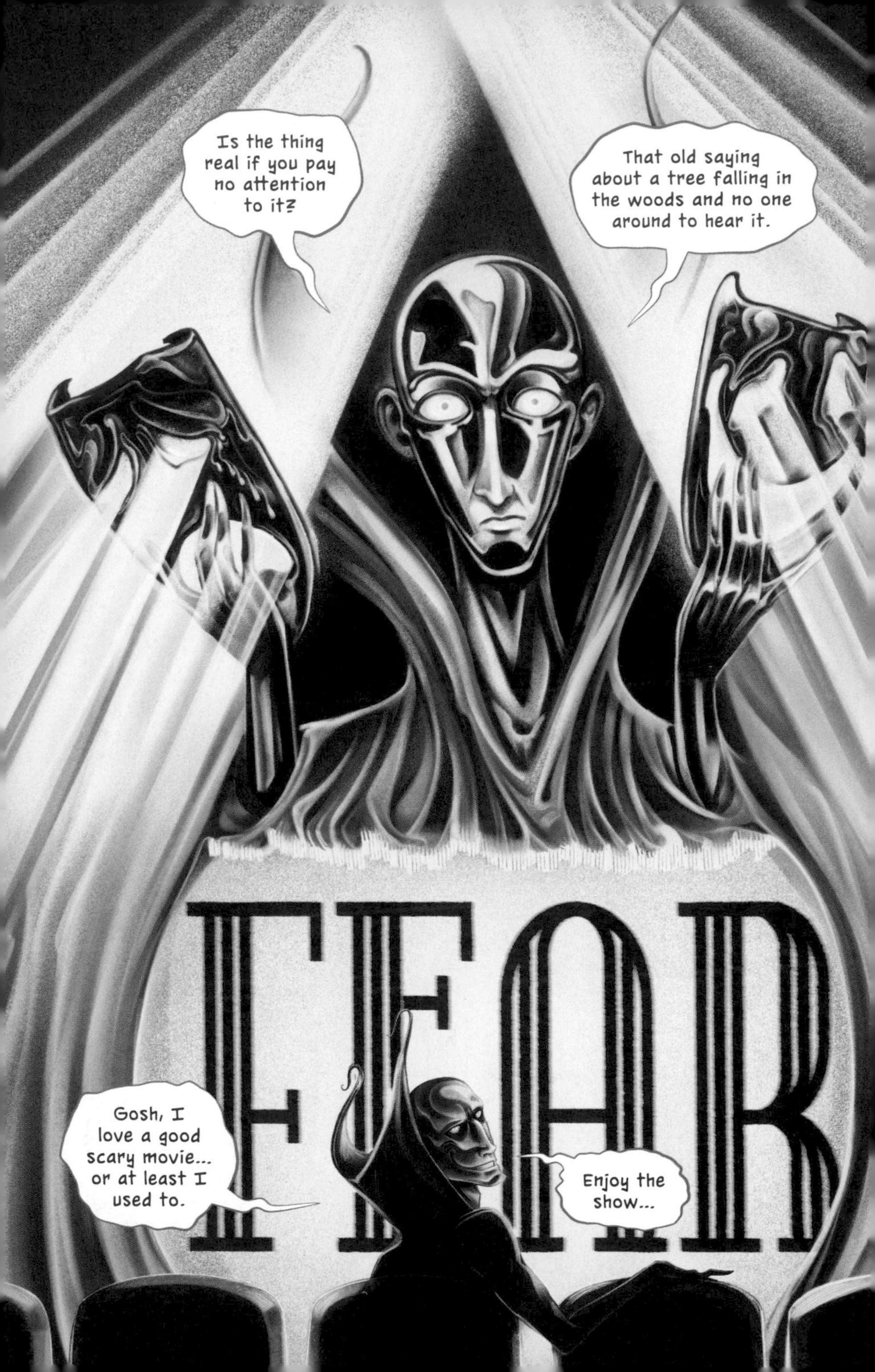
Is the thing real if you pay no attention to it?
That old saying about a tree falling in the woods and no one around to hear it.
FEAR
Gosh, I love a good scary movie... or at least I used to.
Enjoy the show...

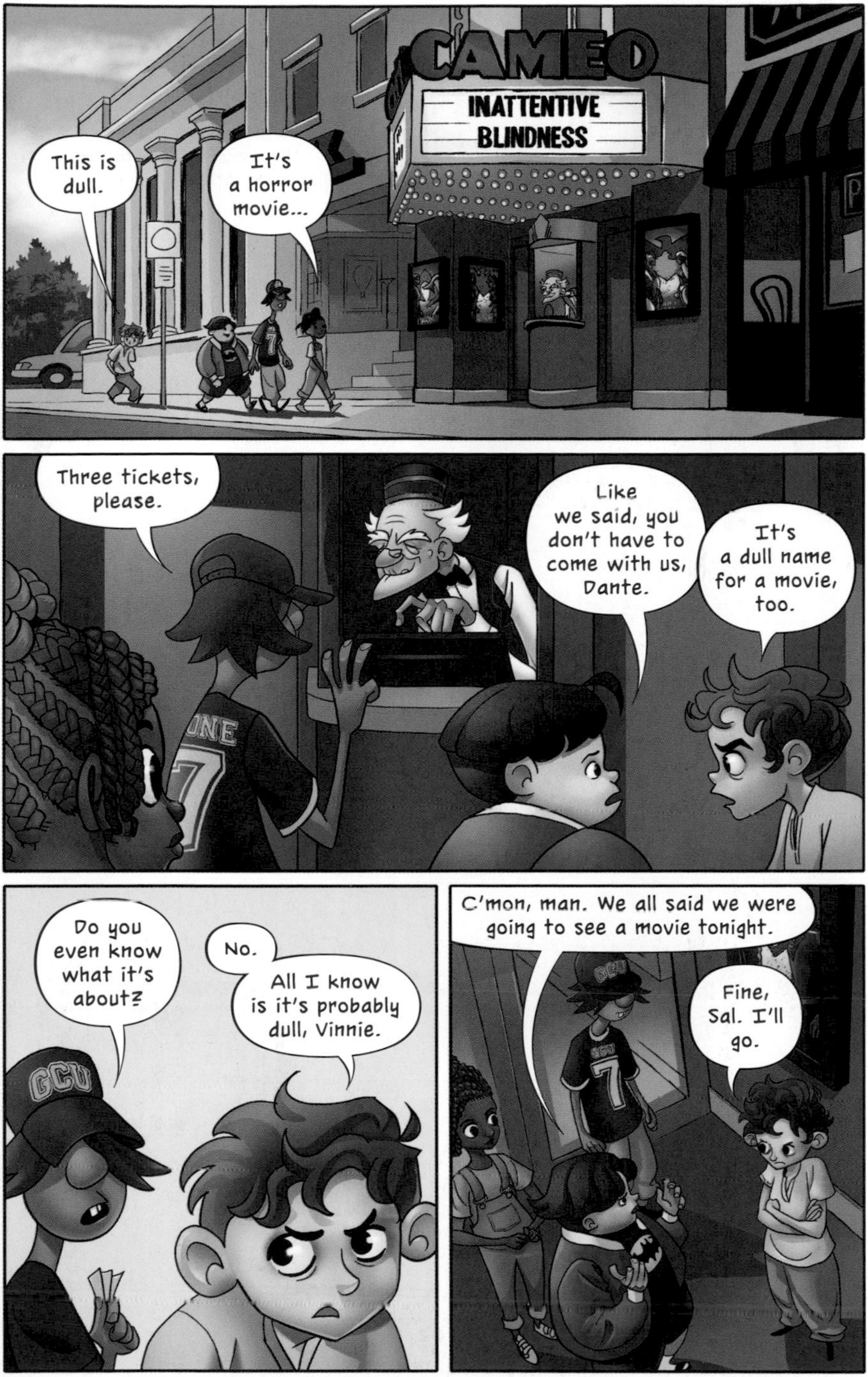
CAMEO
INATTENTIVE BLINDNESS
This is dull.
It's a horror movie...
Three tickets, please.
Like we said, you don't have to come with us, Dante.
It's a dull name for a movie, too.
Do you even know what it's about?
No.
All I know is it's probably dull, Vinnie.
C'mon, man. We all said we were going to see a movie tonight.
Fine, Sal. I'll go.

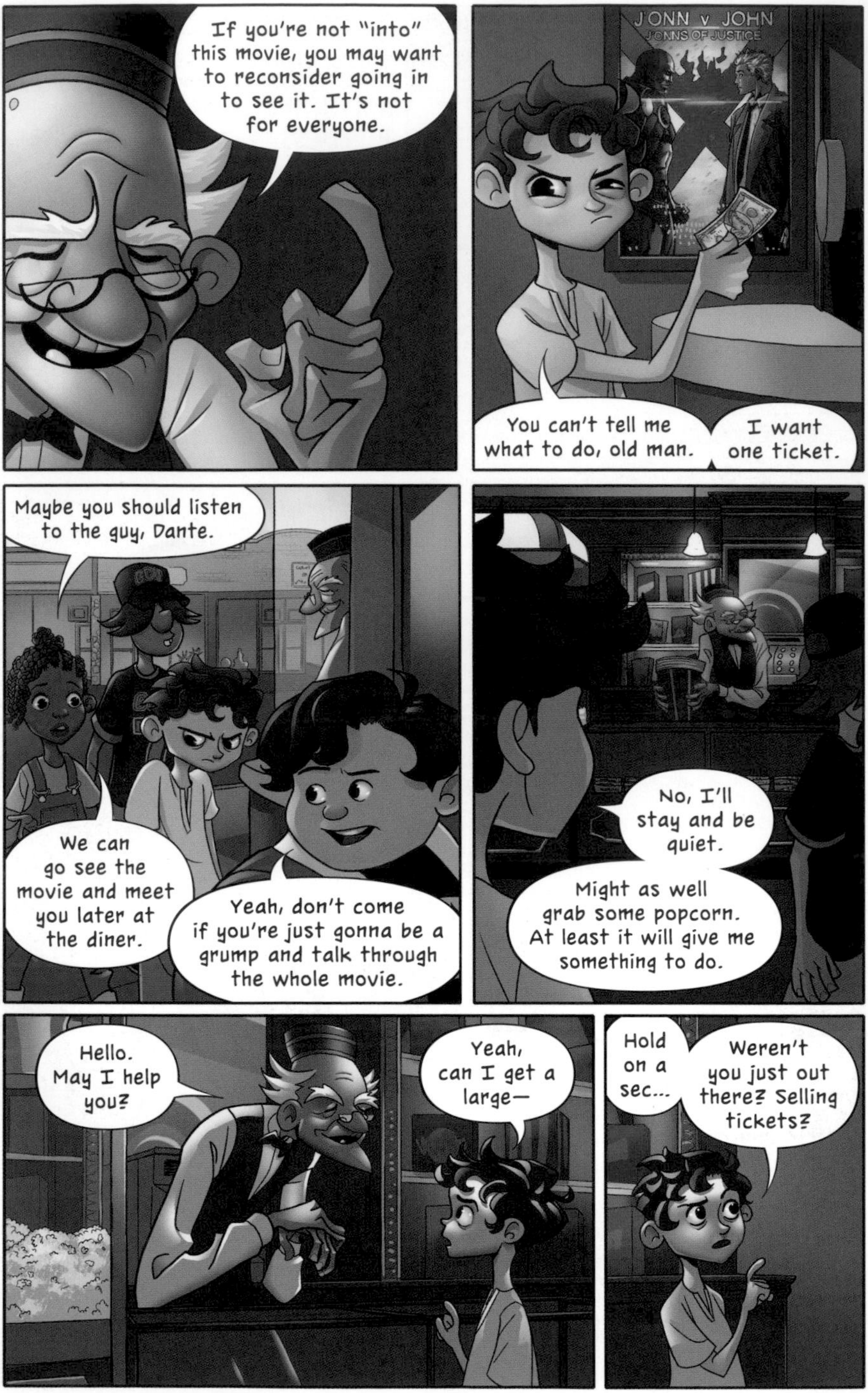

If you're not "into" this movie, you may want to reconsider going in to see it. It's not for everyone.
J'ONN v JOHN
J'ONNS OF JUSTICE
You can't tell me what to do, old man.
I want one ticket.
Maybe you should listen to the guy, Dante.
We can go see the movie and meet you later at the diner.
Yeah, don't come if you're just gonna be a grump and talk through the whole movie.
No, I'll stay and be quiet.
Might as well grab some popcorn. At least it will give me something to do.
Hello. May I help you?
Yeah, can I get a large—
Hold on a sec...
Weren't you just out there? Selling tickets?

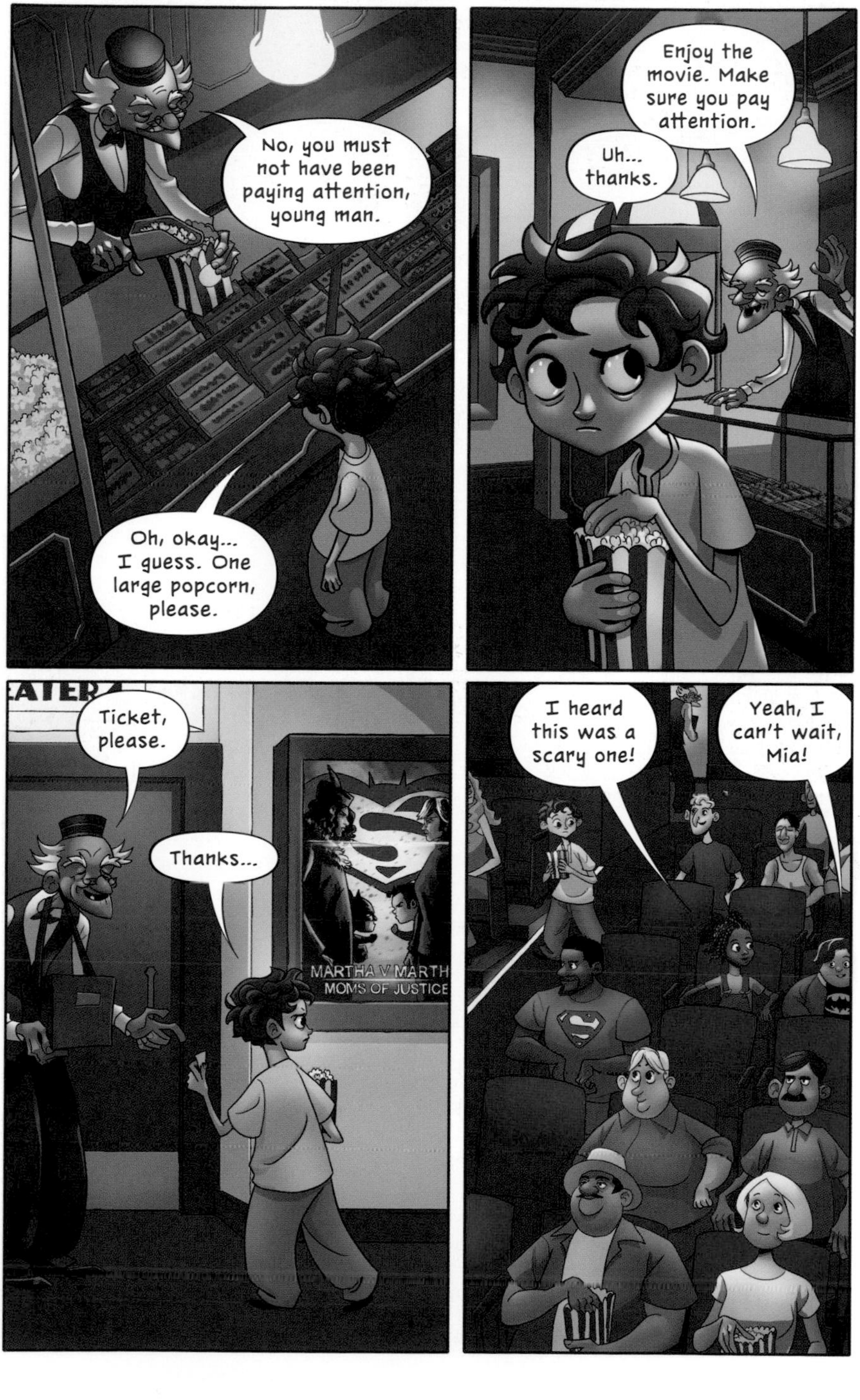
No, you must not have been paying attention, young man.
Oh, okay... I guess. One large popcorn, please.
Enjoy the movie. Make sure you pay attention.
Uh... thanks.
EATER
Ticket, please.
Thanks...
MARTHA V MARTH
MOMS OF JUSTICE
I heard this was a scary one!
Yeah, I can't wait, Mia!

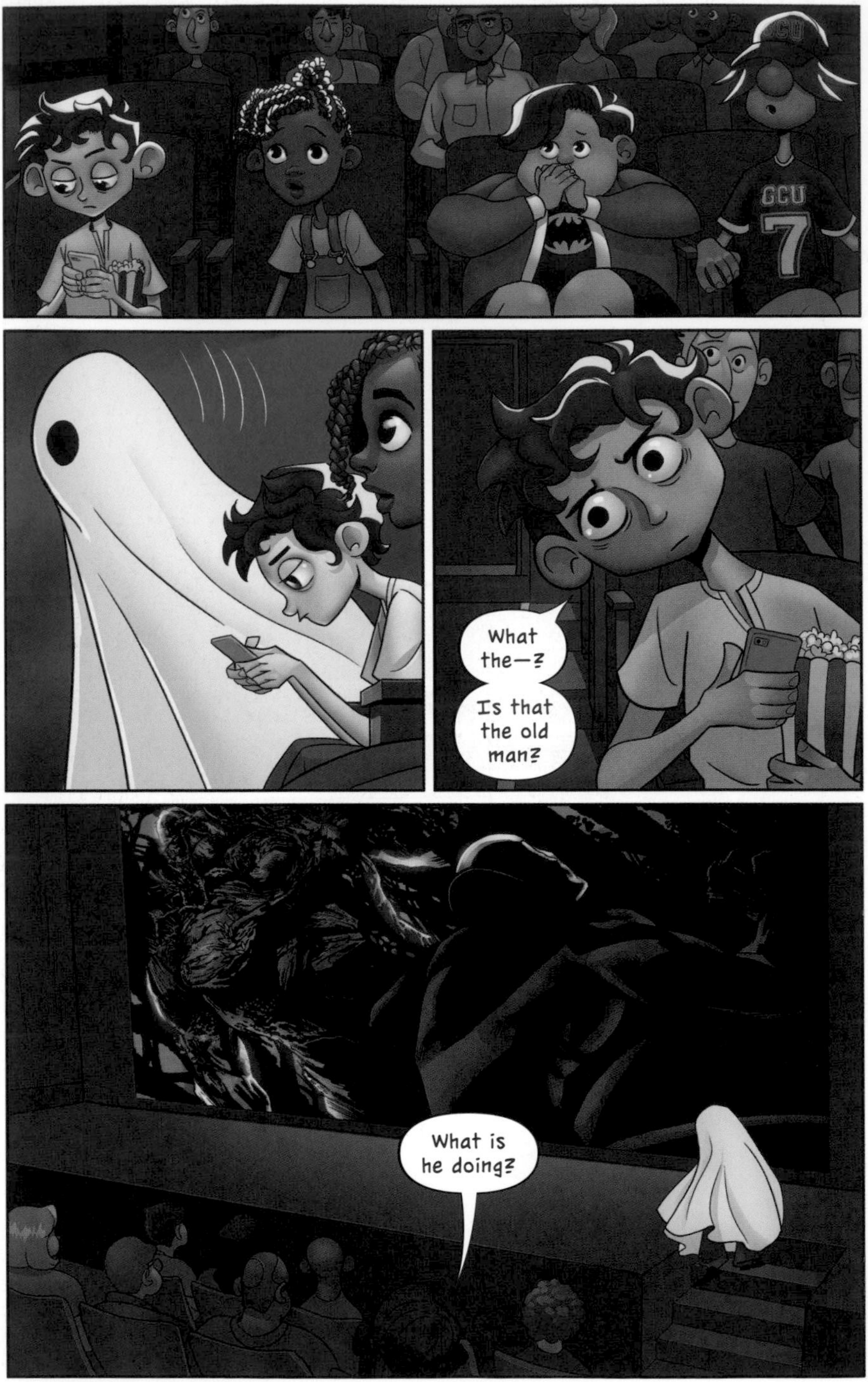
What the—?
Is that the old man?
What is he doing?

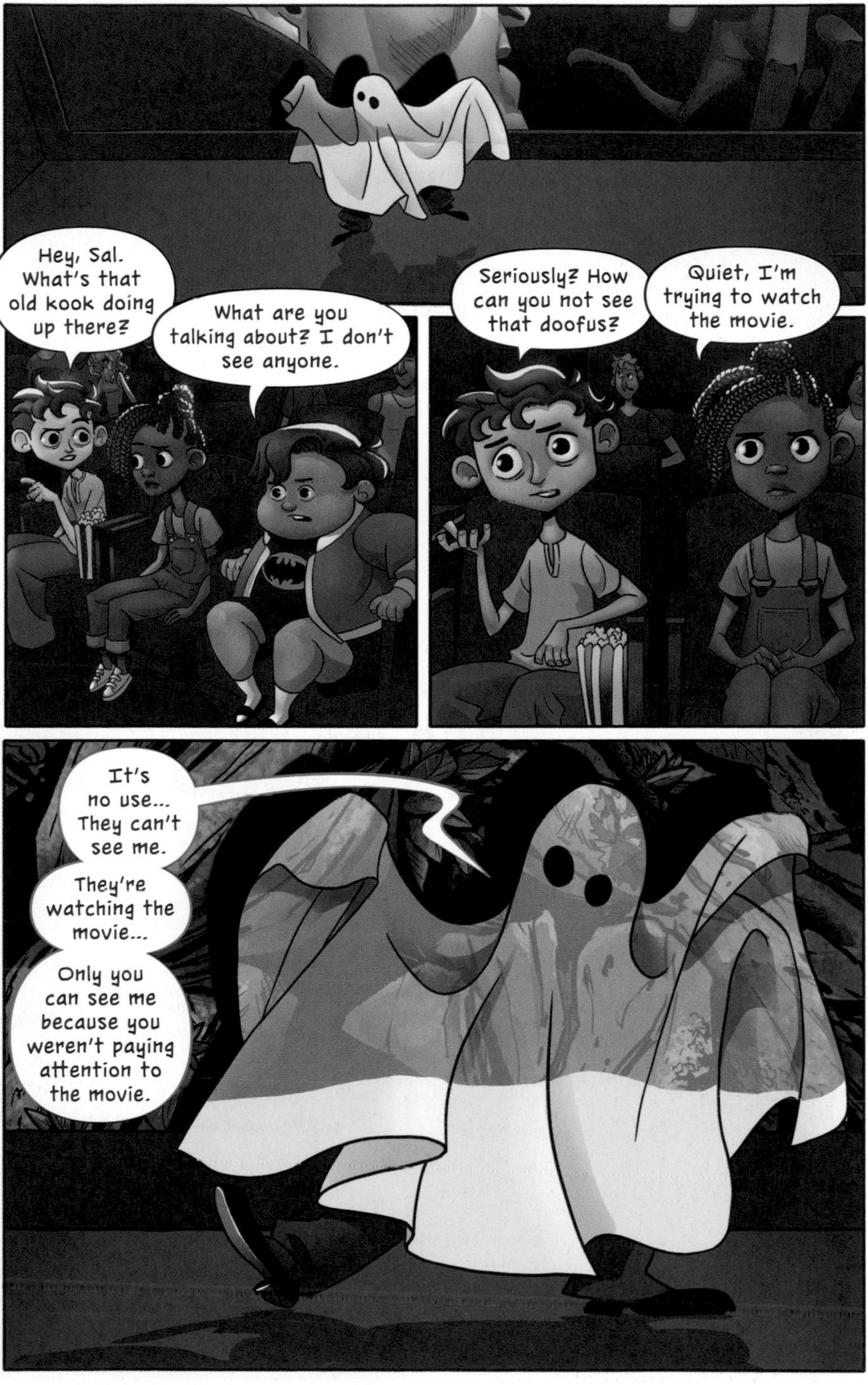
Hey, Sal. What's that old kook doing up there?
What are you talking about? I don't see anyone.
Seriously? How can you not see that doofus?
Quiet, I'm trying to watch the movie.
It's no use... They can't see me.
They're watching the movie...
Only you can see me because you weren't paying attention to the movie.

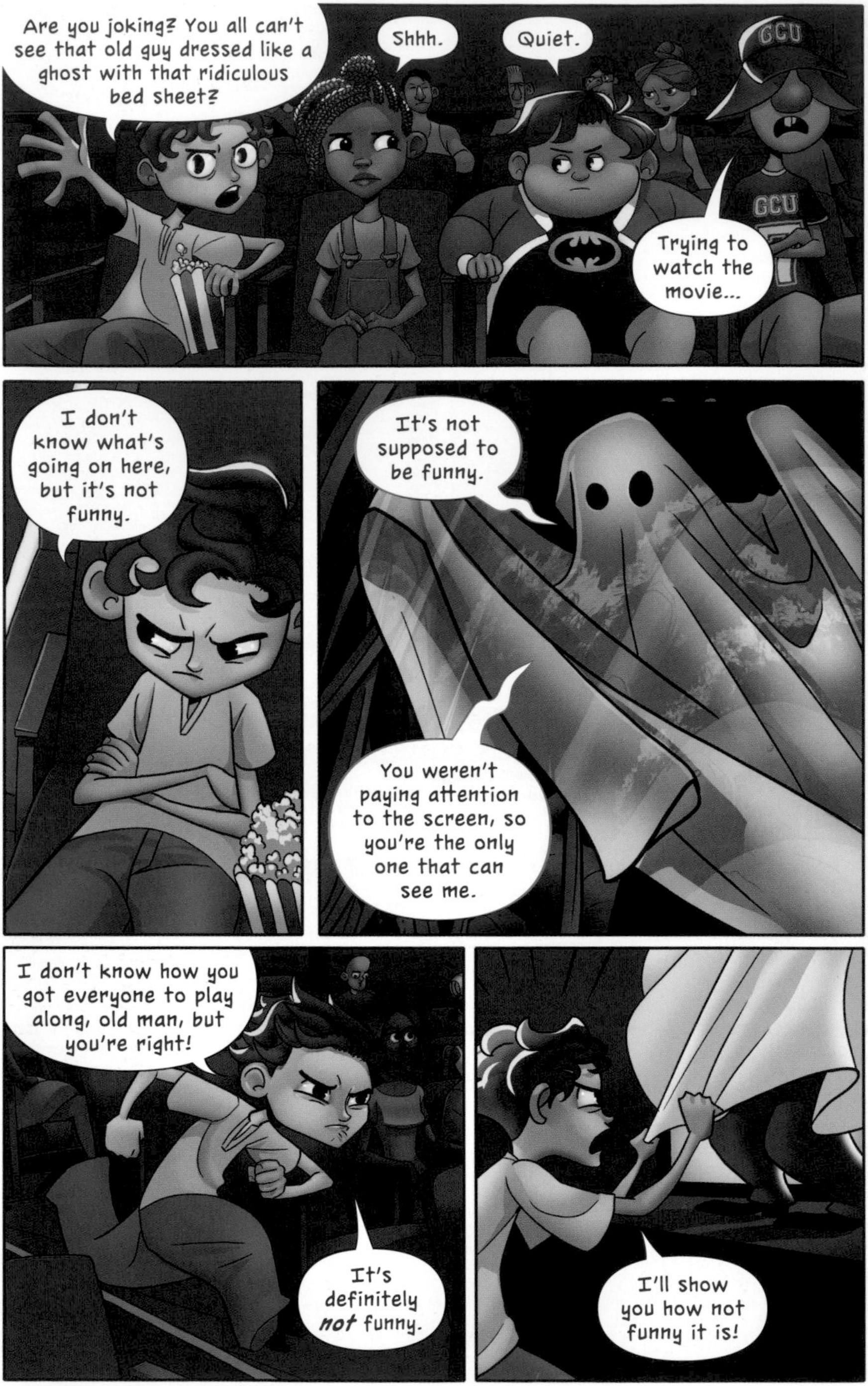
Are you joking? You all can't see that old guy dressed like a ghost with that ridiculous bed sheet?
Shhh.
Quiet.
Trying to watch the movie...
I don't know what's going on here, but it's not funny.
It's not supposed to be funny.
You weren't paying attention to the screen, so you're the only one that can see me.
I don't know how you got everyone to play along, old man, but you're right!
It's definitely *not* funny.
I'll show you how not funny it is!

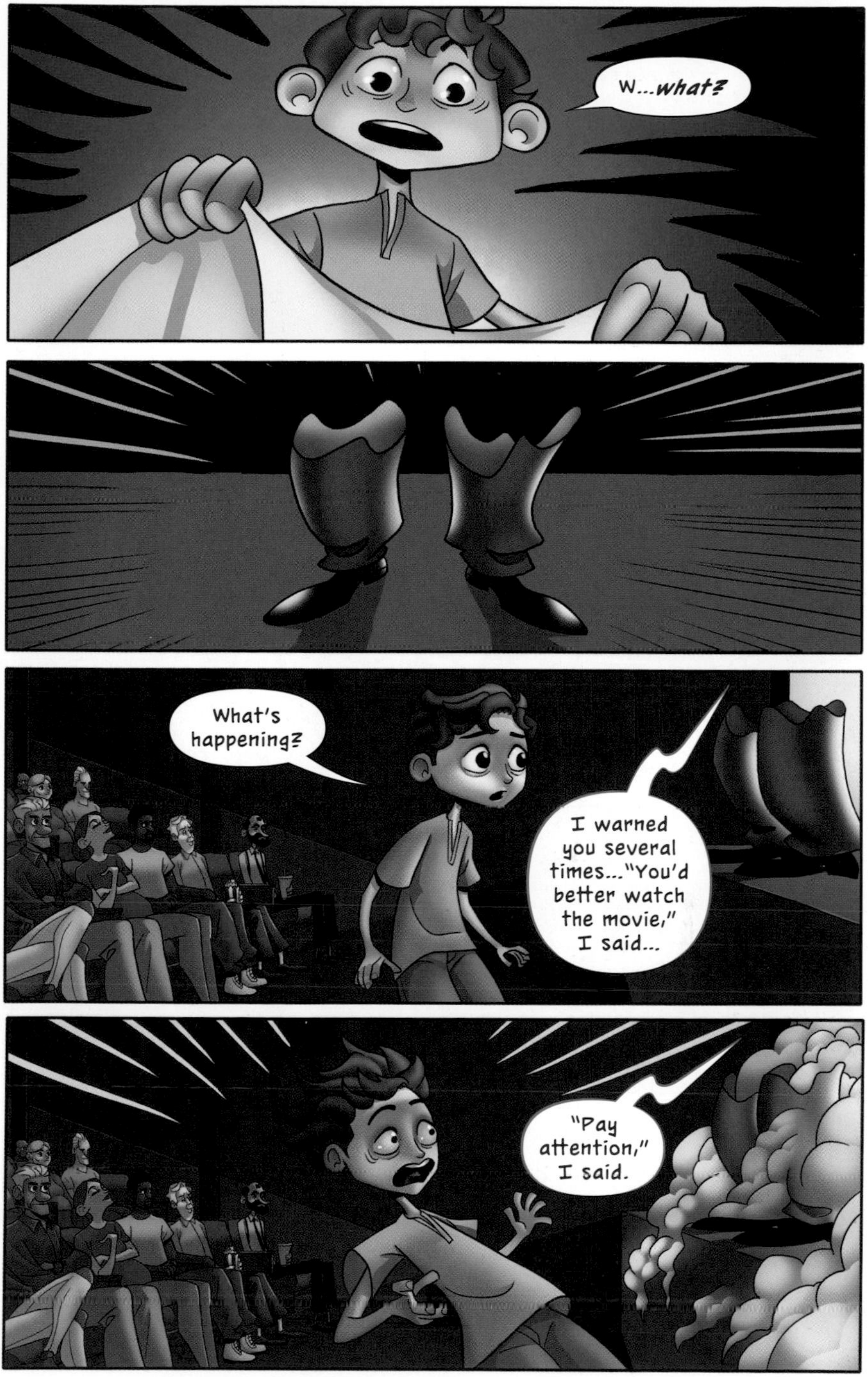
W...what?
What's happening?
I warned you several times..."You'd better watch the movie," I said...
"Pay attention," I said.

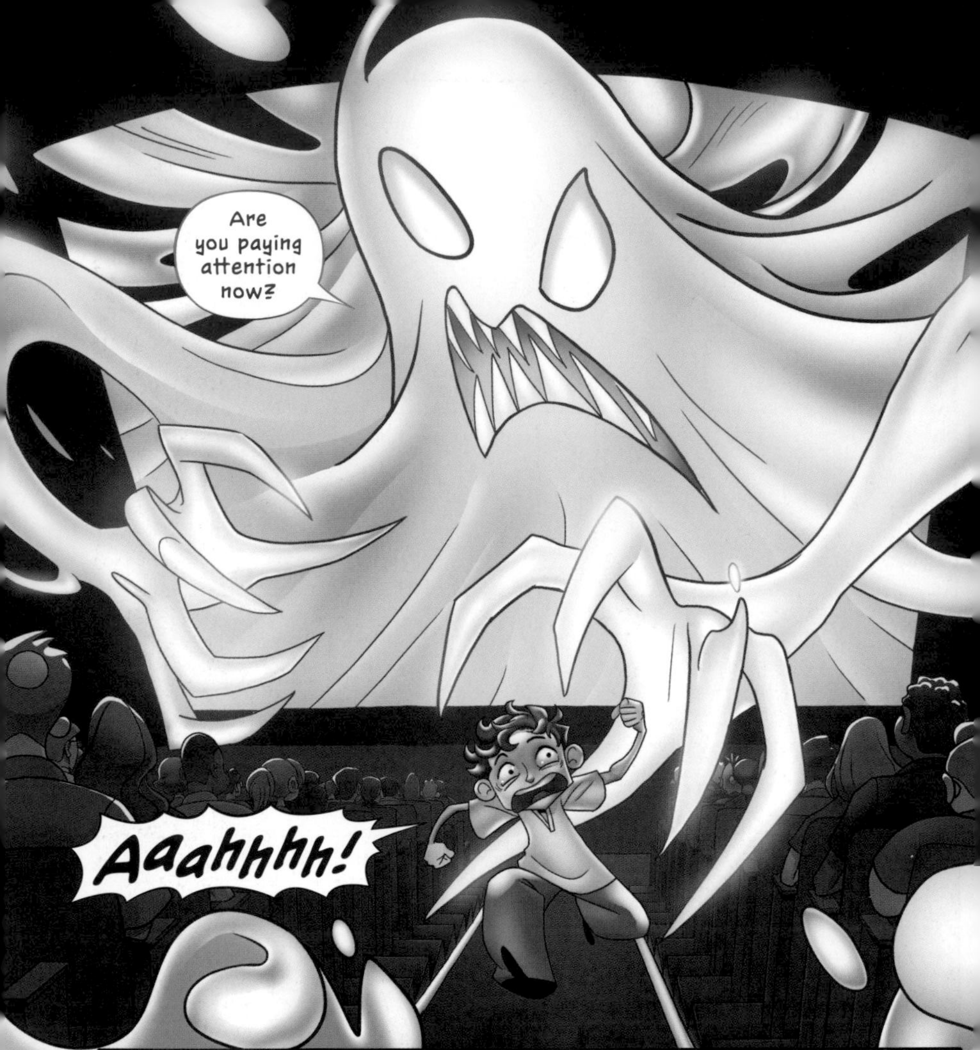
Are you paying attention now?
Aaahhhh!
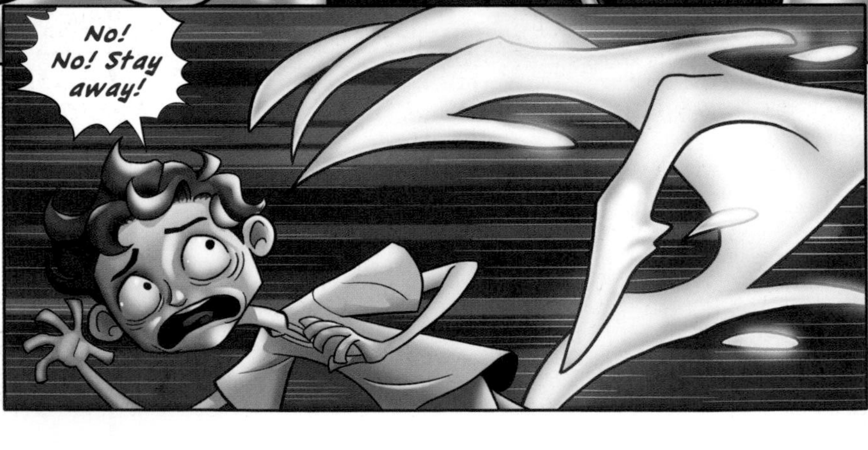
No! No! Stay away!

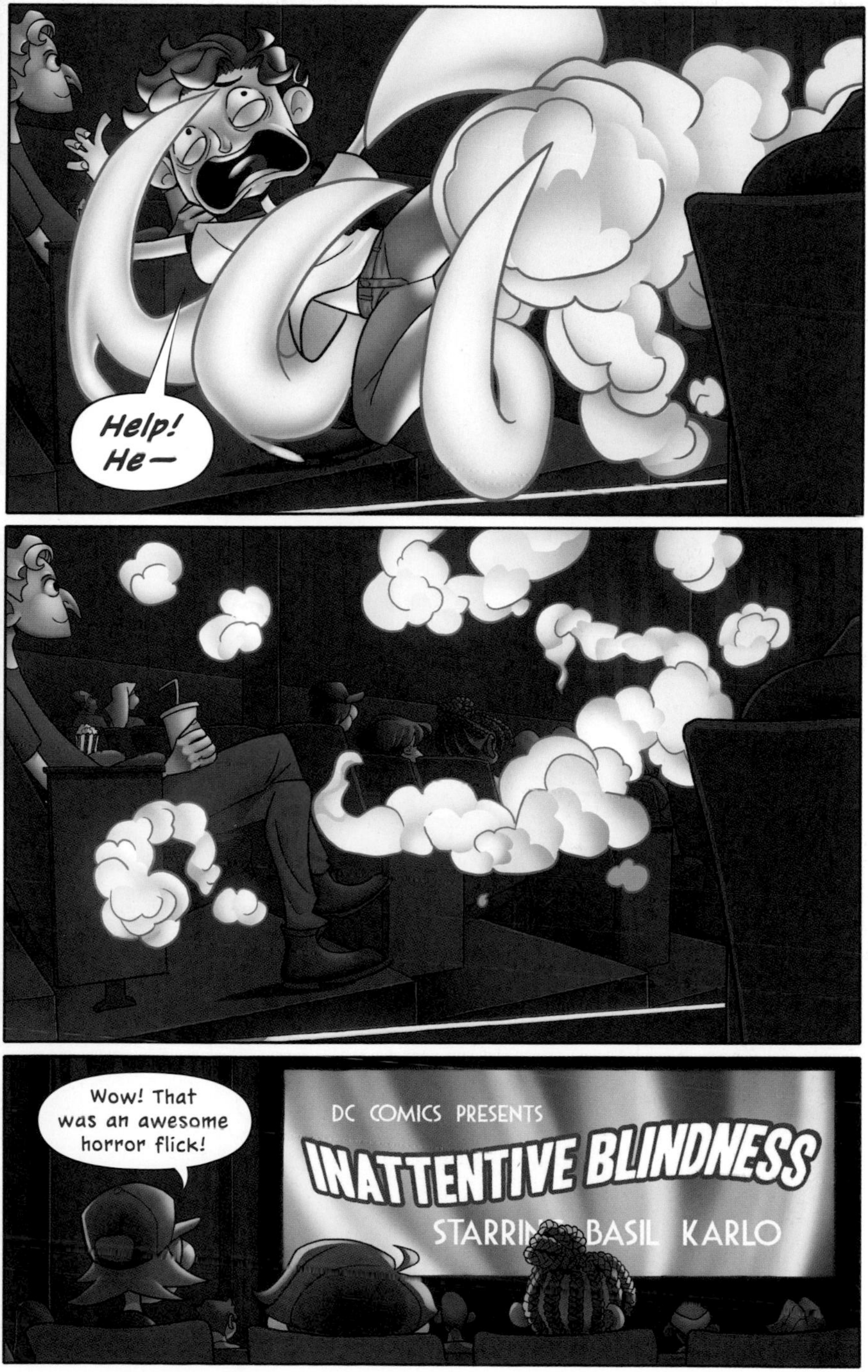

Help! He—
Wow! That was an awesome horror flick!
DC COMICS PRESENTS
INATTENTIVE BLINDNESS
STARRING BASIL KARLO

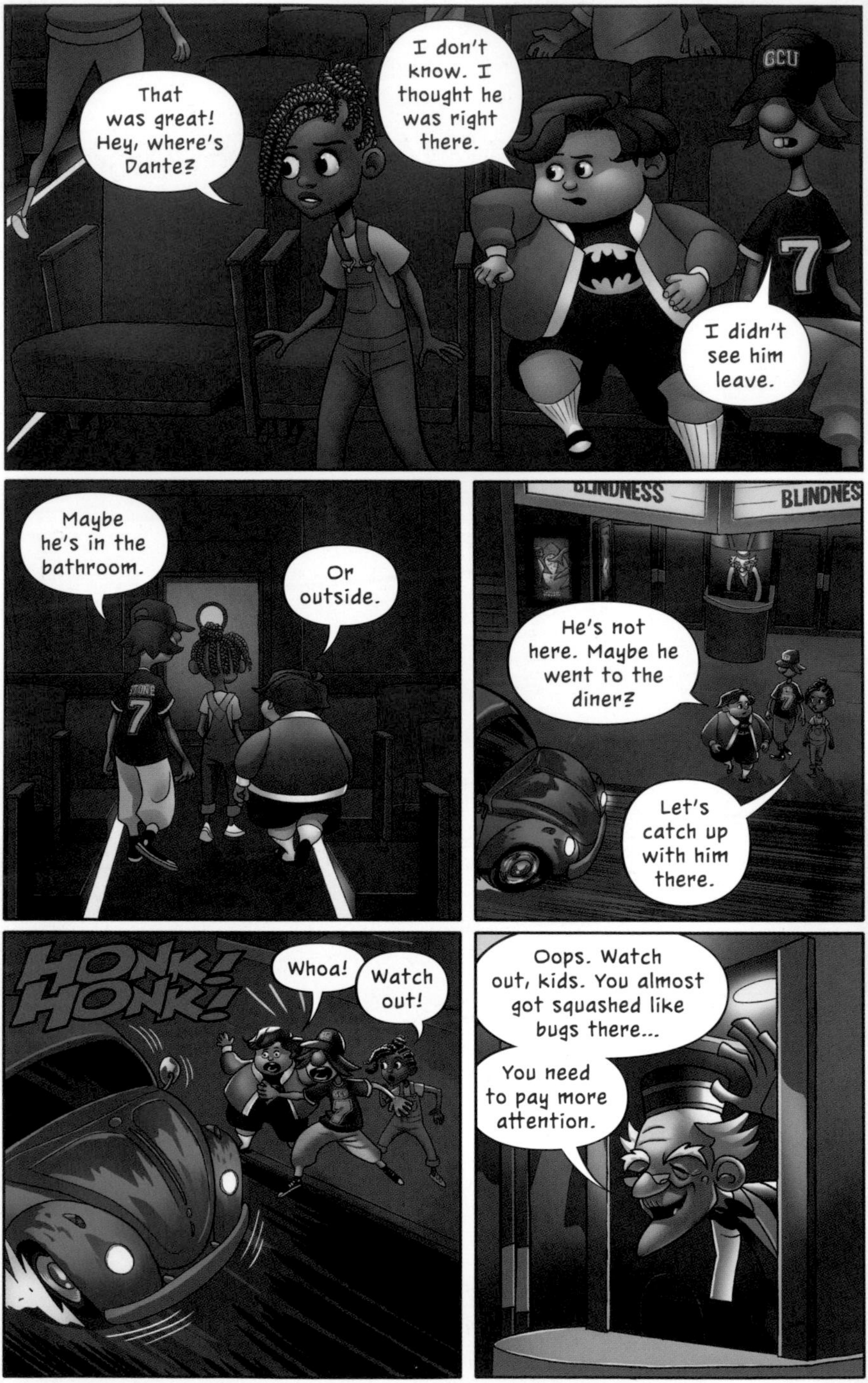
That was great! Hey, where's Dante?
I don't know. I thought he was right there.
GCU
I didn't see him leave.
Maybe he's in the bathroom.
Or outside.
BLINDNESS
BLINDNES
He's not here. Maybe he went to the diner?
Let's catch up with him there.
HONK! HONK!
Whoa!
Watch out!
Oops. Watch out, kids. You almost got squashed like bugs there...
You need to pay more attention.

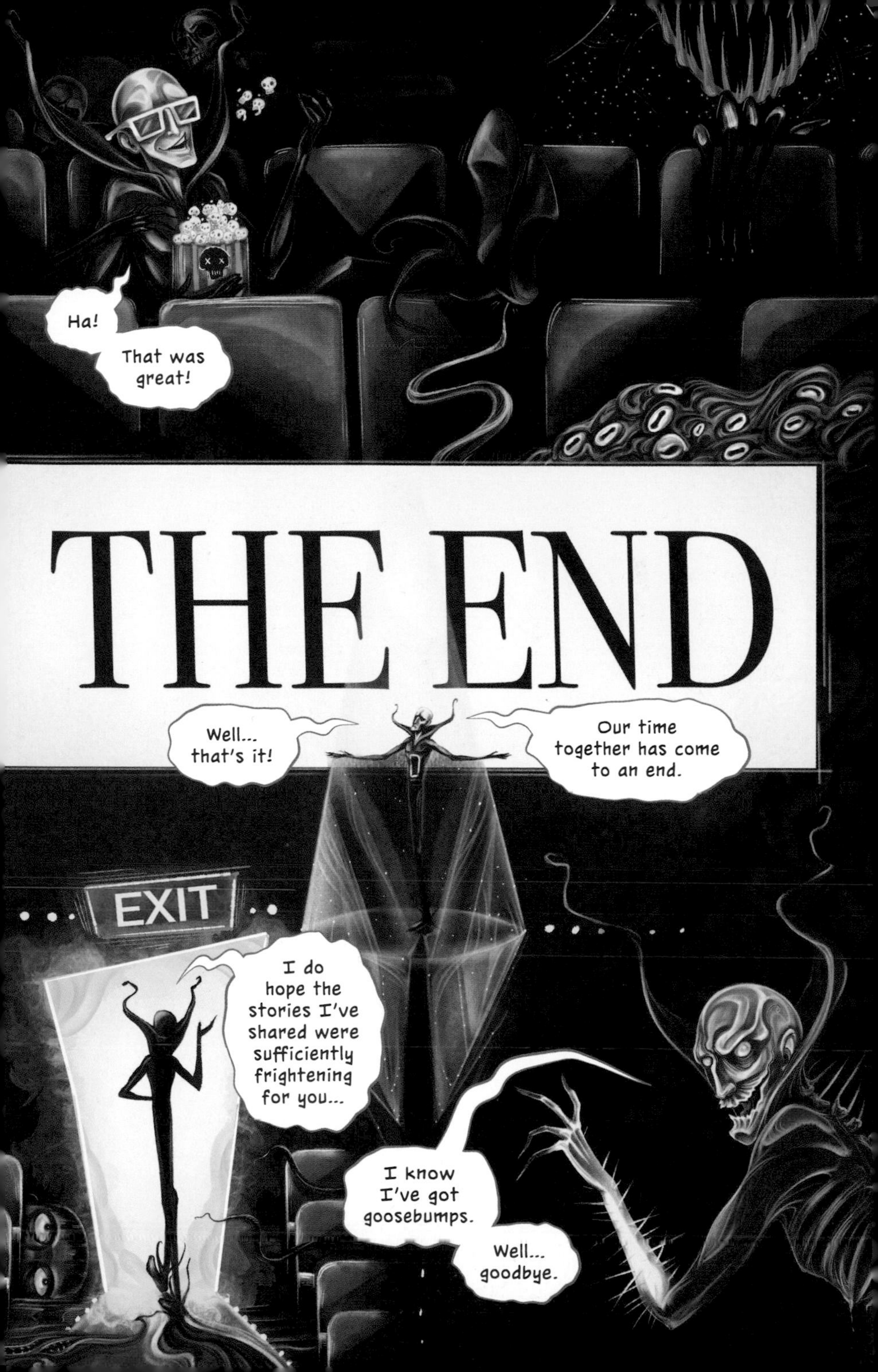
Ha!
That was great!
THE END
Well... that's it!
Our time together has come to an end.
EXIT
I do hope the stories I've shared were sufficiently frightening for you...
I know I've got goosebumps.
Well... goodbye.

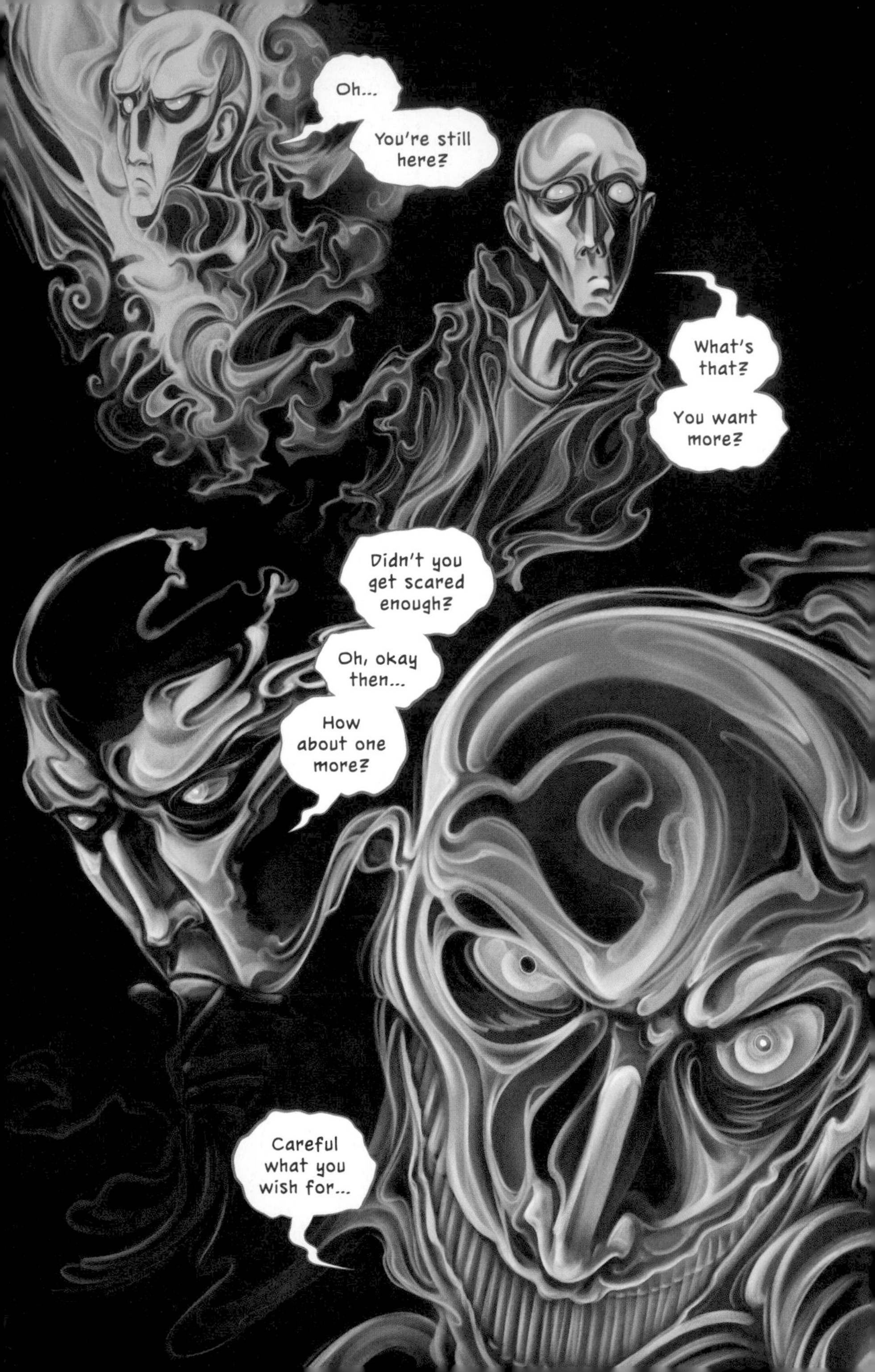
Oh...
You're still here?
What's that?
You want more?
Didn't you get scared enough?
Oh, okay then...
How about one more?
Careful what you wish for...

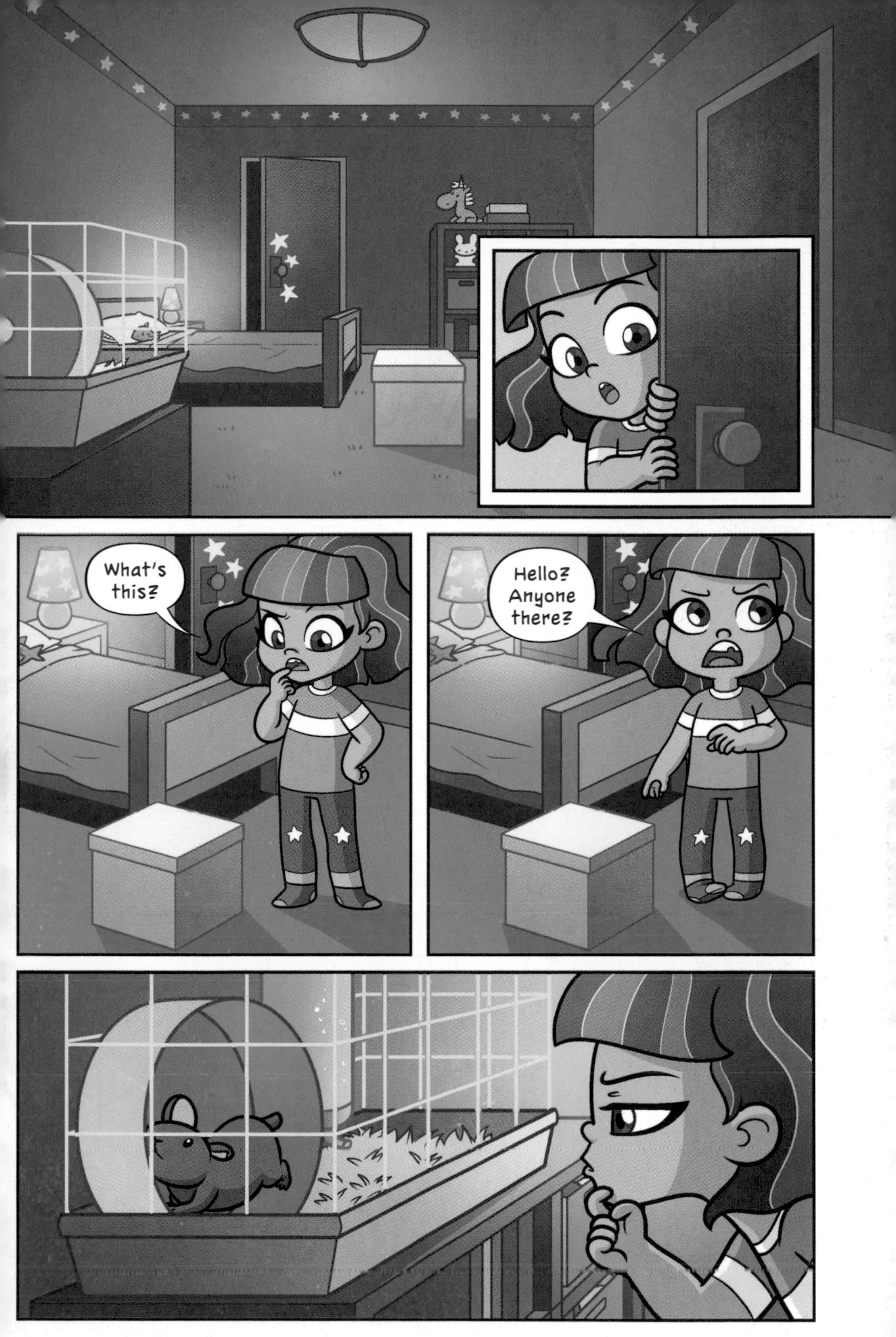
What's this?
Hello? Anyone there?

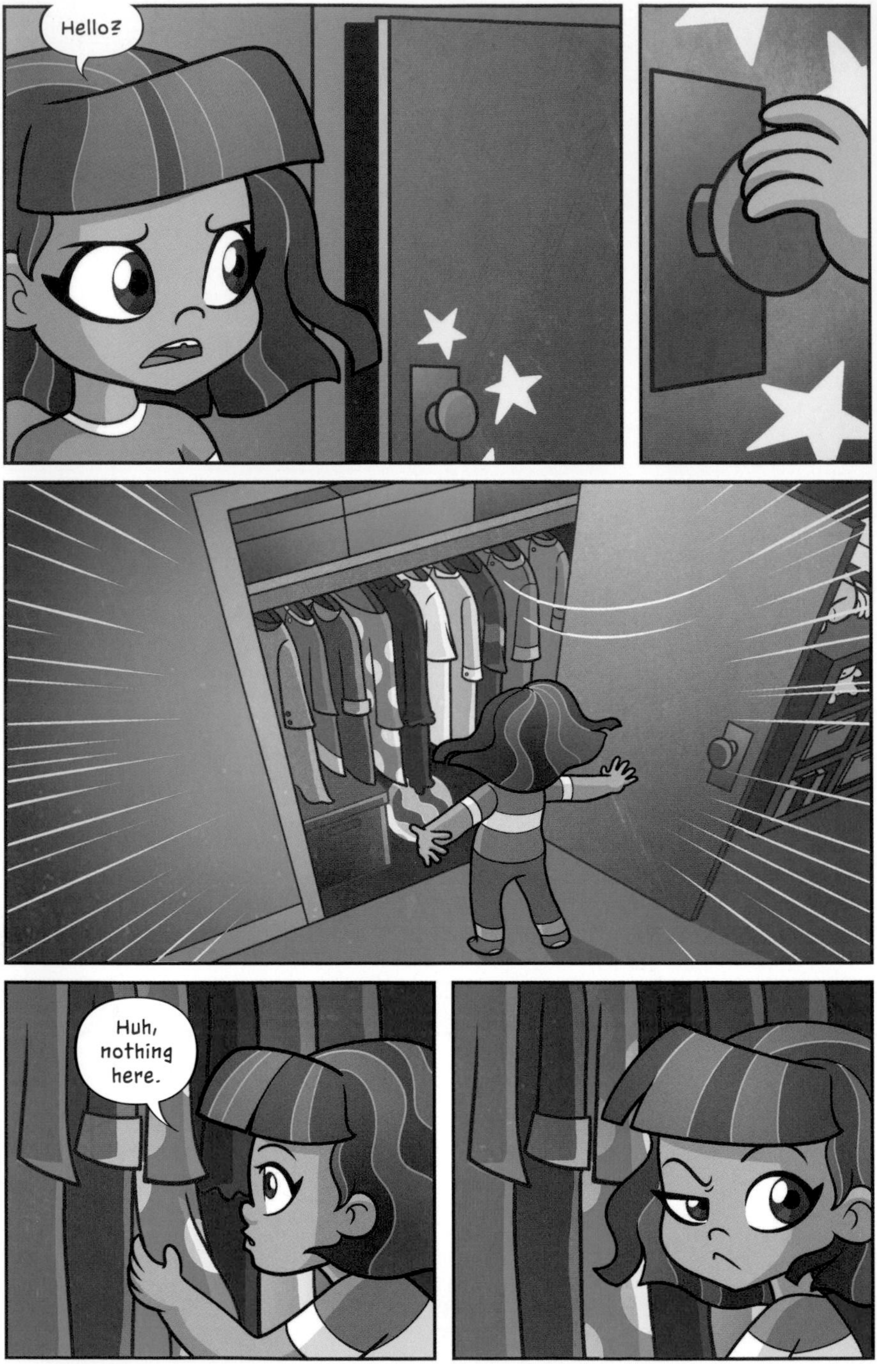
Hello?
Huh, nothing here.

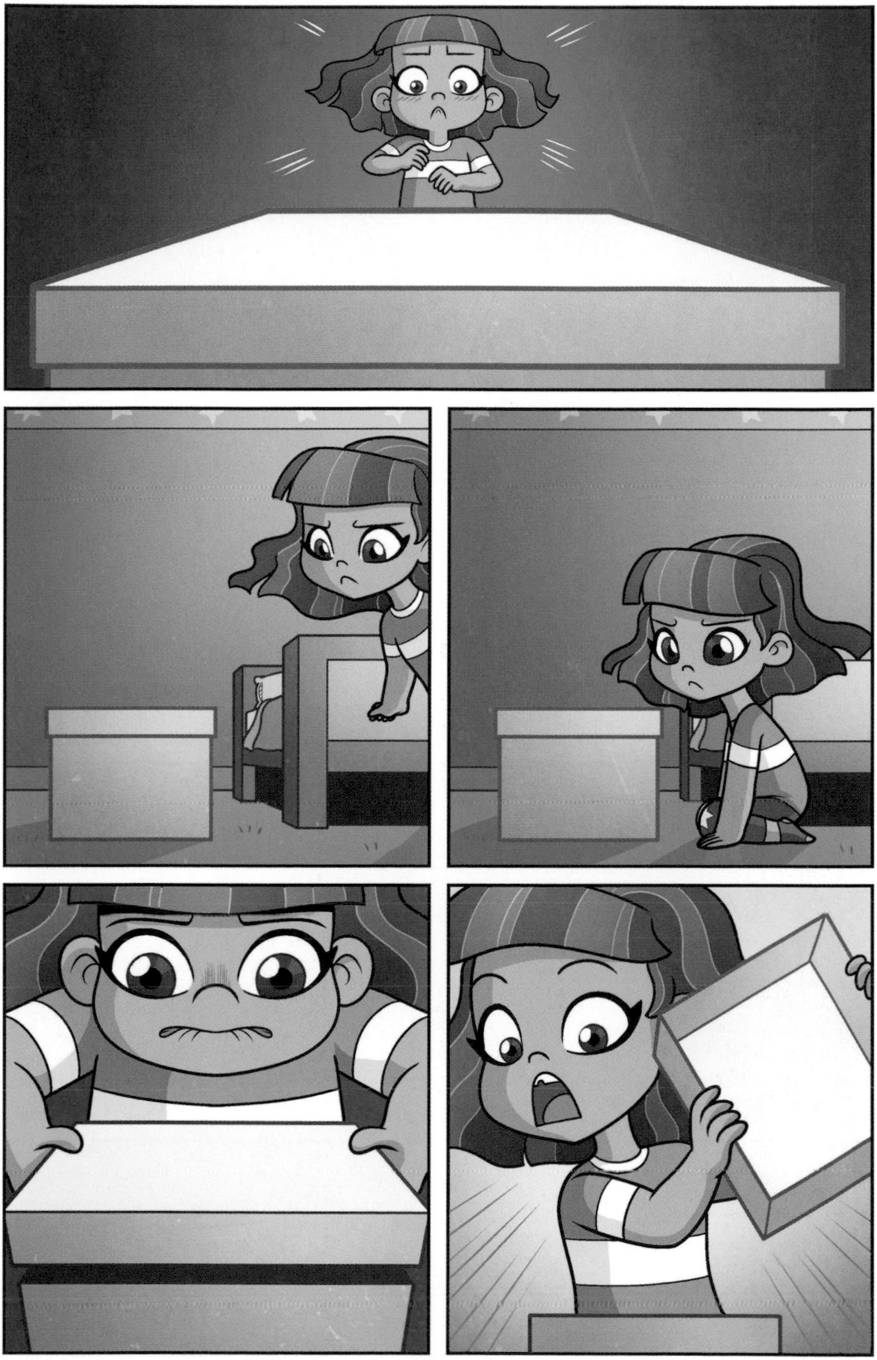

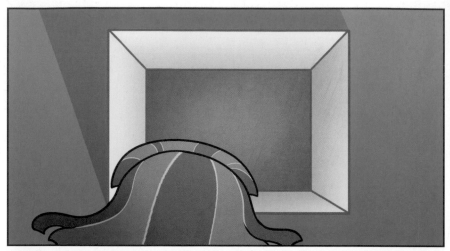

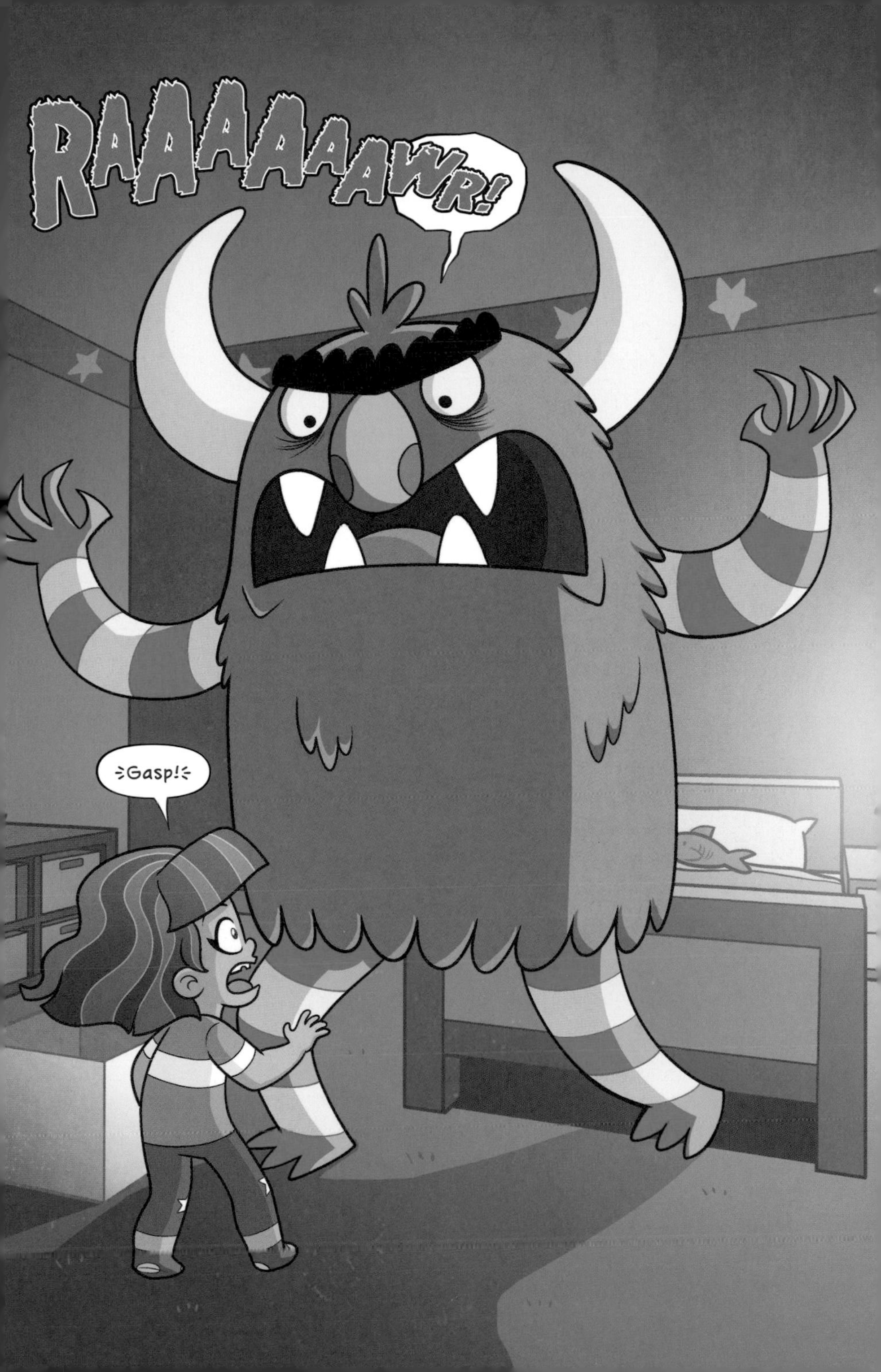
RAAAAAAWR!
Gasp!

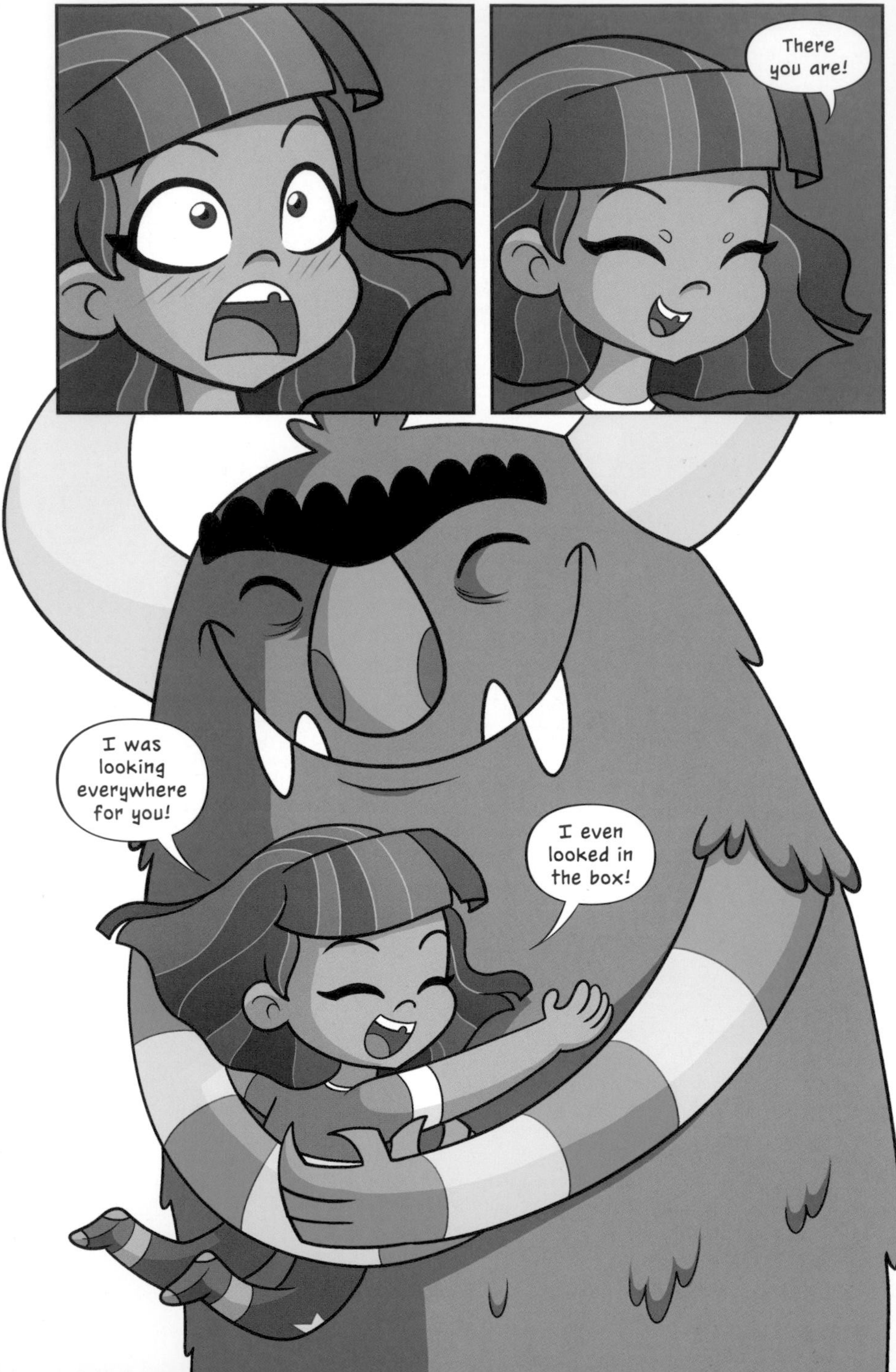
There you are!
I was looking everywhere for you!
I even looked in the box!

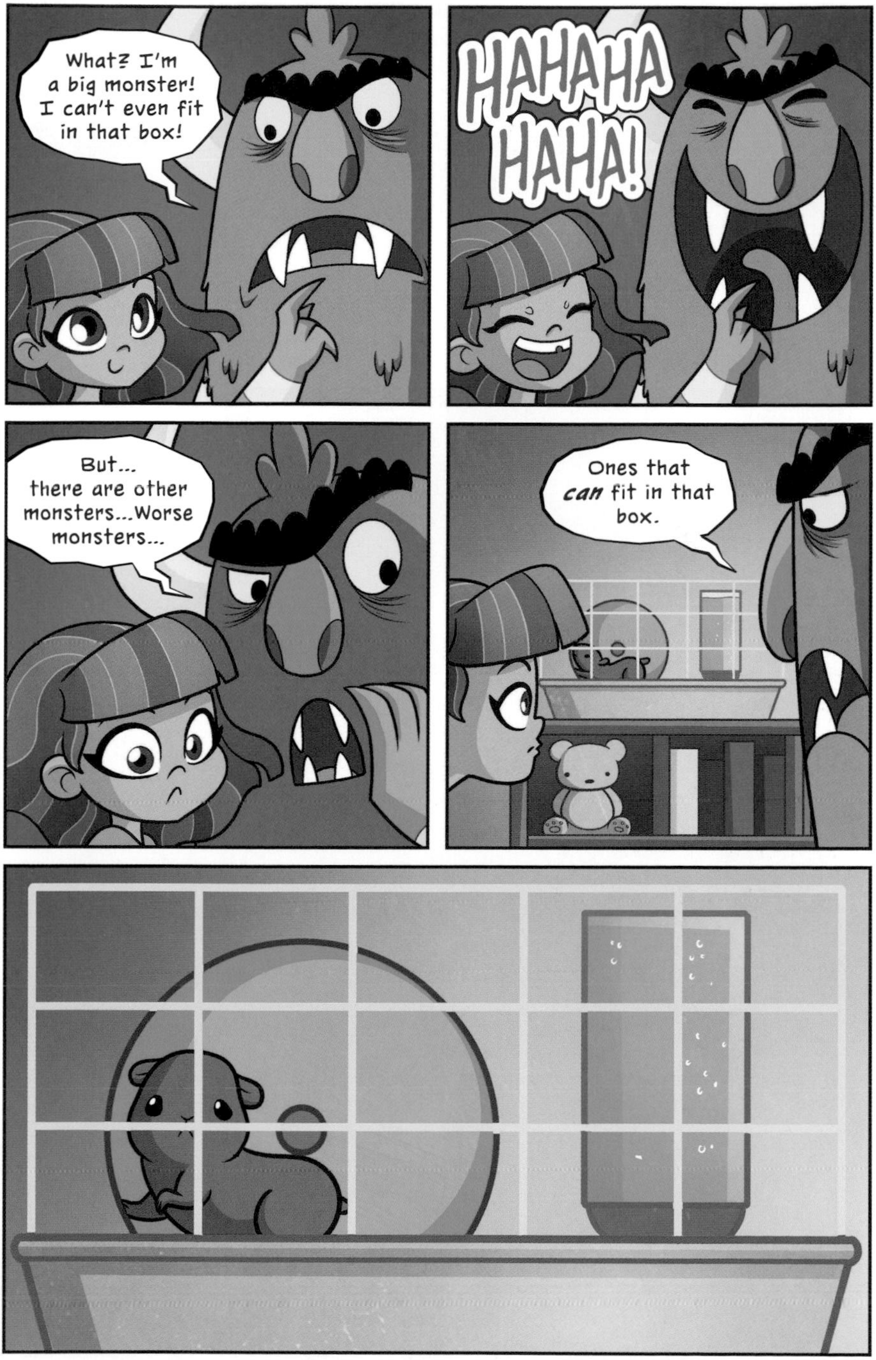
What? I'm a big monster! I can't even fit in that box!
HAHAHA HAHA!
But... there are other monsters...Worse monsters...
Ones that *can* fit in that box.

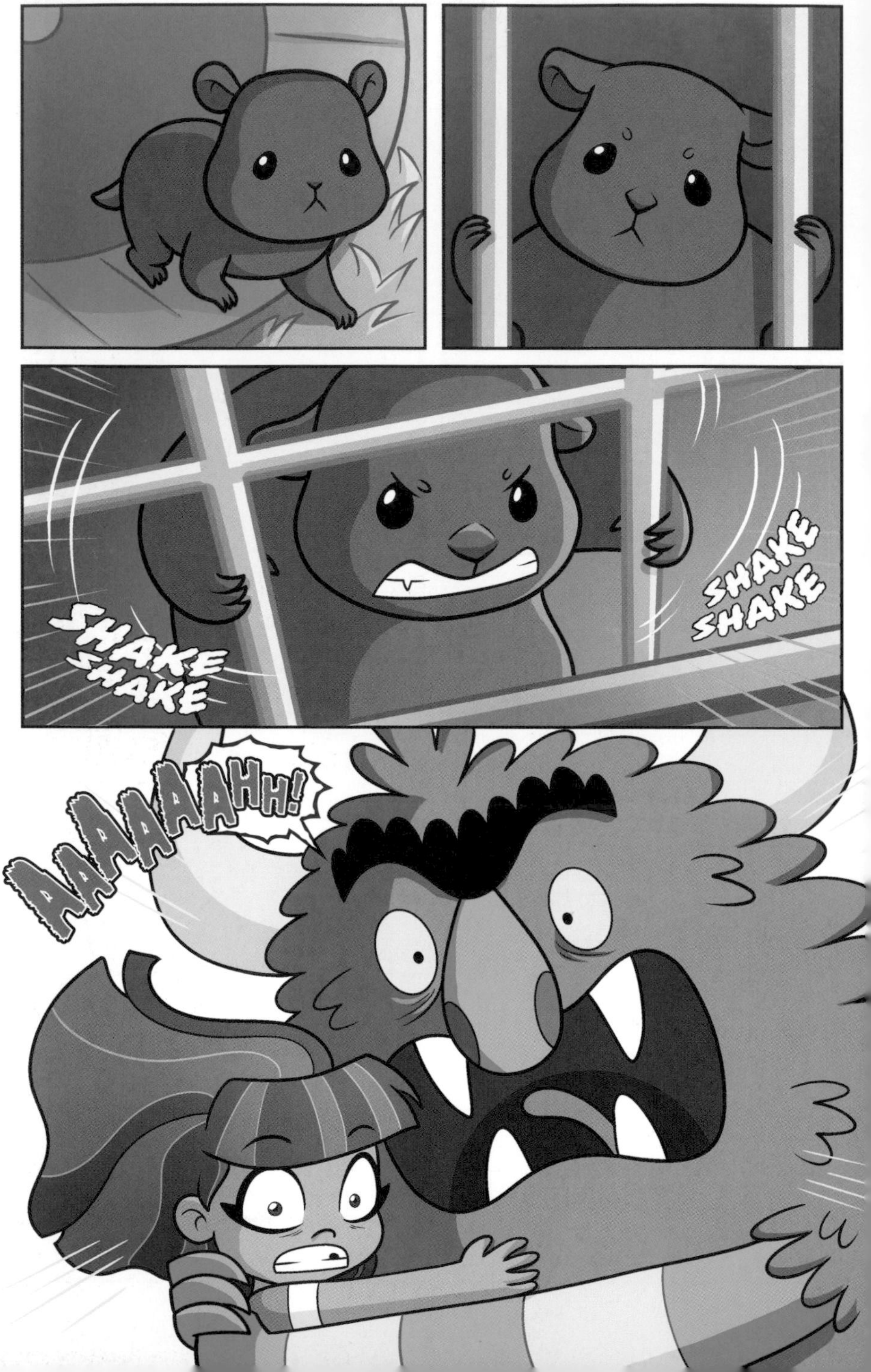
SHAKE
SHAKE
SHAKE
SHAKE
AAAAAAAAHH!

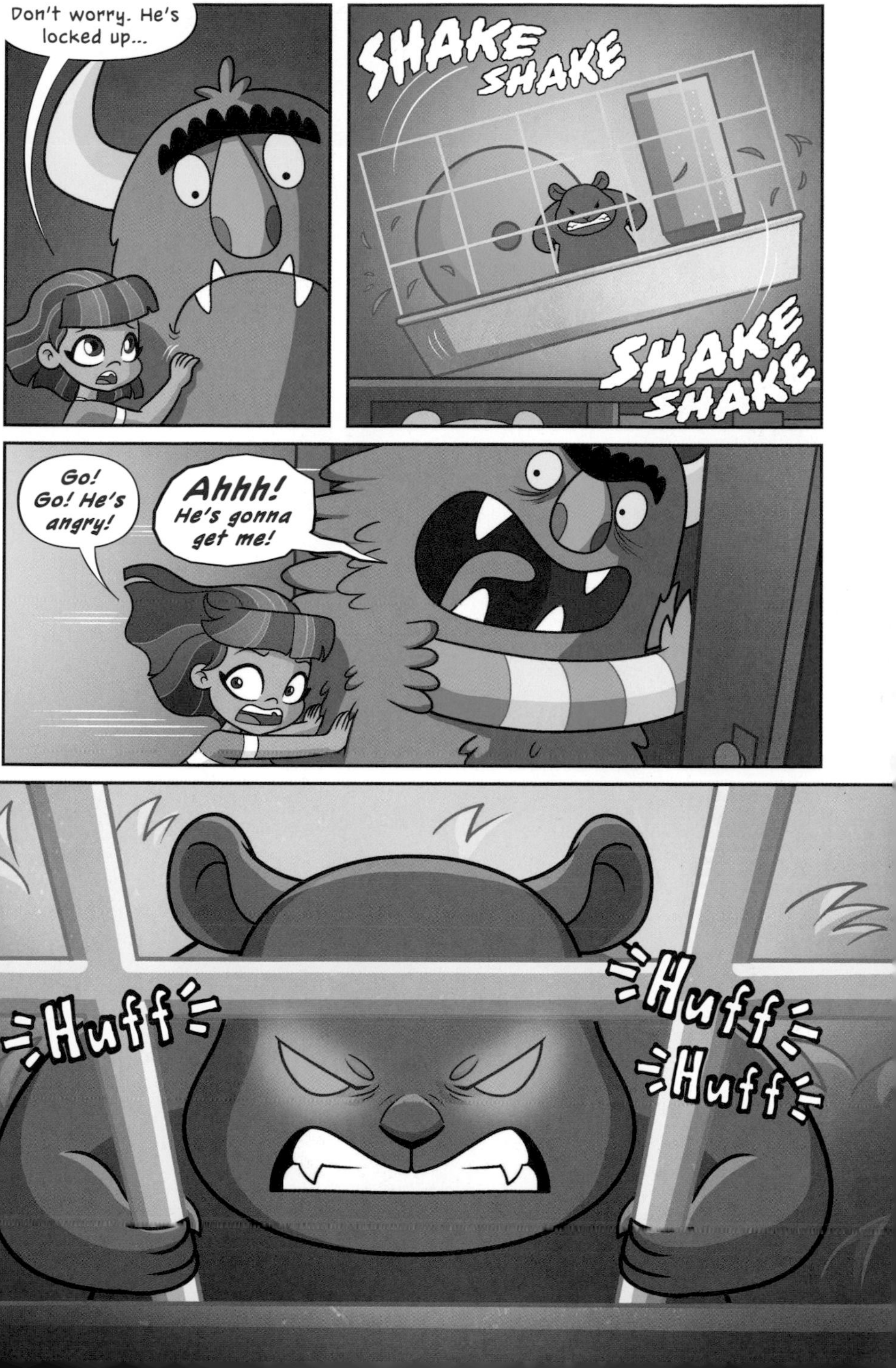
Don't worry. He's locked up...
SHAKE
SHAKE
SHAKE
SHAKE
Go! Go! He's angry!
Ahhh! He's gonna get me!
Huff
Huff
Huff

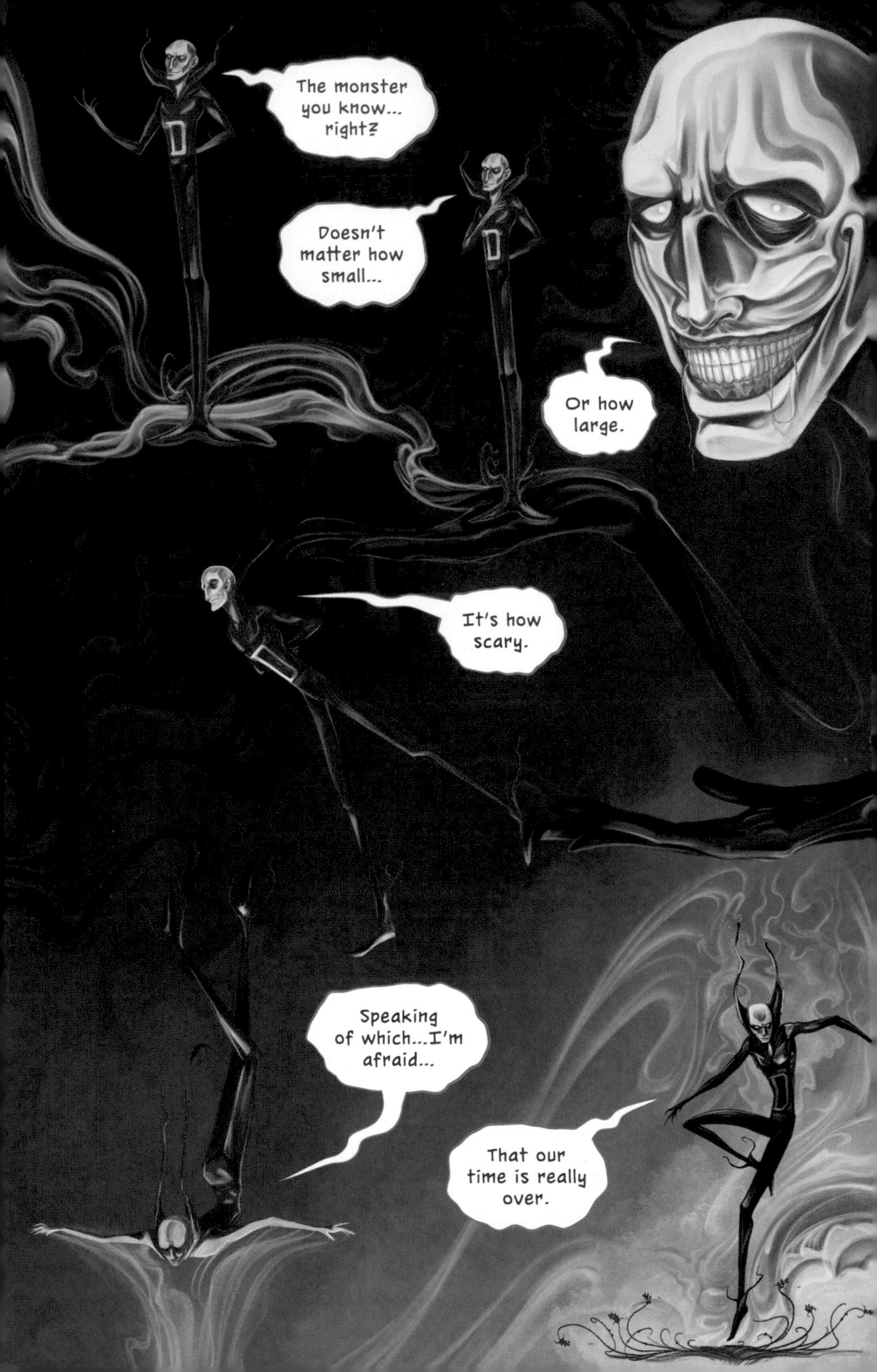
The monster you know... right?
Doesn't matter how small...
Or how large.
It's how scary.
Speaking of which...I'm afraid...
That our time is really over.

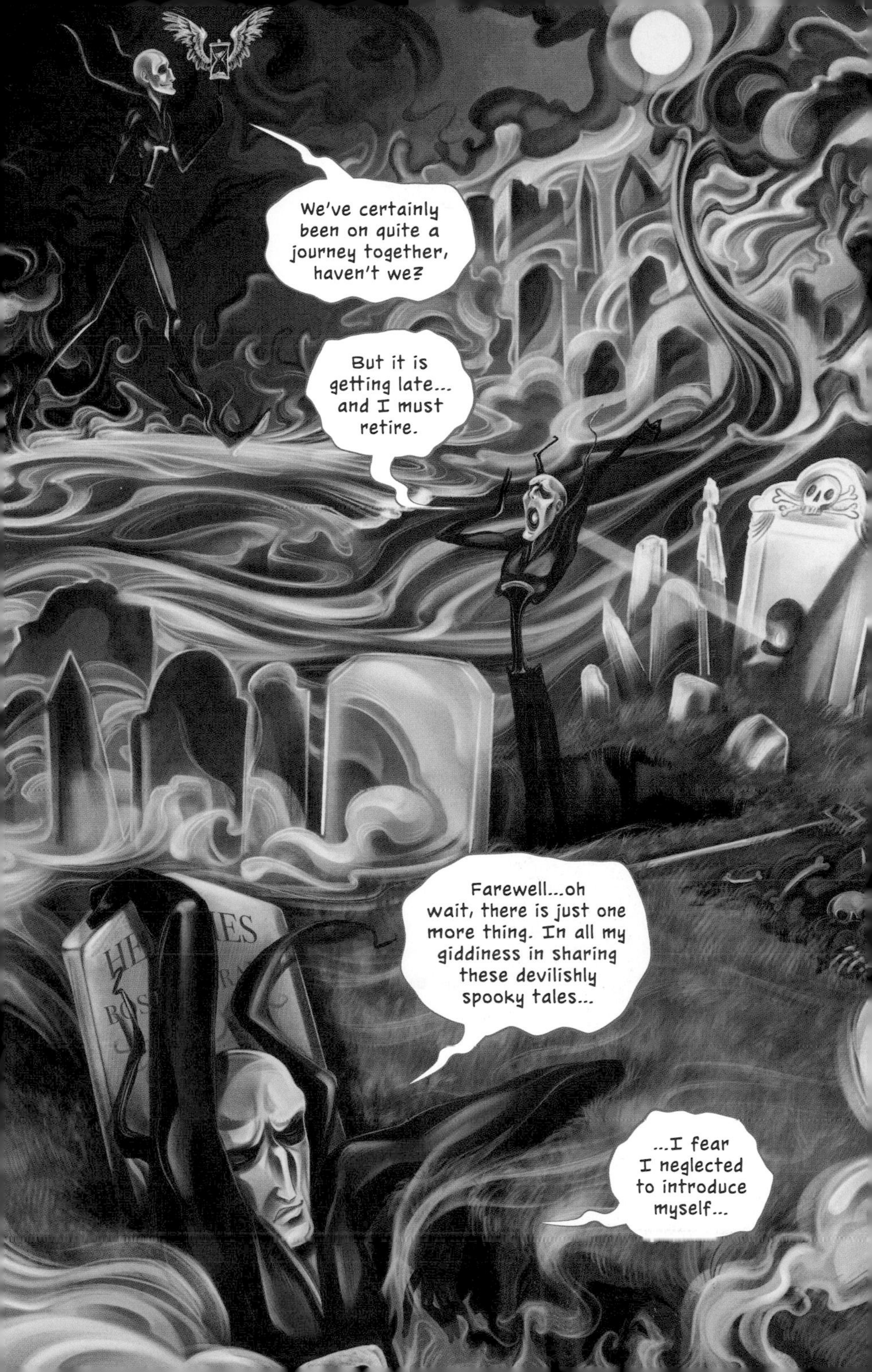
We've certainly been on quite a journey together, haven't we?
But it is getting late... and I must retire.
Farewell...oh wait, there is just one more thing. In all my giddiness in sharing these devilishly spooky tales...
...I fear I neglected to introduce myself...

HERE LIES
BOSTON BRAND
DEADMAN
He always loved a good story.
Goodbye... My name is *Deadman.*

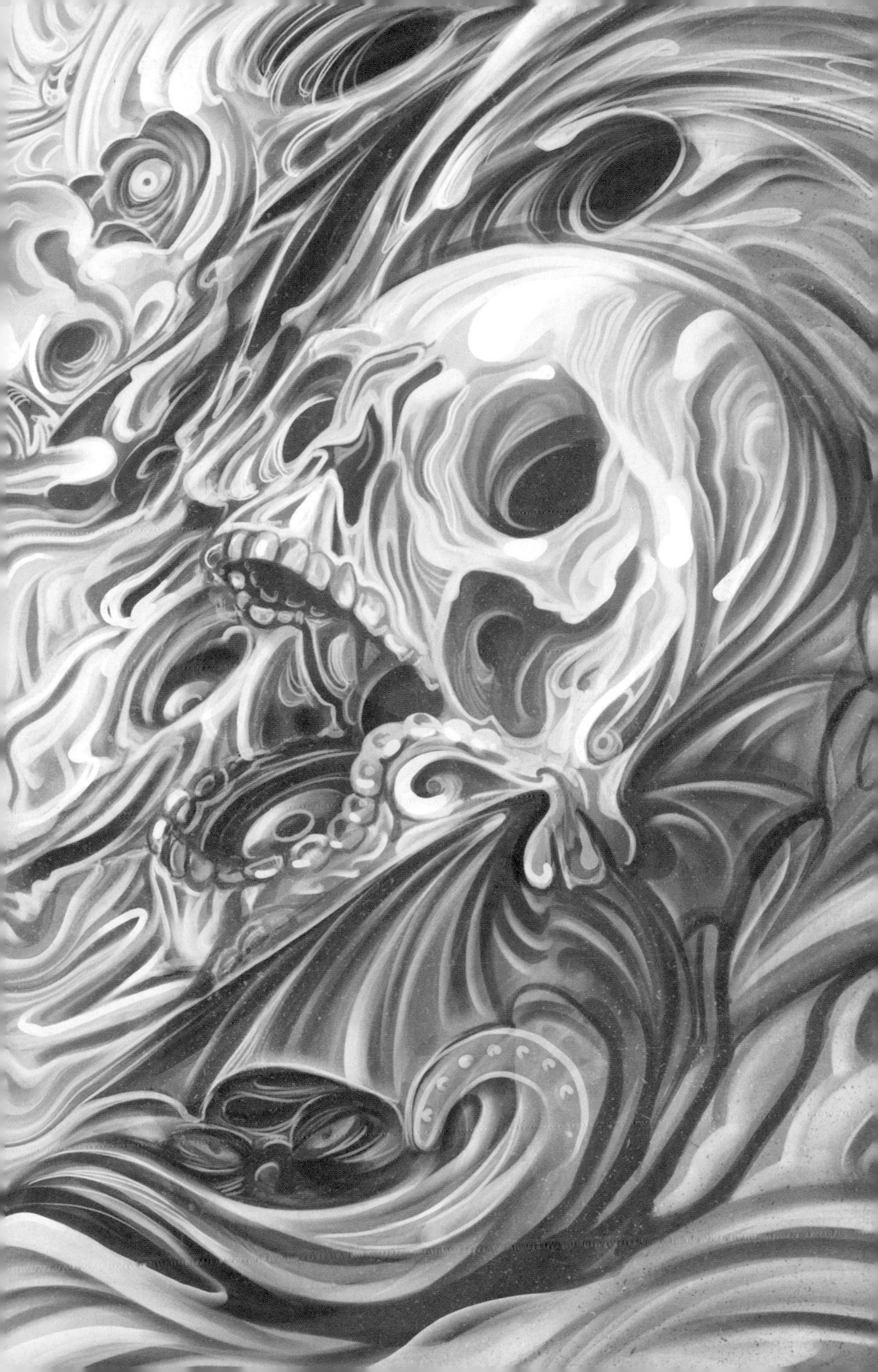

Franco Aureliani is a writer and artist of graphic comics art forms for many companies. He has worked on *Superman of Smallville, Arkhamaniacs,* and *Tiny Titans* for DC Comics. He is also a high school art teacher of 23 years and is one of the proud principal owners of the Aw Yeah Comics line of comics and Aw Yeah Comics retail stores. He lives in New York with wife Ivette, son Nicolas, two dogs Harley and Quinn, and a kitty named Jerry.

Lady **Sara Richard** is a part-time artist, writer, gravestone cleaner, and mushroom forager. Her work has been featured on over 100 comic book covers across a variety of publishers, a Justice League tarot card set, and in the pages of British *Vogue*, *Wired*, and *Vanity Fair*. Lady Sara has earned her Ladyship title for preserving a couple of small plots of land in Scotland, one of her favorite places in the world, as well as for doing her best at promoting environmental protection. Sara is also the great-granddaughter of Margaret Scott, a Salem Witch Trial victim, as well as a direct cousin of Edgar Allan Poe.

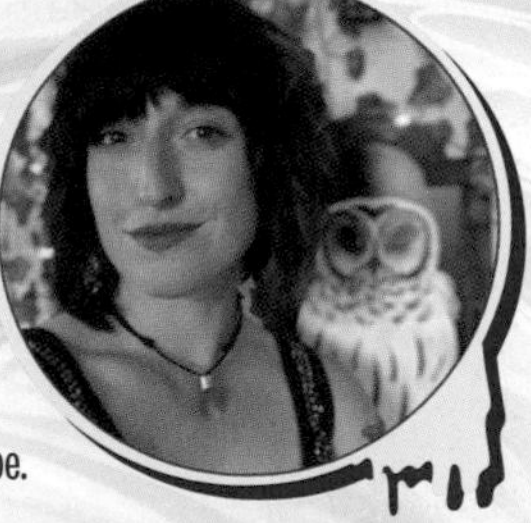

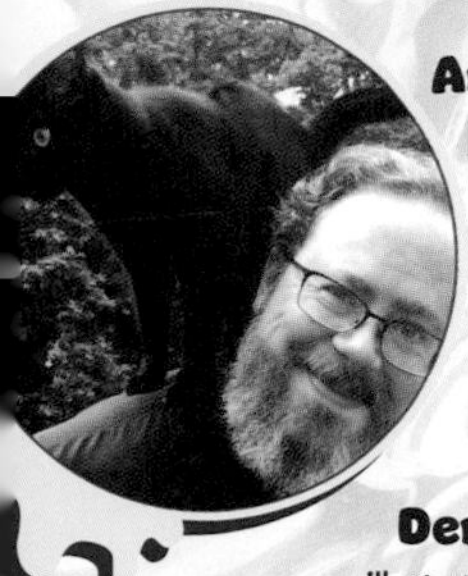

Andy Price has always been immersed in the world of comics and illustration—or at least since he was found as an infant in the wilderness by comics-collecting sasquatches! A graduate of the Kubert School, he has a 30-year career of working for the likes of Storm King Productions, Archie, Marvel, and Boom!, and is best known for his decade-long run on IDW Publishing's *My Little Pony: Friendship Is Magic* and its many offshoots. Andy lives with his wife Alice, six cats, and a mountain of Star Trek and Batman paraphernalia.

Derek Charm is an Eisner Award-winning comics artist and illustrator. He was the artist on *Jughead, The Unbeatable Squirrel Girl, Star Wars Adventures*, and *The Mystery of the Meanest Teacher: A Johnny Constantine Graphic Novel*. He currently lives in New York. PHOTO CREDIT: LEANDREW TABB

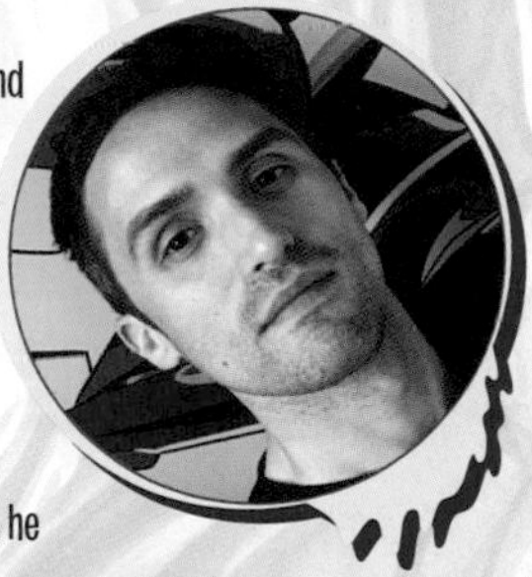

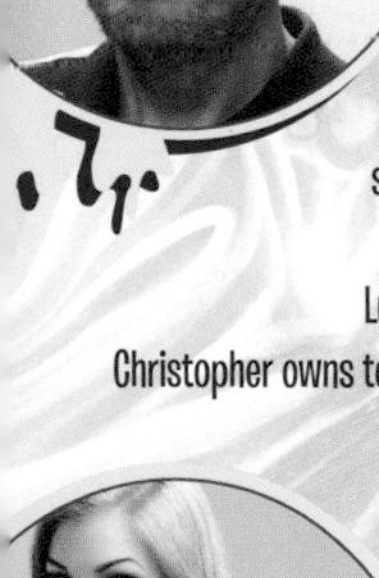

Mike Haritgan is a freelance artist from Auckland, New Zealand, where he lives with his amazing wife, three awesome kids, and a cat named Elvis. When Mike's not busy with that lot, he can always be found with his face buried firmly in his tablet, drawing. His self-published works include *A Bag for Santa* and *The Gift of Time* by author Kendra Esbrook. Mike has big aspirations and he needs more sleep.

Christopher Uminga is a Connecticut-based artist who has spent his career developing a unique style that blends together creepy and cute. He has worked on projects for DC Comics/Warner Bros., Lucasfilm, Foot Locker, Disney's WonderGround Gallery, and others. Christopher owns too many backpacks and loves spending time with his three dogs, Sandwich, Wolfie, and Ketchup.

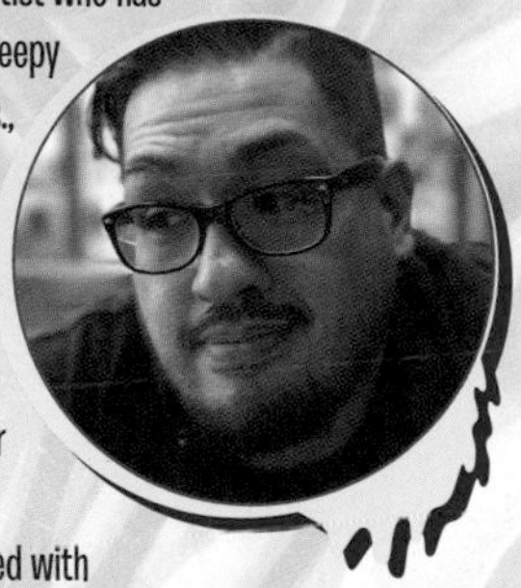

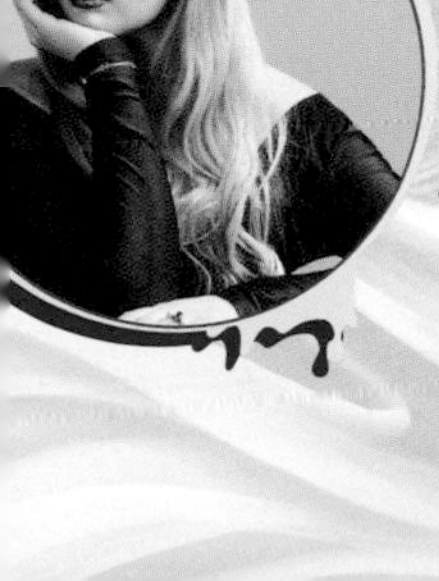

Abigail Larson is an Hugo Award-winning illustrator who has worked on DC titles such as *The Sandman Universe: The Dreaming* and *Teen Titans Go! To Camp!* She's also worked with Netflix Animation and Disney Publishing Worldwide, and loves all things strange and spooky! PHOTO CREDIT: ROGER WALK PHOTOGRAPHY

Morgan Beem is a freelance artist who works predominantly with ink and watercolor. Her work includes *Swamp Thing: Twin Branches*, *The Family Trade*, *Buffy the Vampire Slayer: The Hilot of 1910*, *Adventure Time*, *Planet of the Apes*, and a number of anthologies. She is also a part of Jam House Studio, a comics collective in Denver, Colorado. PHOTO CREDIT: LAUREN ASSOUR

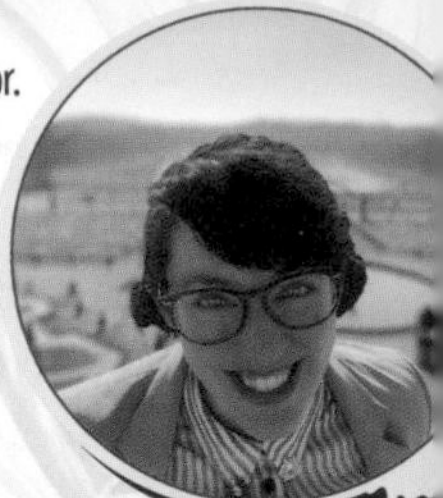

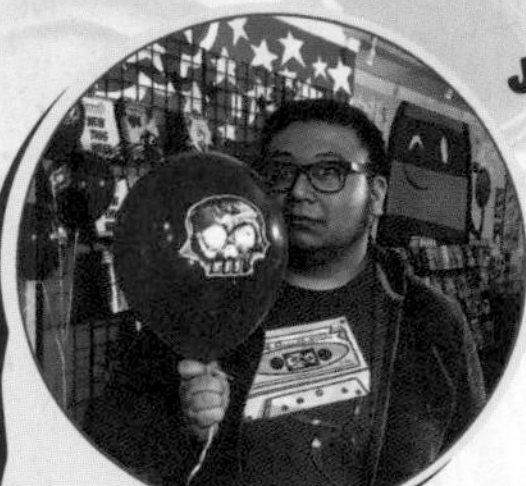

Justin Castaneda is an illustrator and book author from Chicago's South Side best known for his self-published works: *Heart* and *The Murder Balloon*. He is the co-creator of the award-winning all-ages indie comic *Wonder Care Presents: The Kinder Guardians* published by Vantage:Inhouse Productions. He illustrated the children's book *My Very Punny Dad* shortly after becoming a father to a beautiful baby girl.

Tressina Bowling is a Kentucky-based artist. Her work ranges from bright and colorful palettes featured in *Aw Yeah Comics* to dark and moody with works like *A Field Guide to Kentucky Kaiju*. She's thrilled to be featured alongside so many incredible and diverse artists for *Deadman Tells the Spooky Tales*.

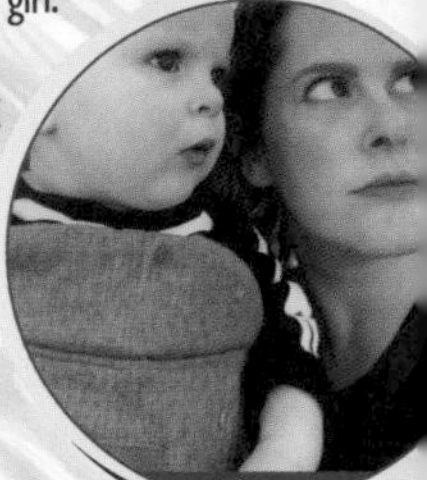

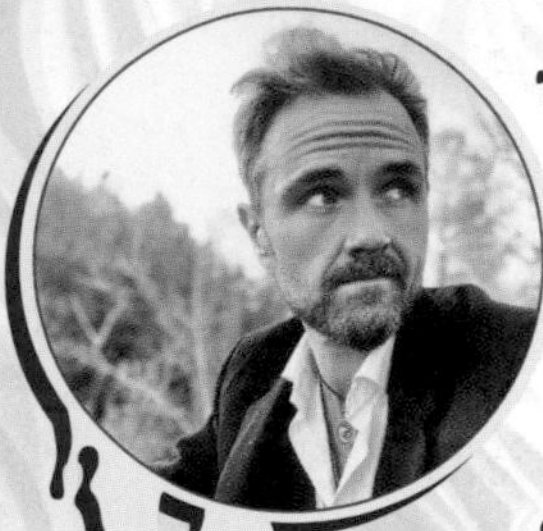

Thomas Boatwright has done illustration for Dark Horse and Image Comics, along with various small publishers. He also enjoys doing freelance art and having a nomadic existence traveling the country. He's sure he'll meet Mothman (his favorite cryptid) in his travels eventually!

Scoot McMahon is a versatile cartoonist from Rossford, Ohio. His catalogue of comics includes *Agents of S.L.A.M.* (Oni), *Wrapped Up* (Oni/Lion Forge), *Tales from the Con* (Image), *Aw Yeah Comics* (Dark Horse), *Sami the Samurai Squirrel*, *Spot on Adventure* (Action Lab), and *The Adventures of Cthulhu Jr. and Friends* (Source Point Press). When Scoot isn't cartooning, he enjoys pizza time, watching pro wrestling, and discovering new parks with his wife and two kids! PHOTO CREDIT: BLUE LUX PHOTOGRAPHY

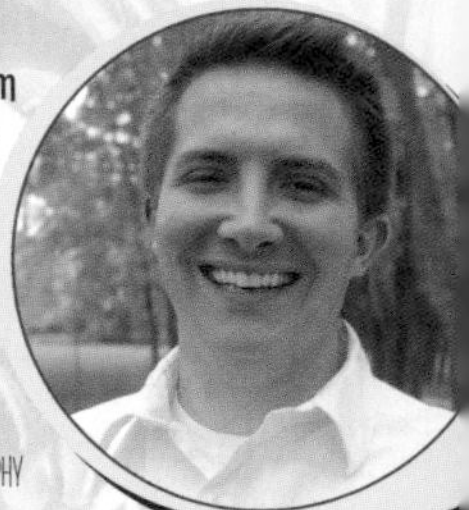

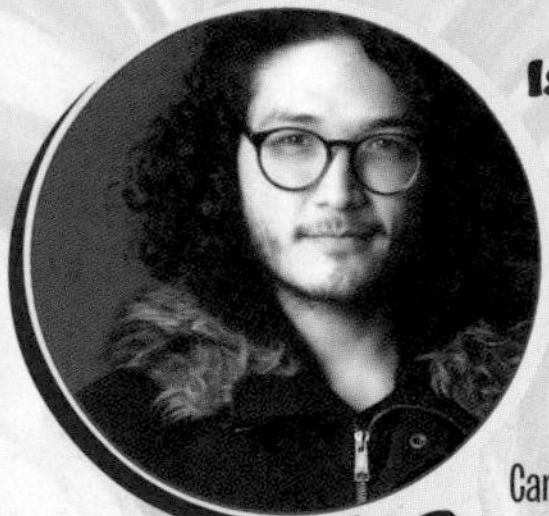

Isaac Goodhart got his start in comics in 2014 as one of the winners of the Top Cow Talent Hunt. After drawing *Artifacts* #38, he moved on to illustrating Matt Hawkins's *Postal* for 26 consecutive issues. He recently illustrated *Under the Moon: A Catwoman Tale* and *Victor and Nora: A Gotham Love Story*, written by Lauren Myracle and published by DC Comics.

Agnes Garbowska was born in Poland and moved to Canada at a young age. An only child, she escaped into a world of books, cartoons, and comics. Agnes has been working in comics for more than 15 years, and is an award-winning and *New York Times* bestselling series artist for the DC Super Hero Girls! She has also worked on Teen Titans Go!, My Little Pony, and Care Bears books. She currently lives in the United States with her two little doggos, Olive and Otis, who are the best studiomates a girl could ask for.

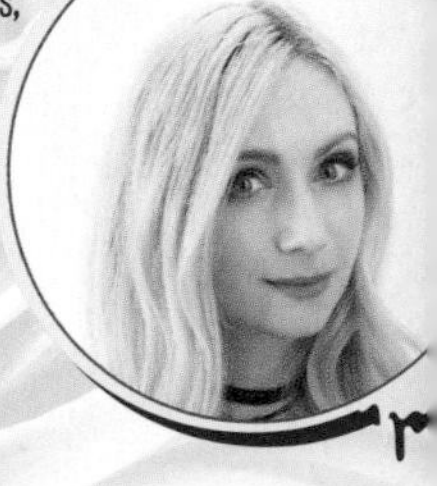

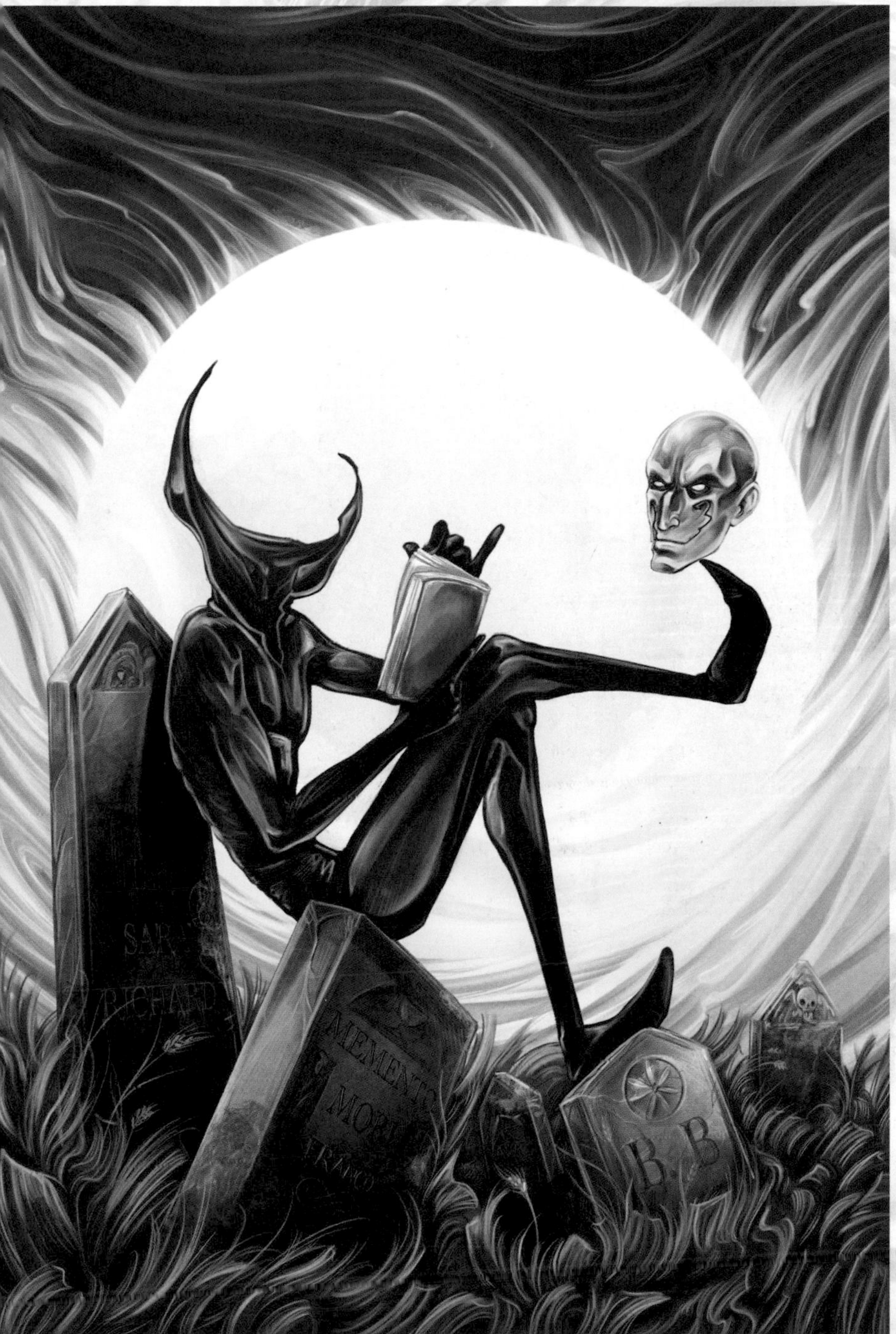
RICHARD
MEMENTO
B B

WANT SOME MORE SPOOKTACULAR TALES?

CHECK OUT THESE STORIES FROM DC BOOKS FOR YOUNG READERS!

DC
the MYSTERY of the MEANEST TEACHER
a JOHNNY CONSTANTINE graphic novel
new york times bestselling author RYAN NORTH
art by DEREK CHARM

THE MYSTERY OF THE MEANEST TEACHER: A JOHNNY CONSTANTINE GRAPHIC NOVEL

Ryan North, Derek Charm

Thirteen-year-old Johnny Constantine has to flee his native England and settles in an American boarding school. But his new teacher may prove to be more dangerous than any of the angry demons he escaped from back home.

ISBN: 978-1-77950-123-3

DC
WE FOUND A MONSTER
A GRAPHIC NOVEL!
BY KIRK SCROGGS

WE FOUND A MONSTER

Kirk Scroggs

Casey Clive has been secretly taking care of tons of monsters—but their needs for a place to stay, something to eat, and lots and lots of attention mean they won't be a secret for much longer...

ISBN: 978-1-77950-052-6

TEEN TITANS GO!
DC
Written by Michael Northrop
Art by Erich Owen and more!
UNDEAD?!

TEEN TITANS GO!: UNDEAD?!

Michael Northrop, Erich Owen, and more!

When zombies invade Jump City, can the Teen Titans cancel the apocalypse?

ISBN: 978-1-77950-785-3

Zatanna and the HOUSE of SECRETS
a graphic novel
MATTHEW CODY · YOSHI YOSHITANI

ZATANNA AND THE HOUSE OF SECRETS

Matthew Cody, Yoshi Yoshitani

Welcome to the magical, mystical, topsy-turvy world of the House of Secrets, where Zatanna embarks on a journey of self-discovery and adventure with her pet rabbit, Pocus, at her side.

ISBN: 978-1-4012-9070-2